EXTINCTION

BY DOUGLAS PRESTON

The Lost Tomb

The Lost City of the Monkey God

*The Kraken Project**

*Impact**

*Blasphemy**

The Monster of Florence (with Mario Spezi)

*Tyrannosaur Canyon**

*The Codex**

*Jennie**

The Black Place

The Royal Road

Talking to the Ground

Cities of Gold

*Dinosaurs in the Attic***

* Published by Tor Publishing Group

** Published by St. Martin's Press

EXTINCTION

A NOVEL

DOUGLAS PRESTON

TOR PUBLISHING GROUP
NEW YORK

EXTINCTION

Copyright © 2024 by Splendide Mendax, Inc.

A Forge Book
Published by Tom Doherty Associates / Tor Publishing Group
120 Broadway
New York, NY 10271

www.tor-forge.com

Forge® is a registered trademark of Macmillan Publishing Group, LLC.

The Library of Congress Cataloging-in-Publication Data is available upon request.

ISBN 978-0-7653-1770-4 (hardcover)
ISBN 978-1-250-34199-0 (international, sold outside the U.S.,
subject to rights availability)
ISBN 978-1-250-90976-3 (ebook)

Our books may be purchased in bulk for promotional, educational, or business use. Please contact your local bookseller or the Macmillan Corporate and Premium Sales Department at 1-800-221-7945, extension 5442, or by email at MacmillanSpecialMarkets@macmillan.com.

First Edition: 2024

Printed in the United States of America

0   9   8   7   6   5   4   3   2   1

TO MY FRIEND AND WRITING PARTNER

LINCOLN CHILD

The real problem of humanity is the following: We have Paleolithic emotions, medieval institutions, and godlike technology. And it is terrifically dangerous.

—Edward O. Wilson

Extinction is the rule. Survival is the exception.

—Carl Sagan

EXTINCTION

1

"Look—over there," said the guide in a hushed voice, handing Olivia the binoculars. "On the far side of the lake."

Olivia Gunnerson took the binoculars and directed them toward the turquoise pond, which lay a mile away at the bottom of the cirque, below their vantage point. It took her a moment to locate the woolly mammoths, four big ones and two smaller ones, on the opposite shore. She touched up the focus, and the animals sprang into sharp relief. It took her breath away. They were so gigantic they looked almost fake— much bigger than the elephants she'd seen on safari in Africa. The bull was drinking deeply. He was fifteen feet at the shoulder, his tusks great scimitars of ivory as long again as his body, sweeping outward from a shaggy domed head. The matriarch of the family was standing guard, her trunk elevated and moving back and forth, warily testing the air, as her calf huddled under her protective bulk, pushing his head upward to suckle. An older calf splashed in the shallows, dipping his trunk and playfully squirting water from it. It was early fall, but here in the mountains, the mammoths were already growing out winter coats, the long brown hair hanging down several feet.

Olivia was thrilled. It was a scene straight out of the Ice Age, the family of mammoths lingering in a lush meadow bordering the pond, with the glittering, snowcapped peaks of the Erebus Mountains of Colorado forming a majestic backdrop. To one side of the group stood a grove of fall aspen trees, their leaves a cloud of shimmering gold rustling with every swell of the breeze.

"*Mammuthus columbi*," whispered the guide. "The largest of all the mammoths, the northern subspecies with fur. That bull weighs at least ten tons."

Olivia continued staring through the glasses. The bull finished drinking and playfully sprayed water from his trunk at the young one, who squealed in delight, the faint sound drifting across the valley.

"Incredible," she breathed. As a girl growing up in Salt Lake City, Olivia had been crazy about dinosaurs and wanted to be a paleontologist, until skiing had taken over her life.

"Don't bogart those binocs," said Mark, Olivia's husband.

"Sorry," she said with a laugh, handing them over and giving his shoulder an affectionate squeeze. She was so mesmerized she had almost forgotten the rest of the world existed. She turned to their guide, Stefan. "What will they do when the snow comes?"

"They'll move lower down in the valley and take shelter in the forests," he said.

Their guide, Olivia observed, was one of those super-fit older men who seemed to be made of cords and cables, with a grizzled beard and leathery skin, exuding a sense of vigor. She wondered if Mark would be like that in his fifties. Probably. He would never let his fitness regimen slide, and neither would she.

"In winter, what do they eat?" Mark asked.

"They'll tear down the aspens and cottonwoods and eat the twigs and buds, and they'll paw up the snow to get at the mosses and bushes along the creeks and bogs. They wreak havoc—but it's an environmentally good kind of havoc. Since being rewilded, they've changed the ecology of the valley, opening up meadows and churning up the ground—which increased the landscape's carbon absorption by fifty percent."

"It looks like they're coming around the lake," said Olivia. Even without the glasses, she could see them on the move, the matriarch leading the way, moseying along the shore. "They're coming our way."

"Nothing to worry about," said the guide. "They're as peaceful as puppy dogs."

The backpack to the campsite had been fourteen tough miles over a three-thousand-foot vertical gain, carrying fifty-pound packs. They had camped in a high meadow at ten thousand feet, not far below the tree line, in a magnificent cirque of mountains called the Barbicans. Olivia had spent much of her thirty years of life outdoors, skiing and backpacking, but she had never seen a place quite as spectacular as this, with its towering, snow-clad peaks, the aspens shivering with gold, the flawless aquamarine of the lake reflecting the evening cumulus—and the crowning glory of it all, the family of woolly mammoths ambling around the lake, their trunks swinging as they went, two little ones trotting along.

That morning, they had left the lodge in a jeep before dawn: her husband, herself, and Stefan. It had been a bumpy eleven-mile drive to the trailhead. They had begun hiking at first light, going up through a deep forest of Douglas firs before coming out on a ridge, with views down into the Erebus Valley and the now distant lodge and its nearby lake, created along the Erebus River by the gnawing and tree-felling of giant beavers, *Castoroides*, another animal that had been "de-extincted," in the jargon of the Erebus Resort.

While at the lodge, every evening, they had watched woolly mammoths and other Pleistocene megafauna coming in to drink at the lake, regular as clockwork. The guests congregated at the glassed-in wall to watch them gather. It was like Disneyland, everyone crowding forward and oohing and aahing, clutching their drinks and trying to get selfies with their cell phones. But here, in the mountains, seeing the mammoths living free and naturally, was a totally different experience. It was like seeing elephants in a zoo versus viewing them on safari in the African bush.

Mark handed her the binoculars, and she looked again. The mammoths were now on the north side of the tarn and had paused at a thicket, pulling twigs and branches off the bushes and stuffing them into their mouths. One of the mammoths paused to take a dump, and an almost ridiculous amount of stuff came out, leaving a giant pile. On the hike up, she had just avoided stepping in a similar mound, so large she had almost mistaken it for a brown rock. If the guide hadn't warned her, she would have sunk up to her knees in it. What a laugh they had about that. Later they had spied a group of glyptodons grazing in a far-off meadow. A more outrageous-looking animal could not be found, Olivia thought. Glyptodons were giant armadillos, the same size and shape as a Volkswagen Beetle. She couldn't see their heads or tails, just five nubbly gray humps in a meadow, moving slowly, leaving cropped trails in the long grass.

But more than anything else, Olivia was dying to see a woolly indricothere. It was the latest animal Erebus had de-extincted, and there were supposed to be two of them in the valley. The indricothere was the largest land mammal that had ever lived, an ancestor of the rhinoceros. It was fully twice the mass of the mammoth, a fifteen-foot behemoth on legs like pillars. The indricothere, she had read in her orientation packet, had been discovered in Siberia in 1916 by a Russian paleontologist named Borissiak, who had named it after the "Indrik Beast," a mythological Russian monster believed to live deep in the Ural Mountains, so large that when it walked, the earth quaked. The Indrik Beast had the body of a bull, the head of a horse, and a giant horn on its snout and was covered with coarse black fur. The woolly indricothere did in fact look very much like that, except without the horn. Despite their size, the indricotheres were shy and hard to find, because they tended to bury themselves in the dense thickets of chokecherries and buckthorn that grew along the streams in the lower areas of the Erebus Valley, or hide themselves in the densest forests on the upper reaches of the valley.

She shook aside her blond hair and took another look at the mammoths, which had moved beyond the lake and had become more visible as they rambled through the thickets, feeding and leaving a wake of ripped-up vegetation.

"We won't get stepped on tonight, will we?" she asked with a laugh.

"They're super careful where they put their feet," said the guide. "And anyway, as soon as the sun sets, they'll bed down."

"Do they lie down to sleep?"

"They're a bit like horses—they mostly sleep standing up but might lie down for thirty minutes or so. They're so heavy that if they lie down too long—such as if they're sick or hurt—they can suffocate."

The last rays of sunlight were spearing across the lake below, and the air was cooling down fast. At that altitude, Olivia knew, it would dip below freezing in the night.

"Let's light a fire and rustle up some grub," said Mark.

"You bet," said the guide, rising.

The two went to build a fire and prepare dinner. She was glad she'd found a guy who not only liked to cook but was good at it—and on top of that, he washed dishes. The menu that night would be freeze-dried, as usual. That was fine. This was not meant to be a luxury safari where they were waited on hand and foot. On the contrary. For their honeymoon, she and Mark had decided on a serious backcountry adventure—an eight-day backpack along the hundred-and-ten-mile Barbican Trek. It was Erebus's most famous circuit, and it offered a serious physical challenge, spectacular scenery, and the chance to see incredible Pleistocene megafauna brought back to life by the science of de-extinction and rewilded in a natural habitat. She was a little sorry Mark had insisted on a guide, but she had to admit he had been a fountain of information, while being quiet and unobtrusive. There were no maintained trails or developed campsites in Erebus; that was one of its attractions: you felt like you were a John Muir exploring an unknown and untouched land. It was silly, of course, because Erebus was one of the most curated landscapes in Colorado, but Olivia was tired of backpacking along heavily eroded trails and camping at overused, beaten-down campsites, even deep in the wilderness. In the years since the COVID pandemic, the wild places in America seemed to have gotten more and more overrun.

She watched from her seat on a log as Mark and the guide busied themselves with dinner. Mark had pulled out a flask of Michter's, and they were trading swigs as they worked. He was such a sweet, eager-beaver guy; you'd never know his father was the billionaire from hell. Mark took after his mom, one of the most wonderful people Olivia had ever met. How those two could've paired up she'd never figure out, but she considered herself fortunate in her mother-in-law. The big, blustery, honking-and-swearing tech-billionaire father wasn't much in the picture anyway. She hoped it would stay that way after she had her baby.

They now had a cheerful fire going. The magic hour had begun, and the peaks were aflame with alpenglow. The temperature was dropping. She pulled on a fleece from her backpack and headed to the fire. She would've loved a hit of that bourbon, but, being pregnant, she had to abstain.

"Sorry, hon, I hope you don't mind," Mark said, waving the bottle with a guilty grin.

"No worries. You two go right ahead."

The mammoths were no longer visible, having disappeared behind a rocky ridge between them and the lake. The guide explained they would spend the night in a protected hollow.

The menu was freeze-dried chicken tetrazzini, along with instant soup, hot chocolate, and Toll House cookies for dessert. She watched Mark eat, his jaw muscles working. He was ripped but not bulked up, with long, smooth athletic muscles, dark curly hair, and white teeth. It was funny how being pregnant seemed to make her hornier than ever. She assumed it would have tamped down those kinds of feelings, but apparently not. They'd have to be super quiet, but that made it even more fun, with his hand over her mouth as she came. It was like high school days when she was in her room supposedly studying with a boyfriend, but instead, they had their hands down each other's pants.

The guide, with his usual sensitivity, had set up his tent discreetly out of sight, behind a clump of trees a good hundred yards from theirs.

Darkness fell, and the stars came out, like God had kicked a bin of glowing dust across the sky. At ten thousand feet, she thought, you could see stars that no sea-level human had ever seen.

The fire had died down, and she could see her breath in the glow of the coals.

Mark stood up. "I'm ready to turn in."

"Me too," she said, pretending to yawn. She was already aroused just thinking about it. Something about the strenuous hike, the glyptodons and the mammoths, the snowcapped peaks and the dome of stars made her horny as hell.

She held his hand, and they crawled into the tent. They had already zipped their sleeping bags together, and they quickly stripped and burrowed into the bag, her arms pulling him close. He was ready, and they wasted no time with preliminaries.

2

Olivia lay in the dark, Mark breathing softly next to her. The night was still, without the breath of breeze, the silence profound. It had dropped below freezing, but their sleeping bags were super warm, and she was used to camping in alpine weather. Her dad had taken her and her brothers camping in the Wasatches and Manti-La Sal in all seasons, sometimes on cross-country ski trips in the dead of winter in ten-foot-deep snow and nights to twenty below. God, she missed him. Mark was a little like that, unintimidated by wilderness conditions, totally cool with anything nature might throw at him. The first thing she did with any new boyfriend was go camping. So many of them, despite their big talk, failed the test—all it took was a little rain or snow, a swarm of mosquitoes, or a rattler, and they were in a panic. Or they just didn't have a wilderness sense—like casually leaving trash or pissing too close to a stream or not knowing how to set up a tent.

She shifted her body, not feeling the slightest bit tired. The sun set so early in the fall, it was still probably only eight o'clock. She wished she could fall asleep like Mark, who could drop off anywhere, anytime, in five minutes. It was a dark, moonless night. The mammoths would be sleeping in their hollow below them. She listened, wondering if mammoths snored. But she could hear nothing.

Her mind wandered, and she thought of her Olympic medal, sitting in its sock in the back of her underwear drawer in Salt Lake. All those years of work, struggle, risks, crashes, injuries, surgery, rehab, recovery, more work, more struggle—and finally Pyeongchang. All that work had been squeezed up and stamped in a piece of bronze sitting in the back of her drawer. Mark had been upset that she wouldn't frame it and hang it with a picture of her receiving it on the stand. Why would she? She hated even looking at it.

It would be different for her child. Son or daughter, it didn't matter. He or she wouldn't make the mistakes she'd made. Olivia had been through it all and knew now how the system worked and what had to be done, and she could guide her child to something a whole lot better than bronze.

She suddenly was hyperalert, tense. She heard a sound. A strange plucking sound. Mark was instantly awake too. And then it started, the loud tearing sound of the tent fly, like it was being cut.

"What the fuck?" Mark sat up like a shot.

She pulled a headlamp out of the tent pocket and switched it on. She shined it through the mosquito netting of the inner tent to reveal a long, ragged cut in the outer fly.

"What was that?" said Mark. "A branch?"

"There's no wind," Olivia said.

"You think it's a bear?" he said.

"They said the bears had been removed."

"Yeah, but one could have wandered back in over the mountains."

Olivia wondered. Maybe it was an animal, smelling the humans inside and reaching out to scratch the fly just to see what it was.

They listened, but the silence was total.

"I'm going out," said Mark.

"No, wait."

"I'm not waiting. If it's a cat or bear, we'd better drive it away. We can't wait for it to come in here."

He took the headlamp from her, put it on, and pulled his buck knife from its sheath, before slipping out of the bag. He was wearing Capilene full-body long johns. He went to the tent door and unzipped it.

He paused. No sound. Then he stuck his head outside the door.

"See anything?"

"Nothing."

She was filled with uncertainty. It could be a mountain lion in wait. Maybe it ran off when they turned on the headlamp. But Mark was right: they couldn't just cower in the tent. They had to do something. Calling out for the guide would only put him in a place of danger, and besides, asking for help from the guide ran against her wilderness ethic.

She felt around and grasped her own knife and put on her own headlamp but didn't turn it on yet.

"Okay, I'm going out," he said, and slipped out into the dark.

She could see the glow of his light indistinctly through the tent fabric as he swept the area. She tensed, gripping her own knife.

The glow quietly moved about for a long thirty seconds. She heard him suddenly grunt—a weird sort of snort—and there was the sound of spilling liquid, and the glow vanished.

"Mark?" Olivia cried. "Mark!"

No sound.

She sprang to the tent flap and looked out, turning on her headlamp and sweeping the area with the light. There was his knife, on the ground. Nearby lay his headlamp in the grass, still lit.

"Mark!" she screamed. "*Mark!* Hey, we need help here!" she cried, leaping out of the tent, gripping the knife. She stopped where he had dropped his knife and headlamp and stared at the ground in horror— just as she felt something strike the back of her neck and slide in, crunching the bone and going through it, as hot as fire and cold as ice at the same time.

3

The whistling cowboy theme of *The Good, the Bad and the Ugly* surged into the dark room.

"Christ almighty," Frankie Cash muttered as she fumbled for the glowing phone by her bedside. She picked it up and stared: five a.m. and the call was from her boss, Wallace McFaul.

"Cash," she answered, trying to keep the thickness of sleep from her voice.

"Frankie," he said, sounding alarmingly alert, "there's a situation up at the Erebus Resort."

"What?"

"Kidnapping, possible murder."

"Oh, jeez."

"We're scrambling a chopper. Detective Romanski will be leading the CSI team." McFaul hesitated. "According to the roster, it's your case . . . Agent in Charge Cash."

He emphasized ever so slightly the *Agent in Charge* part: this would be the first case since her promotion to senior detective in the CBI Major Crimes Division.

Now she was wide awake. "I'll be there in forty."

Frankie Cash punched the phone off and in a single motion rolled out of bed. By sleeping nude, she made sure there was no delay between bed and shower, and the blast of hot water directly in her face cleared her brain. Sixty seconds later, she was out, whipping herself dry with a rough towel, followed by a fast brushing of hair and teeth. Never ceasing to move, she yanked from a chair the light blue silk blouse, gray worsted jacket, and skirt she had set out ready to go the night before. She dressed, clipping her shield to her waist and holstering her Baby Glock 9 mm, followed by a quick touch of lipstick. She stared for a moment into her face as she smacked her lips together. God, were those really new wrinkles around her eyes? She stuck her tongue out at herself. Fuck off with the worrying about weight, age, wrinkles, and ass—and do your job.

Her first case in Major Crimes. And it felt like it could be a big one.

In the tiny kitchen of her apartment, she boiled water in an electric kettle, poured it into a Yeti mug with two tablespoons of Café Bustelo instant espresso, two tablespoons of Cremora, and two of sugar, snapped on the lid, and two minutes later, she was in her car, heading north on Kipling to CBI headquarters in Lakewood, Colorado.

At five forty a.m., the parking lot of the Colorado Bureau of Investigation was almost empty. The stars were just fading in the night sky when she stepped out into the chilly September air and, carrying her coffee, went into the building and straight to McFaul's office.

She found her boss, dressed in his unvarying dingy blue suit with white shirt and gray tie, standing in front of his desk, talking to Bart Romanski, head of the CSI team.

McFaul looked at his watch. "Forty minutes on the dot. Is that a record?"

She gave him a quick grin. "I've always wanted an Erebus holiday."

"Not going to be much of a holiday up there for you, I'm afraid," McFaul said. "At around nine o'clock last night, two backpackers—newlyweds—were abducted from their tent. Names are Mark and Olivia Gunnerson."

"Gunnerson?" Romanski asked. "Any relation to the tech billionaire?"

"His son."

"Holy *fuck*—excuse me, sir."

McFaul frowned and went on. "They were camped up in the high country. Around nine p.m., the guide heard a scream. By the time he'd pulled on some clothes and gotten to their tent, they were gone. The tent was slashed, and there were two areas of bloodstained grass.

Sheriff James Colcord of Eagle County responded with deputies. They immediately called us in to assist." He turned to Romanski. "This is a case possibly involving significant Forensic Services."

"Right," said Romanski.

Cash hadn't worked with Colcord before but assumed he was like the other elected county sheriffs she'd liaised with in Colorado—good old boys, friendly as long as you didn't get into their politics—and always worried about the next election.

McFaul went on. "Erebus security have already mounted a big search with their own people. The sheriff's team is up there now. The crime scene is fourteen miles from the nearest road at an elevation of ten thousand five hundred feet. This is rugged terrain. There's only one place close by to land a chopper. It's a half-mile hike from the LZ to the crime scene, so you'll have to pack your gear. We're flying at dawn in the A-Star. Any questions?"

"Eaten by a mammoth?" Romanski asked.

Cash stifled a smile.

McFaul frowned; he was famous for his lack of a sense of humor. "Bart, take a powder on the jokes for once, okay?" He turned to Cash, his gray eyes appraising her in a cool, but not unkindly way. "Looks like your first case as agent in charge is going to be a big one."

"Yes, sir."

He nodded curtly, and she was relieved not to get a pep talk.

"Let's load up the A-Star. Be sure to stow your gear in packs you can carry a half mile uphill." He looked at his watch. "Sun rises in twenty-nine minutes."

"Yes, sir," said Romanski, turning for the door. Cash followed him out into the corridor.

"This is gonna be a good one," said Romanski, walking fast on his wiry legs, feet turned out. "I can just feel it."

Romanski always had a ghoulish thrill for spectacular crimes, the bloodier the better.

"You ever been up there?" Cash asked.

"To Erebus? On my salary?"

"Looks like we're gonna get to see the place for free."

"Oh yeah." He smacked his hands together with glee, a huge grin on his elvish face. "I get the Jacuzzi suite. See you on the chopper, Frankie."

As the A-Star rose, banked, and headed west over the front range, the sky behind them flushed with the sunrise, the peaks dipped in gold. The first snow of the season had come a few days before, and it carpeted the high country in dazzling white. It was a magnificent sight, and it reminded Cash all over again of why she had moved to Colorado from Portland, Maine. Portland had a lot of snow, but it never looked quite this good.

This promised to be a high-profile case, and she was finally going to see the fabulous Erebus Resort from the inside. On the other hand, with one of the victims being a billionaire's son, this had the potential of blowing up. High risk, high return.

Inside the chopper, the six passengers were crowded together on bench seating as they sped over the mountains. Cash took stock: Romanski had brought along two crime scene investigators, a forensic specialist in latents, firearms, and toolmarks, and another in trace chemistry, fibers, and miscellaneous evidence. Scrunched between them was the CBI's chief medical examiner, Dr. Chris Huizinga, a serious young man with black-rimmed glasses and pale-yellow hair.

As the chopper thwapped through the dawn air, Cash took a certain satisfaction in identifying the mountain ranges below: Mount Evans, where she had thrown up from altitude sickness in her first week in Colorado ten years ago; Grays Peak; Keystone, where she loved to ski; the town of Frisco; Grand Traverse Peak; Keller Mountain—they were heading west-northwest. Finally, as they cleared Pilot Knob and the Flat Tops, the lush valley of Erebus came into view. It was a deep glacial cirque enclosing the upper drainage of the Erebus River, surrounded by a semicircle of twelve- and thirteen-thousand-foot peaks, with one point of entry where the road from below came in. The entire valley was the resort—over ninety thousand acres: a hundred and forty-four square miles.

The helicopter began to descend into the valley. The resort's famous lodge came into view, modeled after Treetops in Kenya, a spectacular timbered structure cantilevered from a mountainside above a lake. Farther up the valley she saw the old ghost town of Erebus, a picturesque mining camp restored into a movie set.

The chopper continued toward the head of the valley. Cash, staring out the window, spied five huge shapes moving slowly through an open meadow.

"Hey, Romanski, check that out."

She pulled her binocs out of her pack and focused. Romanski leaned over her shoulder to see, breathing down her neck. Springing into view was a family of woolly mammoths, traveling lazily in a group. The shaggy bull took up the rear, his immense tusks gleaming in the dawn light, with several cows leading the way, and in the middle, two little ones bumbling along.

"Lemme see."

She handed the binocs to Romanski.

"Amazing," he said. "Jurassic Park for real."

The chopper veered to the northwest, toward a spectacular arc of stone towers, like blunt granite teeth, surrounding a hanging valley. A tiny lake, a turquoise jewel, nestled in the bottom of the valley.

Now the chopper turned and descended toward a meadow just above the lake—evidently their LZ. As it came down at a hover, a sheriff's deputy stood in the field, acting as a flagger, waving orange batons indicating where the helicopter was to set down into the grass. A moment later, they had settled on the ground, and the rotors were powering down.

Frankie Cash grabbed her backpack. She had packed light—coffee, water, a PB&J sandwich, compass, notebook, binoculars, lighter. A crew member opened the door, and she tucked her Red Sox cap over her short hair and hopped down, clearing the rotors at a crouch. The CSI team followed with their packs. They gathered at the edge of the meadow. Romanski came up beside her and thumped his pack down.

"Nice view."

"You're not kidding."

"Here comes the sheriff."

She looked around and saw a guy come striding over, big cowboy hat, fifty give or take, six foot five, wearing a star. He was pretty much what she expected, and that wasn't encouraging. Maybe it was his resemblance to John Wayne, the type of big, macho, slow-talking man she heartily disliked.

He grasped her hand in his, cool and dry, his eyes the color of washed denim. "Sheriff Jim Colcord, Eagle County. My deputy, Teresa Sandoval."

A slender and much younger woman, dressed in a perfectly starched and pressed uniform, nodded a greeting.

"Frankie Cash, CBI agent in charge." She gave his hand a brief, hard squeeze. "Our team—" She pointed to each one in turn. "Romanski, chief detective, CSI Forensic Services; Dr. Huizinga, ME; Reno and Butler, CSI specialists."

A flurry of nods.

"Thanks for coming," said Colcord. "We've got a bit of a hike ahead of us. I'll fill you in as we go."

Cash hefted her pack and swung it over her shoulder.

"I can help you with that, Agent Cash," he said, reaching out to take it from her. "We're close to eleven thousand feet up here."

"No thanks," she said, shrugging into the shoulder straps. "I wouldn't want to put an elderly man at risk for myocardial infarction at this altitude."

Romanski stifled a laugh.

Colcord frowned. "No offense meant."

"No offense taken," said Cash cheerfully. "Let's go."

4

Frankie Cash paused at the perimeter of the crime scene, breathing hard from the steep hike. While she recovered her breath, she gave the area a visual sweep. It was a spectacular location, a high meadow tucked at the base of snowcapped peaks, with views north and west of the Erebus Valley, and beyond that, mountains after mountains as far as the eye could see.

Crime scene tape had already been strung by the sheriff and the deputy, and it fluttered in a cool breeze. It enclosed the campsite in the meadow, next to a grove of aspen trees. A green tent was pitched in the middle. A fire ring of stones stood twenty yards from the tent, at the edge of the meadow, the fire reduced to ashes. The victims' packs were leaning against a tree nearby, with rain covers. Everything was neat and shipshape—apart from a ragged tear in the tent fly and two big, dark, clotted stains on the flattened grass outside the tent.

Beyond the crime scene, the land fell away down a gentle slope to a ridge, and she could see the lake, shimmering like a piece of fallen sky. Beyond that, the mountains rose into scree slopes and cliffs to end in a row of snowy mountaintops—the Barbicans, according to the GPS map on her phone. On the other side of the campsite, a creek ran out of the aspen grove and gurgled downslope in a series of little water-falls and pools, overhung with grass and fall flowers. The early-morning light shone through the aspen trunks and striped the scene in light and shade.

She looked closer at the area where the stains were. They were bigger than she had assumed from what McFaul had described—a lot bigger. That was not good. She could see no obvious evidence of a disturbance, struggle, or the comings and goings of attackers. The grass was flattened down in places by being trod upon, but there were no marks of the dragging of bodies.

She turned her attention to the tent. It was an ultralight backpacking tent, covered by an outer fly. The diagonal tear in its side had been made in the fly only, not the inner part of the tent. The cut was about two and a half feet long. She couldn't tell if it had been done with a knife or something else. Romanski, she knew, would take the tent back to the lab and give the tear a microscopic examination.

Cash had always found it useful to suspend deduction and analysis when first at a crime scene. Instead, she tried to fix the scene visually in her mind. Memorize it. But this crime scene resisted that. The contrast between the beauty of the surroundings and the horror that had occurred was too great to wrap her mind around, at least right away. Above all, it seemed a crazy place for a kidnapping—or a double homicide if those bloodstains were to be taken seriously. Who would hike up here, all this way? That tear, she thought, was just possibly ragged enough to have been done by an animal. Could it have been one of the park's creatures? Was this a Jurassic Park for real?

Romanski came up behind and interrupted her thoughts with a loud sigh. He shrugged out of his pack, dumping it on the ground and mopping his face with the bandanna tied loosely around his neck. Then he too stared across the crime scene tape.

"Man, that's a lot of blood."

"Just what I was just thinking."

"Eaten by a saber-toothed cat?" he said.

Cash shrugged.

The rest of the CSI team straggled in, setting down their packs and taking a breather after the hike up. Sheriff Colcord, who had fallen a bit behind, now arrived with his deputy. Cash was gratified to see him bathed in sweat, his face red, and then upbraided herself for taking satisfaction in that.

The sheriff took a long drink from his canteen.

Beyond the aspen grove, a group of men appeared, walking outside the crime scene tape. Some were in green uniforms and looked official, and Cash assumed they must be Erebus security.

"Time for the monkey suits, guys," Romanski said to his team, pulling out his own from the pack.

As Romanski and his CSI team busied themselves putting on suits and assembling their evidence kits, a man detached himself from the group.

"Andrew Maximilian," he said, approaching Cash and holding out his hand. "Chief of security, Erebus."

"Agent in Charge Frankie Cash, CBI," she said, taking his hand.

She looked at him curiously, trying not to be obvious about it. Here was the Erebus guy she would have to liaise with. Maximilian was a slender man, fit, about her age of forty, dressed in a safari-style khaki outfit, all pockets and pressed canvas, sporting an Australian cowboy hat, and a chrome-plated .45 stuck in a holster on his belt. He had a ruddy, handsome face, blue-steel eyes, and a brush mustache. The Great White Hunter look. To top it off, he spoke with a broad Australian accent. She was impressed by his calm, controlled demeanor—especially striking given that two people had just been kidnapped on his watch.

"So, Mr. Maximilian, could you fill me in on what Erebus has done so far in response to the situation? I understand you've mounted a search."

Maximilian said, "As soon as we got word, we deployed all available personnel on the ground and in the air. We've got almost a hundred of our people out there and both helicopters, with more joining them."

Cash nodded.

"So far, we've dragged the lake by the lodge, and we're surveying the glacial tarns that dot the high country, like the one down there. We're also combing the area in an expanding ring. No results so far."

"What're the search protocols? Are they armed?"

"We divided the searchers into teams of six—five plus one of our security people as team leader. The team leader is armed, but others are also carrying personal weapons. Colorado is an open-carry state, and we're clearly dealing with some bad guys. We're calling in employees from out of the valley and hope to have two hundred on the ground by the end of the day."

"Were you able to pick up a trail?"

"No."

"Not a blood trail, drops, or tracks? The victims must've been actively bleeding, judging from those stains."

"We looked. There was nothing like that. Believe me, we're working on it."

"Dogs?"

"Not yet."

"We'll get some. So tell me about your security."

"All our animals carry video recorders and GPS. We're reviewing the tapes as we speak."

"Your animals are on video?"

"Not *on* video. Each one has a video collar, forward mounted, so we see approximately what the animal is seeing. Those feeds are monitored twenty-four-seven in our central hub. There are also some cameras set up at the high mountain pass at the head of the valley, which goes over to the other side into the Flat Tops Wilderness Area."

"The only pass out?"

"The only one not requiring technical climbing skills."

She turned to Colcord. "Sheriff, do you work with any local dog handlers?"

"We've got a top-notch search and rescue team out of Eagle," Colcord said.

"Can you get them up here ASAP?"

"Already in process. They'll be here in two and a half hours."

Cash was pleasantly surprised. "Can you fill me in on what else you've done, Sheriff?"

He touched his hat. "We've got our own search team out there liaising with Erebus. We brought in a search and rescue helicopter, which has joined Erebus in searching from the air. And . . . we called you."

She nodded. "Thank you, Sheriff." She turned back to Maximilian. "I'd like to talk to the guide who was with the victims. Is he here?"

Maximilian waved over a man, wiry and fit, with a fine head of grizzled hair, clean shaven, skin the color and texture of leather.

"Agent in Charge Cash, CBI," she said, not bothering to stick out her hand. She hated chitchat, social niceties, and handshakes at a crime scene and didn't want to encourage it. She waved her CBI-issued cell phone at him. "Any objection to recording?"

"Not at all."

She turned to Maximilian. "I might have a few questions for you too in a moment."

"I'd like to be in on this conversation," the sheriff said.

"Of course." She pressed Record, slipped it in her shirt pocket, microphone facing the man. "For the record, your name and title?"

"Stefan Dressel. Erebus guide, A level."

"This is just a preliminary interview. We'll want more detail from you later. Totally voluntary. Okay?"

"Understood." Unlike Maximilian, Dressel looked badly shaken up, his face drawn and white, his fingers fiddling with a carabiner loop on his belt. It looked like he'd been up all night, eyes bloodshot and jittery.

"Age?"

"Fifty-nine."

"How long have you worked for Erebus?"

"Ten years."

"Before that?"

"I was a Colorado mountain guide in the summer and taught ice climbing in the Uncompahgre Gorge in the winter. I was also a part-time ski instructor, Keystone and Vail."

"Let's start with your clients. How did you get assigned to them, and what were they like?"

He nodded, eager to cooperate. "The A level guides are assigned the, ah, best clients. Mark and Olivia Gunnerson—you know, he's the son of the tech billionaire."

She nodded. This was getting tiresome, hearing about this billionaire's son.

"And she was on the Olympic ski team. They're both experienced backpackers and mountaineers. They didn't need me. I think they hired me to make sure they'd see plenty of wildlife."

"Nice people?"

"Very nice. Genuinely nice. Not what you might think. They're on their honeymoon—Erebus caters to honeymooners, as you probably know."

"When did you set out?"

"Yesterday morning. Early. We left the lodge at around four a.m. in a jeep, got to the trailhead at first light. It's a fourteen-mile hike up here."

"Were they strong hikers?"

"Oh yeah."

"Anything happen on the hike?"

"Nothing much. We saw some glyptodons."

Glyptodons. What the hell were glyptodons? She'd find out later. "When did you get here?"

"About three. Set up camp. Right before dinner, we saw a family of woolly mammoths at the lake. They come every evening—one reason why we bring people to camp here."

"What time was that?"

"Around five. We watched the mammoths for a while, until they went below the ridge, where they usually spend the night."

"And then?"

"We made dinner."

"Who made dinner?"

"Mark and I."

"Menu?"

"Freeze-dried chicken and rice. Cocoa. Cookies for dessert."

Cash made a face. "Freeze-dried food?" She hated the stuff. "I thought this was a fancy resort."

"Yes, but this is no luxury safari. It's a real backpack. No food drops. We carry all our stuff for a full eight-day circuit, so we have to pack super light."

"Alcohol?"

"He brought some bourbon, which we drank. Not her, but Mark and I."

"How much?"

"We shared out half a pint, I'd say, maybe a little more."

"Any drugs? Pot?"

"No."

Cash nodded. "And then?"

"Sun set around six thirty. We sat around the fire, and then I went to my tent."

"Where's your tent? I don't see it."

"Behind the aspen grove about a hundred yards off." He gestured. "Over that way and around the corner."

"You went to bed that early?"

"They're newlyweds . . . I left them alone so they could have their privacy."

"What time was that?"

"About seven thirty."

"I see the packs over there on the ground, leaning against the tree. How come you didn't hang your gear against bears?"

"There aren't any bears in Erebus."

"No bears? In the Colorado mountains?"

At this, Maximilian, who had been standing nearby and listening, gently interceded. "When Erebus was set up," he said, "we relocated all the predators from the area—bears, mountain lions, bobcats, wolves, coyotes, and so forth."

"Why was that?"

"As I'm sure you know, we've introduced six de-extincted species of Pleistocene megafauna in here. All peaceful herbivores. Each animal we de-extinct costs us millions of dollars. We can't have them being preyed upon. This may look like wilderness, but the truth is, the ecology in the valley is carefully curated and monitored."

"And predators can't get in or out over the mountains?"

"There's only Espada Pass, thirteen thousand feet, which goes over the mountains and down into the Flat Tops Wilderness Area. It's got monitors and alarms, including cameras watched twenty-four-seven. Nothing can get in or out without us knowing."

"You said all the animals are herbivores. No saber-toothed cats, that sort of thing?"

"None."

"It's my understanding," said Cash, "that in Africa, elephants are among the most dangerous animals."

"You are correct about elephants in Africa. But, Agent Cash, let me assure you that this is no Jurassic Park. In resurrecting our megafauna, our scientists carefully removed the genes for aggression. Every single animal is chipped and equipped with a GPS unit and live video collar, monitored continuously. We know where each animal is every second of the day and night. No animal was in or near the camp last night. We confirmed this. There were some mammoths sheltering below the ridge about half a mile away—their habitual spot—and that's the closest any came to the camp."

"So you're saying that it's impossible for an animal to have done this?" She gestured at the two pools of blood near the tent.

"That's exactly what I'm saying." He added dryly, "And animals don't carry knives."

"How do you know it was done with a knife?"

"What else could have made that cut?"

"A sharp claw might have done it."

"It seems to me a clawed animal would have left multiple parallel cuts," Maximilian said. "And anyway, as I said, we know where our animals are, and all predators in the valley have been removed. Trust me, this was done by a human being."

Cash nodded. He was probably right, and she was just being contrary. "We're gonna take the tent back to the lab and do a microscopic examination of that cut."

"I'm glad to hear it."

Cash turned to Dressel. "I interrupted you in your story. Go on."

He nodded and cleared his throat. "So I undressed and got into my sleeping bag."

"Wearing?"

"Um, nothing. I sleep in the nude."

She nodded approvingly.

"It was early, so I read."

"What did you read?"

"A novel."

"What novel?"

"*Bloodless* by Preston and Child."

"Any good?"

"So good I was worried I wouldn't be able to get to sleep."

"Go on."

"At one point, I heard a tearing sound from the direction of their tent. At the time, I just thought it was one of them making a tent repair or pulling off a piece of duct tape. They were experienced wilderness travelers. I wasn't the slightest bit worried about them. So I did nothing."

"How long did the sound last?"

"Maybe two or three seconds. A kind of slow tearing."

"Time?"

"I didn't check my watch, but it was around nine. Anyway, after the sound, there was a silence. I went back to reading, and then I heard another sound, not exactly a scream but a loud grunt, cut short. It didn't sound right. I sat up and listened. That's when I heard a horrible scream."

"How long between the grunt and the scream?"

"Oh, around thirty seconds, maybe less." The guide removed a cloth dangling from his belt and mopped his face. His hand was trembling slightly. He was a good witness, Cash thought. Observant, focused, keeping his shit together.

"And then?"

"I pulled on my clothes and boots and ran up to their tent. When I got there, I saw two headlamps, still lit, on the ground, and two knives—and those two big pools of blood."

Cash said, "How long between the first grunt you heard and your arrival at the tent? Please give your answer some thought. It's crucial we nail down the precise time sequence."

Dressel was silent for a moment. "Well, as I said, there was about thirty seconds between the grunt and the scream. That's when I jumped out of my bag, put on my long johns, socks, and boots. I didn't lace them up, just stuffed the laces inside and pulled them on. Let's see . . . I also got my headlamp and grabbed my buck knife. I ran to their tent, which was about three hundred feet on the other side of the trees . . . I would guess the whole process took me three, four minutes, give or take."

"What route did you take from your tent to theirs?"

"I went around the aspens." He turned and pointed. "You can't see my tent, but it's just behind those trees."

"We'll measure the distance in a moment," Cash said. "And during that time, while you were running to the tent, did you hear anything more? Sounds of a struggle, footfalls, voices?"

"Nothing. But I was in such a panic and moving so fast I wasn't really listening."

Cash paused. Her eyes drifted to the two pools of blood, which had congealed among the matted grass, one a yard across, the other slightly smaller. Romanski and the ME were crouched over them, swabbing, collecting samples, measuring and probing the stain, and inspecting the ground for hair and fibers. She hated to take them from their work, but . . . She called out, "Hey, Bart, can you and the doc come over here for a moment?"

The two finished what they were doing and ducked under the crime scene tape, removing their face masks and goggles, Huizinga's blond hair stuck out in a silly way. He could have been a male model, she thought, were he not so nerdy. Romanski was hollow-faced, and the usual wry expression gone.

"How much blood is in each of those stains?" she asked.

Huizinga shook his head. "We're going to address that question when we get everything back to the lab."

"Take a guess now."

"You *know* I hate guessing."

"Would you prefer having a pissed-off boss?"

The young ME shook his head. "Well, if you insist . . . I'd *guess* two to three liters. Please don't hold me to it."

"Would that be fatal?"

"Two liters is extremely dangerous if you don't get blood volume up right away. For a woman, it might be fatal—they have less blood. Three liters would be fatal for anyone."

"Thanks," said Cash.

Colcord, who had been listening quietly but intently, cleared his throat. "Doctor, could they have been able to walk after that much blood loss?"

"No," said Huizinga. "They would have been unconscious."

"So they had to have been carried. I don't see any signs of dragging."

"I would say so."

"Two bodies, carried, would take at least two, and probably four people," Colcord observed mildly.

Cash was surprised at the insight and wondered if she needed to revise her opinion of Sheriff Colcord.

"Mr. Dressel," Colcord went on, "says he was on-site within three to four minutes of hearing the scream. The bodies were already gone. So my question to you, Doctor, is how did these two victims bleed this much in such a short time? Isn't that a lot of blood to lose so quickly?"

The expression on Huizinga's face was one of great discomfort. "I'd really prefer not to conjecture on that question without more data."

Cash scowled. "Look, Chris, we've got to know *right now* whether we're looking for corpses or kidnap victims."

"Well"—the doctor shifted his weight—"my guess is that they are dead."

"Even at the low estimate of two liters?"

"Yes, because it would be hard to exsanguinate two liters in four minutes unless . . ." He hesitated.

"Unless what?"

"They were decapitated."

5

Sheriff Jim Colcord watched the CSI team doing their thing. From what he could see, they appeared thorough and competent. The team leader, what was his name?—Romanski—had taken off his protective suit and was packing the evidence containers in canvas duffels. Sections of bloodstained turf were being cut from the ground and removed. It amazed Colcord to see what was taken as evidence these days, even bloody sod. No wonder the evidence warehouse back in Denver was vast—Colcord had seen it several times during the course of his two terms as sheriff of Eagle County. It was as big as a Sam's Club.

They had gathered so much evidence that there was no way they could carry it out on their backs. Instead, they were strapping it into helicopter baskets, ready to be picked up by a hovering bird and flown to Denver. Meanwhile, Colcord had learned on the radio that the chopper carrying the dogs had dropped them with their handler off at the LZ and they were now hiking up. He had worked with the dog handler before—Acosta. The guy was first-rate. They'd track down these bastards in no time, he hoped. This was certainly one of the craziest murders he'd been involved in—and he was pretty sure it was murder, given what the doc had said.

While waiting for them to arrive, Colcord got on the walkie-talkie and checked on the status of the search. It was going poorly, apparently, over a hundred people beating the bushes for hours and coming up empty-handed. He could see some of them below, a line of them working their way through a meadow of tall grass. It was close to noon, and the day had turned into one of crisp fall clarity, clouds passing over the mountains, their shadows moving up and down as they traveled over the landscape.

His deputy, Sandoval, came from around the grove of trees, laying out a measuring string, the guide showing her the route he'd taken in responding to the scream. He watched Cash walking around, taking notes in a little notebook. He hoped the pain-in-the-ass CBI agent with the Red Sox cap and Boston accent—was it Boston? He wasn't sure—wouldn't come along on the dog tracking. It remained to be seen whether she was any good at her job. She was big and tough and apparently fit, if heavy. Short auburn hair, green eyes, no makeup except for a touch of lipstick, freckles, obviously some Irish in there, pugnacious expression on her face, lower lip thrust out. New to the job, he would guess, trying to prove herself.

He watched as the CSI guy straightened up from packing the evidence bundles, putting his hands on his hips and stretching his back, first one way and then the other, cracking it. Cash, standing next to him, winced.

"That can't be good for you," she said to him.

"Whaddya mean? It's stretching. Like yoga."

"That's not yoga. You keep that back-cracking up and you'll be using a walker with those little yellow tennis balls by the time you're seventy."

"It's what the chiropractor does to my back."

"Chiropractors are quacks."

Romanski laughed. "You're in an ornery mood, Frankie."

"I'm always in an ornery mood—didn't you know that?"

Annoyed by the banter, Colcord moved away so that he could think in peace. How could two bodies just vanish like that? They'd already looked into the lake—that was one of the first places they'd searched—nothing.

Sandoval came up alongside him, rolling up the measuring string. "Looks like the information we got from the guide was spot-on."

Colcord nodded.

"Think they're dead?" she asked.

Colcord shook his head. "I'd hate to speculate about that now, but . . . yeah." He paused; he could hear the faint baying of the hound dogs from down the trail, gradually getting louder. The dogs appeared—two redbone bloodhounds, droopy ears swinging, tongues hanging out. The handler, a tall, unshaven man with long black hair, half-Arapaho, came up behind, holding the dogs on long leashes—Sam Acosta, well known to Colcord. He raised his hand in greeting and Colcord did the same. Acosta never shook hands—he claimed to be avoiding the transfer of scents.

Acosta ordered his dogs to sit, and they obeyed immediately.

Cash and Romanski came over.

"Agent Cash," said Colcord, "Detective Romanski—Sam Acosta."

Acosta gravely raised his hand again. "Do we have a scent article?" he asked, looking around to no one in particular. "I don't mean to rush things, but the clock is ticking on that trail."

"Bart?" said Cash. "Show Mr. Acosta what you got."

Romanski pulled out two ziplock bags containing socks of each victim.

Acosta took them. "How old is the trail?"

"About fifteen hours."

He nodded and took the two bags she offered. The dogs were sitting, hyperalert, their ears perked and mouths open, panting eagerly.

He turned to Colcord. "Sheriff, any idea where the trail goes?"

"No," said Colcord. "You'll need to start at ground zero—the tent site. It's that flagged area there."

"Who's coming along?" Acosta asked.

"I will," said Cash right away.

"And you, Sheriff?"

"Certainly," Colcord said, trying to maintain a neutral expression on his face. He was relieved that Maximilian was off with his people, a cluster of men on walkie-talkies on the far side of the crime scene tape. He could see one of Erebus's helicopters making yet another circuit farther up the valley. With all the people out there and three choppers no less, he wondered how at least four killers, burdened with two corpses, could get away without leaving a trail—and then stay hidden. And what the heck was the motive? The more he thought about it, the crazier this case felt.

"Okay, here are the rules," said Acosta. "Stay at least fifty feet back. When the dogs hit a corner or a back track, they'll start to circle. So stop when they stop and remain in the rear until they pick up the trail again." He hesitated. "Sheriff, can you tell me how many suspects we're pursuing and if they're armed?"

"Four, at least," said Colcord. "They're probably armed with knives. I don't know about firearms. When you think we're getting close, or if we corner them, hold the dogs back while we call in reinforcements."

"Sure enough. Let's go." Acosta led the dogs under the crime scene tape to the flagged area where the tent was, knelt, gave the dogs a good long sniff of the socks along with issuing a stream of soft commands. He then unclipped their leashes. The dogs sprang up and began circling fast, their noses to the ground. They immediately came to the two bloodstains, spent a few moments there, and then took off heading down the hill toward the pond.

Another soft command from Acosta stopped them. He went on to them and clipped back on their leashes.

"Do they have a scent?" asked Cash.

"You bet they do. These dogs don't run deer or rabbits, only people, and they don't bay while on a scent unless they tree a person."

The dogs, now leashed, moved down the slope at a deliberate pace, sniffing vigorously. The incline was strewn with boulders. The meadow gave way to patches of brush and clusters of scrub oaks, the dogs weaving among the obstacles, moving decisively along the scent trail. Colcord followed with Cash behind him. This was really encouraging. They might wrap this case up by nightfall.

"These look like good dogs," Cash said to Colcord.

"The best. Eagle County includes the Vail Ski Resort, White River National Forest, and the Flat Tops. And a long stretch of I-70. These dogs are working all the time. You wouldn't believe how many people get lost in the mountains." He hesitated. "You know, people from places like . . . Boston."

She looked at him sharply and then laughed. "Oh yeah. Boston. I can believe it. Where I come from, people from Boston get lost there all the time."

Okay, she's not from Boston. He wanted to ask the next obvious question—where she came from and what that accent was—but decided not to.

The slope leveled out into a rocky basin and rose toward a ridgeline of traprock. They intersected a trail beaten down among the boulders, and the dogs followed it eagerly.

Cash leaned toward Colcord. "If they're armed," she said quietly, "we could end up in a shoot-out. What do you carry?"

Colcord liked being asked the question. "Beretta 92. You?"

"Baby Glock 9 millimeter."

He nodded. That seemed like the right kind of firearm for her. He wondered if she could shoot. He was pretty sure nobody from back East could shoot worth a shit, but you never knew. Colcord, like many native Coloradans, had a suspicion of transplanted Easterners.

They continued along the trail, broad and as hard-packed as concrete. They halted as the dogs, up ahead, paused and took a sudden, intense interest in a low, greenish-brown rock.

"I'd guess we're following a woolly mammoth trail," said Colcord.

"Really? How do you know?"

"I've done a lot of tracking, and I don't know any native animal that would leave a trail as beaten down as this one. And also—that." Colcord pointed to what the dogs were sniffing, to the growing impatience of Acosta, who was murmuring disapproval and pulling on the leashes.

"That rock?"

"No. That pile of shit."

Cash stared, then laughed. "Oh my God, it *is* a shit pile."

"They're all over," said Colcord. "Just like a cow pasture, only mammoth pies are ten times bigger."

The dogs finally abandoned the shit heap and continued up the mammoth trail, going up the ridge. When they reached the top, the blue lake sprang into view again, riffled by the breeze. As she looked down the face of the ridge they were on, she saw a big area of trampled dirt in the sheltered hollow below. There were many piles of dung strewn about, along with chewed and frayed pieces of wood and bits of bark and other animal detritus. At the edge of the lake was a giant mud wallow.

"This must be their stomping ground," said Cash.

The dogs had hesitated at the top of the ridge and circled a bit—a "corner" in Acosta's tracking jargon—and then headed quickly down the trail.

"I wonder where the mammoths are now," said Cash. "I'd sure like to see one."

"Right there," said Colcord. He'd spotted a gigantic mammoth just emerging from an aspen forest across the lake, less than half a mile away. It stopped, having seen them too. It raised its trunk into the air and waved it about, furry ears flapping slowly. A second mammoth came out and halted. In the trees, they could see a few more, including a bull with tusks.

"Oh, wow," said Cash. "They are *big*."

Colcord stared. Seeing these animals in the flesh was amazing. Not even Africa had animals like this. And they were *alive*. He found himself entranced by these towering, shaggy beasts, hair springing from their heads like giant toupees, furry ears waggling, trunks swinging. He never would have believed it possible that an animal so large and powerful could be so cute and cuddly. Colcord had been reading and hearing about the Erebus Resort for years, but you really had to see these animals in the flesh, he thought, to understand why it had become one of the most popular destinations in Colorado.

The dogs halted in their tracks, frozen, staring at the mammoths.

"They're supposed to be as gentle as puppies," said Colcord.

"Unless you get stepped on."

The mammoths, unperturbed by the dogs, continued feeding, tearing lower branches off the trees and stuffing them into their mouths, chewing them up, leaves, wood, and all. Even from half a mile, he could hear the racket they were making and the crunching and grinding of their teeth. Out of the trees bounded a little one, trunk swinging, making a high-pitched noise of distress, running to catch up to its mother.

"There's Ping," said Cash.

Colcord had no idea what she was talking about but didn't ask.

The dogs, having recovered from their surprise, resumed tracking, moving faster now and more determinedly. Colcord felt even more encouraged; this was going to lead them right to the bodies, if not the killers. They'd have to be careful and call in reinforcements for the final approach.

At the bottom of the ridge, they turned right, heading for the heaviest concentration of mammoth activity, weaving among increasingly closely spaced piles of dung, much of it having been trampled and spread around into green puddles and skid marks and smears—the elephants walking around in their own shit. Did they also do that in Africa? Colcord wondered.

"Welcome to Uncle Woolly's Watering Hole," said Cash.

In the midst of the thickest area of mammoth activity, the dogs began to circle again. And circle. Acosta finally released them from their leashes, and they went loping around in widening gyres, this way and that, noses scanning the ground. Minutes passed.

Colcord watched as the dogs ranged ever farther afield. It was not an encouraging sight; they seemed to have lost the trail.

"I wonder how the dogs can follow the scent here, with all this dung around," Cash said, wrinkling her nose.

"I believe," said Colcord, "that's the idea."

"Idea?"

"The killers' idea."

"What do you mean?"

"A dung heap like this," said Colcord, "is a perfect place to confuse and shake tracking bloodhounds."

6

Detective Bart Romanski rose to his feet and cracked his back again—this time out of earshot of Cash—and bundled the last duffel of evidence into the helicopter litter, then strapped it down. Cash and the sheriff had returned thirty minutes before with the tracker and his dogs. It had been a bust—they apparently had lost the trail in a mammoth shit-palace down by the lake. The dogs had left for home, heading back down the trail with Acosta, tails between their legs with shamed expressions on their droopy faces.

Romanski had gathered a lot of evidence. "When in doubt, take it out" was his motto. They must have two hundred pounds of evidence in the two litters, much of the weight coming from bloody sections of turf Reno had cut out from the stained ground.

"Lemme see what you got," said Cash, coming over. She was all red-faced and sweaty and annoyed-looking. Romanski had seen her like this before, and at those times, she was to be avoided at all costs.

He handed her the iPad with the evidence list. She took it and, frowning, began flicking through it with her finger, making grunting noises.

"Lot of latents, I see. You think whoever did this wasn't wearing gloves?"

"It's hard to tell," said Romanski, "until we rule out latents from the people we know were here. But there was no wipe-down, no glove smears. I'm not sure there was any reason for the killers to touch the tent or anything—possibly only the knives and headlamps. We got some full and partials off those."

"Swab for DNA?"

"Oh yeah. Swabbed everything. It was a pretty clean crime scene, organized. This was no messy, spontaneous attack—this was planned. Choreographed, even."

She looked up from the iPad and squinted, looking out over the valley, tinged yellow and orange in the setting sun. "Where the hell do you think they went?"

Romanski grunted. "There's a hundred thousand acres out there."

"Why did they take the bodies?"

Romanski had the feeling she was thinking out loud, so he said nothing. In his career as a forensic specialist, he'd seen a lot of criminal behavior that totally defied explanation. Some people were just fucking crazy.

She returned her focus to the iPad and went through the rest of the list, grunting her approval, or at least Romanski hoped that's what those grunts meant. She handed it back. "You done and ready to fly this stuff out?"

"Yes. It's too much to carry, so the chopper's gonna drop a rope for it."

"Good. Let's get this evidence back to Arvada."

"Right." He got on the radio and called the A-Star, which had been waiting at the landing zone for their call, and told them the litters of evidence were ready. Huizinga, Reno, and the rest had already headed down to the landing zone and would be flying back to Arvada with the basket.

"I want you to light a fire under the labs," she said. "I want top priority." She looked at her watch. "Maybe you can get a head start on it tonight—I'll authorize overtime."

"You got it, boss." Romanski loved overtime. Not only did it pay double, but he got to work at night, his favorite time. He was a nighthawk from way back.

He could hear the A-Star thudding up from the LZ, and it soon appeared above the trees. It turned and went into a hover, stabilizing itself, the noise loud and echoing off the mountain peaks. The downdraft from the rotors stirred everything up, lashed the bushes, and sucked up a bunch of leaves from the aspens, which whirled around like golden coins.

A cable lowered from a hoist in the open door. Romanski grabbed it as it descended within reach, guided it down, and clipped it to the first litter. The winch pulled it up, and they stowed it in one of the helicopter's side baskets. After a moment, the cable descended again, and he clipped it to the second litter, stowed in the other basket.

Meanwhile, Romanski slipped into a harness and sling seat himself, and when the cable descended the third time, he clipped into it and was hoisted up and into the A-Star, the door slid shut, and he unclipped and put on his seat harness.

The helicopter, now fully loaded, set off eastward over the Front Range toward Arvada, the Denver suburb where the Forensic Services building was located. As Romanski eased back in the seat, watching the stupendous Rocky Mountains unroll beneath him, he felt the indescribable thrill of being on a big case. This was what he lived for.

Romanski's interest in forensic work had been ignited when he was ten years old and his crazy English uncle gave him a book about Sir Bernard Spilsbury, the man who invented forensic pathology. He devoured those notorious British cases from the early twentieth century, classics that included the Brides in the Bath murders, the case of Dr. Crippen, and the Crumbles murders. Spilsbury was legendary for his fearsome courtroom appearances and his application of scientific methods to what had previously been guesswork and intuition. No jury could resist his unruffled certitude and keen language as he used science to put away killer after killer. Ever since, Romanski had been enthralled by the whole range of forensic science—pathology, fingerprints, hair and fiber, adipocere, blood splatter, the chemistry of poisons—the works. Spilsbury was the inventor of the "murder bag," and as a teenager, Romanski had created his own Spilsbury murder bag, with tweezers, gloves, evidence tubes, magnifying glass, and swabs, which he carried to school and with which he pretended to solve crimes until it was taken away by the horrified principal. He graduated from CU Denver's forensic science program, one of the best in the country, with a master's degree in crime analysis, and went straight into the Forensic Services division of the CBI, where he had risen to chief in twelve years.

In his spare time, Romanski was also an amateur sculptor who welded together giant faces out of junk—boilers, springs, automobile engines, flywheels, gears, and anything else he could find at various junkyards and scrap dealers. It was a strange hobby for a forensic scientist, everyone told him—but he saw building a picture of a crime not unlike building his "portraits" out of discarded steel junk: you had to take a lot of apparently unconnected pieces and weld them together to create a portrait of the crime.

As the chopper cleared the Front Range and began to turn, heading for the CBI lab complex, Romanski thought about the crime scene he had just processed. He knew—he just *knew*—that this would be the biggest crime of his career so far. This was not some one-off crime—this had all the hallmarks of an opening volley, with the main action yet to come.

7

Cash watched the bird carrying Romanski disappear over the ring of mountains. It was getting on toward evening, and the search parties had still come up with nothing—not even a drop of blood. After discussing it with her boss, McFaul, she'd decided to stay at the resort to supervise the case full-time. With the CBI chopper gone, she tagged a ride on the Eagle County Sheriff's Office bird back to the lodge, where, she knew, an all-nighter awaited her.

They took off as the sun hung fire over the mountaintops. As they skimmed past meadows and valleys, Cash glimpsed strung-out lines of Erebus searchers moving steadily across the rugged landscape, and she once again wondered how the hell four people with two bodies could just disappear like that. That was a big area to search, and she wondered if it might be appropriate to request a National Guard deployment, since it would not be best practices to leave the search mostly up to Erebus personnel. There was always the possibility that someone at Erebus might have been involved in the crime.

It was a ten-minute flight to the lodge. The helicopter set down on the heliport on the lodge's roof. Maximilian, who had left the crime scene earlier, met them. No one spoke as the three of them took the elevator down to the main floor of the lodge.

When the doors opened, it was a showstopper. Cash found herself staring into a magnificent space framed in massive wooden beams and log walls that gave her the feeling of being in a great Adirondack lodge. A huge stone fireplace dominated the center, in which burned a real fire. This was surrounded by rustic sofas and chairs of wood and leather, with Navajo rugs on the floor and an immense chandelier of elk antlers above. The log walls were decorated with crossed wooden skis and snowshoes and paintings of mammoths and other extinct animals. A faint smell of piñon smoke from the fire added to the atmosphere of a Western lodge.

The right side of the lofty room opened into a cantilevered deck that extended out into space, ending in a glass wall. The glass was crowded with people looking out, a murmur rising.

Cash paused, wondering what was going on—what they were all looking at.

Maximilian asked, "You've not been here before?"

"No," said Cash.

"Me neither," Colcord said.

"Sunset is when many of the animals come to the lake. We have a traditional gathering on the observation deck every evening. Would you like to see?"

"I sure would," said Colcord.

Cash felt a twinge of impatience; they had more important things to do. But she said nothing. She noticed that Colcord, in the classic Western style, had not removed his cowboy hat inside. She still hadn't made up her mind about him, but at least he wasn't a talker. She hated talkers.

"Follow me."

She and Colcord followed Maximilian past the great stone fireplace and out onto the deck. It offered spectacular views of the lake and mountains, the peaks aflame with the setting sun. The wall was formed from seamless curved glass, and sections of the floor were also glass, looking down. People had gathered, drinks in hand, oohing and aahing as they watched a family of woolly mammoths disporting themselves on the lakeshore and wading in the shallows. A calf, like a fur ball, splashed and stomped in the water, playfully squirting his mother and everyone within reach. On the other side, a herd of giant elk quietly watered.

Cash, despite herself, was entranced. She glanced over at Colcord, but it was hard to read him. She'd been hearing about the Erebus Resort for years but never took much interest in it herself, dismissing it as a kind of Disneyland for rich people. But this—it was genuinely amazing.

"That mammoth family comes here every evening," murmured Maximilian. "The baby is a favorite. Nicknamed Tom Thumb after P. T. Barnum's famous little elephant. We have three mammoth herds in the park. And those"—he pointed—"are Irish elk, *Megaloceros giganteus*. Not an elk at all but a giant deer. The antlers are twelve feet from tip to tip and weigh close to ninety pounds."

"A hell of a trophy that would make," said Colcord.

Cash frowned. What a comment. She couldn't imagine killing one of those animals.

Maximilian pointed. "And here comes one of my favorites, right on time, *Megatherium americanum*, the giant ground sloth."

A sharp buzz of excitement rose from the crowd, and there was a movement of people to one side to get a better view. A creature had just emerged from the trees, seeming more like a freak of nature than an animal. It was as big as the mammoths, twenty feet from its awkward head to its thick tail, covered in cinnamon-colored fur. It waddled on two stumpy back legs and two front legs, in a pigeon-toed gait. It periodically stopped to reach up with a clawed paw to snag down a branch. An enormous tongue then snaked out and, curling around, it stripped off the leaves with incredible efficiency. The creature then moved on, repeating the process left and right, leaving a trail of broken and torn-off branches in its wake.

"God must have been drunk when he designed that creature," murmured Cash.

"We have only one of those," said Maximilian. "It was challenging to de-extinct because its living relatives are genetically distant and much smaller. It's the very hellion of an eater, stripping several acres of trees in a day."

"Doesn't it get lonely?" Cash asked.

"It's a solitary animal in the wild. They only come together to mate . . . but our animals don't mate."

"Poor buggers," said Cash, then re-collected herself. "This is interesting, but the sheriff and I have business to take care of." She made an effort to return to an air of professionalism.

"Right," said Colcord.

"Of course." Maximilian led them away from the glass wall. They crossed the great room and came to a door marked STAFF ONLY. Maximilian used a key card on a lanyard to enter. As he did so, he said, "I'll get you both one of these."

"Thank you."

The change from rustic Western luxury to C-suite elegance was abrupt. A corridor of blond wood paneling with recessed lighting led into a suite of executive offices. One of the first was marked DIRECTOR OF SECURITY, and this they entered.

The outer office was occupied by two assistants, even though it was after six o'clock. They passed through a second door into Maximilian's inner office.

It was a beautiful room, again paneled in blond wood, with a real fireplace, several old Navajo rugs, a capacious desk, and a sitting area of leather furniture. At the far end, a picture window looked out over the lake.

"Please, have a seat," Maximilian said.

They seated themselves.

"Coffee, tea, water?"

"Coffee for me," said Cash.

"Same," said Colcord, finally taking off his hat and placing it on the table. Cash was shocked to see Colcord was almost entirely bald, with just a fringe of blond hair. No wonder he wore the hat most of the time.

Maximilian touched a unit on a table. "Miriam, could you kindly bring in some fresh coffee, along with an assortment of snacks?" He sat back and folded his hands. "Now—what next? We want to help you in every possible way to track down these killers."

"Thank you," said Cash. "I'll start by asking you if you have any idea who might be behind this. Could it be any of your staff or guests? Do you have enemies?"

"We've accounted for everyone on payroll—everyone," said Maximilian. "No guests are unaccounted for either. I think it has to be someone from the outside."

"Any thoughts on who?"

"We've had no end of environmental protesters trying to shut us down. Early on, a radical antidevelopment group set fire to the gatehouse at the valley entrance while it was under construction. They were caught—thanks to Sheriff Colcord."

The sheriff nodded. "They were pretty ragtag, but we're looking into them and their associates now."

Cash remembered how, when Erebus was built some ten years ago, right after she had arrived at the CBI, there were a bunch of protests. "Have there been any recent threats?"

"The protests mostly died down. We still get the occasional anonymous threat. I've asked my staff to compile them, and we'll of course share them with you."

"Thank you," said Cash. "I've drawn up a list of specific ways Erebus can support our investigation." She took out a handwritten sheet she had hastily drawn up. "We'd like to set up a command and control center here, in the lodge. Tonight. Large enough to accommodate up to ten personnel, with a separate room for private interviews."

"Done."

"I'll need a guest room for a Forensic Services specialist, and a storage area. A room for myself. And meals, et cetera."

"We are at your disposal. Sheriff?"

"I'll also need two rooms, for myself and Deputy Sandoval," he said.

"Done."

"Tomorrow morning, early," said Cash, "I'd like to have a tour of the resort. I need to get a handle on the geography of the valley and what you do. I'd like to see everything. Sheriff, you're welcome to come."

"I will, thank you."

"And then I'd like to start conducting interviews. We'll start with you and Maitland Barrow and your CEO, and anyone connected with the victims from the time of their arrival at the resort, including guests. If you could put together a list of the people the two victims interacted with in a meaningful way, that would be helpful. As we collect more evidence, our list of interviewees will grow—that's how it usually goes."

At this, Maximilian folded his hands. "Our founder, Maitland Barrow, isn't here, and I doubt he would agree to an interview. He's quite . . . inaccessible. And anyway, he hasn't been here in at least a month, so I doubt he has any information of value to contribute."

Cash said, "A voluntary interview is always better than a subpoena, don't you agree? But I hear you. I'll let you know when and if we need to interview him."

"As for interviewing guests," Maximilian said, "that might be awkward."

Cash raised her eyebrows questioningly and waited.

"Obviously, we want to keep this incident from frightening the guests." He hesitated. "We've been fortunate in keeping it under wraps so far."

"What exactly are you telling people?" Colcord asked.

"Just that two guests have gone missing in the backcountry. It would make your job and mine much harder if we had a valley full of panicked guests—not to mention the media swarming about."

"There's a simple solution to that," said Cash evenly. "Shut down the resort until we find the killers."

At this, Maximilian displayed a frisson of horror. "You aren't serious."

Cash had gone over this many times in her mind and had conferred with McFaul, who was fully against the idea of ordering Erebus shut, even if the CBI had the authority to do so, which it did not. "At this point, we're not officially recommending a shutdown." She leaned forward on her elbows. "But I'm not sure you're thinking this through, Mr. Maximilian. You've got two victims, who are—let's be real—probably dead. One's an Olympic medalist and the other's a famous billionaire's son. Word's going to get out." She paused. "Have next of kin been notified?"

Maximilian paled more. "Yes."

"I imagine they're on their way right now."

"I believe they are."

"How are you going to keep them from making a scene—and letting the cat out of the bag?"

At that moment, the intercom unit buzzed on Maximilian's desk. He picked up the phone and listened, and his face went just a shade paler. "Tell him I'll see him in a moment. I'm just wrapping up a meeting."

But even before he could put down the phone, a voice roared from the outer office and the door flung open. An enormous man, bulging out of his suit, with a white beard and mussed white hair, stood framed in the doorway like an unruly bear.

"You'll see me now, you son of a bitch, and tell me what the fuck you're doing to find my son!"

8

The man strode in, followed by two men in dark suits. He halted in front of the desk and, placing his forearms on it, leaned forward. "You hear me?"

"Mr. Gunnerson," said Maximilian, recovering his equilibrium, "let me introduce you to Agent Cash of the Colorado Bureau of Investigation and Sheriff Colcord, Eagle County. And let me just say how terribly sorry—"

"Cut the crap." Gunnerson turned to Cash, his eyes darting from her to Colcord. Cash had the feeling he might have been drinking. "So—what're you doing besides sitting on your asses? What *is* the Colorado Bureau of bumfuck or whatever?"

Cash was left momentarily speechless by this sudden abuse. But before she could react, Colcord rose from his chair and spoke, his voice even. "The CBI is Colorado's equivalent to the FBI. We called them in to assist. A comprehensive search for your son is underway. We've put all our top people on this, I can assure you."

Maximilian quickly added, "We've got choppers in the air and a hundred searchers on the ground. They're out there searching nonstop—and will be until we find your son and catch the kidnappers." He took a breath. "Why don't you sit down, Mr. Gunnerson? Can I offer you anything?"

"Scotch, rocks, no water," said Gunnerson gruffly, remaining standing.

Maximilian nodded at his assistant, and she went to the little bar in his office, mixed a drink, and brought it back. Gunnerson took a massive gulp and set it down with a loud noise on a glass coffee table. "I was told this place had world-class security. How the fuck did kidnappers get in here?"

Maximilian remained cool. "We're extremely shocked and extend our profoundest apologies. I can assure you we're doing everything we can—*everything.*"

Gunnerson turned and looked at Cash. "And who is this mute woman over here? What's she doing?"

Cash felt a rush of blood to her face. She managed to say, "I'm the CBI agent in charge."

"Agent in charge? You're in charge—of what?"

Cash stared at the man. She swallowed and told herself he'd lost a son. "Of the case. If you have questions," she said evenly, "please ask them now."

He blinked at her, then pounded down the rest of the drink. "Someone said drops of blood were found at the scene."

"Two areas of blood were found near the tent," said Cash.

"How *much* blood?"

"We're determining that now."

"Enough to kill them?"

"We don't know."

The man was now slurring his words, spittle flying. "You don't *know*? Why didn't anyone tell me?" His two minions moved closer to him, one on either side.

"Mr. Gunnerson—" Colcord began.

Cash held up her hand. "Our assumption is they're still alive. We're working with the utmost urgency."

"But I want to know what *you* think, Agent in Charge Whatever: is he *dead* or *alive*? Tell me the truth, for fuck's sake!"

"Given the large amount of blood found, my personal opinion is that they could not have survived."

He stared at her, his beard quivering. "*I've been lied to.*"

"No, Mr. Gunnerson," said Maximilian hastily. "We're still gathering the basic facts. It's premature to draw conclusions."

With a mighty pivot, Gunnerson slung his drink at the wall, the heavy glass tumbler shattering. He turned with balled fists and advanced toward Maximilian, swaying slightly. *"Liar."*

Maximilian pushed a button on his intercom. "Security, *now*."

The two minions on either side of Gunnerson suddenly closed in on him, and in a practiced move, each took an arm. "Sir?"

He roared and twisted and tried to break free, but they tightened their grip and held him fast.

"Sir. *Please.*"

He abruptly stopped struggling. "My son."

"Let's get you to a room, sir."

"My son." Gunnerson let out a sob.

"We've got it," said the bodyguard to Maximilian. "No worries. It's all good. We need a room for him."

Maximilian turned to an assistant, standing in the door, looking shocked. "Get him a suite. One of the private ones."

It felt to Cash like this wasn't the first time they had been forced to handle Gunnerson like this.

The two men led the billionaire out of the room, holding him up as he staggered and sobbed like a baby.

After a silence, Colcord turned to her. "I'm disgusted at the way he spoke to you."

She stared at him. "Sheriff, I'm not a damsel in distress—understood? I've heard the word *fuck* once or twice before."

She didn't mean to speak so sharply. Colcord's paternal look of concern had annoyed her.

His face colored crimson, but he said nothing.

"I'm so sorry," said Maximilian. "I'll have a conference room cleared for you in thirty minutes. And we'll make sure your rooms are ready."

"I'm going to want to interview that man tomorrow," said Cash. "There's always the possibility his son was targeted because of him. A guy like that's got enemies."

"What about the girl's parents?" asked Cash. "Are they on their way?"

Maximilian hesitated. "Her parents are dead. Her next of kin, a brother, works in Singapore. Apparently, they're . . . not close. I don't think he'll be coming."

As they left the office, Colcord turned to her. "I'm sorry. I didn't mean—"

She held up her hand. "No apologies. Let's just get through this case as quickly as possible."

9

Frankie Cash pressed the keycard against the lock, and it clicked, the door opening on its own. She fumbled for a light switch and flicked it on.

"Oh, Jesus," she said. The room was huge and luxurious, with a sitting room and a bedroom beyond, plate glass windows looking northward into the dark mountains. The sitting room had a kiva fireplace in one corner with an antlered elk skull mounted above it, a fire already built and burning brightly. Pine floors were spread with Navajo rugs, and the walls of the room were like a log cabin, made from hand-adzed logs chinked with mortar. A scroll-pattern crystal chandelier hung from the wood-beamed ceiling. As she looked around, she thought how the room did not make for good optics for a detective on assignment, but it was too late to change, and she was too tired to do anything about it.

Cash groaned and collapsed into the nearest cowhide chair, sinking down into it and leaning back. It was five o'clock in the morning, and she'd been up twenty-four hours straight. She was tired and wanted to get into bed, but her mind was going a mile a minute, and there was no way she could sleep until she'd wound down a bit.

As she sprawled in the chair, her eye strayed to the far wall, which was decorated with an old bamboo fly rod and a creel. It reminded her of her father, a police captain in Portland, who spent every free minute fishing, talking about fishing, and thinking about fishing. He'd taken her fishing as a kid many times, always full of hope that she could be converted. But she'd hated it. Fishing was all about the process, of being present in the moment, about the light reflecting off the riffles and the sound of the stream and the scent of pine needles and fresh water. Cash was too goal oriented. When she didn't catch a fish in ten minutes, she would get annoyed and start lashing the water, getting her fly snagged on brush, pulling too hard and breaking the leader, much to her father's dismay as she ruined pool after pool.

Her dad had retired from the force at sixty-five, looking forward to many long years of fishing—and was dead in six months of pancreatic cancer, cheated by life. At least he hadn't lived long enough to see the shit rain come down on her three years later, from his beloved Portland CID. Her mother was still in Westbrook, outside Portland, playing bridge and attending the bean suppers at the grange, seemingly invincible, leading a full life and in good health . . . so far. Not bad at all for eighty. Cash didn't want to think about what was going to happen when her mother went into the inevitable decline, with her only daughter two thousand miles away.

She groaned again. Maine. It seemed so far away now, the memories softening and dissolving around the edges. She dreamed about it all the time, but each time in the dream, Portland was a little different, changed, a little more foreign. In many of her dreams, she was lost in the back streets of Portland and couldn't find her way home. Or she was in a boat lost on a rough sea, the compass spinning wildly, dark as night, Portland Head Light blinking in the distance through the lashing rain, but she couldn't reach it, couldn't reach the safety of the harbor.

The alarm from her phone cut the air, and she almost fell out of the chair in surprise, morning sun suddenly streaming in the window. For a moment, she was in a panic, wondering where she was. She turned off the cell phone alarm—it was seven a.m. She'd fallen asleep in her clothes sitting in the chair, and now she was stiff and looked like shit.

She eased up from the chair, her back aching from sleeping in an awkward position. She shuffled into the bathroom, a palace of marble and nickel and porcelain, with little soaps and bottles of shampoo and conditioner and creams all lined up.

Looking at herself in the mirror, she frowned, brushed her hair and her teeth, splashed some icy water in her face, and gave it a couple of hard slaps to bring up the color. And then she hunted around for coffee. *Coffee.* And there it was, a gleaming espresso machine as intricate as a miniature nuclear power plant. How wonderful. She fired it up and made two doubles and tossed them down, one after the other.

Another few slaps, a tug on her suit, and she was ready to go.

10

The jeep crawled up the mountain slope through a series of hairpin turns, the final turn disclosing a brace of huge metal doors embedded into the face of a cliff.

"That's some entryway," said Cash.

Colcord said nothing. He looked tired, dark circles, gray pallor. He'd been out with the searchers all night. There were now over a hundred out there beating the bushes, and still they'd found nothing.

"How's your room?" she asked.

"I don't know," he said, "haven't seen it yet. Yours?"

"Over the top."

The jeep slowed at a guardhouse, next to a smaller set of open doors inset into the giant portal. Maximilian showed his badge and was waved through.

The jeep entered a spectacular open space carved into the mountain. Cash estimated it must be at least three hundred feet in diameter and a hundred feet high. A soft light came from a giant rosette window set into the rock above the door, flooding the space with natural light.

"Maitland Barrow loves to impress," said Maximilian. "We bring guests in here all the time, and this just astounds them."

"It's like the volcanic lair in *Goldeneye*," said Cash. "Only bigger."

At this, Colcord broke his silence. "That was *You Only Live Twice*."

Cash looked at him in surprise. "You a James Bond fan?"

"Movie buff in general."

Maximilian halted the jeep in a parking area with many other vehicles, and they got out. The space was like a huge staging area, with rows of vehicles, trucks, and heavy equipment, along with stacks of supplies. Dozens of uniformed employees went to and fro.

"This is incredible," Cash said, craning her neck upward and gazing around. "They must have dug out a whole lot of gold."

"They did, but we enlarged it," Maximilian explained. "This was originally the main entrance to the Fryingpan Mine. Mr. Barrow didn't want to site our labs and offices in visible buildings outside—he wanted to keep the valley as unspoiled as possible—so we retrofitted everything into the old mine complex. The Fryingpan Mine produced wire gold shot through quartz, a beautiful curling form they call ram's horns. The largest of those ram's horns is in the Harvard Mineralogical Museum. There's another mine the next mountain over, called the Hesperus. This was all hard-rock mining, and it left behind a stable system of tunnels and galleries, perfect for our purposes. It happens to be one of the largest hard-rock mining complexes in North America."

"So there are two mines in the valley, Hesperus and Fryingpan?"

"It's really one single mine, hundreds of connected tunnels and shafts driven deep into these mountains following veins of gold."

Cash had a thought. "Could the killers be hiding somewhere in the mines?"

"We absolutely considered that, and the answer is no. When we created Erebus, we carefully surveyed the mines and sealed any open tunnels and shafts with iron plates—riveted shut. We've checked them all—they're intact."

"Could there be openings you didn't find?"

"Not likely."

"Do you have maps of the mines?"

"We do." He hesitated. "Do you need them?"

"We might find them useful."

"I'll send them over—they're in digital form. And they're confidential. We've had problems with security."

"Problems? Such as?"

"Hackers and spies trying to steal our intellectual property. You wouldn't believe the lengths the Chinese have gone to get their hands on our technology. Not to mention the Israelis, the Russians, even some U.S. companies."

"Anyone succeeded?" Cash asked.

"No. We haven't had any security lapses, and we've blocked all cyberattacks."

"Is it possible," Cash asked, "that a competitor might be behind the killings? Murdering guests would be a great way to put you out of business."

"Possible," Maximilian said dryly. "We're looking into that, of course—as should you."

An electric golf cart glided up, driven by a man in uniform.

"All aboard," said Maximilian.

They slid into the buttery leather seats. As they drove across the vast entry space, Cash felt a little disoriented. The amount of money it took to build this must have been staggering.

"We're heading," said Maximilian, "to the main lab, where I'll introduce you to Marius Karman, our chief scientist."

The cart passed through an archway and whispered along a gleaming tunnel lined with doors.

"Media rooms, workrooms, storage, and labs."

The walls and ceilings were painted spring green, with indirect lighting that bathed the space in a pleasing, even light. Many of the workers were wearing uniforms: some an olive-colored jumpsuit with the colorful logo of a woolly mammoth with curving tusks, others lab coats, with security employees distinguished by blue-and-gold insignia.

"Where do you get your power to run this place?" asked Colcord.

"Good question. We bring up power on special DC lines from the interstate, where they're converted to AC in a substation at the Mammoth Gates and run underground from there. We would like to have put in green energy, but it just wasn't practical. The flow of the River Erebus isn't sufficient, and solar and wind power would have marred the landscape." He held out his hands. "We're stuck with Colorado Light and Power. We have two layers of backup power—generators—and three cell towers, well disguised."

The driver arrived at a sealed set of double doors, which Maximilian opened by waving a card. They hissed open, and the cart drove through.

"We're entering a medium-security zone now," Maximilian said. "This is an area most guests don't get to see."

It was another pleasant green corridor with more doors, all unmarked. A few more minutes and the driver halted at a small, unassuming door. They dismounted. Maximilian waved his card, and the door whispered open. Cash could hear, faintly, the sound of someone playing a violin. A beefy security officer with a shaved head met them at the entrance and ushered them down a corridor and through another set of doors into a capacious office. It was handsomely appointed with clean white walls, sleek contemporary furniture, and a large black-and-white rug featuring an abstract design. An old-fashioned blackboard stood at one end, covered with chemical formulae and equations. Opposite the desk was a sitting area, where a man wearing a white lab coat was gently laying down a violin and bow.

He straightened up, a look of displeasure fleeting across his face.

"Sorry to disturb, Dr. Karman," said Maximilian. "I'm with the two people I told you about earlier, who are directing the investigation— Agent Cash and Sheriff Colcord. Dr. Marius Karman, our chief scientist."

Cash looked at the scientist, intrigued. Karman was tall and lanky, with a shock of straight gray hair hanging down over a high forehead, and a craggy face with sunken cheeks and prominent cheekbones. There was an air of old-fashioned European formality about him, reinforced by the fact that he was wearing an elegant suit underneath the white lab coat. He looked to be in his early fifties.

Karman approached, hand extended. "Pleased to meet you," he said, shaking their hands with grave formality.

She noticed that even in here, deep in the mine, Colcord did not remove his cowboy hat.

"Please, have a seat," Karman said, indicating where and waiting for them to sit before he did. "A nasty business. Shocking. Now what can I do to help?"

He had an accent Cash couldn't quite place. Karman . . . What kind of name was that? Hungarian?

"Dr. Karman," she said, "the sheriff and I would like to get a sense of what you do around here."

Karman tented his fingers and leaned back with a frown. "Forgive me, but shouldn't the police be focusing their efforts on finding the killers? I'm not sure I understand how the question is relevant."

This unexpected pushback surprised Cash. "Dr. Karman, this crime may well be an attack directed *at* your organization—so, yes, what you do here is relevant."

She spoke more sharply than she'd intended, but she could already feel a prickle of arrogance from Karman. She had a problem with arrogant people.

"Very well," said Karman. "The Erebus Project was initiated by myself sixteen years ago. I was formerly the director and founder of the celebrated Mammoth Project at MIT, which de-extincted the first woolly mammoth. It died, of course, but it was still one of the great biological milestones in history—as you undoubtedly know."

Cash did not know but said nothing.

"Maitland Barrow hired me away from MIT," he continued, his voice swelling with self-regard. "We shared a vision for creating a park and populating it with de-extincted megafauna from the Pleistocene age—a safari-style park modeled on the great game parks of Africa, with no fences, where visitors could experience the rewilded animals in their natural habitat."

"But it's not really natural," said Cash. "You don't have any predators."

Karman smiled. "Ah yes. How I would have loved to resurrect saber-toothed cats and dire wolves and short-faced bears! But obviously we couldn't do that and have a safe, tourist-friendly place." He turned and picked up a leather-bound portfolio. "We've de-extincted six mammal species so far. Would you care to see?"

"Of course."

He opened it to a dramatic double-spread of a woolly mammoth. "We developed powerful new gene-editing techniques using CRISPR.

Our first successful resurrection was the Columbian mammoth, the northern variety with fur—the largest species of woolly mammoth."

He turned the pages slowly, one after the other, each spread displaying a fantastical beast.

"And here is the Irish elk, *Megaloceros giganteus* . . . The giant ground sloth, *Megatherium americanum* . . . The glyptodon, *Glyptodon petaliferus* . . . The giant beaver, *Castoroides ohioensis* . . . And finally, our crowning glory, the woolly indricothere, *Paraceratherium transouralicum.*"

His voice quavered with pride of accomplishment.

Cash had never heard of an indricothere before, and it had to be the weirdest-looking beast she'd ever seen, an enormous rhinoceros without a horn. It was standing next to a grove of trees, towering above them, its funny little head raised to the sky.

"Is it really that big?" she asked.

"Oh yes," said Karman, his voice thrilling with satisfaction. "It's the largest land animal that ever lived—half again as large as the mammoth and as heavy as four African bull elephants."

Cash stared at the animal, with its ridiculous rubbery, floppy nose and droopy, elephant-like ears—body covered in a dense mat of hair.

"That's a beast straight out of Dr. Seuss," said Colcord.

"I'd love to see one of those in the wild," Cash said.

"You will if you stick around long enough," said Karman. "We have two. They're shy and solitary, but you can hear them coming from quite a distance. And the ground actually shakes when they walk." He lowered his voice. "I'll let you in on a secret: that creature belongs to the Oligocene. Don't tell anyone. It went extinct twenty-three million years ago. It was devilishly hard to resurrect, because of how degraded the DNA was. We found its DNA not in remains of the animal itself but in a leech that sucked its blood, preserved in a flood deposit in Kazakhstan."

"Sort of like *Jurassic Park*?" Cash asked.

A sudden frown. "*Nothing* like *Jurassic Park*," Karman reacted harshly. "*Jurassic Park* was bad fiction *and* bad science. Do not talk to me about *Jurassic Park!*" He almost spit out the name. "What we do here is real."

This was clearly a sore point with Karman, Cash thought. As for herself, she had adored *Jurassic Park*, the book and the movie. "So how do you do it?" said Cash. "How do you resurrect an extinct creature?"

"Please follow me."

He led them out of the office and down a corridor to an observation window. Next to it was a door with a sign that read:

WARNING:

ULTRAVIOLET RADIATION HAZARD

ENTRY BY AUTHORIZED PERSONNEL ONLY

"Have a look through the window."

Cash peered in. She saw not a vast and expensive laboratory but a cramped little room in which two people in full space suits, with air hoses attached, were working. One was grinding a small bone under a hood, while the other was working on a rack of tiny test tubes, sliding it into the side of a big machine.

"This is where we extract and sequence the DNA of extinct animals."

"It looks claustrophobic."

"It has to be that way. We must be extremely careful to keep stray DNA out. A single DNA molecule from a person can ruin everything. When the lab is unoccupied, it's flooded with intense ultraviolet radiation that destroys any DNA molecules that might be floating around. The atmosphere in there is at positive pressure at all times. It's much easier to regulate a small space than a large one—that's why it's so cramped."

Cash backed away from the window and let Colcord look in.

"What are they working on?" he asked.

Karman hesitated. "I'm afraid that's confidential."

"You can share confidential information with them," said Maximilian quickly. "I authorize it."

"Well, in that case, the lab assistant is grinding into the cochlea of *Camelops*, an extinct camel."

"Cochlea?" Cash asked. "What's that?"

"A tiny bone in the inner ear. It's the best source of DNA in most mammals, even better than the root canal of a tooth." He paused.

"That bone comes from the famous Walmart camel, found back in 2007 while excavating a Walmart parking lot in Mesa, Arizona. The fossil is at Arizona State University, but they sent us the cochlear bone. It's the size of a pea. We'll drill into the tiny cavity and extract bone dust mingled with DNA, which we'll amplify millions of times using the polymerase chain reaction."

Karman was warming up, thoroughly enjoying giving them a tour. "Come with me."

They followed him through a set of doors into a room with a huge picture window looking into a gleaming laboratory space. Now this was more like it, Cash thought as her eyes roamed over the shiny equipment and machinery, the racks of computers, the long lab tables and hooded workspaces, the area swarming with scientists moving with purpose and care.

"This is our central CRISPR lab, where we rebuild the genome of an extinct animal. What we do is simple to explain, but extremely difficult to execute. I'll use as an example the first animal we resurrected: the mammoth."

He paused to take a breath and held up a long, elegant finger. "First, we sequenced the mammoth genome—all four-point-seven-billion base pairs."

Another finger went up. "Second, we compared that genome to the genome of its closest relative, the Asian elephant. We mapped the differences."

Another finger. "Third, we took a fertilized Asian elephant embryo, cut and pasted the mammoth genes into the elephant genes in the embryo, while snipping out the genes specific only to the elephant.

"Fourth, we implanted the embryo into the womb of a living female elephant.

"And fifth, the surrogate mother elephant gave birth to a woolly mammoth calf."

His face was flushed with the pleasure of recounting this scientific triumph, all five fingers on his hand extended, his eyes wide open. He suddenly reminded Cash of the mad scientist in *Back to the Future*—Doc Brown. Only calmer and more controlled.

"I was told," said Cash, "that you also edit out the genes for aggression."

Karman nodded. "Contrary to that execrable movie, *Jurassic Park*, herbivores are *not* peaceful animals. Good lord, no! In fact, the most dangerous animals in Africa aren't lions and leopards but elephants, buffalo, hippos, and rhinos—all herbivores. They are violent with each other and extremely dangerous in defending themselves and their young. We couldn't risk our precious animals fighting with each other or attacking people. So we identified those genes that code for aggression and dominance, and we modified them. What we do with our creatures is similar to how early humans bred the fierce and predatory wolf into a dog with floppy ears and a friendly, submissive personality."

"How much does it cost to make one of these beasts?" Colcord asked.

Karman glanced at Maximilian, who nodded his approval to answer the question.

"It's confidential, but between twelve and sixty million dollars."

"Each *one*?" Cash asked, incredulous.

"Each one."

Cash absorbed this remarkable fact. "What other animals besides *Camelops* are you working on?"

"We have plans to resurrect *Bison antiquus*, the ancestor of the American bison. And *Pelorovis*, the so-called monstrous sheep. All our resurrected fauna have to be adapted to the high, cold climate of Colorado. The winters here are fierce."

"Do your animals breed?" asked Colcord.

"No. We'd like them to, but our efforts in that direction have not been successful."

"You've tried?"

"Yes. The problem is, the CRISPR process still introduces errors. Those errors don't usually affect fetal development, but during oogenesis and spermiogenesis, when germ cells divide to form eggs and sperm, things go wrong. Even the tiniest error is magnified. And when defective sperm and egg unite, what results are fetuses with multiple lethal mutations that are not carried to term."

"Stillborn freaks?" Colcord asked. "Monsters?"

"That's a rather crude way of putting it—but yes."

"Getting back to our investigation," Cash said, "do you have any thoughts on who might have done this? Can you think of anyone who might want to destroy your business by killing visitors?"

At this, Karman issued a low, almost sinister laugh. "In other words, do we have enemies? Good lord, yes."

"Who?"

"Where to begin? First, the traditional scientific establishment. They've been implacably against us."

"Why?"

"There are narrow-minded scientists who think de-extincting animals is unethical, that we're playing God. Then there are the scientists who approve of resurrecting extinct animals, but they're against us because we aren't resurrecting these animals exactly as they once were—we've tamed them, made them safer. And then there are those who object to us making money from them." Karman's voice rose a notch. "The environmentalists hate us for altering the ecology of the valley and relocating predatory species. Hikers and climbers hate us because we closed the valley except to paying visitors—even though this has always been private property. Locals hate us because we didn't hire them at high wages but instead brought in people from the outside. Everyone hates us because we're in the vulgar business of capitalism." He stopped, breathing hard. "Sometimes I feel like Columbus, with everyone telling him he was going to fall off the edge of the world. So many are against us!"

"Enough to kill?"

"Of course. The world is full of mentally unstable people."

"But not everyone is against you," said Colcord. "You seem to be doing a good business."

"There are people who have a sense of wonder and awe at what we've done, and they come here for unique and life-changing experiences. We are doing God's work, bringing back species that went extinct—some *because* of human beings. The mammoths, for example, were driven to extinction by humans, as were the ground sloths and probably the Irish elk. So we're in the business of righting ancient wrongs, expiating our species' sins."

He spoke with the fervor of a true believer. Cash hesitated. She wanted to follow up that line with more questions, but it was getting on toward noon, and they had an investigation to run—and many more people to interview.

"Thank you, Dr. Karman, that will be all. For now."

He bowed. "You're most welcome."

11

Sheriff Colcord looked over the conference room they had been loaned for interviews. It was nice—elegant, in fact—with big photos on the walls of the animals and lots of polished wood, soft lighting, and tasteful furniture. An espresso machine in the corner, a fridge with water and drinks, and a bathroom completed the picture.

He turned to Cash, standing next to him. "What do you think?"

"It should be smaller, darker, and uglier, with cinder block walls and a hard metal chair."

Colcord laughed. "Seriously?"

"Hell yes. You want to force people out of their comfort zone. You don't take someone to champagne brunch at the Ritz and expect them to confess to murder."

"Maybe we can turn it to our advantage," said Colcord. "Get them nice and relaxed—and then pounce."

She slapped a folder on the big conference table and sat down. "I drew up a list of people I want to talk to," she said. "You?"

"Oh yeah." He slid a portfolio out of his briefcase and laid it on the table. "Let's combine our lists and get Maximilian to bring 'em in, one at a time."

"Right." She seemed to hesitate. "What would you say to the classic good-guy, bad-guy routine?"

He shrugged. He never put much stock in that game, but he was disinclined to disagree with her.

"You be the gentleman, and I'll be the bitch." She grinned. "That's my forte."

No disagreement there, he thought.

A half hour later, they were set up, and Maximilian brought in the first interviewee. She was a person who had been at the top of both of their lists: Karla Raimundo, the CEO of Erebus. As soon as she appeared in the door, black hair pulled back in a severe bun, gray suit, bright red lipstick, facial skin so tight you could almost see her bones, Colcord sensed an aura of resistance.

She came into the room, walking stiffly.

"Please, have a seat," said Colcord. He took off his hat and placed it on the table next to him.

The woman took a seat on the other side of the conference table. Colcord slid a cell phone over to her. "Mind if we record?"

A hesitation. Colcord waited. Finally, a tight nod.

"Ms. Raimundo," said Cash, "if you don't mind, your responses have to be verbal, since we're taping."

"Yes, you may record," she said crisply.

"Thank you," said Colcord. "We want to confirm that this interview is strictly voluntary, that you've waived the right to an attorney, and that you understand that you can terminate it at any time."

Another tight nod. "Yes."

"For the record, please tell us your name and title."

"Karla Raimundo, chief executive officer of Erebus." Her voice was a few degrees above zero.

"Also for the record, you're speaking to Sheriff James Colcord, Eagle County, and Agent in Charge Frances Cash, Colorado Bureau of Investigation. Now, Ms. Raimundo, could you briefly tell us how long you've worked here and what your responsibilities are?"

She folded her hands to make a tight bundle on the tabletop. "I was hired by Maitland Barrow twelve years ago as president of the company. I was promoted to CEO ten years ago. I am in charge of all aspects of the business, from finance to marketing. I report to the Erebus board of directors. Erebus is a wholly owned subsidiary of RxB Worldwide, a privately held corporation, of which Maitland Barrow is the major shareholder."

It was as if she were reciting a page out of the company manual, her voice flat.

"Thank you," said Colcord. "Now, Ms. Raimundo, can you tell us when you heard about the crime and from whom?"

"The crime occurred at around nine o'clock in the evening of the night before last. I was working late. Mr. Maximilian, our head of security, called me around ten past nine with the news."

"So quickly?"

"The guide had a satphone, and he called the incident in to security."

"And what did you do then?"

"I immediately ordered the full and complete mobilization of our security team to begin a search. We called in everyone we could muster. We mobilized our two helicopters—a third was undergoing repairs. We also began a review of all closed-circuit security video footage in the valley. Every de-extincted animal carries a video collar, and there are security cameras in the lodge, the entrance, and also covering Espada Pass at the head of the valley. We immediately called the Eagle County Sheriff's Office."

"That's right," said Colcord. He turned to Cash. "We got the call at nine thirty." He turned back to Raimundo. "And since then?"

"We've enlarged the search to over a hundred people and are bringing in more as we speak. We had our third helicopter fixed, and it's now in the air. And the CBI has also joined the search. We're doing everything we can."

Cash broke in, her voice edging into stridency. "May I ask *why* you can't seem to find the killers? You've got a hundred people out there, with three helicopters, dogs, and video cameras. It boggles the mind they can't find even a trace."

Raimundo stared at her coldly. "There are one hundred and forty-four square miles in the Erebus Valley. That's ninety two thousand acres. We're dealing with extremely rugged, mountainous terrain."

"But there are at least four killers out there," said Cash, "lugging two dead bodies. They know this valley. And they also seem to be familiar with your security methods, location of security cameras, and even your search patterns." Cash leaned forward on her elbows. "Everything points to the fact that the killers are employees of yours."

Raimundo stared back with narrowed eyes. "We've accounted for all our employees. Every single one."

"And they all have alibis for nine p.m. the night before last?"

A hesitation.

"Do they all have alibis for the night in question?" Cash repeated.

"I can't say."

"How many employees do you have?"

"Two thousand four hundred and twelve."

"How many are living in the valley?"

"About two hundred."

"And you've checked *all* their alibis?"

"We're trying to. That's in process." Her voice was rising in pitch and full of gravel.

"Trying. In process." Cash hesitated. "Where do they live in the valley?"

"The lower level of the lodge is a dormitory. Agent Cash, I can assure you none of our employees did this."

"I sincerely doubt," Cash said, "you can make *any* such assurances. How do you vet your employees?"

"We have a comprehensive process—criminal background checks, employment, credit history. We are meticulous."

"We'd like access to all those personnel files."

At this, Raimundo stared back at her with undisguised hostility. "They're confidential."

"You want us to go to a judge and get a warrant?"

She faltered. "No . . . I will instruct Mr. Maximilian to release them to you."

"Thank you. But what's more to the point: Aren't *you* combing those records for any individuals who might have a problem? It seems to me the perpetrators might well have killed the victims, disposed of the bodies somewhere in the wilderness, and then gone back to work at the lodge the next morning. That's why the killers can't be found by searching the mountains—they're waiting on tables right here."

"That's ridiculous. And we don't know if the victims are dead."

"Of course they're dead."

Colcord was surprised at Cash's aggressive technique. But Raimundo was holding up well, still cool and controlled.

"Why haven't you shut down the resort?" Cash went on.

"Shut down? No. That would trigger panic."

"You've got four killers on the loose—don't you need to protect your guests?"

"We *are* protecting our guests. We've completely closed down the backcountry, and we have high security at the lodge and the laboratory complex. And finally, we have at least a hundred employees who can't leave."

"Why not?"

"In case you haven't noticed, we have dozens of de-extincted Pleistocene animals who need constant care and attention." She leaned forward. "Why don't you start investigating the radical environmental organizations that have attacked us? Why don't you look into the Animal Liberation Army that burned down one of our buildings? Or HART, the Hackers for Animal Rights? They've been trying to take down our systems for years."

Colcord said quietly, "We are, in fact, looking into some of those organizations."

"Thank you."

"All right," said Cash. "Let's assume a radical animal rights organization is behind this. There's only one entrance. How did they get in?"

"There is Espada Pass at the head of the valley."

"Where does that go to?"

"It goes into the Flat Tops Wilderness, Colorado's second-largest wilderness area. Over a quarter million acres. Anyone coming over that pass could gain access to the Erebus Valley."

"But don't you have security cameras on that pass?"

"Yes, but it isn't impossible to get over those mountains elsewhere, with technical climbing equipment. In my climbing days, I could have done it."

Colcord stared at her. *In my climbing days.* She didn't look like the type. He cleared his throat and spoke in a gentle voice. "Ms. Raimundo, is it your theory that radical environmentalists might be behind this and that they entered the valley over the mountains and perhaps went out that way as well?"

"It's as good a theory as any," she said, then she paused and took a long, deep breath. Colcord could see she was making an attempt to keep herself under control.

"On the contrary," said Cash, "the most likely theory is that the killers are insiders—employees or former employees."

Raimundo said nothing, her hands tightly folded.

"No more questions—for now," Cash said.

Colcord said, "Thank you, Ms. Raimundo. We appreciate your cooperation."

"You're welcome," she said tautly, then got up out of her chair and strode from the room. Deputy Sandoval, manning the door, opened and shut it for her.

Cash looked at Colcord and grinned.

Colcord said, "You're a tough lady."

"I'll overlook the condescension in that compliment and say thank you."

He shook his head.

"Who's next?" Cash asked.

Colcord thought, *She's really enjoying this.* He consulted his list. "Gunnerson."

"Oh boy."

"Is he outside?" Colcord asked Sandoval, who nodded. "Bring him in."

"Mind if I take the lead?" said Cash.

"Be my guest."

Sandoval opened the door, and Gunnerson came in, followed by his two minions.

"I'm sorry," said Cash. "No one else is allowed in the interview room."

Gunnerson stopped. He looked much better than the night before, his suit neatly pressed, his hair groomed—and he was apparently sober. "I want witnesses."

"Mr. Gunnerson," said Cash, "the interview is voluntary, but it has to be on our terms. If not, you're free to leave. Next time we speak, it will be under subpoena."

Gunnerson hesitated, then turned to his minions and made a gesture for them to leave. He came over and sat down. "Any news?"

"I'm very sorry," Cash said, suddenly and surprisingly solicitous. "Despite tremendous efforts, we haven't made any progress in the case."

He appeared about to say something but collected himself. "I'm hiring a team with infrared drones."

"Drones?"

"Drones that image heat. The latest thing in search and rescue. You fly them, and they can pick out heat sources on the ground, animals and people. Naturally, you've never heard of it."

Colcord swallowed his annoyance at the jab. Drones might not be a bad idea.

Cash said, "Thank you. We can use all the help we can get."

"You sure as hell can," he said. "I've already got the ball rolling. The drone team is going to be here tomorrow morning."

"Please have them liaise with us as soon as they arrive," said Cash.

Gunnerson folded a pair of knotted hands on the table and leaned forward. "Now—you got questions?"

Cash ran him through the preliminaries. "We need to explore all avenues," she said. "Which means I have to ask you some awkward questions. Of course, this is voluntary, and you can always have a lawyer present."

"Don't need one. Shoot."

"It's possible your son was targeted because of his background," Cash said. "Is there anything you know of in his history that might have made him a target? Drugs, business dealings, womanizing, that sort of thing?"

Gunnerson tightened up, angering. "Drugs? Are you kidding me? He's a health fanatic. He works as an instructor at NOLS—the National Outdoor Leadership School. I don't think they're into killing people. As for womanizing, he was just married and a good husband. They love each other and are looking forward to starting a family. He leads a clean life. I resent the question."

Cash gave him a steady look. "You understand why I have to ask it, don't you?"

He fidgeted. "I suppose so."

"Which leads me to my next question: Could he have been targeted because of *you*?"

At this, Gunnerson sat back. "Me? What the hell does that mean?"

"We have to ask."

"You mean, someone getting back at me by kidnapping or killing my son?"

"That's correct."

He seemed temporarily flummoxed. "Look. I know I'm not a popular man. I've made my share of enemies. The list is long. But to murder my son and his new wife? And to do it up here? You're barking up the wrong tree, Agent Cash."

Cash said, "I understand you and your company are under investigation by the New York AG's office for self-dealing."

"Bullshit!"

"Bullshit that you're under investigation, or the investigation is bullshit?" Cash asked calmly.

"The investigation is bullshit! And what does this have to do with my son?"

"Just exploring every avenue."

"You're wasting your time! Why don't you drag Maitland Barrow in here and ask him what the fuck *he's* been doing?"

At this, Colcord felt a prickle of suspicion. He broke in gently. "What *is* Maitland Barrow doing?"

Gunnerson turned to him. "That's what you should find out! Ask him what he thinks he's doing up here!"

"If you know something, Mr. Gunnerson," said Colcord, "you need to tell us."

Gunnerson made an effort to collect himself. "All I mean is, Barrow's pissed off a lot of people. This attack was directed at *him*, not me. You should look into *his* business dealings, not mine. That's all I meant."

"Do you know Maitland Barrow personally?"

"I've met him."

"In what context?"

"We met at Davos."

Davos, pondered Colcord. *What the hell is Davos?* He'd heard the name but couldn't place it. "Where's that?"

"Switzerland," said Gunnerson, eyeing him with contempt. "You don't know Davos? It's where the World Economic Forum is held every year."

"When did you meet him?"

"Ten, twelve years ago."

"How well do you know him?" asked Colcord.

"Not well. We move in the same circles, that's all."

Cash broke in. "You mean, because you're both billionaires?"

"It's not about money," Gunnerson said. "We're both concerned about economics, finance, development—the future of the world."

"I see," Cash said. "The future of the world. Is that how you learned about Erebus?"

"It was my son's choice to come here. I didn't choose his honeymoon destination."

"What did you discuss at Davos with Barrow?" Cash asked.

"Davos," Gunnerson said, losing his temper again, "has fuck all to do with my son." He rose. "These questions are going nowhere. You find my son." He stabbed a trembling finger at Cash and repeated. "*You find my son.*" He got up abruptly, turned about, and left.

Colcord looked at Cash. "What do you think he meant by saying, *Ask him what he thinks he's doing up here?*"

"I've no idea," said Cash, "but I think it's time we talked to Barrow and asked him that same question."

12

Romanski waited for Cash in the lobby of the Forensic Services division of the CBI. It was located in the suburban sprawl north of Denver, in the town of Arvada, wedged between a garbage collection company and a storage unit compound. The low white building looked more like a JCPenney than a state-of-the-art complex of forensic labs, morgue, and autopsy rooms.

Romanski had made a special effort to comb his hair before the briefing, and he had spent a few minutes more than usual picking out an outfit to wear under his lab coat, which he also made sure was freshly washed. It was still a bit rumpled from the dryer, as he drew the line at ironing. He knew he was the best Forensic Services director the CBI had ever had, and he expressed that by dressing down amid his blue-suited, french-cuffed colleagues.

Of all the agents he worked with, he liked Cash the best. She was a bit foul-mouthed like he was, and she had a solid, working-class background. Her dad had been a cop, and Romanski's dad had been a ski-lift mechanic.

"The conference room's packed," Romanski said, falling into place beside her as they walked down the corridor. He had to hustle to keep up with her; she was big and moved fast. "*Huge* interest. McFaul's pacing around, waiting for us."

"Any news from the forensic front I should know?"

"Here's the big takeaway: At least six killers. And the two victims are definitely dead."

She stopped. "*Six* killers?"

"Or more. I'll go into it at the meeting."

She started walking again.

"So . . . what's it like at the lodge?" Romanski asked. "Nice room?"

"No complaints."

"Deluxe?"

"I barely spent three hours in it."

"Chocolate and flowers on the pillow?"

"Fuck you," said Cash.

"While you've been sleeping between bamboo sheets, I've been messing around with buckets of bloody dirt."

"Poor you."

The doors opened to the biology section, the smell of denatured alcohol washing over them. Beyond, they blew through a set of double doors into the main biology conference room. The loud murmuring from the waiting audience fell into silence, and every face turned. The place was packed—he'd never seen the room so full. It was hard to believe this many people even worked in the Arvada building. A lot must've come up from headquarters. Romanski loved it.

McFaul was on the stage, electronic pointer in hand.

"There you are," he said, waving them up. "Finally. Let's get going."

They joined him onstage. A projector was ready to go, and the AV screen had been lowered.

McFaul launched into an introduction that had nothing new in it— but at least he got the facts straight. He talked about the confidential nature of the investigation and the near miracle that the press hadn't yet gotten wind of it. He then introduced Romanski and Cash and turned the review over to her, as she was the agent in charge.

Cash kept her presentation strictly factual, no speculation, and under five minutes.

Romanski was impressed. She was doing well on this, her first case as AIC.

Cash turned the floor over to Romanski.

He stepped up to the podium. "As you all know, I'm Detective Romanski," he said, plucking the mic out of its stand. "Director of Forensic Services. Okay, let's review our findings so far."

The AV guy dimmed the lights and turned on the projector. Romanski stepped away from the podium and picked up the remote in his left hand.

"Let's start with the tent," he said. "Here it is as we found it in the mountains"—the slide flashed up—"and here it is set up in the lab. Please note the tear—fifty-two centimeters long. We examined it under magnification."

He flashed through the slides, showing a series of microscopic images of the cut.

"The top part of the cut is clean, made by a sharp knife edge. Then, in the middle part, the fabric, as you can see, becomes ragged. It's more torn than sliced. And then toward the bottom, the cut becomes clean again."

He took a turn on the stage. Romanski liked to pace during his presentations, like a preacher. And he did think of himself as a sort of preacher, dispensing truth to the multitudes. "It appears the knife that made this cut was defective, a portion of the blade damaged. When the perp starts the cut, it's with the tip of the knife. But as the knife goes farther down through the fabric, the slicing part reaches the damaged portion of the blade, and the fabric begins to tear. Then the cut ends up clean at the bottom as the blade is withdrawn and the fabric is once again cut by the sharp part."

More slides of the crime scene. It was beautiful, like a postcard—except for the two dark bloodstains near the tent. "The cut," Romanski went on, "was probably made to flush them out of the tent. This has been done before. For example, the famous serial killer in Italy, known as the Monster of Florence, flushed his quarry out of a tent by cutting the fly in exactly this way. The man emerged to investigate and was shot, and then the killer went into the tent to kill the woman."

He paused. Everyone was on the edge of their seats.

"That's similar to what happened here. The man goes out to investigate. He's assaulted. The woman then goes out. She's assaulted. Both are likely killed immediately."

He took another turn around the stage.

"How do we know they were killed and not just injured? Our medical examiner, Dr. Huizinga, estimated that each bloodstain represents three liters of blood, plus or minus fifty centiliters."

More slides of the bloodstains in situ.

"That is not a survivable loss of blood. And . . ." He paused and took a step back from the podium, flicking on a new slide showing a rather gruesome graphic of a cross section of a human neck. "They were also decapitated. It's the *only* way that much blood could be lost in the three minutes between the attacks and the arrival of the guide."

More slides went past.

"Our crime scene reconstruction team mapped the scene—here it is. Note the matted grass, the location and position of the bloodstains, the locations of the dropped knives and headlamps. While the grass didn't retain sharp footprints, our analysis of the number of depressions in the grass, the lack of dragging, and the rapidity with which the killers disappeared with their cargo of beheaded bodies, suggested there were most likely six killers. Possibly more."

He paused for dramatic effect and was gratified by the riveted attention of his audience.

"This was a well-planned operation," Romanski said. "And they must have had body bags or something similar to carry the bodies in, because there was no trail of blood from the scene. Not a drop. Those bodies and heads were immediately placed into waterproof containers and taken away—fast."

He paused. He could sense the shock in the hall.

"No physical traces of a trail were found. We tracked the scent trail with dogs, but lost it among an area of, ah, mammoth dung. These killers knew exactly what they were doing. This homicidal operation, ladies and gentlemen, was *choreographed*."

Romanski paused dramatically.

"Moving on to fiber and latents," he said. "We pulled latents from the knives, tent, headlamps, and a bunch of other stuff. There was no evidence the perps were wearing gloves. After ruling out fingerprints of the victims and guide, we ended up with over a dozen full latents and many partials. No hits in the databases yet." He paused. "Think about that for a moment. The murder was planned like a military campaign, and yet . . . they didn't bother to wear gloves. And none of these latents are in our databases—none of them had a criminal record, or worked for the government, or had any job requiring fingerprinting."

Another dramatic sweep of the audience with his eyes.

"Moving on to hair and fiber: we collected many samples from the campsite—human and animal hairs, as well as miscellaneous fibers. Unfortunately, this area has been used as a campsite for about ten years. A couple of the hairs had roots attached, and we're running DNA on those. We swabbed the area for other genetic traces—the grass, the two knives and headlamps, the cut in the tent, et cetera. We're currently running PCR tests on those samples to sequence the DNA. That's gonna take another eight days."

He paused, cast his eyes over the audience. Even McFaul was transfixed.

"Finally, we did trace tox on the blood. Nothing of note—a small amount of alcohol present in the male victim's blood, nothing in the female's. No drugs present. We confirmed that the female victim was pregnant."

He looked around and pressed his hands together. "And that's it, folks—so far."

McFaul stepped back into the center. "Thank you, Detective Romanski. I'd like to open the floor to questions, comments, theories."

Hands shot up. There were questions. Romanski answered them as best he could, but most were unanswerable as of yet. Several ideas about the crime were mooted about, but nothing that made any sense to Romanski.

When the discussion period was over, McFaul came back to the podium and read out team assignments, and then the meeting broke up.

As they were stepping down from the stage, McFaul came up to Romanski and Cash. "See you two in my office?"

They followed him up to the second floor. He seated himself behind his desk while Romanski took a seat in front, Cash settling down in the seat on the opposite side. McFaul looked better dressed than usual, his suit just a cut above the bargain-basement stylishness he usually sported. He looked fired up.

"This is the most goddamned case I can think of," McFaul said. He looked at Cash. "You got any theories, guesses? I mean, privately."

"Not yet," she said.

He frowned. "The case is two days old. I'm not criticizing, but I have to point out that it doesn't seem you've made much progress. No bodies, no motive, no hot leads."

"We're working flat out, sir," said Cash.

McFaul paused, gathering his thoughts, his brow wrinkling. "It's your first case as agent in charge, and it's okay if you're feeling a little overwhelmed. If you like, we can assign you an experienced partner, a sort of co-AIC, and no one would think twice about it. This is a challenging case."

Romanski could feel the heat coming off Cash. But Cash stayed calm. "Not necessary, sir," she said. "I've got the case firmly in hand, and I'm certain we're making the best progress possible. It does have some unusual elements, sir, but we're going to crack this case, I promise you."

A long silence, and McFaul finally nodded. "Okay. No lack of confidence intended. We're here to throw any and all our resources into this case—all you have to do is ask."

"Thank you."

"And how's working with Sheriff Colcord?"

"Colcord's fine," said Cash. "He's an old-fashioned kind of guy, quiet. The department there in Eagle isn't very big, just him and a deputy and a dozen officers."

"Are you getting cooperation from Erebus?"

"Yes, sir. They've got at least half their on-site employees out there beating the bush. The security chief, Andrew Maximilian, has been cooperative, and they've done everything we've asked." She paused. "There is one thing, though."

"Yes?"

"The sheriff and I would like to interview Maitland Barrow."

"Why? I understand he wasn't there."

"The father of the male victim, Rolf Gunnerson, made a statement that implied Barrow might know something."

"Like what?"

"He wouldn't say."

McFaul fell silent, his short fingers drumming on his desk. "Ask for a voluntary interview." He then leaned forward, folding his hands. "There's something you should know, Agent Cash." He started tapping a finger on the desktop. "Just before the meeting, I got a call from Nicky Boswell at *The Denver Post*."

"Boswell, the guy with the fat cheeks and John Lennon glasses?" Cash said. "Uh-oh."

"He's onto the story," McFaul said. "He's gotten his grubby hands on a source, and I wouldn't be surprised if he's already writing it up. We need to be proactive and control the narrative."

"Which means?" Cash asked.

"A presser," said McFaul. "I'll handle it myself. You won't have time."

"Thank you," Cash said.

"And me?" Romanski asked. He loved pressers.

"You need to get back to Erebus and keep this case moving forward." He looked at his watch. "We're going to announce the presser now and give the media ninety minutes to show up. That'll make it around three. The shit will hit the fan for sure, so be ready."

"You sure you won't need me for the presser?" Romanski asked.

"No, Bart. You're too busy."

Romanski felt pissed. It seemed to him McFaul was hogging the limelight—no surprise.

"We're closing the airspace over Erebus," McFaul said, "so those media people don't interfere with the search. The press will be kept out of the valley for now."

"I appreciate that, sir," said Cash.

"Good." He rose. "It goes without saying that we need to show progress—and *fast*."

13

Cash drove west on I-70, the CBI vehicle climbing into the Front Range, Romanski in the passenger seat. It was another gorgeous fall afternoon, the mountains still topped with fresh snow.

"McFaul's a publicity hound," said Romanski. The whole drive, he'd been grousing about not being invited to the presser. "I can just see him up there onstage, his long pink tongue hanging out, drooling at the cameras."

"If this case goes south," said Cash, "he'll be the one skewered."

"He'll blame us. But do you think the case is gonna go south?"

"No. I don't," said Cash. "How could it? Six killers lugging around two bodies and two heads? I mean, *something's* gotta give. But I feel like we're missing a crucial piece."

"Like what?"

"Why'd they take the bodies?" said Cash. "What are they doing with them? It's a lot of work to haul dead bodies around, and . . . I hate to say it . . . they begin to smell."

"Maybe gonna make a big-toe cassoulet?" Romanski said.

NPR had been droning on the radio in the background, and Cash suddenly heard the word *Erebus* float by.

"Uh-oh." She turned up the volume.

And there it was—the Erebus story was breaking on the national NPR feed. They had many of the relevant details: the kidnapping, bloodstains, possible decapitation and murder, the search, the victims, the billionaire father—on and on. All the ingredients of a scorching story.

"Damn it," said Cash. "I wonder who they got to?"

"It was bound to get out," said Romanski.

A half hour later, as they passed the Vail exit, Cash realized something was amiss when several television vans bombed past them, going over a hundred miles an hour.

"Shall we pull 'em over?" Romanski said eagerly.

"Yeah, right, and get our mugs on the evening news," said Cash.

Far up ahead, she saw the vans take the Erebus exit and disappear. They took the same exit. The road to Erebus wound up a narrow valley toward a dramatic cluster of peaks called the Spiders. As they gained altitude, a number of cars started coming down in the opposite direction, the traffic getting heavier the farther up they went.

"Looks like that NPR report triggered a lot of departures," said Romanski.

"Good," said Cash. "I hope they all leave."

The final turn of the road revealed the dramatic stone Mammoth Gates into the Erebus Valley. It also revealed a traffic jam of monumental proportions, cars and vans lined up to get in.

"What the fuck?" said Romanski as Frankie slowed the car. "This can't all be media!"

"It is," said Cash, squinting ahead. "Look at it. From all over."

"Siren, please," said Romanski.

"Yeah."

She reached over and pressed the yelp button, the siren giving a loud sound. The cars immediately in front tried to move over, but the road was too narrow, and there wasn't enough shoulder on the right for them to get out of the way. The oncoming traffic was steady and growing heavier. There just wasn't the room to pass.

She gave it another yelp.

"This is hopeless," said Romanski.

She put the siren on wail, trying to edge around, but there was no way it was going to work on the narrow road with no shoulders against the steady stream of cars coming out.

She got on her car phone and called Maximilian.

He answered immediately. "Bloody hell," he began. "The story just broke in the news and—"

"I know, I know. We're trying to get in through the Mammoth Gate, but there's a jam of press. Can you stop the flow of cars coming out until we can come in?"

"On it."

They waited and finally, the stream subsided. She put the siren back on wail, and they drove up the final stretch of road on the left side, through the huge wrought iron gates set into walls of stone, forty feet high, that went from one side of the narrow valley opening to the other. A big guardhouse stood on the left, and a large substation on the right.

"You think they call them Mammoth Gates because they're so big," Romanski asked, "or because they're designed to keep in the mammoths?"

"Both."

Once inside, it was suddenly peaceful. An orderly flow of guests was still leaving.

They drove up the road to the lodge, parked, went inside, and headed to the war room.

There she found Colcord, who had continued interviewing while they were absent. A flustered-looking woman was just leaving as they entered.

Colcord got up and stretched.

"Who was she?" Cash asked.

"Head of personnel." He had been taking notes by hand in a hard-cover notebook, which he set aside.

"Looks like someone talked to the press," said Cash.

Colcord shook his head. "Yeah. I know. But . . ." He grimaced. "It was bound to break."

Cash nodded. He was right. No point in belaboring it. "Anything new?"

He shook his head. "No. We've spent the morning with Erebus employees. No one has a history that jumps out. They're paid well, no labor unrest, low staff turnover." He tapped his notebook. "She gave me a list of individuals they've fired over the past three years. I'm asking our department to hunt down and question all they can find."

"And the ground search?"

"Nothing."

"Christ," said Cash, "I could use a coffee."

"Me too." Romanski made a beeline for the espresso machine. "Anyone care for a doppio?"

"Quadrupio for me," said Cash.

"Double for me," said Colcord, starting to rise. "I can make it myself."

"I knew you'd volunteer," Cash said, "being the only gentleman present—but Romanski's on it."

Romanski snorted and began messing with the machine. He made a doppio and two quadruples for himself and Cash, bringing them over.

Cash turned to Colcord. "Okay, Sheriff, Bart and I were talking on the way up, and we've got a number one question: *Why* did they take the bodies?"

Colcord frowned. "I handled a case about twelve years ago, the Poudre River Killer. You remember that?"

"Before my time."

"I remember it," said Romanski. "Weird fucking dude."

"He took the bodies home," Colcord said. "He played with them. Cut them up. Had fun."

"Had *fun*?"

"Yeah. Made things. Sewed them back together in funny ways."

Cash shuddered. "So you think we're dealing with a serial killer?"

"No," said Colcord. "Serial killers work alone or at most in pairs. This is more like a gang." He paused and said, "Maybe they want the bodies for some sort of ritual, Satanic or otherwise."

Cash swigged her bitter drink. God, it tasted good. "Satanic rituals?"

"It's a possibility."

She tossed down the rest of her espresso. Satanic rituals . . . It was a viable hypothesis.

"While you were gone," said Colcord after a moment, "I arranged to interview the director of the film crew. In about half an hour. You want to come with me? We can go in my vehicle."

"Film crew?" Cash asked. "What film crew?"

"They're shooting a film in the old ghost town. You didn't know?"

"How would I know if no one told me? Hell yes, I'd like to go along. Anything else going on I should know about? Ice Capades, Criss Angel, Elvis impersonators?"

"My apologies. I believe the film crew is the only outside group in here now."

"I gotta stay here," said Romanski. "I need to get a whole bunch more DNA swabs from everyone who was at the crime scene."

14

Cash eased into the passenger seat of Colcord's vehicle, a late-model black Suburban with sheriff's department decals. Her hand slid over the luxurious russet leather of the seat.

"Nice wheels," she said. "Eagle County must have plenty of money."

"We're fortunate," he said. "In addition to Erebus, we have Vail and a bunch of other ski resorts. That gives us a rich tax base but not a lot of infrastructure to keep up. Nineteen hundred square miles and only fifty-five thousand people. The county is mostly wilderness."

"You ever ski at Vail?" she asked.

"Oh, sure."

"You good?"

"I used to be. Now I don't take too many risks, just go nice and easy on the groomers. And you?"

"I took up skiing when I moved here ten years ago. I suck."

"Just being in the mountains is what it's all about."

They drove awhile in silence, working their way down the valley. She had been curious for a while about the sheriff's background. He was quiet and unassuming, not like a lot of other elected sheriffs she'd worked with.

"So what's your story?" she asked abruptly.

"My story?" Colcord sounded surprised. "Born here, grew up on a ranch west of Durango. The usual ranching childhood."

"What's the usual ranching childhood?"

"Felt like most of the time I was stretching barbed wire and hunting lost cows. But it was a good childhood. Nothing tragic, no broken home, great dad. I was lucky. We had cattle and horses, an irrigated section of alfalfa. Hunting and fishing in the San Juans. Growing up in Colorado is like growing up in heaven."

"You had your own horse?"

"Oh yeah. Chewbacca. A shaggy, dun-colored grade horse."

"Chewbacca? What kind of name is that for a horse?"

"Named by a kid who loved *Star Wars*."

Cash laughed. "Okay. And then?"

"Did my twenty in the military, moved to Eagle, bought a café, ran for county sheriff, won."

"Which branch?"

"Army."

"Rank?"

"Lieutenant colonel, now retired."

"Wow, that's impressive."

"If you're reasonably competent and get along with people, it's not so hard to make the grade in twenty years."

"You were a commissioned officer?"

"West Point class of '95."

"Did you see action?"

"Iraq. Three tours."

"Was it worth it?"

This question elicited a sudden silence. "I don't know you well enough," said Colcord slowly, "to go into the long answer to that question."

Judging from the darkening tone in his voice, Cash realized she had trod on sensitive ground and changed the subject. "You own a café?"

"The Ore House in Eagle."

"When did you drop the *W-H*?"

"Very funny. It was once an assay office. Pressed tin ceiling, creaking wooden floors, comfortable furniture, woodstove going in the winter, homemade scones and pastries and good, strong coffee."

"My kind of place." She liked the sense of pride in his voice.

"Drop in sometime."

"You going to run for sheriff again?"

"These are a lot of questions, Agent Cash."

"I'm nosy."

"Watch out, I'm going to turn the tables on you."

"You can try."

The road passed through a narrow ravine and topped out in a valley with a stream flowing through it. The ghost town was spread out on both sides of the river, with an old wooden bridge across it—a picturesque cluster of batten board buildings, stables, corrals, and a narrow church with a steeple. At the entrance to the town, a dirt parking lot was filled with movie vans and trailers, along with several cherry pickers, cranes, and other equipment.

They drove up to where the road into town was blocked with a gate. A man at the gate came over and bent down to look in the car.

"We're here to see Slavomir Doyle," said the sheriff, showing his badge.

"He's shooting a scene," said the man. "Does he know you're coming?"

"Yes. I made an appointment."

"Park over there. I'll bring you over to the shoot."

They parked and followed him past the gate into the lone dirt street leading through town. It was a classic Western town, with long boardwalks, saloons, livery, a hotel, dry goods store, sheriff's office, jail, and at the far end, a gallows.

"Who you gonna hang?" Cash asked.

"I don't know. That's for the movie."

"What's it called?"

"*Hannibal and the Baron*. Starring Brock Ballou." He paused with reverence at the naming of the famous star. Then he went on. "It's sort of *Cowboys and Aliens* meets *Jurassic Park*. A herd of mammoths gets caught in a time warp and appear in the 1880s, and a bunch of cowboys catch and break them, and then ride them into town to save it from a railroad baron and his gang of killers."

"Right, okay," was all Cash could say.

"Is it . . . a comedy?" ventured Colcord.

"No, no. It's a Western," the man said.

As they approached, a bunch of lights on towers and tripods came into view, set up outside the main saloon, with a number of camera operators. Two groups of cowboys were facing off on the dirt street. Cash could see that one was Ballou, wearing a tall white hat, standing clean and straight, while the other was a dirty slouching man with greasepaint smeared on his face, a black hat, stubble, and a missing front tooth.

"Gee," said Cash, "I wonder which one's the bad guy?"

The director, Slavomir Doyle, was standing behind a camera, shouting and waving his hand. His voice was shrill and high, and it cut the air like the cawing of a crow.

"Um, it looks like he's still busy," said their escort. "Can you wait?"

"No," said Colcord, his voice suddenly devoid of its usual friendly warmth. "We can't."

This was a side to Colcord Cash hadn't seen before. She decided to hang back and let him take the lead.

"Okay, well, let me check and see . . ."

"You don't need to check anything," said Colcord, brushing past him and striding toward Doyle. "Mr. Doyle?" he boomed out. "Sheriff Colcord."

"Cut! Cut!" The man spun around, his face furious. "What the hell? Can't you see we're shooting a scene here?"

Colcord went straight up to him, opening his jacket to display his star and moving well into Doyle's personal space before halting. "And my associate, Agent in Charge Cash of the Colorado Bureau of Investigation."

Cash watched, amused. Ballou stood in the middle of the dusty street, hands on his hips. He began striding over, an annoyed look on his face. "What's going on here?" he asked. "Who are these people?"

Colcord turned to him. "We have an appointment with Mr. Doyle. You'll have to excuse us, Mr. . . . . Sorry, your name?"

Ballou stared at him, outraged that the man didn't know who he was.

Without waiting for an answer, Colcord turned his back on the movie star and spoke to Doyle again. "That looks like an appropriate place to chat," he said, pointing toward the sheriff's office. "After you. We're in a hurry."

"Hold on!" Ballou demanded in a loud stage voice. "We're in the middle of shooting a scene!"

Colcord turned to him. "Do you mind, mister?"

"I *do* mind. Very much so. My time is extremely valuable." He positioned himself to where he was blocking Colcord's path forward, standing with arms crossed. Cash could see that this was not a good move on Ballou's part.

Colcord said coldly, "Why don't you go back to your trailer and powder your nose while we have a chat with Mr. Doyle here. Or would you rather garner the publicity of being charged with obstructing a law enforcement officer—Mr. Ballou?"

Ballou stared at him for a moment and then stepped aside with a scowl.

"Let's go," said Colcord to Doyle in a decidedly unfriendly tone.

Doyle cursed under his breath and walked stiffly toward the office, leaving the rest of the actors and crew standing in stunned silence. They went inside. Colcord immediately took the chair behind the sheriff's desk and leaned back, hands behind his head. Cash sat on the far side.

Doyle remained standing. "Jesus fuck, you can't talk to my leading man that way. And I'm trying to shoot a movie here—"

"Jesus doesn't fuck," said Colcord. "We had an *appointment*. This won't take long. Of course, it's entirely voluntary." He put his feet up on the desk with a thunk. "I feel quite at home here," he said pleasantly, looking around. "Better than my own office. Have a seat, Doyle."

Doyle sat down.

Cash looked at him curiously. He was a small, intense man, with a head of curly black hair, in his late thirties perhaps. He had an Irish accent and one of those diminutive faces with the features a little too close together, graced by a sharp little red nose. The blue eyes were extremely intelligent, restless, and wary.

"Look, I want to be helpful," Doyle said, "but the incident took place many miles up the valley—nothing to do with us."

Colcord put his feet back down and sat up, placing his cell phone on the desktop, pointing at Doyle. "Could you please state your name and title for the record?"

"Slavomir Doyle, DGA, director of *Hannibal and the Baron.*"

"Thank you. Interviewing are James Colcord, sheriff, Eagle County, and Agent in Charge Frances Cash, Colorado Bureau of Investigation."

He reeled off the date and location, then paused and smiled. His affability had returned.

Cash decided to sit back and let him do the talking.

"Now, Mr. Doyle, could you tell me what you were doing at the time of the killing—that is, at nine p.m. two nights ago?"

"We were shooting a night scene. Wrapped at midnight."

"How much of your crew were there?"

"Almost everyone. Except that the accountant, catering chief, and a few others were off that night."

"How many are you in total?"

"Thirty-two. We probably had twenty-five or so on set."

"Where are you all staying?"

"The lodge has accommodations for film crews."

"Can you account for everyone at the time of the killing?"

"Of course not."

"I'd like you to ask your people where everyone was. Get everyone to write down where they were between eight and ten and who they were with, if anyone. Circulate a piece of paper, have them write down the information, and sign it. We may pick out individuals to interview separately."

Doyle frowned. "Is this really necessary?"

"It's strictly voluntary, like I said. But you know the line they use in the cop shows—you will find the alternative to be most *inconvenient*."

"Funny, I never heard that line."

"Then you're welcome to it." Colcord turned to Cash. "Do you have any questions?"

"I do." She turned to Doyle. "Are you working with trained mammoths?"

"Oh, no. We aren't allowed to disturb the animals. We're shooting B-roll of the mammoths in their natural environment. The mammoth action scenes will be CG."

"What's the financial arrangement between you and Erebus?"

"The ghost town was restored to be used as a movie set. We contracted to use it for five weeks, paying a daily rate."

"Which is?"

"Ninety-five thousand."

"A *day?*"

"It includes room and board and catering on set. And the mammoths."

Cash whistled. "And how far along are you?"

"Three weeks in, two to go."

"Have you had any disputes on set, or difficulties with Erebus?"

"Nothing. Erebus isn't cheap, that's for sure, but they've been fine to work with. Totally professional. Sure, we've had conflicts on set, nothing beyond the usual. No violence, just the usual arguments you have. Nobody accidentally shot by an actor." He smiled thinly.

Cash glanced at Colcord. "No more questions from me."

"Thank you, Mr. Doyle. Please get us that list by the end of the day."

Doyle slapped his arms on the chair and got up. "I'm getting back to my scene, if I can get my star back out of his trailer. Louis will show you out."

After he left, Cash turned to Colcord. "Nice work."

"Aw, shucks," said Colcord.

15

As they drove from the movie town back to the lodge, evening was falling in the valley, a few cirrus clouds drifting through the sky like horses' tails, tinged with gold.

"Where do you think he got a weird name like Slavomir Doyle?" asked Cash.

"Mother was Serbian, father Irish. He grew up in a tiny town called Knockalassa in Ireland. I looked him up on Wikipedia."

That impressed Cash. She should have done that herself. "You handled him well."

"People like Doyle need a firm touch, and then they're okay."

They drove for a while in silence, and then Colcord asked, "How long have you been in Colorado?"

"Ten years."

"If you don't mind me asking, is that a Boston accent or what?"

She laughed. "You think I'm a Masshole? No way. Portland, Maine."

"Masshole? Is that what Mainers call people from Massachusetts?"

"Only in the summertime."

"You don't meet people out here from Maine very often."

"Mainers don't leave. They like where they are."

"But you did."

"So it's my turn to get the third degree?" She was amused to see Colcord blush.

"Just turning the tables."

"Yeah, I left. My grandpop was a cop, my dad was a cop, I was a cop." She halted.

"And?"

"I just decided to get the hell out, start a new life."

He nodded. He sensed right away there was more to it, but he didn't ask. He said, "You've done well since you got here. Agent in charge and all that."

"I work hard."

"Family? Kids?"

"Divorced. Husband turned out to be a two-six-packs-a-night kind of guy, so it was no great loss. No kids—his sperm sucked. You?"

Colcord coughed and cleared his throat. "You're kind of direct, aren't you?"

"I don't like small talk. I get to the point."

"I can see that."

"How about you—wife, kids?"

"Divorced, two kids. One daughter's a ranger with the Forest Service, the other daughter's an archaeologist."

"Archaeologist? That's interesting."

"She's getting her Ph.D. at CSU in Fort Collins."

"You must be proud."

"Of both of them. The ranger works at Mesa Verde. Have you been there?"

"I've been meaning to. Hard to find the time."

"If you do, I'll give you her name. Those cliff dwellings are one of the greatest things to see in the entire country."

The lodge loomed up, windows blazing with light like a giant glowing crystal stuck into the side of the mountain. They parked in the underground garage and took the elevator to the lobby. The evening animal viewing was going on, the guests gathered at the wall of glass watching the creatures gather at the watering hole.

"Fewer people," said Colcord. "It looks like quite a number skedaddled."

They walked over to take a look. The family of mammoths were there, the bull and several cows wading into the shallows. The baby of the family, Tom Thumb, was back to his antics, squirting water at his mother and stomping in the shallows like a mischievous child. They watched for a while.

"I'm dead tired," said Cash. "I'm gonna turn in."

"No dinner?"

She shook her head and headed back to her room. She entered, switching on the light—and was once again put off by the extravagance of it. It was only seven o'clock, but she'd had barely any sleep since yesterday.

There were chocolates and an orchid blossom on the pillow. She looked at them, thinking of Romanski and his wisecrack. Then she gobbled up the chocolates—that would be dinner—stripped, crawled into bed, turned off the light, and instantly fell asleep.

16

"We're fucking wasting time!"

Cash heard Gunnerson's voice booming out of the security station even before she arrived. Maximilian had called to tell her the drone pilots had arrived with their equipment, and they needed to be onboarded and briefed. Colcord had left Erebus at dawn, saying he was going to Eagle on some vague research task. She would be on her own that day.

Cash entered the security annex to see Gunnerson haranguing Maximilian, pounding a table with his fist. He spun around when she came in.

"There you are!" he cried. "Maximilian here tells me I need to coordinate with you. So—let's coordinate!"

Cash took a deep breath. "Very well. Now"—she looked at the nervous drone team standing behind Gunnerson—"who's the leader?"

A woman stepped forward. "I am."

"Thank you. Have a seat and let's go over the plan."

"No time for sitting on our asses! Let's get going!"

Cash turned to Gunnerson and said calmly, "I need to know how this is going to work, so"—she turned to the woman in charge—"your name?"

The head of the drone team was a collected individual with remarkable self-possession, dressed for the mountains, perhaps thirty years of age, with a thick french braid down her back. "Lisa Stein."

"We're wasting time," said Gunnerson.

"*You're* wasting time," Cash said, turning her back on him. "Lisa, I'm Agent Frankie Cash, CBI. Please tell me how you propose using these drones."

With a twisted expression of frustration on his face, Gunnerson fell silent.

"Mr. Gunnerson has hired us to search for his son. What we have here are six drones, each with thermal-imaging sensors. They can see through fog and smoke and are specially designed for search and rescue operations—identifying anomalous sources of heat. They're most effective operating in colder temperatures, which usually means at night, but here in the mountains on a cool day, they also work in daylight. These are Matrice 300 drones, with a thirty-six-minute flight time, nine-mile range, and a maximum speed of fifty miles per hour. They each carry an infrared and 4k combined camera with 640-by-512 infrared resolution with a frame rate of 30 Hertz."

Cash nodded as if she understood. At least Stein seemed to know what she was talking about.

"Are these the pilots?" Cash indicated the group waiting behind her, also dressed for the mountains.

"Yes. Each drone has its own pilot. All are FAA certified. Would you like to see their certificates?"

"Leave copies with security," Cash said. This was all very intriguing. She wondered if the CBI shouldn't get some of these drones. "And how do you propose to search?"

"We divide up the search area into grids, by section. Place a pilot and drone in each grid and fly a lawn mower pattern until the grid is complete, then move on to the next one." She took out a large map from her briefcase and spread it out on a table. "Here's Erebus Valley and the grids we've laid over it—one hundred and forty-four sections, or square miles. When each six-hundred-and-forty-acre section is covered, we proceed to the next section."

"How long will it take to search the valley?"

"Very hard to say. And the problem is, the drones can't see well in areas of heavy tree or vegetation cover, ravines, overhangs and caves, steep mountain slopes, rockfalls. Another difficulty is getting our pilots into the launching zones. Reaching many of these remote sections will involve a hike or helicopter transportation. We're hoping to have use of a chopper and pilot to insert the drones and pilots into their LZs."

Cash considered this. The drone idea was a good one—amazing that a jackass like Gunnerson could have come up with something useful.

"We'll provide one of our helicopters," said Maximilian.

"Very good. Thank you."

"We can't let you go out there without security," said Cash. She didn't express her conviction that the two missing hikers were dead and not giving out a heat signal, but the gang of killers might be visible. "Mr. Maximilian," she said, "could you spare an armed security person to accompany each pilot? And a guide, if needed?"

"Absolutely."

Cash turned to Stein. "Are you one of the pilots?"

"Yes."

"I'd like to go with you. I want to see how this works."

Stein nodded. "Of course."

"I'm coming too," said Gunnerson.

Before she could protest, he went on, "I put this together, and no one's gonna keep me back here while my son is out there. I want to be part of the search. I *need* to be part of the search."

Cash gave this a think. He had taken on a pleading tone, and she felt a pang of sympathy for the old man. Better to have him with her than somewhere else, out of control and causing trouble.

"All right, Mr. Gunnerson, provided you follow my orders at all times."

"Yes. Good. Thank you. Let's get going."

17

Cash decided to start their drone search at the campsite where the hikers had vanished. It was the logical place to begin, a good spot with views, and the original helicopter landing zone was only half a mile away. The five other drone pilots were distributed in adjacent sections, for an initial coverage of six square miles of terrain.

Six square miles. One hundred and thirty-eight to go.

The helicopter dropped Cash, along with Stein and Gunnerson, at the LZ below the campsite. They hiked up, Stein carrying the drone in a special backpack. Maximilian had assigned them a security guard named Vanucci. He wore body armor and carried an AR-15 assault rifle.

They arrived at the campsite around ten a.m. Stein shed her pack and unzipped it to reveal the drone, batteries, and ancillary equipment packed in foam cutouts. Cash watched as Stein removed a launching pad, then unfolded the drone and placed it on top. She used a handheld console with two antennas and a screen to calibrate it. The drone woke up with various beeps and whirring sounds and flashing lights.

Cash was glad that Gunnerson was staying quiet and behaving himself. She thought she had smelled alcohol on his breath earlier, but he didn't seem drunk. The guard, Vanucci, stood watch.

"We're ready to launch," Stein said.

"Tell me how it works—what to expect."

"Of course. I'm going to fly a lawn mower pattern starting with the northern end of the grid and working south. When I hit a thermal signature, I'll bring the drone into a hover to look down and see what it is. It could be an animal or a human being, or even something like a dark boulder warmed by sunlight or a hot spring."

"And then?" Gunnerson asked. "What if they're human?"

"They might be searchers," said Cash. "That we can immediately determine because every search party has comms. If they're not searchers, we call in the cavalry. Maximilian has a chopper standing by with half a dozen armed personnel."

Gunnerson grunted his approval.

Stein held the console in both hands, thumbs on the joysticks. "Clear the LZ. Ready to fly," she announced.

They stood back. With a loud whirr, the drone rose vertically and hovered briefly at ten feet before soaring higher. Cash tried to follow it with her eyes, but the drone quickly disappeared into the bright morning sky. Stein held the controls and was working the joysticks, peering at the image on the screen.

"Okay, right away, we got some nearby thermal signatures," she said, peering at the screen. "Looks like . . . wow, mammoths."

Cash and Gunnerson looked over her shoulder. The screen on the console was divided into two windows—infrared and visible light. The thermal side showed half a dozen bright yellow-and-orange blobs in a background of blue and green. The visible portion of the screen showed six woolly mammoths lounging in their accustomed area near the pond.

"Continuing on," said Stein.

She flew the drone past the mammoths and over the lake, moving past the meadow on the far side and a forest of aspen trees beyond. On it flew, the thermal screen showing blurry blues and greens, the visible-light screen showing terrain.

"We've reached the edge of the search area," said Stein. "I'm now turning and starting the search pattern . . . coming back on the first line. We're going to proceed slower now."

Again an endless sea of blue and green passed by on the screen as the drone flew along the northern edge of the section.

"Got another signature," said Stein sharply.

Several orange-and-yellow blobs were moving next to the edge of a forest. When Stein brought the drone to a hover, Cash could see on the visible screen a buck and several does browsing vegetation.

"Mule deer," said Stein, flying the drone onward. She carried the drone to the end and made another turn, bringing it back along line two.

"How long is this going to take?" Gunnerson asked.

"To cover this section, an hour maybe."

"Can't you fly it faster? You said it went fifty miles an hour."

"That's too fast for this complicated terrain—we could miss something. And we have to return it for a change of batteries."

"Push it a little, for chrissake."

Stein said, "I'm doing my best, Mr. Gunnerson. If you don't mind, I need to concentrate."

Gunnerson tightened his lips and reached into his back pocket, pulling out a silver flask. He unscrewed the cap, took a long pull, and slid it back.

Uh-oh, thought Cash.

A long time passed as Stein continued to fly the drone back and forth, working down the section with methodical precision. Another thermal hit proved to be a pair of gigantic glyptodons, and later, several elk.

"For fuck's sake!" said Gunnerson. "This is going to take days! Goose it!"

Stein continued working the joysticks, ignoring him.

Gunnerson took another pull from his flask.

Cash turned to him. "Mr. Gunnerson? We've got a long day ahead of us. Can you lay off the booze?"

He looked at her with bloodshot eyes and without a word took another suck on the flask.

The minutes dragged on.

"How far along are we?" Gunnerson asked.

"About forty percent of the section," murmured Stein, focused on the controls.

"Fuck."

"A hit," murmured Stein.

Cash peered over her shoulder, glimpsing some yellow dots on the blue thermal screen. Nothing could be seen on the visual screen but a dense forest of fir trees.

Stein brought the drone to a hover. The yellow blips were on the ground.

Stein lowered the drone close to the treetops, trying to get the right angle to get a visual down through the immensely tall trees. Cash counted half a dozen orange-and-yellow blobs, moving slowly on the ground, appearing and disappearing as they went. But on the visible-light screen, they could see nothing of the forest floor—it was cloaked in darkness.

Gunnerson, peering closely over Stein's shoulder, said, "Go lower."

She brought the drone right down to the treetops, but the trees were at least a hundred feet tall, and the forest floor remained in shadow. It was impossible to tell what life-forms were down there.

"Send it down in between the trees."

"Too risky."

Cash could smell the whiskey exhaling on Gunnerson's breath as he peered intently at the monitor.

"There's room between the trunks. Lower the drone down in there, damn it!"

"Mr. Gunnerson, please step back. I'm the pilot."

Stein maneuvered the drone around the treetops, trying to find an opening in which to see down to the forest floor. The blobs stopped and gathered in a group.

"It looks like they heard it," Stein said.

"Flush 'em out," said Gunnerson. "Fly down and get 'em moving."

"Mr. Gunnerson," said Cash sharply, "back off *now*."

Gunnerson stepped forward and reached for the console.

"Hey!" Cash yelled. "What are you doing?"

Stein, holding the console in both hands and working the joysticks with her thumbs, tried to move away and elbow him back, but Gunnerson lunged for the console. He grabbed it, and there was a short tussle as he tried to wrench it from Stein's hands, but in the struggle, he lost his footing and fell, Stein yanking the console back. On the screen,

Cash saw a blurry, thrashing image that lasted a second or two—and then, after a moment, the camera image came back into focus, revealing a stationary floor of pine needles.

"You just crashed my drone," Stein said.

18

Sheriff James Colcord ambled into the Eagle County Historical Society and touched the brim of his hat to the man sitting behind the volunteer desk.

"Hello, Burch," he said.

"Well, howdy, Jim," said the volunteer, a tiny man with a face as wrinkled as an old map. He leaned forward. "What's happening up at Erebus? You catch that gang up there yet?"

Colcord hadn't had time to read the local papers, and he wondered what they were reporting. A lot of nonsense, no doubt. But it was clearly a big national story: on the drive out, he had passed a frantic line of press and television vans that were hoping to get into the valley.

"We're working on it," he said. "That's why I'm here."

Burch rose eagerly. "Well, what can I do for you?"

Colcord couldn't help but smile at the man's wizened face, his blue eyes popping with excitement for information. It was amazing that a man so old—he was close to ninety—could still have so much energy. There were a lot of people like him in Colorado, who lived a long time and had lots of energy and then died suddenly in their sleep.

"Think you can keep it confidential?"

"Absolutely. No problem. You can trust me."

Colcord knew he couldn't trust Burch for one minute, and he was pretty sure whatever he told him would be all over town in an hour or two, but he didn't really see a way around it. He needed the information, and Burch Burchard knew the archives better than anyone.

"I'm interested in the mining archive—of the mines in Erebus. The Fryingpan Mine and the Hesperus."

"You think the gang of killers might be hiding out in the mines?"

Nobody said Burch was dumb, thought Colcord. "It's possible."

"And what about the Jackman Mine? You want that too?"

"Um, what mine is that?"

"It's the third mine up there."

Now this is interesting. Wonder why Maximilian never mentioned that one. "Yes, all three."

"What aspect of the mines? I've got assay reports, partnership agreements—"

"I'm looking for maps—passageways and the location of all the entrances."

"You're gonna also want the ventilation shaft openings too."

"Yes. All the openings to the outside. Everything."

Burch nodded. "Okay. We got a lot of maps. The Jackman-Hesperus-Fryingpan complex is the largest hard-rock mine complex in Colorado. Follow me."

He went and locked the door to the historical society, turned a sign over that said CLOSED. "Right this way."

Colcord followed him through the office and past public exhibits of various mining tools, ore samples, old photographs, framed stock certificates, and miscellaneous bric-a-brac. Burch unlocked a fearsome padlock on a metal door in the back to reveal a warehouse extension behind the historical society building, packed from floor to ceiling with cardboard boxes and files.

Burch made a beeline through the maze of steel shelves, stopping before a big antique flat-file cabinet in polished oak and brass. He consulted the yellowing paper labels stuck into brass holders and finally pulled a file out. "Okay, here is the Fryingpan Mine, front section."

"Can we get a little more light in here? I want to photograph."

"I'm afraid it's about as bright as it gets in here. We'll bring them out into the office to photograph."

"Fryingpan, back section." He eased out sheet after sheet, laying them on top of the cabinet, then went on to another drawer and another.

"Jackman Mine, front section."

He pulled out the drawer and stared. It was empty.

"What the hell?" he said, peering down into the flat-file drawer that had nothing in it. "The maps of the Jackman Mine were supposed to be in here."

Colcord felt a crawling sensation along his spine.

Burch opened and shut more drawers in the cabinet labeled *Jackman*, but all were empty. Finally, he straightened up. "Stolen."

Colcord frowned. "Really? Are you sure?"

Burch shook his head, his beard waggling. "Positive. I have no idea why they'd be taken. These old maps aren't worth much."

"Has Erebus been in here, consulting these maps?"

"Oh yes," said Burchard. "When they first were laying out the place, they copied all these maps. But the Jackman Mine maps were still here, for sure. They must have been stolen recently."

"How do you know?"

"'Cause I periodically check these flat files. I like to keep tabs, go through stuff. I would've noticed. Those maps couldn't have been stolen more than a few months ago."

Colcord pondered this. "Any idea who might've done it?"

"I can check the visitors' log, but . . . it seems to me if you're gonna steal something, you ain't gonna sign in. Anyway, all visitors have to be accompanied by a volunteer, and that's usually me."

"Do you have security cameras?"

"In here? With our budget?"

Colcord asked, "How can I go about finding maps of the Jackman Mine?"

Burch was silent for a moment. "There's a prospector up in the hills, an old geezer named Yearwood—you know him? Augustus Yearwood."

"No."

"He spent most of his life roaming those mountains with a burro, pick, shovel, and gold pan. Most of the gold was sucked out of these mountains a long time ago, but he managed to eke out a living. Old Gus wandered all over Eagle County, up in the Flat Tops and the Spiders— and the Erebus." He pulled a soiled envelope out of his shirt pocket and scribbled the address down on it. "No phone. You'll have to drive out there. Don't let the signs deter you—old Gus is all bark and no bite."

Colcord took it. *Augustus Yearwood. Sawmill Corral, Grundage Creek Road.*

"You know where Grundage Creek is?"

"Sure do." Colcord put it in his pocket. "Thanks."

"Now let's bring these other maps out into the light so you can photograph them."

19

After working the controls for a while and getting no response, Stein turned to Cash. "I'm sorry, but we have to go get it."

"How far away is it?"

"About a klick." She showed Cash the location on the console screen. "That's where we are, and that's where the drone is."

It didn't look all that far to Cash, but it was downhill, through rough country. She turned to Gunnerson. "You stay here. Don't you move."

"You should've flown it down closer, like I asked," Gunnerson said.

Cash turned to Vanucci, the guard. "You watch him."

Vanucci looked uncertain. "Agent Cash, I'm not sure it's a good idea for you to go down there without security."

Cash opened her jacket to show her shoulder-holstered Glock. "*And I know how to use it.*"

Vanucci nodded. "Okay. Fair enough."

Gunnerson sat down, red-faced and sulky, on a fallen tree trunk and took another pull from his flask.

Stein said, "We pretty much go in that direction, downhill, for about three-quarters of a mile." She showed Cash, using the console's GPS, the exact position of the drone and the terrain in between.

They set off hiking down the meadow and quickly entered an aspen forest. Stein consulted the GPS on the console from time to time to guide them.

"What an asshole," Stein said.

"I'm sorry I allowed him to come along," said Cash. "That was a mistake."

Stein shook her head. "Not your fault. It was so unexpected. Nobody's ever done that to me before."

"You think the drone's toast?"

"It's pretty tough, and it has automatic avoidance features—and it landed on pine needles. The blades might be chewed up, but I've got replacements. I think it'll be okay."

As they hiked down through the trees, the slope got steeper. They were soon working their way gingerly down through rocky outcrops and deformed trees with their knuckled roots clinging precariously to the hillside. The footing was slippery, and Cash found herself hanging on to branches to maintain her footing.

After a half mile, they were blocked by a granite cliff with a twenty-foot drop.

"Son of a bitch," said Cash. "This sucks."

Moving along the top of the escarpment, they precariously followed its edge, looking for a route down. After a hundred yards, they came to a ravine choked with boulders. They halted, staring at it.

"I think we could get down that," said Stein.

Cash examined it. An ugly, steep little ravine, it was only a twenty-foot drop before it leveled out into a dark forest of giant spruce trees. There were plenty of foot- and handholds on the way down. It was doable, she thought.

Stein checked the map on her console. "The drone's down there just a few hundred yards ahead."

"I'm game," said Cash.

"Let's do it."

Stein put the console into her pack, zipped it up, and started climbing down among the boulders, moving slowly. Cash followed. It was scary; the boulders were huge and covered with slippery patches of moss, with broken tree trunks lying every which way. But there were lots of handholds, and Cash reached the bottom without much difficulty, putting her feet gratefully on the firm forest floor and breathing a sigh of relief.

Stein drew the console out of her pack and stared at it. "That's funny."

"What is it?"

"The drone's stopped transmitting."

"But you still know where it is?"

"I dropped a pin on its location. It's just a few hundred yards that way. Maybe the battery died."

They set off through the gloomy forest, the trees shagged with moss. After five minutes of walking, Stein stopped and looked around.

"It should be right here," she said. She stared at the console. "This is definitely where it landed, where I dropped the pin."

Cash likewise cast her eyes about. The forest floor was thick with springy needles, and it was cool and shadowy, the tall trees filtering out the sunlight, leaving them in a deep green shade. The fresh scent of pine drifted in the air. There was something awe-inspiring about the grove. She felt a prickling of alarm.

Stein saw something on the ground and bent down as if to pick it up.

"Whoa," said Cash. "Don't touch that."

She brought out a ziplock evidence bag from the small supply she habitually carried and a tweezer and picked up the object—a broken piece of plastic. She slipped it in the bag and gave it to Stein.

"That's a broken blade from my drone. So where the hell is it?"

Cash felt the prickle of alarm grow. "It was taken," she said.

"Taken? What the hell?"

"Taken and, I would guess, turned off. Which is why you lost contact with it." She reached into her jacket and unsnapped the keeper on her sidearm and withdrew it, casting her eyes about. They were surrounded by trees that limited sight in all directions. This was not a good place to be.

Stein stared at the gun. "Really?"

Cash saw, or thought she saw, a brief movement among the trees out of the corner of her eye. She snapped her head around, focusing in that direction, but whatever it was had disappeared. She put her finger to her lips and listened intently, but the only sounds were a sighing of wind in the treetops and the occasional creak of a tree trunk. The usual ubiquitous chirping of birds, however, had stopped.

Stein suddenly spun around. "What's that?"

Cash too thought she saw a brief movement, but when she stared—nothing. She had a feeling of being stealthily surrounded.

"I think," Cash said quietly, "we'd better get the fuck out of here."

Stein nodded.

Cash turned and began walking back the way they had come, Stein following. Cash looked steadily to the left and right as they moved, occasionally looking back to see if they were being followed. She glimpsed flickers of distant movement through the trees on either side of them—they were being paced. She had her Baby Glock in hand. Since she carried it without a round in the chamber, she now racked one in. The noise was loud and unnatural. They were definitely being surrounded. The movements through the trees on either side felt like they were getting closer, in a sort of pincer movement. What the hell were they—people? They didn't seem to be moving like people—more like animals. But animals wouldn't pick up and turn off a drone.

She murmured to Stein, "*Run.*"

They broke into a jog, keeping side by side. That seemed to provoke their pursuers, who kept pace, edging closer but remaining flashes of movement among the many trees, impossible to differentiate or see.

In a moment, the ravine came into view.

"You go up first," Cash said, spinning around with her Glock raised. "I'll cover."

Bracing herself in a firing stance, she aimed the weapon while scanning right to left and back again. Behind her, she heard Stein scrambling up the rockfall, grunting with the effort as she hoisted herself up through the tight boulders. All around her, among the tree trunks, Cash could see movement, fleet and silent—a tightening of the circle. It felt more like circling wolves than human beings.

Christ, maybe they are *animals.* She sighted along the barrel of the Glock, but was loath to fire. Discharging a weapon meant a shitload of paperwork, and her training told her never to fire at anything without an absolutely clear view. She could definitely see forms moving swiftly through the trees, still shrinking the circle—and again, she had the sense they were animals. They were too silent, too fleet, too . . . *feral.*

If she couldn't fire at them, she could at least try scaring them off. It would still mean paperwork, but that was better than being decapitated. She lowered the gun and fired into the ground. The sound of the shot boomed and echoed among the trees.

It seemed to have the desired effect—all motion ceased.

She glanced back; Stein was halfway up the slot. Time for her to start climbing too. She holstered her weapon, spun around, and started up after Stein, grasping the edge of a rock and wedging a boot in a crack, pulling herself up, reaching, finding a handhold and foothold, pulling up again, struggling to get to the top as fast as possible. She'd done some rock climbing before, and it came in handy now.

She heard a sharp cry above her and looked up in time to see Stein slip, hang by a second from one arm, the other gyrating madly, trying to catch a handhold, and then she fell right past Cash, glanced off a boulder, and landed on the bottom with a sickening thud, where she lay on her side.

"Lisa!" Cash cried, almost losing her own grip as she scrambled back down, jumping the last five feet and kneeling over Stein. Her eyes were slits. She was unconscious. She looked dead.

"Lisa. *Lisa!* Can you hear me?"

No answer.

"Lisa!"

20

Bending over Stein, Cash cast her eyes around, looking for her pursuers, but whoever or whatever was surrounding them had either fled or hidden behind trees. She turned her attention back to Stein. Had she hit her head? She gingerly checked, moving her hair, but could see no injury to her head or neck. To Cash's enormous relief, Stein's eyes fluttered, and she gradually came to, her eyes blinking and staring around.

"Lisa?"

She didn't answer, her eyes rolling around in an uncomprehending panic.

"It's okay, Lisa. You had a fall. I'm going to examine you."

Cash examined Stein's body, scanning her limbs for injuries but not daring to move her. One of her legs was badly scraped and bleeding, the jeans torn, and the ankle was at a funny angle.

A groan. Her eyes finally focused on Cash.

"Jesus . . . what . . . ?"

"You had a fall."

"Where . . . ?"

"We're in the woods. Retrieving your drone."

"Oh God." She closed her eyes. "My . . . ankle . . ."

"I see it," said Cash. It looked broken, but she refrained from saying so. She gave their surroundings another scan. Had they run away, or were they still there? She pulled off her pack, fumbled out her radio, and called on emergency channel 5. Right away, she raised a dispatcher at the lodge and asked for Maximilian.

He came on immediately. "What's happened? Where are you?" he asked.

"Stein's hurt, can't walk, maybe a broken ankle. We were being pursued. We need to be evacuated—now." She gave the coordinates of their position.

"Copy. We've a chopper on the pad, ready to go. We'll be there ASAP. But . . . we'll have to find an LZ near you. I see from your coordinates that you're in a forest."

"Yes. And I think we're surrounded," Cash said.

"Surrounded? By what?"

"I don't know. Animals or people. Bring armed security. Hurry."

"Copy that. I'll leave the frequency open," said Maximilian. "Stay on it."

She placed the radio next to her. "Did you hear?"

Stein nodded, wincing. Her face was pale and beaded with sweat, but otherwise stoic.

Cash saw a fresh trace of movement and turned her attention back to the wall of forest surrounding them. The same covert flitting among the trees had started again. The shapes were moving closer, in a more deliberate way. It was hard to make them out—they were the same color as the tree trunks, a dark brownish gray. It was mostly through movement that she could even see them at all. What the hell were they? She yanked the Glock back out and raised it with both hands, still kneeling, panning the view. She had nine shots left, but the weapon was only accurate at short range—not much good beyond ten yards.

She kept the gun raised in case there was a rush. It was unnerving, being cornered against the cliff with no corridor of retreat and a partner who couldn't walk.

More darting movements among the trunks. They were definitely closing in, but still staying well behind cover.

Another groan from Stein.

"How're you doing?" she whispered.

"Okay," Stein said, swallowing. She didn't look okay. She might have been going into shock. "Are they still there?"

"Yes. We're gonna have to hold out for a bit."

It would take about ten minutes, Cash figured, for the chopper to reach where they were after it took off. But then they would have to find an LZ and hike in. Or could they abseil down through the trees? Not possible with these hundred-foot giants.

She continued to scan the forest, but it was silent and still.

"I'm sorry," Stein said, "that I fell."

"Forget it."

She saw a flash of movement on both sides, weirdly coordinated, as if they all moved at once. And now she saw clearly they were human—they couldn't be anything else, even if they moved so quickly she couldn't see anything but a blur. And being human, they must be the killers. How many were there? More than six.

"Hey! You out there!" she cried. "Agent Cash, CBI! Identify your-selves!"

Her words dissipated in the trees.

"Stay the fuck back. I'm armed, and I *will* shoot to defend myself. Do you understand?"

Nothing but the faint hiss of wind.

She turned to Stein. "Are you carrying a weapon?"

"A knife . . . in the pack . . ."

Cash dipped into the pack and pulled out a fixed-blade buck knife, unsheathing it and laying it down on the ground between them. No way were they going to take her without a fight.

She squinted, staring into the trees. God, it was so thick and dark.

Another organized movement: this time unmistakable. On her right. And then one on her left. They were stealthy, quick, and wary—and they were coordinating.

"I will shoot to kill!" she yelled. She waited, gun raised, the tension almost unbearable, the silence broken only by an occasional whimper of pain from Stein. It felt like an eternity. Her hands on the Glock's textured grip were sweaty. She waited.

Another sudden coordinated movement. They were closing in. This time, she caught a clear glimpse of a human outline—dressed in some sort of camo.

She grabbed the radio. "Cash, calling Maximilian, over."

"Maximilian here."

"We're being surrounded by people wearing camo. Closing in. Maybe six, eight—impossible to tell."

"Copy that. Bird lifted off five minutes ago."

She lowered her voice to a whisper. "Forget the LZ for now. We can't wait that long—they're closing in. Have the chopper fly straight to our position and hover. Make a lot of noise. Drop flash-bangs, fire weapons, do whatever to drive 'em off."

"Copy that."

Another sudden flurry of movement as the attackers moved in closer. She heard something—a weird sound. At first, she thought it might be the approaching chopper, until she realized it came from all around, a high-pitched keening that gradually rose in volume and morphed into an ululation or yodeling that cut the air like a razor blade, throbbing and coming from everywhere and nowhere at once. An unmistakably human sound, which made it all the more frightening—and they were now much closer, crouching behind the massive spruce trunks.

These people were crazy, weird fucking fanatics. She had to accept they were about to be attacked and respond accordingly. She aimed, waited for another movement, then swiveled to it and fired.

The boom echoed and died as the sound erupted into a squealing, yowling chorus that was spine-chilling, even demonic. Had she hit one of them?

It abruptly ceased. At the same time, she heard a low throbbing sound—the helicopter. It rapidly grew in volume, and soon she saw the dark shape of the bird itself visible above the treetops, hovering and coming down lower, the backwash thrashing the treetops and sending down a shower of twigs and needles, the trees groaning and creaking. There was a burst of automatic gunfire, and a second burst, as the chopper rotated slowly a hundred feet above them, more stuff cascading down from the upper canopy.

The gunfire did the trick. There was an explosion of movement as figures—human figures—burst out from behind trees, scattering and vanishing into the forest.

21

Grundage Creek Road went up a steep gorge, the creek rushing below over boulders and through pools. The old road had been carved and blasted by hand out of the rock walls of the gorge, and it went to the old sawmill and ghost town of Grundage. Colcord fly-fished this river on occasion. It was here, as a teenager, he had caught a four-pound cutthroat trout on a two-pound test line. It was the indelible memory of that day—the sunlight glittering off the water, the fish leaping and fighting, the aspens rustling in the breeze—that he replayed again and again in his mind like a mantra during some of his worst days in Iraq.

He slowed down as he passed by the hole where he had caught that trout. There was a teenage boy there, just like he'd been, lashing the water. It gladdened his heart.

The road went from bad to worse and finally, where the gorge opened up into a broad valley, petered out into a rutted track. A hand-painted sign said, NO TRESPASSING THAT MEANS YOU. And then another sign, with a crude painting of a six-gun aiming at the viewer: YES YOU.

Colcord shook his head with a smile. Colorado was full of these old-timers, these independent backwoods types. God love 'em.

The track soon ended in the ruins of the old Grundage sawmill, a batten board structure now caved in, with a scattering of log cabins beyond it, the remains of the former settlement. One cabin appeared lived in, with cheerful red curtains in the windows and smoke issuing from a stone chimney.

Colcord pulled up well short of the inhabited one. There was no car out in front, but a horse grazed in a pasture nearby, tossing his head and nipping away flies. Colcord got out of the vehicle and stood next to it, waiting for the inhabitant to see him, if he hadn't already. He saw one of the curtains over the window move. He waited a moment, then reached into the Suburban and gave the horn a little toot.

A moment later, the door opened, and out came Yearwood, looking just as Colcord expected: moth-eaten cowboy hat, overalls, and a beard as long and white as one of those ZZ Top band members'. A double-barreled shotgun, broken open, was draped over his left arm.

"Mr. Augustus Yearwood?" Colcord called out.

"What you want?" came the shrill reply.

"Sheriff Colcord, Eagle County. I'm investigating the murders up at Erebus." He held up his star.

Silence. Colcord wondered for a moment if Yearwood had even heard of the murders, but then the old man raised a hand and in a much friendlier voice called out, "Welcome, Sheriff. Come on in!"

Colcord followed him into the interior of the log house. Yearwood shut the shotgun and propped it up next to the door. He was about the skinniest old man Colcord had ever laid eyes on, a string bag of bones.

"Coffee, Sheriff?"

"Yes, please."

"Take a load off while I git it." He pointed to a seat.

He disappeared into the back of the cabin while Colcord sat down in a homemade chair constructed of screwed-together oak branches, with an old Navajo rug draped over it. It was viciously uncomfortable. A big stone fireplace with a woodstove built into it issued a welcome heat.

Yearwood returned with two steaming mugs. Colcord took his while Yearwood sat himself down in the only other chair in the room. The old man leaned forward on his elbows, his beard draped over his knees, his eyes flashing with a fierce eagerness. "Now, tell me about the murders up at Erebus."

Christ, thought Colcord, *this guy's as excited for news as Burch.* It dawned on him that this must be a huge news story in the outside world to have reached all the way up here. He felt a momentary chill. If this case didn't get solved, and fast, he might as well kiss reelection goodbye.

He pushed that idea out of his head and focused on the interview at hand.

"Mr. Yearwood," said Colcord. "I hear from my old friend Burch that you might be familiar with the mines up in the Erebus Valley."

"Yes, sir, I am. I spent five years up there prospecting. That's some of the most beautiful country in our God-given land. Shame those bastards at Erebus took it over."

Colcord nodded. "Are you familiar with the Jackman Mine?"

"Sure. There are three mines up there, sort of—Hesperus, Fryingpan, and Jackman. I say 'sort of' because they started out as three mining claims, but they all eventually connected inside the mountains. I prospected in all three of them, especially Fryingpan. They call it that because the two partners who filed on the claim got into a disputation, and one bashed the other's brains with a frying pan."

"I see. Interesting. Did you, ah, find anything in the mines? Gold?"

"Hell yes. There's still little bits of wire gold in there, just enough to make it worthwhile. That complex is the biggest hard-rock mine in Colorado, yielded over a billion dollars in gold and silver. What you got there is the so-called Cronus Pluton, a magma intrusion into Precambrian rock that was uplifted during the Laramide orogeny fifty-five million years ago. The Cronus Pluton is mostly quartz-rich granitoid and diorite with dispersed silver and gold in wire form, following quartz veins going every which way. So to git it, they had to take out a hell of a lot of rock, just blast the shit out of the mountain. You could put Notre Dame in some of those stopes in there, but the pluton is so hard and consolidated that they got away with it, mostly without shoring and bracing."

Colcord had temporarily lost the geological thread. "So you're saying the Jackman Mine is big?"

"Big? It's huge. And like I said, it's all just one mine. Started out as three, but eventually, the adits and stopes linked up inside the mountains. Those miners were chasing a bunch of diffuse ore bodies and veins that were like a maze."

"I went to the historical society," Colcord said, "but someone stole the maps to the Jackman Mine."

"That so? Those maps were there back when I was prospecting."

"It seems they were recently taken. Any idea who?"

"No, sir. Not a clue."

"Burch said you might remember where the openings to the mine were."

"I got better than that. I got my own hand-drawn maps of Jackman. Those filed maps were never accurate. Mine are better."

This was almost too good to be true. But Yearwood didn't make a move to get them. Instead, Yearwood asked, "So you think them killers are hiding inside Jackman?"

"It's a possibility," said Colcord.

"How many?"

"At least six."

"Six? That's a gang. They say they beheaded their victims. That so?"

Colcord realized Yearwood expected a fair exchange of information. "Yes, that's what the medical examiner thinks."

"What do you think they done with the bodies? Et 'em?"

"There's no evidence of cannibalism."

Yearwood was clearly disappointed. He shook his head. "There's a lot of tough terrain up there. You may never find 'em."

"Mr. Yearwood, you know that country as well as anyone. Where would you hide?"

The question was immensely gratifying to Yearwood. He leaned back and stroked his beard. "Aside from inside the mines—that's your best bet—there are some couloirs up above the tree line with rockslides—granite boulders as big as houses. There are all kinds of holes and crawl spaces and caves in those rockslides. There are some deep forests in there a man could disappear into, thickest in Colorado. There are rock shelters, crevasses, prospect holes, ravines. You got a big problem on your hands trying to find that gang."

"Where are these couloirs and ravines?"

"They're on every mountain up there, especially the Barbicans, then going northward on Mount Erebus and below Espada Pass over into Flat Tops, in a place called Hookers Canyon."

Colcord asked, "Can I get copies of those maps of yours?"

Yearwood rose and went to a padlocked wooden door at the far end of his sitting room. He unlocked it to reveal a closet stuffed with

rolled maps, hundreds of them stacked like cordwood. He began pulling them out, and the rolls cascaded into the room. He sorted through
them and brought one over to Colcord. "There it is: Jackman Mine."

"Can I take this and copy it?" Colcord asked.

"No. I don't let them out of the cabin."

Colcord took out his cell phone. "Photograph it?"

After a moment, Yearwood nodded. "Why not? My prospecting
days are over."

Colcord unrolled it near the window. It was surprisingly detailed,
drawn in a careful, neat, sure hand.

"What about this area here?" he asked, pointing to where the map
petered into blankness.

"I didn't map the whole damn place, just what I prospected."

"So you don't know how much farther these tunnels go?"

"I don't, but I've no doubt some of them adits connect to Fryingpan
and Hesperus."

Colcord weighed down the corners with ore samples and photographed it, sector by sector. As he did so, he wondered just who might
have stolen the maps—and once again he wondered why Maximilian
never mentioned the Jackman Mine.

22

"Over here!" Cash called out as she saw, through the trees, four guys with assault rifles moving cautiously, bulked up with body armor, helmets, and gear. Maximilian was with them, along with two paramedics carrying a stretcher.

The security guards quickly established a perimeter while the paramedics went to Stein, gave her an injection, and began working on her. She seemed very much out of it, lying back, her face white and bathed in sweat, her eyes half-closed.

"Thank God you're safe," said Maximilian, striding over. His face was pale and slick with sweat and carried a frightened look. It was the first time Cash had seen him break out of his cool demeanor. "What did you see? How many were there?"

Cash brushed herself off. "Maybe eight people in camo."

"Did you get a good look?"

"It was hard to see them. At first, I almost thought they were wolves or some kind of animals as they circled us, keeping to the trees."

"When you say camo, what kind of camo? Soldier's camo?"

"It was more like homemade camo, leaves and bark stuck on them so they blended in. Really effective. I could hardly tell them from the background."

"But definitely human?"

"Oh yeah."

"So how did you get out here? What happened?"

Cash shook her head and explained about Gunnerson and the drone crash. "But when we got here," she said, "the drone was gone. They took it."

"They *took* it?" Maximilian asked, incredulous.

"Yes. All we found was a broken propeller blade. And then we realized they were surrounding us. We tried to climb up that ravine—Stein fell."

Maximilian turned to the guards. "You two"—he motioned to two of them—"go up to the old campsite and escort Gunnerson to the other chopper waiting at the LZ."

"Yes, sir."

The two men set off, scrambling up the ravine and disappearing. Meanwhile, the two paramedics hefted Stein on the stretcher and began carrying her through the woods. Cash followed with Maximilian.

"Does the drone have a GPS?" Maximilian asked. "We might be able to track them with it."

"They turned it off. Stein told me it will only transmit its location if they turn it back on and keep the GPS setting to auto."

Maximilian shook his head. He had grown even paler. "Did they give any indication of *why* they were stalking you?"

She swallowed. "I had the distinct impression we were being hunted—that they were going to kill us."

"Bloody hell," said Maximilian under his breath.

The forest thinned out, and the trees gave way to a meadow where the helicopter had landed. From the other side of the meadow, Cash could see several guards hiking down from the campsite, one helping Gunnerson down the trail.

Cash said, "That man"—she pointed at Gunnerson—"must be removed from any contact with the investigation and confined to his quarters at the lodge. He's responsible for this."

Maximilian nodded. "I hear you. Clear as a bell."

23

As the chopper descended on the heliport on the lodge roof, Cash saw parked at one end a sleek black corporate helicopter.

"Whose is that?" she asked Maximilian.

"Mr. Barrow's," he said, not sounding thrilled about it.

"Did you know he was coming?"

"No. He arrived unannounced. That's how he usually operates."

Their bird settled down not far from the black helicopter, which Cash could now see had the corporate initials *RxB* emblazoned in gold on the door, above the Erebus logo of a woolly mammoth.

They stayed on the chopper while the paramedics unloaded Stein in the stretcher and carried her to the elevator, taking her to the infirmary. Vanucci, the guard, took a subdued Gunnerson away. Cash followed Maximilian out of the chopper.

When the elevator doors opened into the main lodge hall, Cash could see that Barrow's arrival had caused a stir. The lobby was abuzz with activity and the staff were scurrying about. The guests had also gathered and stood about in chattering groups, apparently hoping to catch a glimpse of the famous billionaire. There were many fewer guests than before the news of the killings had broken, but Cash was surprised at how many had stayed.

She made her way past the crowds to the conference room. It was empty—Colcord hadn't yet returned from his research trip to Eagle. She made herself a double espresso and eased down in one of the plush conference chairs, throwing her feet up on the table in the blessed silence and privacy of the room, and dialed her boss to check in.

After a ring, McFaul answered.

"Jesus Christ," he said. "I just heard that you were stalked! Are you okay?"

"I'm fine," Cash said. "I'm calling because Barrow's just arrived. I want to interview him while we have the chance. Since they're saying he won't talk voluntarily, I'd like to get a subpoena started."

There was a short silence. "Agent Cash," McFaul said, "I want you to understand the situation out here. It's crazy. The media is all over this thing. They're pouring in from the coasts. Our parking lot's jammed up; they're buttonholing everyone coming and going. I just got a call from the governor, wanting to know what the hell we're doing."

Cash waited out this rush of words. "What does this have to do with interviewing Barrow?"

"My point is, we've got to be careful. All eyes are on us. If we go chasing a subpoena to compel the testimony of the world's fifth-richest man, that's front-page news, and there'd better be a good reason. He wasn't there when all this happened. He doesn't have any direct knowledge. If you can persuade him to talk voluntarily, hats off to you, but *no subpoena*. Now, anything else before I hang up? We're swamped here dealing with the media."

Cash took a deep breath. "I'm pretty sure from what I saw today that there were at least eight killers."

"Jesus. We've got some kind of crazy cult on our hands."

"I believe the risk to civilians is too high. We need to shut the resort down to all but investigators, security personnel, and the minimum of support staff."

A silence. McFaul then spoke, his voice unnaturally calm. "Erebus is the fourth-largest employer in Colorado after Lockheed Martin, United Airlines, and Vail Resorts. Did you know that?"

Cash didn't answer.

"What you're proposing would cause economic damage not just to Erebus but to the entire state. And not just for the duration of the shutdown. It could hurt their business long-term."

Cash took a long breath. "Sir, consider the economic damage that more killings would cause." She paused. "And the damage it might cause to the CBI's reputation." She stopped herself from mentioning the damage it might also cause to his own reputation—and hers.

"Erebus has already pulled their guests out of the backcountry. The only guests remaining are at the lodge, which is like a fortress, or so I'm told, with armed guards around the clock."

"What about the movie team shooting in the town? Or the laboratory up in the mountain?"

"They have their own armed protection. Look, Cash, the bottom line is: I don't have the authority to close the place down."

"You could talk to the governor."

"This conversation is verging on insubordination."

Cash swallowed. McFaul was a wimp who'd never backed her up before, and she'd been stupid to think he'd change now.

"Sorry, sir," she said. "Just trying to do what's right for the investigation."

"I know you're under a lot of pressure," McFaul said, softening his tone. "I have faith in you. Just get me something, anything, in the next twenty-four hours, because if not, we're in trouble."

She hung up. This was bullshit. Her head reeled from stress and lack of sleep. What she really should do was head back to her room and snatch a few hours of sleep, but she was worried if she did that, she wouldn't be able to get up and would sleep through to the next day. No, what she needed to do was tank up on coffee and think through this thing.

As she was making her second double espresso, Colcord entered. He looked at her with concern. "I heard about what happened to you," he said. "You okay?"

"Fine," she said curtly.

Colcord laid his hat on the table and sat down next to her. "I made a rather interesting discovery today," he said in a low voice. "Rather, two discoveries."

"Yeah?"

"There's a third abandoned mine up here, called the Jackman."

"Maximilian never mentioned it."

"Exactly. Why didn't he? I went to the Eagle County Historical

Society and looked at their map collection. The maps of the Jackman Mine have all been stolen."

"No shit."

He grinned. "But I found an old prospector who had drawn his own maps." He held up his phone. "Got 'em all photographed."

"You think the killers could be hiding in the mines?"

"It's a definite possibility. But why were the Jackman maps stolen, and why did Maximilian never mention that mine? I feel like they're hiding something."

Cash nodded.

"I'd like to give Maximilian the third degree on those two points," said Colcord.

"Me too," said Cash. "And that brings up something I've been thinking about—what would you think of asking the governor for some National Guard troops in here? I'm a little uneasy leaving all the security and most of the searching to Erebus. I mean, what if they're involved?"

Colcord looked at her. "That would be a big step. But yes, I think you're right." He hesitated. "You know that's your bailiwick, not mine—right?"

She nodded. "Yeah, I know. Just glad to know you'd support it."

"I'd back you up one hundred percent."

She'd have to ask for it through McFaul. No way would he agree to it now, but maybe in another day—or if something else happened, god forbid. She looked at her watch. Three p.m. "They won't let me subpoena Barrow. But maybe we can get a voluntary interview."

Colcord picked up his hat. "It's worth a try. Let's go find him."

They found Maximilian in the security monitoring room. He turned to them as they arrived, his face flushed. "We're launching an armed sweep of the forest where you were cornered," he said. "We're going to find those attackers. We're also monitoring the drone camera in case whoever took the drone turns it back on. We're also allowing the drone search to continue."

"All good," said Cash. "The sheriff and I'd like to speak to Barrow."

"You want me to set up a meeting?"

"No meeting," said Cash. "I'm talking about an interview."

Maximilian paused. "Why?"

"It's not up to you to ask why," Cash said in a surge of irritation. "This is standard investigative procedure."

"I'm sorry, but Mr. Barrow is not available."

"How would you know without checking?" Cash demanded.

"Because he never speaks to anyone. Ever."

"I'm asking you, Mr. Maximilian, to tell Barrow we're seeking a voluntary interview."

"No point. He's going to say no."

"*Who's* going to say no?" came a booming voice from the doorway.

Cash turned to see a stocky man of medium height, wearing white slacks and a blue blazer with brass buttons and an ascot, close-clipped white beard, and intense blue eyes. He looked uncannily like a shorter Hemingway. He came striding into the room, a charismatic presence so strong that everyone fell momentarily silent.

"Well?" he asked.

"Mr. Barrow," said Maximilian, "I was just telling Agent Cash that you're not available for an interview."

"I'm not?" He turned to Cash. "Agent in Charge Frances Cash, I believe? And this must be Sheriff James Colcord. Pleased to meet you."

He stuck out a big, rough, workingman's hand and shook both of theirs with vigor. He had a British accent.

"Now—where shall we chat?"

"We have an interview room all set up down the hall," said Cash. "Please follow us, Mr. Barrow."

Maximilian started down the hall with them, but Barrow waved him off. "I can handle this myself, thank you, Mr. Maximilian!"

They entered the room, and Barrow, before seating himself, stood behind Cash's chair to help seat her as one might do at a formal dinner party. Cash hesitated, momentarily incredulous, then she said, with a cool smile, "Thank you, Mr. Barrow, but I prefer to seat myself."

"Independent. Good!" He took his own seat. "Now—what questions do you want to ask me? I am at your service."

24

Barrow gave them both a smile, displaying a row of very white, fine teeth in a deeply tanned face. He sat on the other side of the table, hands clasped, looking the very picture of cooperation.

"Thank you, Mr. Barrow," Cash said. "Do you mind if I turn on a recorder?"

"No problem."

She turned on the phone recorder and went through the preliminaries, identifying herself and Colcord, ID'ing Barrow, and making sure it was a matter of record that this was a voluntary interview.

"Mr. Barrow," Cash began, deciding to get straight to the point, "it appears there are half a dozen or more killers in Erebus. They appear to be deeply familiar with the resort, the terrain, and your security procedures. They are clever. They have evaded a hundred searchers now for three days."

He nodded.

"In other words," she said, "the evidence strongly points to the Erebus killers as being employees—former or current."

"That also occurred to us," Barrow said. "We've scoured our employment records every which way, looking for disgruntled employees, spies, foreign operatives, hired guns from rival companies. We've found nothing—yet. We've turned over reams of records to the CBI too, and I assume you're looking through them also?"

"We are." Their investigative team had so far found nothing, but it was a big task. She glanced at Colcord. He was jotting notes in his book.

"Do you have *any* idea who they might be?" she asked.

"I don't."

"Surely you must have *some* thoughts on that question."

"I have enemies. Everyone knows who they are. My enemies are misguided environmentalists, scientists, PETA militants, NIMBY activists. They may be unpleasant people, but are they killers? Would they infiltrate half a dozen people into my valley to start brutally killing people? It seems unlikely."

"It was my impression, being surrounded in the forest earlier today, that they were back-to-the-land crazies or radical environmentalists—dressed up in homemade camo and playacting like wild animals."

"It's possible that a truly fringe group might be behind this."

"I understand you know the father of Mark Gunnerson, one of the victims."

"Yes."

"How well?"

"We met at Davos about ten years ago, I believe. We've kept in touch, off and on, as casual business associates will. We do not socialize on a friendship basis." He said this with a certain tightening of the voice.

"Why is that?"

"We move in different circles. He's in finance; I'm a scientist. I don't find financial people interesting—unless they're making *me* money." He gave a laugh. "We are both members of Bohemian Grove, I might add."

"What's that?"

"You don't know? It's a—how to explain? A retreat of cabins in the redwoods of Northern California, where influential men gather once a year for two weeks of relaxing, sports and games, amateur theatricals—that sort of thing."

"I'm not sure I quite understand. You and Gunnerson are members?" said Cash.

"That's right. The club dates back to 1870, and the all-male membership includes—let me speak frankly—some of the most influential people in the world—business leaders, former U.S. presidents, powerful media executives."

"And you spent time with him there every year?"

"Just once. I don't go every year. I'm very busy. And as I said, he's not really a friend—more like an acquaintance."

"Did you know his son, Mark?"

"I never met him. Nor his new wife."

"Have you had any financial dealings with Gunnerson?" she asked.

"None whatsoever. Obviously, his son paid to come here, but I had nothing to do with that." He sat back in his chair, tenting his fingers and looking at her with a placid, self-satisfied face.

Cash had the urge to shake him up, he was so self-assured and comfortable. "Are you British?"

"No," he said.

"Where are you from originally?"

"Born in Kansas City, grew up in LA."

"Why the British accent?"

"Oxford. Rhodes scholar."

"Hard to pick up a plummy accent like that in just a year."

"I imagine you think it's pretentious. And perhaps it is. We all re-invent ourselves—as *you* did, relocating from Maine to Colorado after that unfortunate incident with the Taser. How tragic."

Cash was mightily startled, but then she realized she should have anticipated it. A man like this would naturally have looked into her background. She glanced at Colcord. He seemed angered by the comment but was, for the moment, holding his tongue.

"Excuse me," said Colcord. "I've got to run out for a moment. I'll be back."

Cash looked at him incredulously, but there was a knowing look in his face that stopped her from asking what the hell he was doing, leaving in the middle of an interview.

Colcord departed. Cash turned back to Barrow. She had interviewed people like this before—savvy, experienced, polished, impenetrable.

"Mr. Barrow, you say you're a scientist. But really, you don't have an advanced degree in genetics. You made your money in the tech business. Isn't it really Dr. Karman who did the real science?"

She could see she'd hit a nerve.

"I financed this," he said. "Sure, Bill Gates didn't build the first personal computer or even write the software, but he was the genius behind Microsoft. We were the first to de-extinct and rewild the woolly mammoth."

"Okay, but why did you take it so much further—buying this valley, building this resort? That's entertainment, not science."

"A great scientist," said Barrow, "is like a great artist. You love what you do for its own sake—but you *also* crave an audience. Michelangelo would never have painted the Sistine Chapel if he thought no one would see it. I wanted to share my creations with the world. Hence"—and he spread his hands apart with a big smile—"Erebus."

"What's your ultimate goal?" Cash asked.

"Here?"

"Anywhere."

Barrow leaned back in his chair, tented his fingers, and half closed his eyes. "To make the world a better place."

What pabulum, she thought, making an effort not to roll her eyes. She was going to get nothing out of this man.

"I see you're skeptical. But let me explain. Think about the miracle of life on this planet. A dust cloud in space condensed into a wet dead rock orbiting an average star. And then, somewhere on this rock, a microscopic bag of chemicals made a copy of itself. And copied itself again, and then again. Because these copies were imperfect and differed slightly from each other, some chemical bags survived better than others. That's it. That dumb little rule, iterated a billion times, produced us and everything else in our glorious natural world! But you and I are still a bag of chemicals, fabulously complex, that somehow acquired this mysterious thing called consciousness. Look at you and me—it blows the mind that we evolved from a dust cloud left over from an exploded star!"

Cash had never heard it explained quite that way, and she was struck by his passion and sincerity, different from her initial impression of him as a manipulative businessman interested only in money.

He went on, his voice rising. "'There is grandeur in this view of life,' Darwin wrote, 'with its several powers, having been originally breathed into a few forms or into one; and that, whilst this planet has gone cycling on according to the fixed law of gravity, from so simple a beginning endless forms most beautiful and most wonderful have been, and are being, evolved.'"

He paused, his eyes shining with childlike earnestness. "But now, we've reached the point where we can *resurrect* the dead. We can actually *reverse* the extinction of a species and bring it back to life. What a beautiful thing! Not only have I brought back to life some extraordinary animals, I've created a place for human beings to enjoy and learn about the richness of life itself."

He sat back. "So, yes, I *am* making the world a better place."

Cash didn't know how to respond to this enthusiastic flood of words, which put Barrow in a different and more complex light in her mind. As she was collecting her thoughts and looking for the next question, she heard a sound in the hall, then a loud voice.

"Where? In here?"

Good god, it was Gunnerson.

The door opened, and Colcord entered, holding it open for Gunnerson.

Barrow was struck dumb, all his composure vanishing. "Mr. Gunnerson, what a surprise. I didn't expect—"

Gunnerson cut him off with a chopping motion of his hand. "You said it was safe." He advanced, his finger shaking, pointing. "*You said it was safe.*"

It was remarkable how quickly Barrow recovered his composure. "I'm truly sorry for your loss, Mr. Gunnerson," he said. "I want to assure you we're doing everything—"

"Cut the bullshit," said Gunnerson. "You killed my son."

"I will not accept that accusation, sir."

"Oh yes you will. You know what I'm talking about." Gunnerson took a step toward Barrow, his fists clenching.

Barrow pressed his hand to the side of his suit jacket—and instantly, two security guards entered the room.

"Don't touch me," Gunnerson roared as the two security guards interposed themselves between him and Barrow. "I'll kill you, you bastard."

Barrow turned to the security guards. "See that Mr. Gunnerson is returned to his suite and remains there. I will not be threatened and insulted on my own property."

"You son of a bitch—" Gunnerson lunged forward, trying to get past the two guards, but they seized him.

"Let me go!" He struggled briefly and then stopped, breathing hard, sweat pouring off his red face.

"Mr. Gunnerson," said Cash quickly, realizing she had a rare opportunity to take advantage of the situation, "why do you say he killed your son?"

Gunnerson didn't answer.

"*Why?*" she repeated forcefully.

"Ask *him*!" he shouted.

"This way, sir," one of the guards said as they propelled him backward toward the door.

"You tell me!" Cash said to Gunnerson. "What is he hiding? Why did you say to him, *You know what I'm talking about*? What *did* you mean?"

"*Ask him!*" he repeated as he was wrangled out the door.

"Get him out of here!" cried Barrow.

The door slammed, and Gunnerson was gone.

Barrow turned to Colcord, his face furious with anger. "Sheriff, what did you mean by bringing that man in here to threaten me?"

Colcord returned the look with a cool one of his own. "I thought you might want to see him, give him your condolences. I'm sorry he threatened you—I had no idea."

"I'm going to file a complaint."

"That's certainly your right," said Colcord placidly.

Cash said again, "Mr. Barrow: Why does he think you killed his son?"

"He's grieving and irrational. What could I personally have to do with his son's disappearance? I wasn't even here!"

Colcord interjected, "When Gunnerson shouted, *You know what I'm talking about!* and *Ask him!* and *You said it was safe!* What did he mean by those statements? What was supposed to be safe?"

Barrow looked at Colcord, then at Cash. "Can't you see the man's crazy with grief? You had no business bringing that man in, threatening my life. You heard him. If he weren't the father of a victim, I'd throw him out of the resort."

"I can't help but think," said Cash, "that there's more behind his accusations than mere grief. If you know something we need to know, you've got to tell us now. If we find it out later and it turns out you've withheld information, you could be charged with obstruction."

"I don't know anything more, and I resent the implication. I'm sorry, but my cooperation with you is over. From now on, you'll talk to my lawyers, and if you want further questions answered, it will be by subpoena."

He rose, turned, and strode out of the room.

Cash stared at Colcord. She was amazed at his audacity. "That was some trick."

"You disapprove?"

"Well, no. We got some valuable information. But there's gonna be blowback."

"I wanted to shake him up. I'm convinced both of them—Maximilian and Barrow—are hiding something."

"I agree, but then why wouldn't Gunnerson tell us what he knows? Especially if he thinks Barrow's responsible for his son's death?"

Colcord shook his head. "It's almost like they each have something damaging on each other. They're playing chicken." He paused. "Let's get Maximilian in here and confront him about why he never told us about the Jackman Mine."

25

Cash went to fetch Maximilian and brought him in. Colcord remained seated and did not greet the security director, focusing his attention instead on a file of papers.

"What's this about?" Maximilian asked.

Colcord ignored the question and looked up from his papers only after a long moment had passed. His idea was to establish at the outset who was in control of the room. Maximilian was a carefully measured personality, and Colcord did not have much faith they'd be able to get anything from him—but you never knew.

"Have a seat," he said, then went back to studying his papers.

"Look," said Maximilian after a moment, "I've got a lot on my plate right now."

Colcord slid his cell phone into the center of the table and turned on the recorder. "State your name and title for the record."

After a hesitation, Maximilian sat down and did so.

"And you agree to have this voluntary interview recorded?"

"Yes."

Colcord read out the other preliminaries. Then he finally looked Maximilian in the face. "I was in Eagle today, at the historical society archives." He paused. "I was getting maps of the mines up here."

He let a beat pass.

"*All* the mines. And I made a discovery. There aren't two mines up here. There are three. There's the Jackman Mine."

"What about it?"

"When we asked you about the mines, you said there were two—the Fryingpan and the Hesperus. You never mentioned the Jackman. Why is that?"

At this, Maximilian visibly relaxed. "Sheriff Colcord, there really is only one giant mine up here—they all connect with each other. The three names are a historical oddity. We never used the name *Jackman* among ourselves, and to be honest, I haven't heard that name in years. We at Erebus got in the habit of speaking of the two mine areas we're using. What's more, we completely sealed up all the mine entrances except the ones we're using, which includes all the Jackman Mine entrances and ventilation shafts. And internally, we sealed up with steel all the tunnels that connect Jackman with Hesperus and Fryingpan. If you're implying we're trying to hide something, I can assure you there's no basis to that. It just didn't seem worth mentioning, and as I said, the Jackman portion of the complex is completely sealed up. Completely."

"The Jackman maps were recently stolen from the historical society."

"I can assure you we had nothing to do with that."

Colcord felt a rising frustration. The man was an impenetrable shield. Of course, he might be telling the truth.

"Have any search parties gone into the Jackman Mine?"

"No. There's no point. As I said, all the entrances to that mine have been sealed with steel plates that can't be opened. Solid steel. To get in, you'd have to cut your way in with a torch. At the outset of the investigation, we did, in fact, inspect all the openings and found the steel intact and undisturbed. The killers are not in there, I can assure you."

"Could there be openings you failed to find? Ventilation shafts?"

"No. We copied those maps that you say were stolen and tracked down every opening. We'd be happy to share those maps with you—I'll email them to your office. We have no secrets. We used those maps to identify every single opening, and we sealed them up completely. And as I mentioned earlier, those tunnels from the Jackman that connected with the other two mines were also plated with steel. There's no way in or out of Jackman."

"Please do send me those maps," Colcord said. He wasn't going to say he had other, better, maps. "So you're sure the killers are not in Jackman?"

"Positive. However, if you want to search Jackman, we've no objection. We'll be happy to cut open one of the entrances and initiate a search."

"Thank you. We might ask you to do that."

"Trust me, Sheriff, when I tell you we are as anxious to get these killers and close this case as anyone. There's no reason for us to hinder your investigation in any way."

Colcord nodded. He was half-convinced that Maximilian wasn't hiding anything, that he was telling the truth. The man was persuasive. He turned to Cash. "Do you have any questions, Agent Cash?"

"I do. Mr. Maximilian, you were with us when we toured the labs. What *didn't* we see in that tour?"

"Well, actually, there's quite a bit more to the labs. We have freezers where we keep remains and sections of frozen Pleistocene mammals, we have storerooms, we have preparation areas and a morgue where we dissect animals that die, experimental failures, that sort of thing. And there are also quarters for scientists and Erebus staff who might be working late or don't wish to stay in the lodge. We have guest quarters for visitors."

"Could we see those?"

"Of course. Anytime."

Cash looked at Colcord. "No more questions."

Colcord said to Maximilian, "That will be all—thank you."

The security director rose. "Always glad to help."

He left.

Colcord turned to Cash. "What do you think?"

Maximilian had shut the door on his way out, but outside in the hall, Colcord heard a sudden sound of running feet and muffled voices. He opened the door to see security personnel sprinting by the door, heading to the main security office.

"What's going on?" he asked Maximilian, who was speaking to a security guard.

"The drone camera has been turned back on. And it's transmitting something . . . totally bizarre."

26

Cash sprinted along the hallway, following Maximilian and Colcord to the C-suite elevator and down to the security complex, joining other personnel streaming to the main CCTV room.

As they entered, Cash could see everyone crowded around a flat-panel screen that was playing the feed from the drone console. She halted in surprise. The drone camera was transmitting a view of some sort of ceremony. In a cathedral-like forest of old fir trees, a sort of altar had been set up, made of sticks, bark, and green moss. A tall, lean man stood at the altar, hands raised, palms upturned, like a priest. The figure was wearing a bizarre outfit, a sort of body covering made of bark, leaves, twigs, and grass all woven and pressed together, creating a remarkably effective camo outfit that almost made him invisible in the forest. On his face was a mask made out of birch bark. It had two holes for eyes and a hole for a mouth, rimmed with red paint, with a grille of twigs like teeth. On his head was a pointed cap made of woven grass, from which a mane of long blond hair cascaded down, woven into a loose, thick braid.

He was standing with his back to a group of people, dressed in similar camouflage outfits—a congregation of sorts—also wearing masks and caps. Cash was shocked to see a few women and even some children in the group. Absurdly, they were all wearing puffy white athletic shoes—Nikes.

Set up in a semicircle around the congregation were six poles stuck into the ground, each with a hook on the end from which dangled a round, fuzzy ornament.

"Is it transmitting a GPS location?" Cash asked.

"Yes. In transmission mode, it sends its GPS location. We're scrambling a chopper to go to the location."

"Where is it?"

"Twelve miles north, near the Barbicans."

"You see the kids?" said Colcord.

"I do." This was even crazier than she imagined—it was a Jim Jones–like cult, parents and children. She did a quick count: there were nine of them in total.

The congregation, if that's what you could call it, began to chant, which was more like a loud humming than anything with words. They had their eyes closed and were swaying as they gradually raised their arms, following the lead of the man at the altar.

The leader suddenly called out a singsongy mantra of the kind you might hear at a Little League game, flapping his hands and crooning in a strange, breathy way.

"They . . . will . . . die," he intoned.

"*Oh yes they will,*" the congregation responded, hands rising and fluttering toward the sky.

"How long until the chopper gets there?" she asked Maximilian.

"Bird's in the air," said Maximilian, holding a headset to one ear. "Only four minutes. I think we've got them."

It was pure madness. The entire spectacle boggled the mind.

"We . . . will . . . fly . . . ," the leader droned.

"*Oh yes we will,*" responded the congregation, hands aflutter.

"The bird's reached the site," said Maximilian. "It's hovering, but it can't see down through the trees. It's now looking for a place to hover so the team can fast-rope down."

"They . . . will . . . cry," the priest intoned.

"*Oh yes they will.*"

"We . . . will . . . purify . . ."

"*Oh yes we will.*"

The chanting abruptly ceased at a gesture made by the priest, or whatever. Then the man turned to face the drone camera directly. Silence fell. He pointed at the camera.

"We hope," he said in that same breathy voice, "that you enjoyed the show." And he began to sing:

> A great while ago the world begun,
> With hey, ho, the wind and the rain.
> But that's all one, our play is done,
> And we'll strive to please you every day.

He let out a laugh, walked up to the drone, and picked it up from its resting place, holding it close to his own face. "We'll strive to please you every day," he repeated and then gave the drone a toss. The camera recorded it spinning around until it landed on the forest floor, coming to rest. The camera continued displaying a view from ground level of pine needles and a tree trunk. Distant laughter and singing could be heard, fading away into the forest.

"They're fast-roping down," a security officer said. "They're going for it. They're only fifty yards away. They're hitting the ground now. Those crazies aren't going to get away."

"We've got them for sure," said Maximilian, his voice tight. There was a silence in the room. They were all waiting for the guards to appear on the screen. But nothing happened, just the view of pine needles.

"Son of a *bitch*!" Maximilian cried, slamming the earphones on the table. "They're telling me nobody's there—they're gone. *Long* gone . . . There's just the drone sitting on the ground . . . " He cursed again. "It was transmitting a prerecorded file."

27

The ATV followed a faint track through the forest before emerging into a sunny meadow dotted with yellow flowers. No one was allowed to go into the backcountry now, but even though they were less than half a mile from the lodge, it felt like they were in the wilderness. On the far side of the field, Doyle could see the local family of mammoths browsing some bushes at the edge of the trees—a bull, two cows, and two calves. He was glad to get away from Brock Ballou and his exhausting demands and relieved to take a day off from the grueling film schedule and the constant importunities of his crew. This shoot, to get some establishing shots and B-roll of the mammoths in their habitat, was like a mini-vacation.

The ATV halted, and the two others being driven behind them, carrying his three-person camera crew and two other guides, pulled up alongside. They got out with their equipment and began gearing up—two handhelds and one Steadicam on a harness. Depending on what they got, the footage would be integrated into the movie as needed. But in looking across the meadow, Doyle felt a faint shiver: those animals were big. Gigantic hairy mountains.

"So," said Doyle to the chief guide, "how do we get close without spooking them?"

"They won't run away," said the guide. "They're used to seeing people. In fact, the opposite might be a problem—they'll come over and want to take a look at us or even interfere with us. The little one is Tom Thumb, by the way, one of the favorites around here."

"What do you mean by . . . interfere?" Doyle asked, alarmed.

The guide laughed. "They associate us with feeding, and sometimes they'll try to search our pockets for treats."

"If they come over," said Doyle, "so much the better. As far as I'm concerned, they can't get too close—as long as they don't step on us."

"Not a chance. They're quite dainty about where they put their feet."

"Let's go, then," said Doyle, turning to his crew. "Let's get some footage."

Carrying their gear, Doyle, the DP, and two camera operators set off walking across the meadow. The mammoths were immediately aware of their presence and turned to look at them, several with their trunks in the air, chasing their scent.

"Let's get a few shots at a distance," Doyle said to the DP, "then some medium shots, then get as close as possible."

The DP issued some instructions to the two camera operators, and they began shooting, spreading out to get the advantage of several angles and backdrops. The mammoths looked alert and curious, having halted to watch them.

"It'd be nice if they were moving," said Doyle to the guide. "How do we get them to move?"

"If we stay here for a while, they might start browsing again."

They waited. Sure enough, after a few minutes, the bull turned his attention away from them and began uprooting a bush with his tusks, then tearing it apart and stuffing the branches into his mouth, munching away. The others followed behind him, plucking and ripping at twigs and bushes.

"Let's get closer," Doyle said.

They advanced to the middle of the field, where they paused again for the camera operators to shoot B-roll. When that was done, they continued forward, moving closer to the mammoth family. As they approached, the mammoths again stopped eating and stared at them. Tom Thumb went to hide behind his mother. The bull raised his trunk and suddenly gave a tremendous blast, a trumpeting sound that caused Doyle to jump. When it ended, the echoes of it came back from the mountains, rolling around the valley like dying thunder.

"What did that mean?" he asked the guide. "Is he angry?"

"No, that was a greeting call. I believe they might be thinking of coming over and investigating us."

And sure enough, the bull took a step toward them, raising its trunk and giving another blast.

This was going to be killer footage, Doyle thought.

Now the bull was ambling toward them, cows and calves trailing.

"Okay, they're coming to investigate," the guide said.

"What do we do?" Doyle asked. They loomed up like big hairy mountains—they could be trampled so easily.

"Just stay cool; stand in one spot and don't move around. No sudden movements or noises. They might explore you a little with their trunks. Put away anything loose in your pockets—they're curious, and they sometimes take things."

As they closed in, Doyle felt a thrill of excitement. "Just shoot and keep shooting," he murmured to the DP. "And, everyone: total silence."

He knew he didn't even have to tell her any of this, but he didn't want the guides talking while they were shooting.

Now as the mammoths loomed above him, he felt his heart beating fast from both the thrill of it and apprehension at how small and vulnerable he felt. He could now smell them—a not unpleasant, dusty, horsey scent. They moseyed closer, trunks swaying back and forth, the tips up and pointing at them.

Doyle held himself still as the bull came up to him, tusks polished and gleaming in the sunlight passing close to his face. The animal's two warm brown eyes stared down at him, blinking. Then the bull reached out with his trunk—slowly, tentatively—and touched Doyle's head, mussing his hair. The tip was surprisingly soft, and he felt the animal's warm breath wash over him as the bull gently pulled and plucked at tufts of his curly hair. The trunk then snaked down and poked itself into Doyle's shirt pocket, but not finding anything went down to his pants pocket and tugged on that, then ran his trunk up his back. A surge of emotion washed over Doyle, triggered by the extreme gentleness of a creature so staggering in bulk and powerful in mass. He found this close contact with the magnificent creature incredibly stirring.

Meanwhile, Doyle could see that Tom Thumb had come out from behind his mother and was tentatively sniffing at one of the camera operators with his little trunk. The bull eventually got bored with Doyle and turned to reach out with his trunk toward the DP and her handheld camera. She continued taping even as his trunk explored the camera, touching the lens and sniffing around, fogging up the glass with an exhale of breath, and then feeling around to every little knob and lever.

Everyone was silent. The only sounds were the creaking of the mammoths' bodies, the rustling of their stiff hair, the sounds of their breathing, and the occasional rumbling of their stomachs. And then there was an abrupt razzing blast of air—one of them farted.

The bull seemed very curious about the camera. He wrapped his trunk around it and gave it a gentle tug. Doyle didn't want to speak, but he hoped the DP would let him have it—and she did, releasing it as he grasped and raised it. He held it up to his eye to examine more closely, staring into the lens while tilting his massive head this way and that, ears flapping. The camera was still running, and Doyle could see it was capturing the shot of the century. After peering at it for a while from different angles, the bull—instead of dropping it as Doyle expected—held the camera back out to the DP, who silently took it back, still running.

After a few more minutes of snuffling and exploring, poking and prying, the herd moved on past them and lumbered back toward the verge of the forest, their curiosity satisfied—if a little disappointed, perhaps, that no one had food or treats.

He looked at the DP. Her face was glowing with suppressed excitement. She knew as well as he the priceless footage she had just captured. This was going into the movie—they'd rework the script if necessary. It was as real as it gets—no CGI, no VFX—just actual footage of a real woolly mammoth. They wouldn't even need to Foley it—the sounds the herd made were already so fabulous. David Attenborough himself would cream his shorts to get that footage.

Doyle finally breathed. "That . . . was totally fucking *awesome*."

28

Romanski stood at the crime scene perimeter tape and watched two CSI colleagues moving slowly through the area where the drone had been left lying on the ground, which was also where the ceremony had taken place earlier and been prerecorded. They were on their hands and knees, crawling across the forest floor with head-mounted macro-binocs, looking for the slightest specks of evidence—hair, fibers, drops of sweat or blood—and sticking little numbered flags into the ground where they found something and tweezered it in a test tube. The altar stood in the center, and around it, the ground was trampled and scuffed. The ritual—if that's what it had been—appeared to have taken place several hours earlier. It had been recorded on the drone video in non-GPS transmission mode. Then, later, the video had been turned on with GPS and issued the prerecorded broadcast.

Whoever figured out how to do that was either clever—or possibly even a drone operator himself.

The light from the setting sun had just vanished from the treetops, and gloom was collecting in the forest. There was a lot more work to be done—they'd be laboring well into the night with a generator and lights.

The weirdest thing they found were the ornaments hanging around the altar. They were about three inches in diameter, woven out of grass and pine needles and tiny twigs. The six objects now sat neatly arranged in an evidence container, nestled in acid-free paper, and they looked to Romanski like Christmas ornaments being put away for the season.

He stared at them. They were amazingly well crafted, the needles and grasses tightly woven, forming a three-dimensional, filigree-like sphere.

Cash came over. "What do you think?"

"It's fucking nuts," Romanski said. "And them quoting Shakespeare? These are crazy people, for sure." Romanski was proud of himself for identifying the little song at the end as being the last lines of *Twelfth Night*.

"And the Nikes? It's so random," Cash said. "But the guy who quoted Shakespeare—his diction was good. He might have been an actor before. That and the long yellow hair might help us identify him. And another thing—was it my imagination, or did they not seem to be native English speakers?"

"I think they were disguising their voices," said Romanski.

"Could be. What's the plot of *Twelfth Night*?" Cash asked. "Could there be a message in there?"

Romanski shook his head. "It's a play about a shipwreck and a girl disguising herself as a boy and a whole bunch of comic misadventures— it's quite a silly play, actually."

Cash gestured toward the evidence box. "What about these ornaments? You think something might be inside?"

"I do. When you heft them, they feel heavier than you might expect if they were grass and twigs all the way through."

"Why don't you open one up?"

"Here?" Romanski asked. "I'd rather do that in the lab."

"You got five others to dissect in the lab. I don't want to wait a day for results. Use your tweezers and pull one of them apart now."

"You're the boss." Romanski reached into the evidence box with a gloved hand and removed one. He held it up to the light and tried to look through it, but it got denser toward the middle and he couldn't see. "Okay. Here we go."

He placed it on an empty plastic container top to use as a sort of operating theater, and then, fishing out a pair of rubber-tipped tweezers and a small scalpel, he began to tease it apart, while Cash hunched over behind him, taking photographs.

The first layer was mostly grass, but then he reached an inner layer of thin willow leaves, wrapped in a tight ball around something. Using the tweezers, he grasped the tip of a leaf and peeled it back, and another leaf, and another—to expose an object: a tiny metal shoe.

"What the hell?" Cash asked.

He turned it in the light. Romanski recognized it immediately. "It's a Monopoly game piece. One of the classic ones."

"Holy crap," breathed Cash, staring at it.

Romanski held up the old beaten-up shoe with the tweezers. "There were six Monopoly tokens, right? Let's see—the shoe, thimble, top hat, iron . . ."

"Cannon and battleship," said Cash.

Romanski nodded.

"You think the other tokens are in the five other balls?"

"Seems logical."

"This is just too crazy," said Cash. "Quoting Shakespeare, wrapping up Monopoly pieces—could it be some kind of comment on American culture?"

"Or maybe an anti-capitalism rant," said Romanski. "Not to mention that chant about *We will purify*. And did you see the women and children? This is like the Branch Davidians or that weird UFO cult, Heaven's Gate."

"God, I hope not," Cash said.

Maximilian came over. He looked like he was falling apart, his face mottled, his hair damp and mussed up. "What'd you find in there?" he asked.

"Mr. Maximilian, do you play Monopoly?" Cash asked.

He looked puzzled. "I did when I was a kid. Not recently."

"Does Erebus, the company, or anyone here have a connection to Monopoly in any way?"

"Not that I'm aware of. Why do you ask?"

"We found a Monopoly game token inside the ball. The metal shoe." She nodded to the box. "Take a look."

Maximilian's eyes narrowed. He finally breathed out, "Bloody hell. Monopoly?"

"Yes. Does it mean anything to you at all?"

He shook his head.

"Are there any Monopoly sets up here, that you know of?"

"We have a game room in the lodge—maybe there's one there."

"We'll check that out. But let's keep this under wraps," said Cash. "This is the kind of thing that'll bring all the weirdos out of the wood-work with conspiracy theories."

"Right," said Maximilian. "Agreed."

Romanski put the dissected ornament back in the evidence con-tainer, sealed and labeled it.

"On another note," Cash said, "Sheriff Colcord's back at the lodge waiting for the dogs to arrive. They're flying them back in tonight. We'd like to keep them here for now so they can track right away if the need arises. Do you have a kennel for them?"

"We've got state-of-the-art animal facilities," said Maximilian. "I'll arrange it."

Romanski began packing the evidence boxes in a suitcase. "I need to get this stuff back to the lab." He called out to the CSI guys. "What's your status?"

"Got a ways to go."

"Okay." He turned to Cash. "Can you get a second chopper to pick you all up? I want to take this evidence directly back to Arvada."

"That can be arranged," said Maximilian.

As Romanski knelt and continued to seal and secure the evidence cases for the ride back to Arvada, he heard Cash say to Maximilian, "Don't you think it's time to shut this place down? You saw the video: we've got a homicidal cult out there with at least nine members."

29

Cash passed through the main lodge hall in time to see the evening crowd at the windows, watching the mammoths gather at the lake. There were many fewer guests, but, Cash thought, even one civilian was too many. Romanski was on his way back to Arvada with the ornaments and other evidence. She desperately hoped something would come out of his work, because if they didn't get a break in this crazy case soon—she didn't even want to think about that.

"I would like to see Mr. Barrow—now," she said to Maximilian.

"Let me see if he's free."

But Cash was not going to wait. She walked fast to the C-suite door and used her card to enter, with Maximilian hurrying to keep up with her.

"It'd be better if I spoke to him first," he said.

Cash ignored him, walking faster. She turned the corner. The door to Barrow's office was closed. She went up to it and, instead of knocking, turned the knob and walked in.

Maximilian came right in after her. Barrow's secretary leaped up from his desk. "What's going on?"

"Agent in Charge Cash would like to speak to Mr. Barrow," said Cash.

"He's busy—"

Cash strode past him and opened the door to the inner office. She saw Barrow rising from his desk. "What's this?" He turned. "Maximilian?"

"I was trying to tell Agent Cash she needed an appointment—" said Maximilian, but Cash interrupted.

"Mr. Barrow, you saw the drone video?"

"I did," he said coldly.

"Then you know that there are at least nine deranged individuals in this valley."

"Mr. Barrow, my apologies, she just barged in—" began Maximilian, but Barrow held up his hand and said to Cash, "I'm listening. Keep going."

Cash took a deep breath and struggled to moderate her tone. "Mr. Barrow, the time has come to close down the resort until we find the killers. We can't have vulnerable civilians up here any longer."

Barrow responded calmly, "We have animals up here that need constant care and monitoring. We have essential personnel, maintenance and power plant workers, sewage and water treatment facilities that need operating, animal caretakers and wardens. We can't just shut down."

"I get that, but you need to close the valley to all guests and nonessential workers."

"Do you have any idea what kind of damage that would cause to my brand?"

Cash felt herself losing her temper. "Mr. Barrow, your brand is already damaged." Barrow flushed, and Cash realized he was unused to being spoken to this way. She went on. "The risk is just too great. There is a deranged cult roaming this valley. They're capable of anything. You saw the video."

Barrow said nothing, gazing at her a long time. Then he sighed. "I understand where you're coming from, Agent Cash. But you have to understand: if we shut the place down, that in itself is going to be a huge story. Big, *big* news. It'll just blow everything all out of proportion. And . . . I'm not sure they're as unhinged as you say."

She stared at him, astounded at this comment. "What do you mean?"

"I think it's more performance than anything else at this point."

She shook her head. "They *decapitated* two people. You call that performance?"

"These are obviously some sort of radical cultists, back-to-nature extremists. They sent us a message. Well, message received."

Cash stared at Barrow. "Do you know something about these people that I don't?"

"I wish to hell I did. I have no idea who they are or what they want. All I'm saying is, I don't believe we're going to see more killings."

"You heard the chant. They *specifically* threatened more killings."

"Agent Cash, we're not going to shut down. We've pulled everyone in from the backcountry. Our guests are restricted to the lodge, which is like a fortress, and they only go out during the day in vehicles with an armed guard."

"What about the movie crew? The lab workers?"

"The lab is heavily fortified, and the doors are now locked twenty-four-seven—and it also has armed guards. The film crew is in the movie town way down the valley, far from where these maniacs have been operating, and they come back to the lodge at night. They also have their own guards."

Cash looked at him, then shook her head. "I'm taking this to the governor."

Barrow gazed back at her, untroubled. "Perhaps you should check with your boss first?"

"Are you referring to Wallace McFaul?"

"Yes, McFaul. Because I understand he's arriving tomorrow morning. I wouldn't be surprised if he isn't coming here to, ah, take over the investigation."

30

"Midnight shakes the memory like a madman shakes a dead geranium," intoned Romanski, his eye moving from the clock to once again lock on the six Monopoly pieces standing in a line on the stereozoom stage. It was late at night, he'd been working eighteen hours straight, and he was getting a little punchy. They had, earlier that evening, gotten back some long-awaited DNA results, but they were inconclusive, and some of the batches appeared to have been contaminated.

"I hope you're not losing it," said Reno with a laugh.

"I've already lost it," said Romanski. "Have you ever seen anything quite this messed up? It's like an Agatha Christie mystery: *Six Monopoly Tokens.*"

"You should write a novel," said Reno.

Romanski and Reno had delved deeply into the history of Monopoly tokens—it was amazing how much information was already out there on the Web—and they had determined these particular pieces had been manufactured from a pot metal alloy of lead and tin by the Dowst Manufacturing Company sometime in the late 1930s. They were not the original tokens but from a second-generation Monopoly set. Millions had been made—it was the most popular game in America for decades.

"I always picked the shoe," said Romanski.

"The ratty old shoe?" said Reno. "No way. I used to fight with my brother over who got the top hat. That was boss." He slipped on a fresh pair of nitrile gloves and used rubber-tipped tweezers to put the tokens back in the evidence bag. "You think this is some sort of anti-capitalist statement?"

"Seems likely," said Romanski. "Anti-capitalist back-to-the-land anarcho-primitivists, sending a message about our corrupt society. I was doing some googling on radical environmental organizations. You know what the symbol of Earth First! is?"

"No."

"A monkey wrench crossed with a Stone Age hammer."

Reno gave a snort. "You think these are Earth Firsters?"

"Something like it, I'd bet, only more radical."

Romanski turned his attention to other evidence they'd recovered from the dancing ground—dead leaves that had drops on them of some pungent liquid. "Before we wrap, let's do a quick analysis on these."

"Jesus, Bart, it's after midnight."

"It'll take fifteen minutes to analyze. Dissolve the substance in distilled water and check it out under a microscope, plug it into the electrophoresis machine, and let it run all night. See what we got in the morning."

"All right, but you're gonna owe me."

Romanski took one of the leaves—a dried aspen leaf—and placed it under a stereozoom. He examined the droplets, which were recent, and then, taking a medicine dropper, placed a drop of distilled water on one spot, stirred it slightly with a tiny swab, and then transferred it to a well slide. He brought that over to the microscope and took a look at it through the eyepiece.

"What you got?"

"A lot of *E. coli*, digested plant fiber, cellulose, grit."

"In other words, you got shit," said Reno.

"Exactly." He increased the magnification. There was a whole lot of wood cellulose, well digested and broken down. "I'd say what we have here is herbivore shit, from an animal that eats wood."

"Mammoth shit?"

"Bingo." Romanski continued peering. "But it's mixed with other compounds. There's protein in here too, which I can see from the agglutination taking place. And it is highly acidic." He took out the well slide and brought it close to his nose and sniffed. "Bile."

"Bile? You mean, mammoth bile?"

"Bile from some animal, not necessarily a mammoth. It has a very distinctive smell. And color. Biliverdin is a greenish color. Bile is found in shit, but this is *fresh* bile, taken directly from the liver of a dead animal. We'll confirm this with electrophoresis, but that's my working hypothesis."

"How do you know what bile smells like?"

Romanski grinned. "One of the things you learn when you go into forensics is that your nose is a chemical analyzer of excellent sensitivity. You learn to pay close attention to smell. Almost everything at a crime scene has a distinct smell—whether it's blood or propellant, mouthwash, cigarette smoke, aftershave, fear. You just take a moment to stand there, empty your mind, and sample the air with your proboscis. Try it sometime."

Romanski found Reno looking at him in disbelief.

"I'm serious," said Romanski. "Those crazy dancers anointed themselves with a smelly concoction of mammoth shit and bile and possibly other exotic compounds—as we'll discover from electrophoresis."

"They put it on like perfume?"

"Exactly."

"Bart, you're not trolling me, are you?"

"No. And I can make an educated guess as to *why* they're wearing this particular kind of perfume."

"Why?"

"To cover up their own human scent. To throw off the bloodhounds with bile-and-shit cologne."

Romanski watched with amusement as understanding finally blossomed on Reno's face. He let out a long, low whistle. "That's amazing."

"Stick with me, Reno, and someday you might be running this lab."

31

Cash awoke in the dark. For a moment, she felt panic, unable to remember where she was, until everything came flooding back and she knew she was in the lodge and had gone to bed at eight o'clock, exhausted.

She reached for her phone and checked. Four a.m. *Son of a bitch*, she thought. *This is what happens when you go to bed too early.* She checked for messages from McFaul, found nothing, and then lay in bed in the dark for a few minutes before realizing it was hopeless to sleep longer.

She got up, took a shower, pulled on her bathrobe, and made coffee on the fancy espresso machine. She took her coffee to the window, which looked northward over the valley. She turned off the room light to see better into the ocean of blackness. In the dark room, the shape of the landscape became visible. The peaks rose up like black teeth, and above them, the Milky Way spread across the sky like a glowing river. She thought back to her conversation with Barrow, who claimed that McFaul would be arriving. The fact that Barrow knew before she did was a serious violation of investigative protocol. While Barrow wasn't a direct suspect, she felt he might be withholding information from the investigation. It was improper for McFaul to be in touch with him at all, let alone confide in him details about the investigation and broadcast his own movements. If McFaul really did show up, what was she going to do about that? He surely wasn't going to take away her investigation— was he? More likely, he would show up for public relations purposes, to emphasize that the CBI was doing everything possible to solve the case.

She took another sip of coffee, gazing into the darkness. The night searchers were out there even now, over a hundred strong, trying to search a hundred and forty-four square miles. The drone team had also been busy, but so far they hadn't found any more traces of the crazies.

She wondered if it was worth taking Maximilian up on his offer to open the old Jackman Mine for a search. They claimed to have sealed up every opening into the mine, but you never knew. There might have been a cave-in somewhere, which created an access to the tunnels, or a missed air shaft that the killers were using to come and go.

She made a second cup of coffee and realized she was famished. Aside from the chocolates gobbled up from her pillow, she couldn't even remember when she'd last eaten. There was a snack bar in the room with seven-dollar candy bars and nine-dollar cans of Pringles. That would not look good on her expense report, but what the hell— she had to eat something.

She pulled out a can of Pringles and a twelve-dollar packet of smoked almonds and practically inhaled them. Then she scarfed down a Snickers bar, chasing it with another espresso. That was followed by a can of Diet Coke and a packet of Reese's Peanut Butter Cups. This was getting gross, but the more she ate, the more famished she got.

As she was munching, she saw a glimmer of light out the window. She stuffed the last Reese's candy into her mouth and peered into the darkness. Half a mile away, on a slope, lights were moving in the forest. A group of searchers, it seemed. But as she watched, more lights were coming up the slope to join them, including some powerful ones that cast long beams sweeping through the trees. They began to cluster around something in the woods, all in a circle.

They'd found something up there, no more than a thousand yards from the lodge. She turned to pick up her phone, but it rang before she could reach it, *The Good, the Bad and the Ugly* theme sounding in the dark room.

It was Maximilian.

"What's going on?"

"They killed Tom Thumb."

It took a moment for Cash to process this. "The baby mammoth?"

"Yes. Butchered him. I'm up here on-site. It's not far from the lodge.

Go to the guard station on the basement level. I'll have a jeep waiting for you to bring you up here."

"Killed how?"

"I can't say yet. There's blood everywhere. It's a mess."

As she went through the lobby toward the elevator, she saw Colcord crossing ahead of her, zipping up his sheriff's jacket. They got into the elevator together.

"You know what the hell's going on?" he asked.

"A dead mammoth."

At the bottom, they went to the guard station, where they were hustled into a jeep. It was a short drive up the road to an area where a dozen vehicles were parked.

"Follow me," the guard said, pulling out a big Maglite and pointing it into the trees. "Watch your step."

They hiked up a slope in a forest of old-growth fir trees. She could hear Colcord becoming winded, but the guard didn't slow down, and she was able to keep up, thanking herself silently for sticking with her workout plan. Even if she wasn't losing weight—it annoyed her that no matter how much she exercised she couldn't shed those damn pounds—at least she was in good physical condition.

Soon they could hear the hiss of radios and see lights through the trees. As they arrived, klieg lights were being set up, powered by a generator. Maximilian was there, directing the placement of lights. The woods were thick, giant firs rising over a hundred feet, the ground crisscrossed with fallen timber. Draped over a fallen tree was a dark mound. As the lights were turned on, one after another, the mound was revealed to be a monstrous heap of bloody gore, organs, and ragged hunks of meat, steam rising. The head of the little mammoth lay off to one side, its trunk curled up, eyes open and cloudy, tiny tusks just peeping out next to its open mouth.

But what surprised and angered Cash more than anything were the hordes of workers around the body of the animal, setting up lights and running power cords to a generator.

"This is a crime scene!" she said loudly. "What's going on here?"

Maximilian came hustling up. "We're setting up lights—"

"I can see that, but haven't you handled a crime scene before?" She turned to the group of workers, milling around, looking confused. "You're messing everything up! Aw, Jesus, will you look at that guy's boots, covered with blood? You're compromising the scene, for chrissake!"

"But how are we going to see—?" Maximilian began, but Cash cut him off.

"Preserving evidence is number one." She raised her voice. "Hey! Everyone! Stop! Just *stop* what you're doing and stay where you are. Don't move. We're gonna set up a perimeter. Then we'll move you out in an orderly fashion."

She turned to Colcord. Before she could even ask, he held up a roll of yellow crime scene tape.

"God bless you." She took it, selected a small tree some distance from the dead mammoth, and wound the tape around it, tying it off and using it as an anchor, then she began unrolling it while she circled, creating a perimeter with a radius of about fifty feet. She and Colcord then escorted everyone out of the sealed-off area.

"No one go in there," she said. "Stay out."

"What now?" Maximilian asked, sweating and red-faced. "Shouldn't we be doing something?"

"We *are* doing something. We're waiting for the sun to rise and the CSI team to get here."

32

Romanski arrived at nine a.m. with the rest of his team, lugging packs filled with forensic gear. He was exhausted, having gone to bed at four a.m., only to be woken at six. Making it worse, there was no helicopter available, which had meant yet another two-hour drive from Arvada. It had been a crazy scene, approaching the resort. A stream of cars with guests was leaving, while another stream of vehicles filled with press was trying to get in. The lodge itself was a scene of confusion and panic, with people packing up and making demands on the staff, who were running around like chickens with their heads cut off. Security swarmed everywhere. The killing of the park's favorite animal could not be kept under wraps.

When Romanski and his team arrived at the scene of the killing, Cash was there. She waved him over.

"Look at this," Romanski said, eyeing the dead mammoth while sliding the pack off his shoulders. He added, "Whose bloody footprints are those?"

She jerked her chin at the workers. "They were wading around in the gore, setting up lights."

Romanski groaned.

"I apologize," said Maximilian. "We wanted to illuminate the scene."

"Right. Okay," Romanski said. "We'll do our best." He pulled out a Tyvek suit from the pack and began putting it on, as did the rest of his team. He pulled the hood up and slid on nitrile gloves and booties, then ducked under the tape. He was joined by the photographer, the latent specialist, a hair-and-fiber guy, and Reno, sampling chemistry and swabbing for DNA.

Because the animal had been butchered and gutted, it was going to be hard to determine the cause of death. On top of that, even though it was a baby, there was still at least a ton of meat, flesh, organs, and bones to deal with. They couldn't transport it back to the lab, so they were going to have to do their best with it right there.

Jesus, what a mess, Romanski thought.

He began by making a slow walk around the dead animal, looking for evidence, spent shells, tracks, shining his light around the shady forest floor. The ground was hopelessly compromised with regard to tracks, and he could see no shell casings indicating the mammoth had been shot. But as he poked around, he caught a faint scent of charring. He followed the scent, moving upwind, and that led him to a dead torch lying on the ground, its end circled with the burnt remains of woven grass and shredded birch bark. He bent over and looked at it closely—fresh. He signaled to the team to take it as evidence.

He continued his circuit, shining a bright light under the fallen tree trunks and roots and forest litter, but he found little else of interest. He stopped to watch the crew pick through the mammoth gore, the photographer taking photos while the two others examined everything with tweezers and evidence tubes out. He removed his mask and ducked under the perimeter to speak to Cash, who was talking to Maximilian. What they really needed was a forensic vet.

"Got anything?" Cash asked him.

"There's a used torch over yonder, lying on the ground. Probably used by the killers to drive the animal or scare it."

Cash nodded.

"And the animal was wearing a video collar," said Romanski. "It's over there, next to the head. It's been cut off."

"There's supposed to be a camera attached," said Maximilian. "It looks like they took it."

Romanski said, "We're gonna need a forensic veterinarian in here to help us determine cause of death. We don't have one on staff, but there's a good one we've worked with in Denver."

"Right," said Cash. "Get him up here ASAP."

"Her. Already made the call."

Cash turned to Maximilian. "How was the animal found?"

"The animal monitoring team was watching the herd's video feed, as is usual. They work twenty-four-seven. There was some sort of disturbance and attack, with burning torches, and then the video feed from Tom Thumb stopped. His GPS unit also stopped registering movement at the same time. So they sent a team out here to check—and found this."

"What time was that?"

"Two fifty-nine a.m. was when the herd seems to have been attacked."

"Did you get any of the attackers on tape?"

Maximilian hesitated. "We got a fair amount of the attack, but not of the attackers. I'll run the loop for you back at the lodge."

"You can't see the attackers?" Colcord asked.

"They stayed out of the viewing area of the cameras. The cameras on the animals point forward, and the attackers stayed behind, out of view."

"So they're knowledgeable about how the cameras work."

"It would seem so."

"What happened to the other mammoths in the herd?" Colcord asked.

"They ran away."

"Leaving their baby?" Cash asked.

"You have to understand," said Maximilian, "these creatures have been genetically modified. In removing the genes for aggression, they pretty much run at the slightest sign of danger."

"Programmed to be fraidycats?"

"You could say that. You can't genetically separate courage and aggression—take out one, and you lose the other."

She nodded. Her awe of the mammoths felt diminished somehow—instead of the noble creatures they appeared to be, they were big furry cowards.

Reno came up, pulling off a pair of nitrile gloves and lowering his mask. "I think we've got evidence of . . . consumption."

"You mean, *eating*?" said Romanski. "They ate something?"

"Yes. The liver seems to present some cut marks. Knife cuts. The gall bladder was also cut away and taken."

"Oh yeah?" said Romanski. He turned to Cash. "That's to make more of the perfume they use to evade the tracking of dogs. Last night, we analyzed some drops of fluid found at the scene of the dancing. It's a concoction made of bile, mammoth shit, and some plants."

"Good work, Bart," said Cash. "Get the liver into a freezer ASAP. And swab those cuts for DNA."

Romanski shook his head. "Mammoth liver. Jesus."

Colcord said, "A beloved animal, killed and mutilated within a thousand yards of the lodge. That's a message for sure."

"I would say so," said Cash. "A pointed message." She turned to Romanski. "There's nothing more I can do here until the vet arrives. You've got it under control. Right, Bart?"

"Yes, boss."

"So let's go back and look at the video," said Cash. "You coming?" she asked Colcord.

"Of course."

33

As Cash and Colcord entered the lodge, she saw her boss, McFaul, surrounded by a gaggle of security personnel. He had apparently just arrived by helicopter. She felt a freezing sensation in the pit of her stomach.

"Ah, Agent Cash, there you are!" McFaul said, seeing her come in. He came striding over. "A quick word?"

Cash didn't say anything. He drew her away from Colcord and the others to a quiet corner. Arms crossed, she waited for him to speak.

"I came up here, not to interfere," he said hastily, "but to provide assistance. I know this might be a bit of a surprise—"

"It is."

"You aren't fully aware of what's going on in the outside world. This is huge. I mean, it's not just front-page news in Colorado—it's national. We have to show *everyone*—the governor, the citizens of Colorado, the politicians—that we're on top of this. That we're pulling out all the stops."

Cash waited.

"So I'm here to support you."

Cash nodded but didn't say anything. Not speaking was making McFaul nervous. She wasn't going to make it easier for him.

"The fact is," he went on, "the investigation is three days old, and frankly, it seems the killers are running circles around everyone, with their crazy rituals and now this—the killing of an animal. We need to show progress, and I mean *now*. I'm sure you understand."

He stopped. She waited and then said, "Is that all, sir?"

"Yes."

"Can I ask a question?"

"Certainly."

"How did Barrow come to know yesterday evening that you were coming up here today?"

He stared at her and flushed. "Well, of course, we had to inform him. Nothing unusual about that."

"Right." She told herself she'd made her point and not to pursue it further. "Sir, may I make a recommendation?"

"Of course."

"I think we should ask the governor to call in the National Guard. To aid in the searching, at the least, if not to relieve Erebus security of some responsibilities. I'm uncomfortable that almost all the searchers and security in here are Erebus personnel. There's always a possibility that someone at Erebus might be involved."

McFaul looked at her steadily. "Agent Cash, I respect your idea, but such a step might terrify the public. Also it's an overreaction. Think what the media would do with that. It would garner huge headlines—NATIONAL GUARD CALLED IN. It would make us look like we're panicking. Erebus security is top-notch, and you yourself tell me they're being cooperative. Correct?"

"Yes, sir, but—"

McFaul held up a hand. "Do you have any reason to suspect Erebus is involved?"

"A couple of things. The killers seem awfully familiar with Erebus's security and routines. And Maximilian omitted telling us about a third mine up here, which we're going to search later today, if possible."

"I spoke to Maximilian about that—in fact, he brought it up. It was an oversight. And he gave you maps of the mine right away, and he volunteered to open it up for you. Right?"

"Yes, sir." Once again, McFaul was communicating what might be privileged information to a potential suspect.

"Surely you can see that calling in the National Guard would create problems," McFaul said.

Cash said nothing.

"What's your plan now?" he asked.

"For right now, I'm going down to security and take a look at the video of the mammoth attack."

"I'll go with you."

"Very good, sir." She had to suck it up and not do or say anything stupid. It was her first case as AIC, and it wasn't going well. If she valued her career at the CBI, she needed to be careful.

She and McFaul headed down to the main security station, through the central monitoring room, to a door in the back, which led to a private screening room with plush leather seats, like a fancy home theater.

Maximilian met them at the door. "Our scientists often use this room to observe the animals," he said. "Behavioral research, wellness checks, food consumption, that sort of thing. Please, have a seat in the front. I'll stay back here with the projectionist."

Cash took a seat next to Colcord, McFaul on the other side. She hoped McFaul wasn't going to tag along with her everywhere.

"What I'm going to play for you," Maximilian said, "is the video feed from Tom Thumb's camera. Which, by the way, appears to have been taken. And turned off, with the batteries removed—which also disables the internal GPS."

"Where's the buttered popcorn?" Colcord murmured to Cash.

"I was about to make the same joke," Cash murmured back, "until I realized it was in bad taste."

"Thanks."

"Okay, here we go," said Maximilian. "The video includes sound. It was shot in visible-wavelength light using night-adapted CCD video. We find that offers more clarity and color than thermal night vision."

The screen sprang to life. They were suddenly in the midst of the herd of mammoths, seeing from the point of view of Tom Thumb, in the center of the group. Once again, Cash was floored by how big they were—so much more massive and bulkier than elephants, made even larger by the addition of heavy mats of three-to-four-foot-long hair. The mammoths were huddled together, in the deep forest, surrounded by giant trees, bluish moonlight filtering down. Their combined breathing sent clouds of condensation into the cold night air, and there was a gentle sound of sighing and, underneath that, a low chorus of gentle rumbling sounds.

"What's that?" Colcord asked.

"Mammoths purr," explained Maximilian. "Just like cats. Especially when they're sleeping. So do elephants, by the way."

"They're asleep now?"

"Yes. They mostly sleep standing up."

A minute or two in, the purring suddenly stopped, as did the heavy breathing. The ears of the mammoth in front twitched and swung out, and it raised its furry trunk to test the air, waving it this way and that. Meanwhile, the rest of the herd awakened and became alert, eyes open, ears moving. Tom Thumb pressed against the flank of a big mammoth, evidently his mother.

The herd now stirred, and several others raised their trunks, including the large bull, who raised his head and trunk, his great coiled tusks, each one the length of a truck, glistening in the moonlight. They had definitely sensed something they didn't like. The animals were nervous but didn't seem to know from which direction the menace was coming. Tom Thumb huddled even closer to his mother.

There was a soft *crack* like the striking of two sticks together, which sent a ripple of apprehension through the animals, ears swinging, trunks probing the air. The mammoth in front began to move, and the others followed suit. They lumbered through the forest, staying together, walking over small trees and breaking fallen trunks with their gigantic feet, making a racket as they moved. These were not quiet animals.

Another *crack!* came, louder this time, and closer.

Now the animals were alarmed and moved a little faster.

A *crack!* emanated from in front, and the lead animal halted abruptly, turned, and started off at a right angle. But a crack sounded from that direction, and the animal halted again, backing up. It raised its trunk and gave a trumpeting sound of alarm, ears flapping. Tom Thumb struggled to stay with his mother. After a moment of confusion, the herd started moving in another direction.

Suddenly, a bright light flared briefly from behind, an orange blaze of fire. The mammoths wheeled away from it and started moving fast, not exactly running but striding swiftly, trunks in the air. The bull trumpeted loudly again. Cash could see they were close to panic.

Another flash of fire, and a third, one side and then the other. The mammoths were now spooked and almost running.

Something zoomed out of the darkness, spiraling in—a flaming torch, thrown from behind. It struck Tom Thumb's mother with a shower of sparks, bouncing off her flank. She let out a screech and began running.

Now the mammoths fully panicked, breaking into a full-on stampede, running pell-mell through the forest, crashing through bushes and small trees. Tom Thumb struggled to keep up with his mother, trumpeting piteously, while the mother raced ahead. Waving torches on either side panicked them further. Cash tried to see who was holding the torches, but all she could see were the dark outlines of people, wearing, it seemed, the same bizarre masks and camouflage as before.

"The attackers are taking advantage of the mammoths' great fear of fire," said Maximilian.

The mammoths were running like mad. The mammoth mother had abandoned her baby and was tearing along far ahead, while Tom Thumb fell farther and farther behind, stumbling and crying and trumpeting shrilly. The whole herd was leaving the baby behind in its panic. Cash found it hard to watch.

Another thrown torch arced through the air and struck Tom Thumb on the back. He let loose a terrified squeal, and then stumbled over a tree trunk, going down with a crash, while the rest of the herd continued fleeing through the forest.

The little mammoth struggled to get back up, flailing and screaming hideously. There was a thumping sound—the sound of blows on flesh—followed by a wet ripping sound, and the animal's screeching turned into a cough, the final piteous sounds of horror choked off by a gurgle and then subsiding into silence.

The camera's point of view had been thrashing about as the mammoth was attacked, but suddenly went still, showing a portion of the ground.

A hand swooped around and covered the lens, and moments later, the video cut off with a crunch, followed by static.

"Show that sequence again," said Cash. "Slow motion."

Maximilian backed it up to the point where the mammoth went down and played it in slow motion. The sound too was slowed down, and the high-pitched screams became a throbbing, deep groan. The hand finally appeared, and then it was over.

"I didn't hear any gunshots. It sounded like the animal was being stabbed."

"That's right," said Colcord. "That gurgling sound of blood toward the end sounded like a blade or something went into the animal's lung."

Cash swallowed. "How much was that animal worth?"

"Tom Thumb cost us twelve million dollars to de-extinct. He was actually the least expensive of our animals, being one of the latest. We're getting better at the techniques. The large cow was his surrogate mother, of course."

"I thought you said they couldn't breed."

"They can't. She carried him as a fertilized, implanted embryo."

"It wasn't nice to see how she abandoned her baby," Cash said.

"I want to see that hand again," said Colcord. "Play it frame by frame."

Maximilian went through it.

"Stop."

A frame froze on-screen. Behind the approaching hand, she could see the blurry, partial outline of the upper form of a person, a man's torso, evidently the owner of the hand, reaching around.

"Can we get that enhanced?" Cash asked.

"Yes," said Maximilian. "We have some editing tools here. Hold on."

The image disappeared and then reappeared, framed in an editing box. Cash watched as the projectionist sharpened it, added contrast, goosed up the color. But it wasn't much help, except to reveal a little of the strange homemade camouflage of leaves and grass and twigs. Definitely a he, though, considering the broad, muscular torso. The head was, unfortunately, out of frame.

"Send the office the full-res of that entire video," said Cash. "We'll have our imaging lab back in Arvada see what they can do."

"Will do."

"Did any of the other cameras on the mammoths record anything useful?"

"Unfortunately not."

"Send all the videos along too, just in case. And what about the stolen camera. No way to track it?"

"Only if the batteries are put back in."

Colcord's cell rang. He answered, spoke for a moment, then hung up. "The dogs are here."

Maximilian escorted them back through the CCTV room and to the main guard station. Sam Acosta had just arrived in the parking lot outside, his van parked. He came over, gave Colcord and Cash each a quick nod. "What we got today?" he asked.

"A murdered mammoth."

"How fresh?"

"Trail is about four and a half hours old," said Cash. "But I have to tell you something—Detective Romanski tells me that the killers are disguising their scent with some concoction made with mammoth dung and bile."

Acosta stared at her. "Wow. Okay. That's a problem because there's mammoth scent all over the place. But we'll see. Let's get going, no time to waste."

"I want you to take along security backup," said Cash. "Just in case." She waved over two Erebus guards with assault rifles, geared up with body armor and helmets. "You all got radios?" Cash asked. "Make sure you're able to communicate. There's spotty cell reception beyond the lodge."

"Great. Thanks."

"If you get close to them or corner them," said Cash, "don't be heroes. Radio for backup."

"Very good."

McFaul said, "I'm going to stay back here, get settled, and wait for the forensic vet. You go on ahead with the dogs."

"Yes, sir." *Thank God*, she thought.

Cash and Colcord and the two guards loaded into a jeep and drove up the road to the mass of parked cars below the kill site. Acosta followed in a van with his dogs. He parked behind them and unloaded the dogs, and the five of them hiked up the slope to the dead mammoth.

34

"Oh boy," said Acosta, staring at the dead animal. "What a mess."

The dogs were excited by all the meat and blood, pulling on their leashes and baying until Acosta told them to shut up and sit.

"I'm going to cut for scent," he told Cash. "When I get it, I'll give you a call on the radio."

He wrapped the leashes around his hands and gave the dogs a command, and they leapt up and went off, straining ahead as Acosta controlled them. He soon vanished into the trees. The sun was now rising, the morning light invading the forest, chasing away tendrils of mist. The chill of the night was receding.

Cash's radio crackled. It was Acosta. "Got a scent trail. Northwest of the site, at ten o'clock, one hundred yards. Heading out."

"Keep in touch."

Cash turned back to Romanski. He looked like a polar bear in his white suit, on his hands and knees poking around the forest floor. He was a good worker, meticulous, and never seemed to get tired.

"How much longer is this going to take?" she asked.

Romanski shook his head. "This is a bitch of a crime scene."

"Has anyone found anything I should know about?"

"Like what, Boardwalk or Park Place?"

"Ha ha."

"Nothing yet," said Romanski. "Just a shitload of what I'm sure will turn out to be useless evidence, but gotta bag it all."

Cash could hear the deep, mournful baying of Acosta's dogs in the distance fade away into silence. She began to feel uneasy and called him on the radio. "Everything okay?"

"All good," said Acosta. "A strong trail for a change—you can hear it in their baying."

"Where's it heading?"

"Upslope, into the mountains. Into fallen timber. Steep. These sons of bitches really went into dense country. Looks like maybe they forgot to dab on their bile perfume."

"Okay. Be careful."

She heard voices, and now McFaul arrived, huffing and puffing, his face all red and dripping with sweat, with a woman in tow, whom Cash figured must be the forensic vet. She quickly donned a monkey suit, ducked under the tape, and went over to the dead mammoth, crouching by the head and examining it with a pair of magnifying goggles. Cash watched as the vet tipped the head over, looking at the severed neck and spinal cord. She could see McFaul eyeing the scene with a look of horror and disgust on his face.

"Sir?" she said.

He turned. She hesitated. *Proceed strategically*, she told herself. "I wonder, sir, if you've thought more since our last conversation about the possibility of closing the resort—especially considering this new development."

McFaul puckered up his face, irritated. "Well, as I said, that would be a drastic step. It would inflame the press and attract even more attention. And you know, we've got a problem with that man Gunnerson."

"How's that?"

"He's making phone calls to the press, saying a lot of crazy stuff. Barrow won't let him leave his suite, but he's causing plenty of trouble even so."

Cash shook her head. "I'm not surprised. We questioned him, and I think he knows more than he's letting on. But getting back to closing the resort—consider, sir, what would happen if another guest were killed. The press would naturally ask why we hadn't shut the place down after the first two killings. And think of all the threats from that cultist priest on the video. An excess of caution is better than a lack of it—don't you think?"

She could see the wheels in McFaul's head working. "You make a good point, Agent Cash."

"If you feel we don't have the authority, we could recommend a shutdown to the governor. Then we'd be on record having made the request—if anything should happen, we'll be covered . . ." She let her voice trail off. She could see she'd finally hit on an argument that found traction with McFaul.

"Yes. I believe you're right."

"You might call him now, while it's early and his day is just beginning." She had to get him to act before McFaul contacted Barrow and got talked out of it.

McFaul checked his watch, took out his cell phone, looked at it thoughtfully as if composing his thoughts, and then dialed. It took a while to get through, and she could hear him finally speaking to the governor. The conversation went on for a while, and she saw it was not going well. Finally, he hung up.

"Well, we tried."

"Barrow got to him first," she said.

He looked at her. "I would guess he did. But at least . . ." He hesitated. "We're now on record."

McFaul, she thought, was never so concerned about a case as to when it might impact the CBI's public image and his own career. That call provided excellent ass-covering, and even someone as dumb as McFaul could see that.

For the next hour, she watched the forensic vet work on the pieces of the mammoth, even as Romanski and his team continued their evidence gathering. Finally, the vet left off her work and came out from the perimeter, taking off her now-bloodied hood.

"What you got?"

She shook her head. "The animal was butchered and some cuts of meat and sections of organs taken." She worked to catch her breath. Despite the chill air, she was sweating. "It's a known fact that human hunters butcher an elephant from the inside out. The skin is just too tough to hack through, and it's a lot easier to crawl inside the animal and get your organs and meat that way. And that," she said, "is what was done here."

"Right. And how much did they take?"

"Not all that much. Just the choicest cuts—part of the liver, kidneys, heart, and the tenderloin. Tongue and testicles too."

"Jesus. How much more time do you need?"

"A few more hours." She pulled the hood back up and ducked under the tape, soon disappearing into the body cavity again.

Cash pulled out her radio and called Acosta. "How's your progress?"

"Trail is still strong," said Acosta's staticky voice. "This is damned rough country, though." She could hear through the radio the baying of the dogs. "Pretty steep, and we're now in a ravine, heading up toward the tree line."

"Call if you find anything."

Cash lowered the radio. Something about this bothered her. The mammoth, killed within a thousand yards of the lodge. The "good, strong" trail leading away, up into a narrow ravine. The fact that the killers hadn't apparently used their dog-confusing scent, so that their trail was easy to follow.

"It's a trap," said Cash.

Colcord stared at her sharply. "What do you mean?"

"Acosta and his dogs are being deliberately lured up there. This feels planned." She hit the radio call button. "Acosta, do you read?"

His voice came through a hiss of static. "I read, barely. We got a lot of cliff around us blocking the signal."

In the background, the dogs were baying wildly now.

"Where are you now?"

"Way up in the mountains. At the tree line. The ravine's opened up a little into a meadow. A real bitch of a climb to get here . . . Hey, we've got something here . . ."

She could hear him breathing hard, hear the dogs going crazy.

"There's a rock shelter up there . . . Looks like a campsite hidden in it . . ."

"Fresh campsite?"

"What the hell?" Acosta's voice carried a note of horror. "Jesus Christ."

"What is it?"

The dogs continued baying madly.

A long hiss of static, his voice unintelligible.

"Acosta! You cut out. What is it?"

More static, and then his voice emerged, high-pitched. "Bones . . . *Human* bones. We got a campsite, firepit . . . two human skulls . . . burnt and broken up . . ."

More static.

"Acosta?"

"Bones . . . Chopped up . . . I think . . . they were, like, *cooked* . . ."

"What's your GPS location?"

He gave it to her. Colcord scribbled it down in his notebook as she repeated it out loud. Then she said, "Acosta, get your ass out of there! You're in a possible ambush situation. You copy?"

"Copy that. I just can't believe this shit . . ."

"I'm calling in choppers for backup, out."

She changed channel and reached Maximilian at the lodge. "Scramble two choppers with armed guys up to this location." She read off the GPS coordinates.

Everyone on-site had stopped work and was now staring at her.

"What is it?" McFaul asked, rushing over. "What's happened?"

"Looks like Acosta and his dogs found the bodies of our two missing hikers," she said. "It seems . . . they've been cannibalized."

35

Cash scrambled over the last few rocks and arrived at the small meadow edged with bonsai-like spruce trees, gnarled and twisted from years of high wind and deep snow. It was a beautiful spot, perched high on the mountainside, filled with fall wildflowers, offering an extensive view of the valley below. Above it extended a couloir that ran up to a high ridge above the tree line, topped with snow. A rivulet gurgled through the middle and tumbled over the edge, becoming a series of small waterfalls as it made its way down.

She looked around. On the right side of the meadow, below the steep couloir, stood a cluster of boulders the size of houses, jammed together. At their base was a small, dark triangular opening. That, she assumed, must be where the campsite was hidden, because a group of Erebus security guards, who had already been dropped into the site, were standing guard in front.

She walked over to it, and the guards separated to let her pass. She stepped into the darkness of the opening, formed by two boulders leaning together. In the large space beyond, she could see the remains of a stone circle, the ashes of a campfire, and a scattering of bones. It was a perfect sanctuary, she thought, this little hideaway tucked into a giant rockfall, hidden from below while offering a view of anyone coming up, sheltered from wind and severe weather, with a natural opening above to allow the campfire smoke to escape through the gaps in the boulders. No wonder it wasn't found.

She paused at the edge of the area—CSI protocol prevented her from going in—to take in and memorize the crime scene. She could see, scattered in the dimness about like so much trash, various chopped-up bones and a partially burnt human skull. At the back of the cave-like space stood an altar, not unlike the one in the video, made of sticks and bark and moss—beautifully crafted—with four poles around it from which hung four ornaments like the ones that contained the Monopoly tokens. She wondered what might be in those little packages. There were also some scattered playing cards and Monopoly money, wrinkled and dirty.

She eased the pack off her shoulders as Colcord arrived. Thank God McFaul had decided to go back to the lodge. Hiking was not his gig anyway, judging from the double chins and pasty complexion.

"Another day, another crime scene," said Colcord. "How many have we taped off so far?"

Cash thought a moment. "Four. Let's set up a perimeter."

She and Colcord began stringing the police tape in a wide circle around the rock shelter and its entrance.

As they worked, Romanski arrived with his team, followed by the doctor, Huizinga. They began to unpack their equipment and suit up.

Cash went over to Romanski. "Got a suit for me?"

He looked up. "You going in?"

"I'd like to do a walk-through, get a closer look."

"Of course."

He handed her a suit from his pack, and she climbed into it, the fabric smelling new. Mask, goggles, hood, and booties followed. She glanced back at Colcord, who gave her a thumbs-up, and then she stepped over the tape, following Romanski.

The ring of stones surrounded a long-dead fire, once quite large, with many broken and burnt bones mixed with charcoal. She took a closer look at the trash lying about—scattered Bicycle playing cards, wet Monopoly money, a Monopoly board tossed in a corner with some game cards, an old wooden checkers board split in half, with scattered pieces. And a soggy paperback book.

She bent down to read the title. It was a novel—*The Cider House Rules* by John Irving. It struck her as almost absurdly incongruous—not some anarchist manifesto or radical screed but a sentimental novel about orphans—and one of her favorite novels, no less. Who were these cultists?

Cash turned her attention to the ashes of the fire. She saw a glint and knelt.

"Bart?"

He came over and knelt next to her. She pointed. Lying among the ashes was a partially melted silver medal of Saint Christopher on a broken chain. The photographer came over and photographed it, and then Romanski picked it up with long tweezers and sealed it in a bag. He then used the tweezers to stir the wet ashes—it had recently rained—and another glint came up.

"Oh God." It was a human tooth with a silver filling.

Romanski scooped that up too.

Cash stood up and looked around. The dirt area surrounding the firepit had been heavily trodden. The bones were flung everywhere, willy-nilly, and she had a vision of the feasters holding a meat-covered bone in one hand, gnawing and stripping off the flesh and flinging it away when done.

"Crazy fuckers," muttered Romanski.

Cash next walked over to where one of the skulls was lying face down. The back of the cranium was singed and blackened. "Looks like they burned the head."

"Right," said Romanski. "I would guess that what we're looking at here is a classic sign of cannibalism. It's been documented at other cannibal sites across the world. The brain, which is one of the most nourishing organs in the body, is roasted by placing the head in the fire, face up, and letting the brains cook inside. And then the skull is broken open from the back and the brains consumed, using the cranium as an eating bowl." He peered in, leaning close. "You can see marks where they scooped out the cooked insides."

"Lovely," said Cash.

Romanski used the tweezers to turn the skull over and shined his light in, illuminating the eye sockets. "This is the woman, I'd guess, based on the lack of brow ridges and the slightly more gracile morphology."

Cash felt slightly sick to her stomach. She stood up and nodded at the poles holding the balls. "Let's see what are in these," she said.

She and Romanski went over. They were similar to the objects that had held the Monopoly tokens, balls of finely woven grass, pine needles, and twigs. As the wind shifted, she caught a foul smell from one of them. On closer inspection, she saw that a vile fluid was draining out of the bottom.

"Uh-oh," said Romanski. "I don't like the look of that."

Cash felt a second wave of nausea. "I've seen enough."

He clucked his tongue. "We'll get all this back to the lab and start working on it right away."

"Be sure to collect DNA from those gnawed-on bones." She hesitated. "And what's with the DNA results from before? They should have come in by now."

"The first run was contaminated. There was a lot of human DNA at the earlier site, and it was all mixed up and it proved difficult to separate. They're doing another run." He nodded at the bones. "The saliva traces on these might be easier."

Cash went back out into the sunlight and took off the suit, taking deep breaths and trying to shake off the feeling of nausea and horror. She was dreading finding out what was in those hanging ornaments.

"I have a nasty feeling," she said to Colcord, "that this thing's a setup."

"How so?"

"We were led up here. They *wanted* us to find this place. They killed the mammoth near the lodge—and then they laid a scent trail way up here that they knew we'd follow." She gestured. "Before, they covered up their scent, but this time, they didn't. They *led* us up here."

"But why?" said Colcord. "So we could find these cannibalized bones?"

"Exactly."

"What's the message?"

"I wish I knew. Strange that they haven't made any demands or written a manifesto. Even the Unabomber tried to explain what he was doing."

Colcord took out his phone. "While you were admiring the Christmas ornaments, I was taking a look at our location on the GPS. Here." He handed her the phone, and she looked at the map and the little orange arrow showing their location.

"Eleven thousand feet," she said. "We're pretty high up."

"Yeah, but I noticed something else," Colcord said. "This ravine is marked on the map as Hookers Canyon. Up at the top end of this gulch, according to that old guy I visited on Grundage Creek, is an adit to the Jackman Mine."

"What's an adit?"

"An access tunnel into the mine, to reach the ore zone. This is a minor one that maybe wasn't on the main maps that Erebus used. Maybe this adit never got closed."

Cash looked up the couloir beyond the meadow. It rose steeply between spires of granite to a series of upper mountain slopes, covered with rocks and granite outcroppings, before ending in the snowy ridgeline. "Up there? I don't see anything."

"According to his description, it's only about a quarter mile up from here."

She squinted. "You think we should go up there?"

"Yes, and go inside. I've got the maps on my phone. Are you game?"

"You mean—*now*?"

"We're here. We've got armed guards we can take with us." He looked at his watch. "It's noon. We've got time."

She stared at Colcord. This was a side of him she hadn't appreciated before, and she liked it. "Okay, hell yes. Let's go."

"Better not tell Maximilian," said Colcord.

She nodded. "I agree." She looked around and waved over two guards. "How are you guys doing?"

They nodded. "Good."

"What are your names?"

"Holder," said one. He was a young man, buff and solid, with a friendly kid-face.

"And you?"

"Johnson."

"Holder and Johnson. Nice to meet you."

They nodded.

"The sheriff and I want to climb up this couloir to where we think there might be an opening into a mine. We want to check it out—and we'd like you to come with us."

They nodded. "No problem."

"Locked and loaded?"

"Oh yeah. But no night vision—we'll have to use flashlights."

"That'll work. Let's go, then, Holder and Johnson."

36

The couloir rose up abruptly from the far end of the meadow, a slide of interlocking boulders between two walls of rock. It was a classic hand-and-foot scramble. At least there were plenty of handholds and footholds, and the granite boulders were well locked in and unlikely to move.

As she picked her way up, grasping one boulder and pulling herself up to the next, making sure each time she had good footholds, she could hear Colcord behind her, breathing hard, and once again, she was glad for her yoga and workouts. Colcord was a good-looking man, but he could stand some trimming around the middle—but then again, so could she. The two guards, on the other hand, were quite a bit younger and having no problems at all.

As they worked their way up, the little stream cascaded down to their left, making a merry splashing sound, with clumps of tiny alpine wildflowers along its course. Once in a while, someone would dislodge a pebble, and Holder or Cash would call out, *Rock!* as it tumbled down. Toward the top, they hit sloping granite slabs that were a little scary. The wind picked up, and the view looking down became nerve-racking. After surmounting the final slab, they came over the edge into another alpine meadow, a few hundred feet across, beyond which rose the upward thrust of the mountain into fresh snowfields, ending in a jagged ridge of rock against bright blue sky.

"I think I see the mine opening," said Colcord, coming up beside her, pointing.

She took out the binoculars she always carried. On the far side of the meadow, about a hundred feet up the side of the mountain, there was a small tailings pile. Above that, she could see what looked like a square opening framed in rotting timbers. It was almost hidden by an overhanging cleft of rock and a lone dwarf pine.

She handed the binoculars to Colcord, who used them to examine the opening for a long moment. "That's the opening we're looking for."

"So they didn't seal every mine opening like they claimed," said Cash.

"No. Yearwood doubted it would have been possible. He said that most of the time, they were digging out gold ore like crazy and not stopping to make maps."

"This one's pretty well hidden," said Cash.

They crossed the meadow, through which the stream gurgled in a runnel.

"I'm looking for signs of people having been up there before," said Colcord, "but the area looks undisturbed."

Holder led the way, hiking fast despite his burden of weapon, ammo, body armor, helmet, and pack. Cash felt reassured; both he and Johnson seemed competent and levelheaded. If these crazies were armed only with knives, they'd be no match for these two guys.

On the barren slopes, the wind picked up. They weren't far below the recent snow line, and it was chilly, despite the sun.

In fifteen minutes, they had reached the mine entrance, almost completely hidden behind the twisted pine. The mine opening was a rectangular hole about seven by six, cut straight into the rock of the mountain and going back into the darkness.

"That's a bristlecone pine, by the way," said Colcord. "Rare in Colorado."

"Looks like a hobbit tree," said Cash. "If you all could stay back for a moment, I'd like to examine this area before we tramp all around—see if there are any traces of people coming or going."

She stepped just inside the entrance and peered at the ground. It was solid rock, with a few little patches of sand, but there were no marks anywhere showing recent activity. She sniffed the air. It was damp and clammy, redolent of mildew and a touch of smoke.

"Are we going in?" asked Holder.

Cash turned to Colcord. "You said you had maps of this mine on your phone, right?"

"I photographed them at Yearwood's place."

"Can I see?"

Colcord loaded the pictures and handed her the phone. She swiped through them. The drawings were precise and labeled in a neat, block-lettered hand. She was surprised at how complicated it was. The tunnel went straight into the mountain for a ways, and then branched into four horizontal tunnels, like the fingers of a hand, which connected with what must have been a complicated ore body, since the tunnels suddenly forked into all kinds of twisty shapes and odd directions. It looked like a giant ant farm.

There was a lot to search, and some of it looked inaccessible. There were also quite a few dangerous vertical shafts to watch out for.

"Yearwood told me he made these maps as he explored the mines, so I think they're pretty accurate. More accurate, he claims, than the maps at the historical society that were stolen."

She nodded, handing the phone back. "How much juice you got on that phone?"

He grinned. "Good question. Fifty percent."

She looked at her watch. One o'clock. Was this a good idea? She paused to consider. They were all four armed, with two guards carrying AR-15 assault rifles and spare ammo magazines. There was no evidence the killers had guns—just knives. The idea wasn't to confront anyone—just reconnoiter and get out.

"What kind of flashlights you two got?" Cash asked.

Holder removed a flashlight from his pack. "TC1200."

The best. She looked at Colcord. "You still want to do this?"

"If we went back and organized a search, it'd take at least a day, and Maximilian would find out about it. So yes, I think we go in now."

"If we find any evidence of recent occupation," she said, "we beat a retreat and order backup."

"Right."

"Hand signals only," said Cash. "Holder, you go first, then me, then

Colcord, then Johnson. Stay in line. Take it slow. And keep an eye on the ground ahead—if you see any trace of recent human occupation, stop and point it out."

Holder went in and paused, shining the powerful beam around, and Cash followed. The cooler air of the tunnel wafted over her, bringing with it the scent of wet rock and humidity. The tunnel had been cut into the hard rock of the mountain, with wooden shoring beams placed at regular intervals. Cash pulled her own small Maglite out of her belt and clicked it on, directing the beam at the floor of the tunnel. There was no sign of recent entry, no prints in the occasional patches of sand. But there was also plenty of naked rock to walk on and leave no trace.

As they proceeded down the tunnel, the mine opening grew distant and the light it cast fainter, until a turn in the tunnel cut it out completely. Cash felt a slight twist in her gut—she was somewhat claustrophobic, and thinking of the weight of the mountain on top of her was not pleasant. She pushed the thought away.

The cool air flowing through the tunnel suddenly turned colder, as if they'd passed through a thermal layer. Holder, ahead, paused as his beam illuminated a flat wall of rock: the tunnel had come to a T. Colcord, consulting his phone, pointed to the left. They turned the corner and came across an abandoned ore cart, lying on its side, and beyond that, a wooden platform on the ground with a square hole cut in it, with a rotting superstructure above made of wooden beams. Holder paused and stepped on the wood, which groaned ominously. He took another step and shined the light down into a void so deep, and so terrifying, that the bottom couldn't be seen.

There was no way to proceed except across the wooden platform, which was sagging and rotten. It was also covered with a thick layer of dust, with no evidence of any recent passage.

Cash signaled to turn and go the other way.

A moment later, they had passed the T. The tunnel began sloping downward, and the ground was scattered with old mining trash—a rotting coil of rope, rusting chewing tobacco tins, a broken pick, an earthen whiskey jug. The air began to feel closer and stale, more humid, with less oxygen. And there was a swampy, gassy smell.

The shaft divided, and Cash signaled Colcord she wanted to look at the map. They consulted it together, staring at the little rectangle of light that was the cell phone. The tunnel divided again and then entered the former ore body, where it expanded greatly into a series of barnlike spaces, separated by narrow tunnels, with many deep shafts and lots of little tunnels going every which way.

Cash pointed to the right, and they continued, the tunnel ceiling lowering to the point where they had to stoop. They inched past another vertical shaft, with a stream of foul air rising from it, and then came to a large open area.

It was like a giant black void, so high that even the powerful beams of the TC1200s could barely reach the top. They paused at the threshold, sweeping the beams around. There had been a cave-in on the far wall, a pile of rock tumbled out from a gap in the roof. More trash lay about—old wooden packing cases, piles of rusted cans, broken bottles, several more ore carts and some warped ore rails, and an old boiler. Rocks lay strewn about, many evidently having fallen from the roof. Cash examined the floor but could still see no marks or signs of any recent occupation.

She gestured for them to keep going, pointing toward a small doorway, shored by heavy creosote-treated beams, at the far side, which the map indicated led to a complicated series of tunnels. They moved across the open area, picking their way among the detritus and rocks. Halfway across, Cash halted, her flashlight beam illuminating a small patch of sand. Imprinted on the sand was the clear impression of an athletic shoe sole—fresh. Nikes?

She pointed, and they gathered around it in silence. She took out her phone and snapped pictures from several angles. She would send them to Romanski; he could identify the brand. An unsettling feeling crept down her spine: they were finally on the right track; someone had recently been in the mine, most likely the killers. This was an important breakthrough in the case. She would come back in force and sweep the mines.

They passed through the doorway, and now the warren of tunnels began in earnest, as the miners of old had chiseled and blasted ore from wherever the seams went in the rock. She examined the ground closely, but she could see no indications of anyone passing through. She checked her watch—two o'clock. They would go only another half hour and then turn around.

She picked the most accessible tunnel, and they headed down it. It curved left and right. They had to edge around a terrifying deep shaft, covered with rotten wood platforms. At one point, Holder dislodged a piece of wood, and it fell into the void. There was a long period of silence and then the sound of the crash echoed up, eerie and distorted. There were so many branching corridors and so many turns that Cash became concerned about finding their way out. She touched Colcord and whispered, "You keeping track of where we are?"

He nodded and gave her a thumbs-up.

According to the map, they were approaching another large chamber. Abruptly, Holder halted and held up his hand. He made a signal for them to hood their flashlights.

In the sudden darkness, they listened. Amid the distant sound of dripping water and an intermittent creaking, Cash could hear something: the low, rhythmic beating of a drum at the edge of audibility.

She touched Colcord and leaned over to whisper, "We need to leave."

He nodded and they turned around. She gestured for them to dim down to five lumens on their flashlights. Her heart was pounding. She wanted to get out of there. They had definitely found them. Now was the time to retreat and come back in force.

Colcord led the way, consulting his phone, the glow from it illuminating his face in a bluish wash. Johnson, taking up the rear, suddenly stopped and made a sign, pointing back, and then indicated they were to extinguish their lights.

They did so and were enveloped in darkness.

Cash strained to listen, but the sound of the beating drum had either stopped or they were now too far away. The absolute darkness frightened her, and she struggled to stay calm.

Suddenly, in the blackness, a light flared, moving swiftly, and then disappeared. No one reacted; no one said a word. Cash blinked, seeing a streak left in her retina from the moving light. She heard a rustle of fabric and the faint clink of metal, and she realized Holder was un-shouldering his weapon.

They needed to get out as fast as possible. But even as she thought that, there was another flare of light, like a firefly streaking in the darkness, and it came not from behind them but from in front.

37

This was the part of moviemaking that Doyle loved the most: the explosions. As a kid growing up in County Clare, Ireland, he'd learned how to make gunpowder using common household ingredients: potassium nitrate from a product called Stump Remover, charcoal from charcoal briquettes, and sulfur sold in garden stores as a fertilizer. He'd grind the three ingredients separately into fine power using a mortar and pestle, mix them together with water, dry the mixture, and corn it, or break it up into kernels of gunpowder. He made explosive sticks by packing it into tubes, sticking in a fuse, and capping it with plaster.

And then he would hike far out into the Burren and blow something up. He started with discarded crates and barrels but then quickly graduated to such things as a derelict chicken coop, an icebox, an abandoned car. There were ruins out there in those desolate lands, old failed farms, that offered lots of good things to blow up. He financed his pyrotechnics habit by charging kids in the neighborhood a shilling to watch. Before he was caught and punished, he'd earned over fifty pounds.

Now, he made millions blowing things up. Doyle took great pride in the gigantic explosions in his films; it was his directorial signature. The critics called it puerile and fatuous, but they didn't get how much young audiences loved a big bang—and the proof was in the box office receipts. CGI just didn't cut it—it was too fake, too fluttery, too goosed, and it lacked the authenticity of an actual, fiery, incredibly loud and gloriously destructive blast.

He admired once again the train they were going to blow up tomorrow. It was life-size—no sissy scale model. It was a work of art, sculpted from giant blocks of Styrofoam that had been shaped and rasped, painted and fauxed, to reproduce, in incredible detail, a classic Old West narrow-gauge steam locomotive with a funnel and cowcatcher, four cars, and a caboose. It had cost over a million dollars to build, and he would have one shot at blowing it up. That was one of the challenges of real pyrotechnics—you didn't get a second take.

For two days, they had been setting up the gigantic pyrotechnics scene, the linchpin of act 3, in which the bad guys blow up a train. Doyle had hired the most expensive pyrotechnics guy in Hollywood, Jack Adair, to do it. The train had been built on a section of track outside the movie town, against a breathtaking backdrop of mountains. Adair was busy wiring it with real dynamite, to get the concussive effect Doyle wanted, which would be enhanced with spectacular incendiaries and squibs, including large hidden balloons filled with propane that would create giant balls of fire upon ignition. It had taken a ton of testing and all kinds of safety reviews and standby firefighting and safety equipment to get to this point. One of the things about explosive F/X in films is that once they're set up, they have to be blown up as soon as possible. You can't keep an explosively wired set hanging around for days—once it's ready to go, you've got twenty-four hours at most to detonate it, or you have to start all over again.

In this case, the detonation was scheduled for two p.m. tomorrow.

Doyle loved the challenge. He'd worked with Adair on half a dozen films, and together, they'd blown up everything from castles to spaceships to intricate models of entire cities and even planets. He watched approvingly as Adair and his crew moved about the fake train, measuring things, marking out areas with stakes, laying down wires, and setting up secondaries. It was a science, with every little thing planned in advance so that when the explosion occurred, there were no surprises, nothing unrealistic or fake-looking.

Doyle saw Ballou come out of his honey wagon, and he hoped he wouldn't come over to chat—but of course he did.

"Going to be quite a show tomorrow, hey?" Ballou said. He was all duded up in his hat and leather pants, wearing six-guns no less, even though he had no scene that day. Method acting.

"Yes, it'll be a big one," said Doyle pleasantly. "I hope you'll be here to see it." He actually hoped not.

"I wouldn't miss it for the world," said Ballou, lighting up a cigarette and blowing out a long stream of smoke. "Not for the world. And that's a beautiful train—you'd hardly know it was just a pile of cheap Styrofoam."

"No, you wouldn't."

"I almost hate to see it blown up."

"When it goes up, it'll be *spectacular.*"

Ballou nodded. "I've got a good feeling about this film, Slavomir. I think it's going to be a terrific hit."

Doyle flushed at the praise. Ballou was a pain in the ass, but he could also be charming when he wanted to. "Thank you, Brock," he said. "And I'm delighted you're starring in this film. It's going to make all the difference. Your name is going to hoover in the audiences."

Ballou nodded, taking another drag. "Yes, that's true. Too bad the script is so weak."

Okay, thought Doyle, segue back to asshole Ballou. What he meant by a weak script was that he wasn't in *every. single. scene*, something he'd been complaining about since the beginning. They'd worked on it, written him into a couple of scenes where it made no sense—his appearances would end up on the cutting room floor anyway—but Ballou never seemed to be satisfied.

"Two o'clock tomorrow, right?" said Ballou. "It go boom."

"Right."

Ballou winked and turned, heading back to his trailer. Doyle watched him saunter off with his John Wayne swagger. He was basically just an insecure, overgrown kid, a lucky bastard born with killer looks, a gorgeous deep voice, and a modicum of acting talent.

It go boom. It certainly would. Adair was utilizing a hundred pounds of real dynamite to create a shock wave and percussive effect that would literally shake the ground and the cameras, no need to Foley anything. This was going to be the best explosion of his moviemaking career. He could hardly wait for tomorrow at two p.m.

38

After the flash of light vanished, they were again enveloped in blackness. Cash carefully felt down to her holster, unsnapped the keeper, and eased out the Glock. She waited in the tense darkness with her hand on the slide, ready to rack in a round. The killers were playing with them, trying to spook them. Well, they wouldn't be spooked.

The silence engulfed them as they waited—waiting for her to lead, she realized. It was clear they needed to get the hell out; they were in an unknown environment, facing an unknown number of enemies who were carrying unknown weapons.

"Okay," said Cash in a low murmur. "We're gonna move fast. Colcord, you navigate, calling directions to Holder in front. Johnson, you cover us from the rear. Stop, look, and clear every turn. Fire at will. No point in silence—they know where we are. On my signal, flashlights on full lumens and we move." She paused, listening and waiting. She had a terrible feeling that they were being set up and that the longer they waited, the more time the other side had to surround them.

"*Now,*" she said.

The flashlights sprang on, and ahead she saw the scramble of dark shapes, vanishing from the beam.

"Straight ahead, and then left at the T," said Colcord, phone in hand.

They started forward at a jog, the flashlight beams bobbing as they moved. At the T, Holder paused at the corner and then spun around, flashlight and rifle pointing ahead.

"Clear," he said.

They continued, moving fast, Colcord calling out the directions and Holder pausing at each turn and fork to check the way ahead. Cash wondered where the figures shadowing them had gone—had they retreated? If they only had hand weapons, it would be madness to engage in a firefight with two guards carrying assault rifles. Or so she hoped.

"At the branch, take the middle passage," Colcord said as they made progress retracing the crazy warren of tunnels, passageways, holes, and channels.

Suddenly, a sound filled the tunnel, loud and distorted: mocking laughter, coming from everywhere and nowhere at once. Holder halted, shining the light up and down, back and forth, evidently searching for the source of the sound.

"Ignore it," said Cash sharply. "Just keep going."

Another burst of laughter erupted around them, freakishly close, and it continued to echo and roll about through the spaces after it ceased.

"What the fuck?" Holder crouched instinctively, swinging his rifle around with the light. They were in a space with a dozen or more cracks and channels going off in different directions, and it seemed to Cash their pursuers were using these channels for sound propagation.

"Keep going," said Cash. "It's just a cheap trick."

A sudden, deafening burst of gunfire erupted from Johnson, in the rear, as he fired his weapon on full automatic, the rounds stitching across the roof of the tunnel, triggering a shower of rock. They all instinctively dropped to the ground. For a moment, Cash wondered what the hell had gotten into Johnson—until she saw, as he fell backward, that a small spear had gone right through his neck, from one side to the other. His rifle ceased firing and clattered to the ground as he landed on his back and writhed, silently clutching and scrabbling at the imbedded spear, blood gushing out.

Holder rushed back to his fallen partner and knelt in front of him, firing three-round bursts into every dark hole and crack from which the spear might have come—resulting in more mocking laughter surrounding them. A second spear came flashing out of the darkness, striking off Holder's body armor. He pivoted and fired in the direction it came from.

They had been ambushed in a really tight place. "Holder!" she yelled. "Help me grab Johnson—take his other arm. Colcord, get his weapon and cover us as you lead us out."

Colcord shoved his Beretta back in its holster and grabbed the AR-15, sliding the strap off the body and over his shoulder, holding his smartphone in his left hand.

Cash wrapped her arm around Johnson's shoulder and Holder took the other, and they began dragging him down the tunnel. She could see he was a goner, nobody could survive a wound like that, but no way was she going to leave his body to these monsters if she could help it. Johnson was heavy, weighed down by his body armor and pack.

Now the air was filled with a kind of chanting, like what she'd heard on the tape. It was strange, distorted, resonant.

"Left up ahead," said Colcord.

Dragging the body, she and Holder took the left. Holder held his flashlight in one hand, aiming it behind them, the beam wobbling. Cash saw several flashes of torches among the side tunnels and channels, and she could smell burning grass and moss.

Holder gave a yell and dropped Johnson's arm, lowering his weapon and firing into the darkness behind. He'd been hit with a spear, which flew out of the darkness and struck his shoulder just above the body armor with a loud smacking sound and penetrating right through the clavicle and shoulder blade, coming out the other side.

Colcord fired a short burst in the direction from which the spear had come, and Cash fired several rounds into the darkness behind them. But it was stupid to be shooting into the dark, without even muzzle flashes to aim for.

There was no way Holder could continue pulling Johnson's body with the wound he had just received. Colcord had to navigate and cover them. She alone was left to pull Johnson along, struggling to drag his body, but the man was heavy. She took out her knife and cut off his pack and tried hauling him again, but still it was not going to work. Holder tried to help, grabbing an arm with his other one, took a few steps, and fell to his knees.

"Leave the body," said Colcord. "We gotta keep going."

"No," Holder said, staggering with his hand on the end of the spear sticking from the top of his shoulder, blood pouring down. "You go on. I'm gonna make a stand."

"That's flat-out suicide," said Cash. "Johnson's gone."

Holder tried to stand and managed to get to his feet but was having trouble remaining upright. Blood was pouring out of his shoulder, more than she ever thought possible from a shoulder wound, and she realized the spear, in going through the clavicle, must have struck an artery.

"Press your hand to the wound," said Cash. "I'll support you. Don't pull that thing out."

He followed her instructions, pressing on the wound with the spear sticking out between his fingers. She wrapped her arm around his good shoulder, keeping him steady. "Okay, let's go."

After a hesitation, Holder acquiesced, and they went on, leaving Johnson's body behind. Colcord covered them from the rear, while at the same time looking at his phone and yelling out directions. Cash supported Holder, who was quickly losing blood and soon barely able to stagger. They finally reached the central gallery. The laughter and chanting grew more distant as they moved across the open space and retraced their journey back to the outside.

They emerged into the bright afternoon sunlight, dazzling after the dimness of the mines, Cash gulping down the fresh air. Holder sank to the ground, and she helped ease him down, slipping off his pack. He lay heavily on his back on the ground. "We need to go back in . . . My partner . . . Johnson's body . . ."

"I know," said Cash. "We're gonna call in SWAT teams right now, get them up here ASAP to go back for your partner."

"My partner . . ."

"Don't think about it." Cash opened Holder's pack, pulled out the medic kit, and took out the roll of gauze. She unrolled it, folded it, and pressed it down on the still bleeding wound. Christ, it was hard to believe a shoulder could produce so much blood. Holder began passing in and out of consciousness.

"Sheriff, cover the entrance in case they come out," Cash said as she pulled out her radio and called the lodge, one hand still pressing down on Holder's wound. She got McFaul.

"We have a man down," she said. "He's bleeding. Get a chopper and medic up here—bring blood and saline."

"What the hell happened?"

"We were attacked in the mine. Johnson is up there, dead. We need the immediate deployment of SWAT teams up there to retrieve Johnson's body, sweep the mine, and go after the killers. And I mean *now*."

39

The first chopper arrived fifteen minutes later and went into a hover above them, lowering a rescue basket. Cash and Colcord lifted the now unconscious Holder into it, spear still sticking through his shoulder. The bird hoisted him up and took off.

Not long afterward, two Black Hawk helicopters belonging to Denver PD landed in the meadow below, and a SWAT team poured out, along with EMTs and paramedics.

That was fast, Cash thought. She watched them with her binoculars but did not see McFaul in the mix of people exiting the bird. He wasn't in good shape and wouldn't be able to climb up the ravine anyway, she thought, which still left her in charge.

"I count twelve," said Colcord, looking down. "Well armed."

"I'm going back in with them," said Cash. "You?"

"Damn straight. I need to lead them to Johnson."

The sun was hanging low over the mountains, the valley filling with golden light. A fall chill was settling down. They waited for the SWAT teams to climb up to the mine entrance. The soldiers arrived, led by a young redheaded woman, who gave Cash a crisp salute. "Lieutenant Commander Graves," she said. "Denver PD."

Cash covered up her surprise at seeing a woman SWAT team commander and then upbraided herself. "Agent in Charge Cash. And this is Eagle County Sheriff Colcord. There's a man down back in the mine. We need to get him out now."

Graves organized her people efficiently, and they went in, six soldiers in front with Colcord and Cash, and the rest behind with two medics and a stretcher. Colcord called out directions.

Going back into the mine set her on edge, but she found her fury at the killing of Johnson drove her forward. The men had bright head-lamps that starkly illuminated the tunnels, reaching every hole and crevice. They moved quickly and silently, passing through the series of tunnels that led to the open gallery. As they came out into the large room, Cash could see it for the first time in sharp relief, the irregular space where, apparently, a large ore body had been removed and then turned into a staging area. Derelict mining equipment lay about, as well as rotting piles of rope and timbers. The tunnels were silent, the sounds of laughter and chanting gone.

Colcord directed them to the small opening at the far side, and they entered the labyrinth of tunnels beyond. There was still the faint smell of smoke but no sign of the killers. Colcord continued calling out the directions until they came around a corner where Johnson's body had been. There was nothing there but blood on the rocky floor.

"Bastards," said Colcord darkly, the lights playing on a small pool of blood, with a long trail behind it. "They took his body."

There was a moment of silence. Cash struggled to master her own rage, mingling with a sick feeling of horror at what they might do to the body. She turned to Graves. "We need to sweep these tunnels. We need to run these fuckers down."

"How big is the mine?" Graves asked.

"It's big," said Colcord. "I've got JPEGs of maps on my phone."

"Can you Bluetooth them to the team?"

He did so.

Cash turned to Graves. "We should break the group up into teams to increase coverage."

"Right. Three teams of four. You two go with whichever teams you wish." She turned and issued the orders.

"I'll accompany your team," Cash said.

Graves called up the map on her phone and looked at it while Col-cord explained where they were. "It's not complete," she said. "Where do the tunnels go from this point?"

"The guy who drew this map didn't explore any farther."

"Okay. We'll divide it up into sectors." She proceeded to do so, assigning leaders and navigators to each team and explaining the rules of engagement. "Unfortunately," she said, "we can't be in radio contact. We meet back here without fail at 2000 hours."

The three teams set off, Cash's team taking a tunnel to the left off the gallery. It appeared to be another feeder to the big space and the ore body beyond. They soon hit it, the tunnel branching into many side channels, vertical shafts, and crawl spaces. Where the seams broadened out, columns of rock had been left, with roof-shoring beams that looked rotten. The air became close and clammy, and the ceiling got lower, so much so that they had to stoop as they went along. Cash could almost feel the weight of a billion tons of mountain above her, and it set her on edge. She kept up near the front, next to Graves, scanning the cave floor with her beam, but there were no signs or marks of passage.

Every few minutes, they stopped to listen, but the only sounds they heard were the dripping of water and the occasional creaking of the mountain. As they swept the tunnels, it was all Cash could do not to think of those brutes desecrating Johnson's body. At a certain point, the ceiling dropped farther, until they could not proceed unless they got down on their hands and knees. They crawled forward, the gritty, fractured rock floor digging into Cash's knees. The entire tunnel began to slope upward, getting steeper so that they were half crawling, half climbing—until they abruptly emerged into a large cavity.

Now Cash faintly smelled something burnt drifting in the thick air. She signaled a stop, and they listened intently. Nothing.

They continued on. It was strange, she thought, that nothing seemed to live in the cave—none of the usual spiders or rats. They came to a partial cave-in—not on the map—and had to scramble over loose boulders and rocks, below other rocks still hanging precariously from the ceiling. Beyond, a small stream flowed along the bottom of the tunnel, the wet rocks stained orange, red, and green with metal oxides. The burnt smell grew stronger, acrid and metallic. Cash signaled at Graves, pointing to her nose, and Graves nodded.

Graves stopped, checking the map on her phone. "By my reckoning, we're approaching the edge of the map now, or maybe a little beyond."

The tunnel ended in a vertical shaft, with several chains hanging down, swaying and clinking back and forth in a strange movement of air. There was no way to cross. Graves edged up to it and gingerly shined her light down. She suddenly stepped back, her hand over her mouth, her face expressing shock and disgust.

Cash looked down.

The shaft ended about thirty feet below in a tangle of old iron cables and rotting wood. Among the detritus, Cash could see a horror—a scatter of dismembered limbs, a torso, and a debrided human skull in two pieces, with much of the flesh and hair still on it. Torn pieces of an Erebus security uniform lay scattered around.

Johnson.

"Good god," said Graves.

Cash averted her eyes and backed up, struggling to suppress the sudden nausea that rose in her gorge.

The others came and looked down, issuing quiet expressions of shock and rage.

This was followed by silence.

"We'll need special equipment to retrieve these remains," said Cash. "And a forensics team. For now, I think we should keep going—if you agree, Commander?"

"I do agree. We need to run down the freaks who did this."

But first they would have to cross the gap formed by the shaft. Cash could see there was a ledge, about a foot wide, running along the wall on one side of the pit. She turned and pointed to one of the team, who had a rope coiled up and attached to his pack. "You a rock climber?"

"Yes, ma'am."

"Cross that ledge and set up a fixed rope at either end so the rest can edge across, clipping on to the rope as a safety."

The man immediately went to work. Anchoring the rope at one end on an old beam, he worked his way across and tied it to an iron ring projecting from the rock, which he tested and found sound. He tightened it.

"Okay, let's cross," Cash said. "Cover both directions; this is a point of vulnerability."

They crossed, one at a time, using a harness and carabiner clipped to the fixed rope, and continued on. The tunnel now plunged downward and narrowed vertically, as if following a vein into the mountain, becoming so tight they had to turn sideways in places.

"By my reckoning," said Graves, "we're now definitely off the map."

"At every dividing point from now on," said Cash, "we'll lay down a marker."

But the narrow tunnel did not branch. It ran straight for what seemed like hundreds of yards. Suddenly, Cash saw a flash and gleam in the distance. They stopped and crouched, playing the beam down the long crack—and as they moved their light, the light at the end of the tunnel moved accordingly.

"Something's reflecting," murmured Cash.

They went forward and moments later found themselves in front of a polished, stainless steel door that blocked the tunnel.

Cash was astonished at the mirrored surface of the door, seeing her own dirty, outraged reflection staring back.

"What's this?" Graves asked. "This looks totally new."

"I'm pretty sure this leads to the Erebus labs," said Cash. "Built into the mountain. The Erebus security director said they had blocked some tunnels with steel barriers."

Graves frowned. "What should we do . . . knock?"

Cash shook her head. "Nah. Why warn them? They can't open it anyway. We need to get a warrant—and surprise the hell out of them."

40

Sheriff Colcord took the lead for his search team, navigating using his JPEGs of the mine layout. He was impressed by the Denver PD SWAT team—they were well-trained men and women, not all that different from what he'd experienced in Iraq, where forty percent of the troops he'd commanded were women.

They moved fast and silently through their sector, which was complex and random, as the nineteenth-century miners had followed every vein and seam to the end. Now that it was brightly illuminated, he could see that it was the perfect environment for an ambush, with many holes, stopes, drifts, and risers going every which way. The scent of burning hung in the air, but as they examined the ground, they found no evidence of any recent occupation. Colcord was a hunter and an experienced tracker, and it amazed him how careful they must have been to leave no trace of their passage, when even a few overturned pebbles or a layer of grit or sand could capture the brush from a foot, a skid, or a drag mark.

When they reached the far side of the sector, they turned back and swept the next set of tunnels leading back through the zone, and then back again. As time went on, it began to seem like a fool's errand, all the tunnels empty and silent. The killers were evidently not there. But if they vacated the mine, where did they go? And how did they get out?

Yearwood had said clearly that Jackman connected with the two other mines, Fryingpan and Hesperus. But those two mines had been retrofitted for Erebus's labs, and he'd seen with his own eyes that the security in those labs was tight. He had no doubt the tunnels into the lab area had all been sealed by Erebus.

Something was not right about this. The stolen maps and Maximilian's failure to mention the existence of the Jackman Mine had shaken his confidence in Erebus's cooperation and made him suspicious. But why would they try to hinder the investigation? One of their own security guards had been murdered and his body desecrated. Maximilian and Erebus had every reason to cooperate and in fact *had* cooperated overall. But he still felt uneasy.

They needed to go back into those labs. Not a tour, but a surprise search. Were they engaged in some sort of forbidden research? Making a doomsday virus or some other biological WMD? Or breeding killer saber-toothed cats or genetically altered freaks or monsters? It felt preposterous—the stuff of thrillers. But whatever it was, he felt that Erebus was hiding *something*, maybe even from most of their employees. Gunnerson had implied as much. That something might be in those labs.

The search party came to another intersection of tunnels, and he checked the map on his phone.

"Straight through," he said. "There's a large cavern up ahead."

They moved through the intersection and continued on. The air was particularly dead in this zone, and Colcord found himself breathing harder. He thought of Cash—she was amazingly fit, despite her rather heavy size. Fitter than he was. He vowed to do something about that as soon as this case was over, join a gym or start hiking regularly in the mountains. His thoughts drifted back to her—the more he got to know her, the more he liked and respected her, despite that sharp tongue. He wondered what had happened back in Portland, Maine, that sent her out to Colorado.

The tunnel emerged into the cavern labeled as a stope on Yearwood's map—an area where a large amount of ore had been removed. The blazing lights of the team illuminated the space. In the center stood an ancient ore crusher, used for breaking big rocks into smaller ones, with a huge, rusted flywheel, crusher bed, and a long, operational handle.

Dangling from the handle were two small, neatly woven ornamental balls.

41

By the time Cash and her group came out of the mine and rendez-voused with the others at eight o'clock, the sun had set and the stars were out in a brilliant show. As they were waiting for the last group to exit, Colcord came over.

"We found his mutilated remains," she said. "At the bottom of a shaft."

"I'm very sorry to hear that." He lowered his voice and said, "We found two more ornaments."

"Jesus," she murmured. "You think inside they're the, ah, eyeballs of the victim, like the others?"

"Yes."

"And beyond that," Cash went on, "we ran into a brand-new steel door that, it seems, blocks off a tunnel leading into the labs in the Fry-ingpan Mine."

Colcord stared. "No shit. Did you try to go through it or knock on it?"

"We almost did. But then I thought twice about that. There's some-thing to be said for the element of surprise."

"This just reinforces what I was thinking: we need a no-knock war-rant."

"Really?" said Cash. "You think you could get a judge to sign off on that?"

"I think so. We base the warrant on Johnson's murder. The steel door was just beyond where his body was found—that's proximity. We make it a no-knock so we don't have to warn Erebus ahead of time. Barrow would have a fit and try to quash it. We just go in."

"Hundred percent agreed," said Cash. "But . . . I hate to tell you, McFaul won't go for it. He's always worried about his tender sweet ass and who might try to mow it for him."

This comment was a little strong for Colcord's taste, but he said nothing—and it was true. Colcord was not impressed with McFaul at all. Probably a political appointee.

Cash said suddenly, "Okay, here's what I'm going to do. I'm gonna bypass McFaul. I'm still AIC, and normally, the CBI director doesn't get involved in subpoenas and warrants. We'll take it directly to a judge."

Now the third team came out of the mine entrance, their lights bobbing in the dark as they unloaded their packs. They had found nothing.

It seemed incredible to Cash, and it made her furious, to think that Erebus had known of this mine all along and never said anything. Was it deliberate? Was it possible that Erebus didn't *want* them to find the killers? That all this searching and promises of cooperation were phony and just for show?

Cash turned to Colcord. "Let's go back to the lodge and put in a request for that no-knock. And then we better get some sleep because tomorrow is going to be one hell of a day."

42

When Cash and Colcord arrived back at the lodge, McFaul intercepted her at the elevator from the rooftop heliport. "We need to talk," he said. "In the conference room." He looked at Colcord. "In private."

She followed him across the main lodge floor, wondering what shit McFaul was going to dump on her now. There were still a fair number of guests, taking selfies and watching the evening gathering of beasts at the lake. She had the suspicion that some of them were hanging around not despite the killings but because of them. What an Instagram moment.

They wouldn't be there long, if she had her way. After all this, after Johnson's death, they simply had to shut down the resort.

McFaul held open the door for her. "Take a seat," he said.

She was dead tired, but tried to keep up an alert and energetic appearance.

McFaul took a seat opposite her. "First, I just want to make sure you're all right."

"Absolutely all right, sir," she said. She was determined to keep this as formal as possible.

"Good. Fill me in on what happened up at the mine—everything."

Cash went through it—the attack, the killing of Johnson, finding his body, the search of the mine. She mentioned the steel door, only because he would hear about it anyway, but said nothing about the warrant. After she was finished, there was a long silence from McFaul as he stared at the tabletop, tapping a finger. Then he looked up.

"Agent Cash," he said, "you made a serious error in going into the mine under-armed and underprepared."

This was not altogether a surprise. "Sir, we had two armed guards with us, plus the sheriff and myself were also armed. Going into the mine didn't seem imprudent under the circumstances, and time was of the essence. You yourself have emphasized how badly we need to make progress on the case."

"And how did that work out for you?"

Cash said nothing. The awful thing was that in a way McFaul was right: they got their asses kicked, and a man died.

"I see your point, sir."

"Good."

"It should be noted we made some crucial discoveries and pushed the case forward."

There was a long, thoughtful pause, and then McFaul said, "Under the circumstances, Agent Cash, I feel it is only prudent if I take over the case."

She felt the blood rush to her face.

"We needn't make a big deal out of it. You'll become my lieutenant, so to speak. We'll let Erebus know, quietly, and that's it. No need to make an announcement." He paused. "May I have your agreement to that?"

What could she do?

"Yes, sir."

"And now, I think it's past time to shut down the resort. I've spoken to the governor, and he agrees. We'll make the announcement at the press conference tomorrow morning."

"Press conference?"

"That's right. I'm leading a press conference tomorrow, to present our findings to date. This is a huge story in the press—an international story, in fact—and the public is hungry for information."

Cash felt hot. It was so unfair, and she realized that, now that a major breakthrough had been made on the case, McFaul was stepping in not just to take over the investigation but to make sure he got the glory.

"So the resort is being closed?"

"Of course. And high time it was. I'll expect you at the press conference too. We need a show of force."

What a waste of her time. "When and where?"

"One. At the lodge, main hall."

"Wait. We're gonna let *reporters* in here?" Cash asked.

"Not everyone. We're organizing a pool situation, selected reporters from each sector of the media, that sort of thing."

"But if we let them in, we'll never get them out. And they'll be at risk."

"Not at all. The lodge is like a fortress, and they'll only be here for a few hours. One of your problems, Agent Cash, is that you aren't thinking about the media impact of this case. It was on the front page of *The New York Times* this morning and also on all the morning shows. *Cannibalism*—that's really drawn people's attention." His voice surged with enthusiasm. "We have a responsibility to provide information to the public in a timely manner."

"How are you going to stop the press from wandering away from the lodge?"

"I'm tired of arguing with you, Agent Cash. I'm in charge now, and you are verging on insubordination. Now tomorrow morning, I want you to be in charge of the evacuation of the resort, making sure there's no panic, that everyone leaves in an orderly and safe manner."

Crowd control. What a bunch of bullshit. They should have closed the resort days ago, but it would be useless to remind him she had recommended it multiple times. "Does Barrow know about shutting the resort?"

"Oh yes. We warned him about it ahead of time. He complained, but there's little he could do, now that the governor finally heeded my plea to order it closed. A small number of staff will have to remain to keep things running, including a contingent of security guards."

"How about calling in the National Guard?"

"No. That's a step too far. We've got a top-notch SWAT team up here from Denver PD—that's plenty."

"Have the guests been told?"

"They will be informed tonight. Everyone's getting a notice under the door. They'll have to be gone by eleven tomorrow morning." He placed his hands on his knees and looked at her. "Now, are we clear?"

"Yes, sir," she said.

"You need to get some sleep, Agent Cash."

It was true, she felt exhausted. She rose and he extended his hand, and she had no choice but to take it.

The main lodge room still had a number of guests hanging around and drinking, despite the late hour. She texted to see if Colcord was still around, and he quickly appeared, looking as haggard as she did.

"What was that all about?" he asked.

"McFaul took over the investigation."

Colcord said, "I'm sorry. So unfair."

She shook her head. "We've got a warrant to obtain. Are you going to help me serve it?"

"Hell yes, but . . . are you going to get fired for doing this?"

She thought about that. It all depended on what they found. If nothing, she would almost certainly be cashiered. But if they uncovered significant evidence or a cover-up . . . and especially if she let McFaul take credit . . . She reminded herself that her first loyalty was to apprehending the killers. Everything else, even her career, was secondary.

She glanced at the clock. Eleven p.m. "We need to get it to a judge tonight, damn it, and look at the time. I know a couple of judges in Denver, but I don't have their home phone numbers. To reach them this late, I'd have to go through channels—meaning McFaul."

Colcord hesitated. "I know the Eagle County Fifth Judicial chief judge. Would that help?"

"Are you kidding me? You have his home number?"

"Sure."

"Will he be pissed?"

"Probably. But this is a big case, and he'll understand." He held up his phone. "Last chance to back out. Gonna make the call."

"Do it. And . . . thanks."

43

They were reaching the end of another midnight lab session, and Romanski had lined up the remains of the two hikers on a long lab table, each bone and fragment with its own tag. It had so far been impossible to identify which bones belonged to which individual, except for the major bones of the pelvis, the skulls, femurs, and a few others. The rest would have to wait for DNA sequencing, which would take some time.

Despite not knowing exactly which bones belonged to whom, what had happened couldn't be clearer. The forensic literature on cannibalism was extensive, and Romanski was familiar with it. It had been developed not by forensic pathologists but by physical archaeologists and paleoanthropologists who had discovered grim assemblages of human bones at prehistoric archaeological sites. The bones were strewn about or heaped up willy-nilly, broken and burnt. They did not look like burials or ritual displays—they resembled food trash. But no one had dared make the leap until a physical anthropologist in Arizona named Christy Turner published a series of papers and a book claiming that the prehistoric American Southwest had gone through a frenzy of cannibalism during the 1100s and 1200s. Turner had uncovered dozens of charnel deposits of individuals who, careful examination showed, had been butchered, cooked, and eaten. He and other anthropologists had developed a set of six criteria for determining if a set of human remains had been cannibalized or not. Since that time, archaeologists all over the world had established the unsettling fact that cannibalism was widespread in the human record and extended way back. People had been killing and eating people for a hundred thousand years or more. Romanski had found the work to be fascinating, if disturbing, but this was the first time he had actually been able to directly study cannibalized human remains.

He had spent most of the evening examining the bones of the two hikers, while Reno had carefully examined and dissected the "ornaments," which, as they feared, had contained the eyeballs of the murdered guard.

Now Reno joined him at contemplating the arrangement of bones. "You done?" he asked.

"For the first round."

"What you got?"

"All six classic signs of cannibalism," said Romanski. "First, you can see cut marks on the joints, where the limbs were chopped, severed, and separated. Second, there are long scrape marks down the bones, indicating the flesh was stripped off with knives. The marrow channels show scraping as well. Third, the areas of cancellous bone tissue were carved or pounded to extract the fat. Fourth, there are anvil marks on the long bones, indicating they were placed on a rock and broken with the blow of another stone to get at the marrow inside."

He turned to the skulls. "Sign five: the skulls were placed upside down into the fire to roast the brain inside the cranium—and then broken open. You can see here and here the burn marks and anvil marks, along with scraping marks inside as the brain was scooped out. And then there's the final proof of cannibalism, the sixth tell: pot polish."

"What's that?" Reno asked.

"You see how all the long bones have been broken into segments no longer than eight inches? That's the diameter of the pot they used. The bones were boiled to make bone broth, and if you examine the broken ends of the bone, you'll see they are microscopically polished by turning round and round in the boiling water, the ends brushing the sides of the pot."

"Pretty awful," said Reno. "At least they didn't eat the eyeballs."

"Is that supposed to be a joke?"

"No, no," said Reno hastily. "It's just an observation."

"The point is," Romanski said, "the bodies were processed to extract every gram of nourishment. That's a characteristic of cannibalism in prehistoric times, when food was scarce. Deer and other food animals were similarly processed."

Romanski drew a sheet over the remains. "Did you find anything unusual in your dissection of the, ah, ornaments?"

"They're simple in construction," said Reno. "Sort of a basket woven around the eyeball, using pine needles, grass, and some willow twigs. Very well crafted, though. I mean, whoever did this had some prior experience weaving something." He hesitated. "I was wondering what the symbolism of it was—as in, *We're keeping an eye on you*?"

Romanski shook his head. "Could be." He lapsed into silence and then decided to share a thought he had had. "In his book on prehistoric cannibalism in the Southwest, Christy Turner divided cannibalism into different types."

"Different types? Like what?"

"First, there's survival cannibalism. That's when people who are starving eat other people as a last resort—like the Donner Party in California, where they had to eat their dead companions and relatives to keep from starving to death."

"Ew."

"Then there's ritual cannibalism. This is where a person will be consumed after death as part of a funerary rite. The Fore of New Guinea ate the brains of deceased loved ones to incorporate their essence back into the living."

"Double ew."

"They got a disease from it, called *kuru*, a prion disease, which almost wiped them out. And then there's sacrificial cannibalism, in which people are offered up to the gods as a sacrifice and their bodies eaten. That was the kind of cannibalism practiced by the Aztecs of Mexico.

"But Turner described a fourth kind of cannibalism, and that's what he said occurred in the American Southwest. That's cannibalism as a tool of terror. If some really evil dudes want to show everyone how badass they are, what better way than to kill your enemies and then cook and eat them and leave the bones for all to see? He theorized that the outbreak of cannibalism in the Southwest was caused by a militant group who invaded from the south and used cannibalism to terrify and subjugate the local people."

"Jesus."

"Which makes me wonder . . . what kind of cannibalism are the Erebus killers engaging in? Are they eating people because they're starving? No. Is it ritual cannibalism? No. Did they sacrifice these people to the gods? No. *They're eating people because they want to terrify.*"

"To what end?" asked Reno.

"I'm not sure. They may be crazy, but they're also clever. They're strategic. They plan ahead. They want to terrify, yes, but why? Because they have some goal in mind. There's a method to their madness."

"A goal? Like what?"

Romanski shook his head again. "I wish to hell I knew."

44

Cash woke up at six, not having had enough sleep but unable to sleep longer. Her mind was going too fast. She checked her phone: the warrant hadn't come through. But of course it wouldn't have at that early hour—after writing it up, the judge would have to put through the paperwork and register it, and that couldn't happen until court staff came in to work in the morning. She'd be lucky to get the warrant by noon.

She threw off the covers, took a long shower, dressed, fired up the espresso machine, and tossed down three doubles. She needed to get some real food, but then she saw they'd stocked the bar fridge. Real food would take too long. She ate a packet of macadamia nuts, a can of Pringles, and two packets of Reese's Pieces. The fruit basket had also been filled, and she ate a banana and an apple, trying to make herself feel better about her terrible food choices.

Six thirty. She texted Colcord and got an immediate reply. He hadn't heard from the judge either.

And now it was time for her to babysit the guests as they left. She left her room and went down to the main hall of the lodge. Even at that early hour, it was a scene of controlled chaos, with guests rushing this way and that, bellhops wheeling around carts piled with luggage, and valets bringing up cars from the garage.

She saw Maximilian to one side, speaking into his radio.

Okay, Maximilian, here we go. She walked over to him. He finished his call. "Good morning, Agent Cash."

She wondered if he knew she'd been demoted. Probably, since Mc-Faul was so free with information that should remain confidential.

"You know, of course, all about what happened up at the Jackman Mine yesterday."

"I do," Maximilian said, "and I'm extremely upset to hear about the death of our security employee Johnson. That was a tragedy, and Erebus is deeply concerned. On the other hand, I commend you on the discoveries you made."

She let him talk for a while, and when he fell silent, she continued looking at him steadily.

He faltered after a long moment. "Is there . . . a problem?"

"Yeah. A *big* problem. If you had told us about the existence of the Jackman Mine, we could've searched it five days ago. Maybe Johnson would still be alive, the perps caught, the case solved."

He returned her look with a cool one of his own. "I firmly believed that twelve years ago we completely and totally closed off that mine, every shaft and entrance. We even blocked some of the interior tunnels with steel. In retrospect, yes, I wish I'd mentioned it, but I didn't, because it simply didn't seem relevant." He looked at her intently. "Frankly, we blew it."

She continued staring at him, saying nothing.

"I see you're not happy with my answer," he said. "I don't blame you, and I apologize. But I'm not sure searching the mine would have made much difference. They weren't camped in the mine or living there."

Cash continued looking at him. Christ, he was so sincere and convincing. But she wasn't convinced. They were hiding something.

"You said something about steel doors?"

"Right. The Jackman Mine had tunnels that connected with the Fryingpan and Hesperus. When we built our labs, we blocked those tunnels with steel plates. They're not doors, they're solid steel."

She let the uncomfortable silence build again.

"Agent Cash, I don't blame you for being suspicious. I would be too. But we want to catch these bloody madmen as much as you. They killed one of *my men*. Why would we want to hinder the investigation?"

Why indeed? she thought.

45

Slavomir Doyle was seriously pissed and trying hard to control it. The contract he'd negotiated with his star, Brock Ballou, required the actor to work only two hours a day—for which he was paid twenty million dollars and five gross points. It was outrageous, but there had been no other way to land the son of a bitch for his movie, and the two-hour clause had added weeks to the shooting schedule. And now, after all this, he had received notice the night before that the valley had to be evacuated by eleven, the movie set shut down—everyone had to pack up and leave. This, after paying ninety-five thousand dollars a day, three million dollars total—to be given twelve hours' notice? Who was going to reimburse him for continuing to pay the entire crew, all the rental equipment, and everything else—while they sat around on their asses waiting for the killers to be caught? The worst of it was that Ballou had a penalty clause in his contract that called for big payments to him if shooting ran over schedule, which now it would.

On top of that, today, of all days, was when his train was set to blow.

He looked at his watch. Nine a.m. Barrow should be arriving at any moment with that cop, Cash, and the sheriff. Brock Ballou was in his damn honey wagon, and for once—for *once*—the jackass had promised to be cooperative. Even he saw what was needed and was willing to do it, but mostly it was because Ballou wanted to meet the billionaire Maitland Barrow, a bigger celebrity than even himself.

He saw Barrow's big red Karlmann King SUV appear where the road came out of the trees. It sped along to the parking and base camp area just outside the movie town. Now it was time for Ballou to strut his stuff, Doyle thought. He texted Ballou and told him Barrow had arrived, although no doubt the actor had noticed the giant SUV.

The driver jumped out and opened the door for the billionaire, who stepped out, followed by another man, a little dumpy, wearing an ill-fitting blue suit. Who was that? Another cop? Here was someone new.

The door of Ballou's honey wagon opened, and the star came out, dressed in a nineteenth-century white linen Western suit with a white cowboy hat, string tie, and snakeskin boots. For once, Doyle was grateful for his sartorial excess.

"Mr. Barrow," said Doyle, his hand outstretched, "welcome!"

Barrow took his hand and gave it a shake. "And you are—?"

"Wallace McFaul, director, Colorado Bureau of Investigation."

A bigger cop. "And I'd like to introduce you to our star," continued Doyle, "Brock Ballou."

Ballou stepped forward with a dazzling smile and gave Barrow's hand a good manly shake. "So pleased to meet you, Mr. Barrow," he said. "I can't tell you how much I've enjoyed working in your gorgeous valley. What a special place. Thank you for making it available to us."

Barrow chuckled. "We're delighted to have you, Mr. Ballou."

"Please, call me Brock."

"Brock. Perfectly delighted to host your movie here. I only wish we hadn't run into this little difficulty."

"Not at all," said Doyle, turning the conversation smoothly in the direction he wanted to take it. "We're so far from where the incident occurred—miles away and far up the valley—that it hasn't affected us at all. At least, not until now . . ."

He let that sentence die away.

"I'm truly sorry," said Barrow, "that we're forced to temporarily close down the set. The investigation, I'm told, is making excellent progress now that Mr. McFaul has arrived, and it might only be for a few days."

"Thank you for your concern. That's actually the reason I invited you down here—to make a little appeal in that regard." Doyle went on quickly, "We have a problem. You see, Mr. Barrow, we were just about to shoot a crucial scene—today—a scene involving some major pyro-technics. No doubt you've seen our beautiful narrow-gauge train over yonder." He pointed beyond the town to the train. "It's set to be blown up in one of the most spectacular pyrotechnical displays you will see in any film ever, I promise you. The problem is, it's already wired to blow, with explosives in place. We can't walk away leaving it like that. We either have to shoot the scene of it blowing up, or we have to dismantle the entire pyrotechnical setup—which is a delicate and dangerous operation—and it simply can't be done by the eleven o'clock deadline."

Barrow said, "I understand the problem. It wasn't my idea to shut down Erebus in the first place." He glanced at McFaul.

Ballou now spoke, his legendary plangent voice cutting into the conversation. "Mr. Barrow, the heart of the film is when the gang of outlaws blows up the train. It's going to be spectacular. I believe it could win an Academy Award for best visual effects. Nowadays, everything is CGI, but this is going to be real. Nothing beats good old-fashioned pyrotechnics. All we ask, Mr. Barrow, is to be given enough time to shoot the scene." Ballou finished up the appeal with a big smile.

"How much time?"

"Just six or seven hours," said Doyle. "We'll shoot the scene at two this afternoon, wrap at five, and then we can shut down the set and evacuate the entire film crew. I understand you're worried about risk, but we're miles down the valley from where the killings took place. And look at how many we are. We have our own security. No one's going to come after us."

"I'm all for it," said Barrow. He turned to McFaul. "What do you say, Mr. McFaul?"

McFaul was sweating. "Well, the order to evacuate nonessential personnel came from the governor. I can't contravene that."

"Of course," said Doyle, "but I think the argument could be made that these *are* essential personnel. At least until the pyrotechnics scene has been done. We can't leave it like this: it's way too dangerous."

"I strongly agree with Mr. Doyle," said Barrow.

McFaul nodded. "I understand." There was a silence as the cop furrowed his brow. "Well, I think, under the circumstances, we'll give you those extra hours."

After McFaul and Barrow had left in the Karlmann King, Doyle turned to Ballou. "Thank you, Brock. You're a true gentleman, and you handled that very well."

Ballou looked at him coolly. "You owe me, Slavomir. You *owe* me." And he walked back off to his trailer.

What an asshole, Doyle thought as he watched him go. But he was an asshole who could perform when needed. He picked up his radio and called his pyrotechnician. "Get ready to rock and roll, Jack. We've got the rest of the day."

46

The main hall of the lodge was now quiet and almost empty. The valley had been evacuated smoothly, with all guests and nonessential personnel leaving by eleven. But the calm, Cash thought grimly, was not going to remain so for long: workers were busy preparing for the one o'clock press conference in the hall of the main lodge for the "select" group of media. As workers began setting up a podium with multiple mics and cables and plug-in power units going every which way, she began to wonder just how "select" this group might be.

She told herself it wasn't something she had to worry about. This was McFaul's deal. Even though she had to be there, she knew McFaul would do most of the talking and her role would be minimized. So much the better—she had bigger fish to fry.

The warrant hit Cash's phone at eleven thirty, arriving as an email attachment. She texted Colcord and met him in the conference room.

"We got it," she said.

"Good."

She printed it out and laid it on the table. The judge in Eagle had come through big-time: it was the no-knock warrant they sought, and it was broadly worded, allowing them to search anywhere in the laboratory complex they deemed appropriate for evidence connected to the homicide of Johnson.

"So," said Colcord. "Now we have to figure out how we're going to serve it. At the main door?"

"No," said Cash. "If we walk in there, even with a no-knock, we'll get the same treatment we did last time: *cooperation*." She made air quotes with her fingers. "They'll let us look around everywhere, but we'll get nowhere because what's hidden stays hidden. This time, we go in the back door."

"You mean, the steel door from the Jackman Mine? How are we going to get through that? Knock and say, 'Avon calling'?"

"We torch it open."

Colcord stared at her. "How in the world are we going to do that?"

At this, Cash gave him a big grin. "My right-hand guy, Detective Romanski, is a wizard with an acetylene torch. One of his hobbies is cutting and welding junk to make sculptures. We take him and his torch."

"Does he know about this?"

"Not yet. But he's authorized to go with a warrant party and often does. He's been in the mine and knows all about it, he's part of the investigation, and we've got a legal warrant. I'm still the nominal head of the investigation. So what we're doing is strictly legal in every sense."

"*Will* he do it?"

"As the director of Forensic Services, he's technically still responsible to me since I am the agent in charge. But he's a good guy—he'll do it because he'll realize it's important for the investigation. And it's the kind of thing that'll capture his interest. I know him—as soon as he hears about that steel plate, he's gonna want to see what's behind it."

Colcord let out a big sigh. "Agent Cash, why don't we just take this whole idea to your boss, lay it out for him, and do it that way? This guerrilla operation makes me nervous."

"Because he'll put the kibosh on it. You know he will. He's too chummy with Erebus already—sharing with them details of the investigation, making sure they're informed of what we're doing. He's way too impressed with Barrow. Trust me, there's no way he's gonna agree to this, and besides, he'll be rip-shit when he finds I went behind his back to get a warrant. The only way we're going to get through that door is to do it ourselves, on the q.t."

"We're going to need security going into the mine."

"We'll enlist some Denver PD SWAT guys to go with us. But I'm pretty sure the mine's been abandoned. Those crazies are long gone."

She paused, looking at Colcord's face creased with doubt. "Are you in? Can I call Romanski?"

He pursed his lips, took off his hat, ran his hand over his balding head, and fitted the hat back on. Then he grinned. "I'm in."

She checked her watch. "And now, Sheriff, it's time for the bullshit news conference. You ready?"

"Hell yeah, I'm all for a bullshit news conference. I've got a reelection coming up."

She shook her head sadly. "What is the world coming to?"

47

McFaul had choreographed everything. He was good at that, Cash thought. He'd arranged law enforcement personnel in a standing semicircle at the head of the room, flanking him on both sides of the podium, all in uniform with their hands clasped in front. It was impressive, reassuring, and a colossal waste of time.

It was ten minutes to one, and McFaul was still fussing with the way people were lined up, where their hands were, whether they were straight-backed and had wiped any inappropriate smiles from their faces. There was the sheriff on one side of her, his deputy next to him, and two other sheriff's office undersheriffs. Cash was to his right, with Commander Graves and several uniformed Denver PD guys flanking her. McFaul was like a damn wedding photographer, adjusting people's positions and making sure their heads were upright and turned the correct way.

"We want to show a solid wall of confidence and poise," he said. "This is what we need to project to the public. This isn't just about image—it's about *reassurance*."

He had even suggested including Maximilian in the lineup, but the security director had demurred, saying Erebus security staff needed to stay in the background. It was Cash's distinct impression that Erebus did not want to take part in the news conference at all and that both Maximilian and Barrow were unhappy at the whole spectacle. Barrow, in fact, had disappeared.

Then, when all was ready, the media pool was let in like a bunch of dogs released into a run. First came the news television crews wielding cameras and boom mics, jostling and pushing each other, with their anchors in front. That was followed by the rest of the media—radio, newspapers, online news outlets, and bloggers loaded down with equipment. There were no chairs—this was standing room only—and there was quite a bit of noise and raised voices as everyone jockeyed for position. Cash was astonished; this was not the select pool McFaul had described—this was forty or more people.

When the hubbub had settled down to a murmur, McFaul stepped up to the podium. A hush fell, and he looked around the room, his face a mask of gravitas, and delivered a statement in a classic police monotone, all in the passive voice. It was one of those jargony speeches, full of the kind of phraseology you hear on television, about *perpetrators* and *persons of interest*, *ingresses* and *egresses*, and such. But it conveyed, quite magnificently, the impression that the case had stalled until he arrived—and then the breakthroughs came thick and fast. They had discovered the opening to the mine; they had entered at great risk; an officer had bravely sacrificed his life; they had found the killers' lair; and they were now hot on their trail. No mention was made of the eyeball ornaments—that was one detail they had managed to keep secret, thank God—but the cannibalism aspect of the case had gotten out, and McFaul addressed that with expressions of outrage, condemnation, and promises to bring the monsters to justice. Cash was praised just faintly enough to throw shade on her efforts, but Sheriff Colcord and the Denver PD were applauded, as was Erebus for its "exceptional cooperation."

The electricity in the room was intense. The press was hanging on every word. Cash had been so focused on the investigation and so isolated in the valley that she hadn't quite grokked just how huge this story was in the outside world. As soon as McFaul concluded his statement, it was as if the entire room raised its collective hand with a frantic roar, trying to attract McFaul's attention.

McFaul was just eating it up. He pointed to a famous anchor in front. "Ms. Ross, of CNN?"

"Do you have any idea who these killers might be?" she asked as boom mics swung around.

"We have reason to believe we're dealing with a cult—an anarchistic, anti-capitalist, radical environmental group that opposes the scientific work of Erebus and are intent on driving them from the valley. Unfortunately, it appears families and even some younger children might be involved—which adds even more urgency to solving this case."

More shouting. He pointed to another.

"Have you any ransom notes or demands?"

"No. We've received taunting videos and cryptic messages of sorts, but nothing that makes any sense or presents any demands."

"What kind of videos? Can we see them?"

"They're strictly confidential for now."

"Do you have any theories as to why these cultists are cannibalizing their victims?"

"We believe it is to send a message of complete hatred and rejection of society. They are establishing that they are entirely outside of all societal and cultural norms."

"You mentioned cryptic messages. Can you be more specific?"

He paused. "They left for us six Monopoly tokens, wrapped in grass, which we've interpreted as a possible anti-capitalist gesture."

This was new, and it generated more shouting.

"What about DNA? Do you have any DNA of the killers?"

"Our Forensic Services Division has collected a great deal of DNA, which is being analyzed. The DNA is mixed and contaminated, and it's been a tough problem to sort it out—we're still working on that and will have results shortly."

"Why weren't the mines searched right away? Why did it take five days?"

Now they were getting down to the nitty-gritty, thought Cash. She was damned glad she didn't have to answer that question.

"We weren't aware of the Jackman Mine's existence until yesterday. It was believed by Erebus that the mine had been thoroughly sealed a decade ago."

"Where did the killers go? Where do you think they are now?"

"We're searching the entire valley, quadrant by quadrant, on foot, with dogs and infrared drones. Trust me, we're going to find them."

"Why did it take so long to close the resort?"

"It was initially decided that it wasn't necessary, but when I arrived, I promptly reversed that decision and persuaded the governor to agree. Only the governor had the power to do that."

The questions went on and on, until it became clear they were never going to end as long as the press conference remained open. Finally, McFaul called out, "One final question. Ms. Dixon, KOAT?"

"Agent McFaul, as head of the investigation, what would you say to the family of the guard who was murdered and then, ah, cannibalized by these killers?"

Cash could see McFaul was taken aback by the question. He spent an uncomfortable moment with his face furrowed in thought. "I would say this: I extend my sincerest and most heartfelt condolences. Your son was a hero who died in service. Second: We're going to bring these monsters to justice. You have my word on that. They *will* be brought to justice, and I can promise you the law will come down on their vile heads like the full weight of the Rocky Mountains."

It wasn't the happiest of metaphors, Cash thought, but it was effective, and she had no doubt it would be the lead on the national news across the country.

The press conference began breaking up. The press had been told they could remain in the lodge, asking questions and doing their thing, until a four p.m. deadline, when they were required to be gone.

She exchanged a glance with Colcord. They had a warrant to execute.

48

Romanski had gotten the call from Cash that morning, and he was intrigued. While collecting evidence the night before, he'd also seen the steel plate in the back of the mine and had dusted it for prints, finding quite a few, which they were running through the databases. Cash's idea of using a no-knock warrant to cut through it appealed strongly to his sense of drama and curiosity. Romanski had never yet seen a blocked door he didn't want to open, he told himself, and this one was more intriguing than most. Of course, it might lead into a boring lab full of test tubes and microscopes.

At the same time, he was apprehensive about the scheme. Cash had explained at length how cutting through the plate and executing the search warrant was by the book in every way: they had a legal warrant, she was still officially the agent in charge, and, as lead investigator, she could tell Romanski what to do. McFaul in his usual weasely way hadn't officially and formally taken over the case. It was typical of the CBI director, Romanski thought, to work both sides, hedging his bets—hoping to take credit if the case were swiftly resolved, but ready to pass the buck if it went south. Cash had promised to have his back—or, as she'd put it in her usual blunt way, *They sure as hell aren't going to mow your ass as long as I'm around.*

The problem was, she might not be around. Cash could get fired for this stunt. That, Romanski thought, would be a damn shame, as she was maybe the best agent they had. But he agreed to it, eyes wide open.

They'd worked up a cover story that, while not exactly a lie, wasn't the entire truth. He had put in a request to do one final round of evidence collection at the mine, which included the ore-cart handle from which the eyeballs had been hung. That would require an oxyacetylene torch to cut off the handle since they couldn't lug the whole thing out. They would need a chopper ride to and from the mine entrance and two Denver PD SWAT team people as security.

All these thoughts were passing through his mind as he and Reno drove the forensics van past the traffic jam of press outside the valley and up through the Mammoth Gates of the resort. They parked in the underground garage, and he took out the portable oxyacetylene setup he used in his studio. It consisted of two small tanks—oxygen and acetylene—sitting on a utility cart with regulators and brass torch assembly. It was cleverly designed to be quickly turned into a backpack with the addition of shoulder straps, and it weighed only twenty-five pounds. He had brought along Reno with the standard forensic evidence collecting kit.

They took the elevator to the main floor, and the doors opened. Romanski could see that the press conference had just broken up, and media people were wandering around like a bunch of hungry rats, poking their noses everywhere, shooting video, and trying to snag interviews.

Romanski turned to Reno and said in a low voice, "Want some advice? Tuck your ID lanyard away."

Reno slid his inside his shirt. "Who decided to let the press in here?"

"You know who," said Romanski as he wheeled the oxyacetylene cart through the crowd. The press paid them no attention—just two working stiffs.

"They're like ants, and they're gonna be everywhere," said Reno. "And they'll never get 'em out."

"Not our problem."

They passed by the giant glass windows and had a glimpse of a woolly mammoth family wading in the water, squirting themselves. A cluster of news crews milled around, shooting footage. Romanski wondered how long it would be before some intrepid reporter ventured outside and got stepped on and squashed. That would be fun to see.

"Thank God you're here," said Cash, detaching herself from a swarm of press and coming over with Colcord. A gaggle of press followed them, waving their microphones, calling out questions. "Let's get the hell out. We've got a chopper waiting on the roof."

They got on the elevator. A burly cameraman tried to push his way in to ride with them. Colcord placed his hands on the man's shoulders and gave him, to his great surprise, the bum's rush back out.

"What the hell?" the man cried as Colcord ducked back in, the door shutting in the man's face.

"That's one way of dealing with the press," said Cash approvingly.

The elevator took them to the roof. The CBI's A-Star was waiting for them, warming up, rotors turning.

Romanski and Reno loaded the chopper with their gear and climbed in, Cash and Colcord following, tossing their packs in and climbing after.

Cash put on a headset and spoke to the pilot over the channel, Romanski and everyone hearing the conversation.

"Where's our Denver PD detail?" she asked. "We're supposed to have two guys up here."

"Don't know anything about that, Agent Cash. Sorry."

"Call McFaul on channel 16 for me, please," she asked.

The pilot made the radio call, and a moment later, McFaul's voice came on her headset. "What is it?"

"Sir? We're at the helipad about to take off, but we're supposed to have two DPDs here as escorts."

"Look, I'm up to my eyeballs with the press, and we just don't have the personnel right now. The mine was swept clean, and it's been sealed and guarded since—you're not gonna have a problem with security. Go in, get the evidence, and come back out."

There was a silence and then she said, "No escort into the mine?"

"You heard me. We're shorthanded." He disconnected.

She shook her head at Romanski. "Okay, pilot, let's go."

The bird took off from the roof and rose vertically before heading northward. As the lodge dwindled beneath them, Romanski thought he could see some figures outside, down by the lake—one with a camera—trying to get a closer shot of the mammoths.

49

What a glorious afternoon for a career-ending misadventure, Cash thought sourly as the helicopter thudded up the valley. She wondered why she had thought this was a good idea. She had been having second thoughts about it ever since the warrant had come through. This was what had gotten her into trouble back in Portland: caring too much about a case and not enough about respecting the chain of command. Even if they found something, McFaul might never forgive her for going around him. And if this turned out to be just a wild-goose chase, it would certainly be the end of her career at the CBI.

The other question was . . . what might they find? It was hard to find something if you didn't know what you were looking for. Cash had racked her brains trying to think of what Erebus might be up to or what illegal activities they might be conducting in their labs, and she couldn't come up with a theory that made sense. Brewing drugs? Breeding saber-toothed cats? Genetically engineering monsters? It all seemed so unlikely and far-fetched. She might find herself staring some illegal activity in the face and not even be able to recognize it. Her background in biology was nonexistent. If Erebus was up to its neck in some nefarious biological plot, how would she even know? She didn't know the first thing about genetic engineering. She could be looking at a lab that was concocting a doomsday virus that would wipe out the human race and not have a clue. And why would a billionaire like Maitland Barrow risk his fortune, his freedom, and his expensive resort by getting mixed up in something criminal? She'd seen little evidence of a cover-up, beyond Maximilian's failure to mention the existence of the Jackman Mine.

Maybe this was a wild-goose chase, after all.

On top of that, going back into the mine after the horrors of the previous day did not exactly appeal to her. She had always been susceptible to claustrophobia, something she had discovered as a child playing hide-and-seek—she always lost because she wouldn't go into tight spaces. And that fear had been exploited by her older brother, who one day thought it would be funny to tell her there was an antique doll in the attic crawl space and then lock her in for half an hour.

On the other hand, the mine, she reassured herself, was no longer dangerous. People had been coming and going all the previous night, collecting evidence, taking photos, and mapping. The mine entrance had been sealed up with a locked gate, guarded by two DPD SWAT team members. She would enlist one of them to come along.

With these thoughts in mind, she took out her Baby Glock and ejected the magazine, checking to make sure it was full, although she knew perfectly well it was. She resisted the impulse to rack one in the chamber, and then she slid the gun back in its holster. As she did so, she felt the stiff envelope containing the warrant in her inside pocket.

The helicopter slowed and turned. Through the glass windows, she saw the landing zone come into view, a high mountain meadow tucked among the rocky slopes. As the chopper came into a hover and descended, she spied the opening to the Jackman Mine. A moment later, the helicopter touched down with a gentle bump onto the grass. Cash hopped out first, followed by Colcord and Romanski, then Reno. They cleared the LZ, and the chopper rose once again into the blue sky and vanished over the ridges, the thwapping of its rotors fading into silence.

For a moment, she stood there, looking up the mountain ridge. The air smelled of crushed grass. The meadow looked out over the valley, and she spied, far below, a huge prehistoric animal—she wasn't sure what—moving slowly across a stream.

"Well, gentlemen," she said, taking a deep breath in the thin air. "Are we ready for this?"

Colcord gave her a grin of encouragement. "You bet."

Reno gave a thumbs-up.

Romanski nodded. He worked with the oxyacetylene torch kit, turning the cart into a case with straps that he could carry on his back. He lifted it up and shrugged into it. "All ready."

They hiked across the meadow and started up the scree slope leading to the mine entrance. After a brief but intense climb, they arrived. Two SWAT team members were standing guard at the entrance, a man and a woman, carrying AR-15s. The opening to the mine had been blocked with newly fitted heavy steel bars, into which a steel padlocked gate was set.

They came to attention when Cash and her group arrived.

"I'm Agent in Charge Cash, CBI." She tried to sound friendly but with an authoritative note. "How are you doing?"

The woman introduced herself as Specialist Watkins and the man as Officer Hadid. She was tall and willowy, with a tight Afro, and he was massively pumped up, with a dark five o'clock shadow.

"This is Detective Romanski," Cash went on, "CBI Forensic Services, and Technician Reno, evidence specialist."

She looked over Watkins and Hadid appraisingly. They were both armed with assault rifles, and they looked like they knew what they were doing. "We're here to collect evidence in the mine and"—she hesitated—"we'll be executing a search warrant. Which one of you would like to accompany us?"

They both volunteered.

"Okay. How about you, Hadid?" Cash wasn't a sexist, she told herself, but he was bigger and beefier, and that reassured her.

"Yes, ma'am," Hadid said. "I have to check in with my superior officer."

"You do that."

He made the call on his radio, murmuring into it for a few minutes, then re-hooked it on his belt. "I'm sorry, ma'am, but the orders are that we're to stay here and guard the entrance while you go in."

Cash looked at him steadily. "Whose orders?"

"My superior officer, Lieutenant Commander Graves."

Cash got on her radio and called in to the DPD frequency. After a few moments, she was put through to Graves.

"Commander, this is Agent Cash," she said. "We're at the entrance to the Jackman Mine, and we'd like to borrow one of your soldiers stationed here to go in and, ah, collect evidence. I hear there's a problem with that."

"I'm sorry, Agent Cash," Graves said, "but Director McFaul issued orders that the soldiers were to remain on guard outside."

"I see. Thank you, Commander."

She hung up and called McFaul. He got on the line right away, his voice high and irritated. "Cash, if this is about borrowing DPD officers, I already told you the answer is no. You've got a simple assignment here: go in, grab that evidence Romanski wants, and come out. There're no bad guys in the Jackman Mine—it's been thoroughly cleared. You don't need an escort. Is that understood?"

Cash swallowed. "Yes, sir."

"Thank you." He disconnected.

Cash turned to the soldiers. "Thanks, anyway," she said, her voice tight. "Let's go."

Hadid unlocked the padlock and opened the gate, and they went through. Cash turned to him. "You're gonna be here for sure when we need to come out—right?"

"Yes, ma'am," he said. "But we're under orders to keep the door locked."

She thought for a moment, staring at the padlock. It could be accessed through the bars. "How many keys do you have to that padlock?"

"We each have one."

"Give me one. Just in case. We don't want to get locked in."

He hesitated and began to reach for his radio.

"No, Officer Hadid. Don't call. Just give me the damn key."

Hadid hesitated again, his face clouded with doubt, but Watkins reached in her breast pocket and pulled out a key, handing it to Cash. "Here, take mine."

"Thank you, Specialist Watkins."

Cash thought she should have been dealing with Watkins all along, instead of the pumped-up guy. She turned to Hadid. "You know what? Here's a secret: not every little thing has to be checked with the CO."

Hadid's face continued to look doubtful.

The door was shut behind them with a clang and the padlock re-locked. Colcord pulled out his phone to navigate, and they took out their flashlights and proceeded down the long tunnel into the mine.

50

With meticulous care, Doyle had arranged the DP, assistant directors, camera operators, line producer, and drone pilots in carefully choreographed positions, poised to capture every detail of the pyrotechnics scene. He had placed himself in a strategic position about four hundred yards from the train, where he had an expansive view of everyone, and he was also in constant contact with them via headsets. Adair stood next to him, hands on the pyro console and laptop controller. Thick bundles of wires came out and ran across the ground to the train, where they spread out and connected to every pyro device. Adair was murmuring into his headset to his own crew, going through a final checklist before the shoot.

Doyle had gotten used to Adair's eccentric dress—stained tan Carhartt overalls, a dirty straw cowboy hat, three-day growth of beard, long greasy ponytail, and shit-kicking boots. It was remarkable how much he looked like a bum or maybe even a serial killer. And yet here was a guy who made ten thousand dollars a day blowing shit up.

The train had been primed and mined the evening before. Detonator boxes of dynamite—repurposed Styrofoam coolers—had been strategically located behind the train, buried under piles of stuffed animals. The stuffed animals were one of Adair's signature inventions. The plushies had been dusted with accelerants and various mineral powders, the bigger ones cut in pieces. When the dynamite went off, the stuffed animals would become dramatic pieces of flaming debris streaking from the explosion like so many fiery comets, trailing sparks in all colors. Stuffed animals were ideal because they came in many different shapes and sizes, they were loose and gangly, they burned well and broke apart in flight. And they had no hard parts; if they flew too far and hit someone, they were soft. Everything involved in the explosion had to be soft and light, especially when using real dynamite. Anything hard or heavy could fragment and act like shrapnel or fly a long distance and brain someone.

That morning, they had positioned and filled the gas bags, the gigantic balloons inflated with propane that, when ignited, would send up huge but harmless balls of fire. They had spent most of the morning blocking, lighting, placing the cameras, getting the crane in place, mapping out the drone flight paths, and working out the kinks. Filling the bags with propane was the last thing on the checklist, because of the danger of a premature ignition.

Once an explosive set had been primed and mined, it was off-limits for safety reasons except to the pyro people. Wired sets had been known to go off prematurely, triggered by a freak lightning strike or some jackass tossing a cigarette—or, in a famous case in Arizona, by a discharge from a blank weapon during a shoot-out scene that sent a burning wad into a propane bag.

And now, finally, Ballou came out of his trailer, his PA with cell phone and clipboard skipping along beside him. Doyle had hoped the actor would not show up—there was no reason for him to be there—but no such luck.

Ballou came striding over. "Howdy, Slavomir. Afternoon, Jack."

He came up beside them, the leather of his tight pants creaking, and took out his silver cigarette case.

"So sorry, Mr. Ballou," said Adair. "No smoking until after the scene is over."

"Right." He slid it back in. "You sure we'll be safe over here?"

"Of course," said Adair. "I've done this a hundred times before."

"Good," Ballou said, taking his hat off, smoothing down his hair, and fitting the hat back on. "I've always enjoyed a fine fireworks display."

"You're going to see a lot more than mere fireworks, Mr. Ballou," said Adair, a rare note of pride in his voice. "But you may want to put on a pair of those headphones—we got some real dynamite that's gonna go off." He pointed to a rack of noise-canceling ear protection.

Ballou reached out and took one off the rack, inspected it suspiciously as if it might have germs, and then fitted it over his ears. His PA, standing behind him, did the same.

Doyle checked his watch. One fifty-five p.m. Five more minutes. He felt his heart accelerate with the joy of it, the thrill. The explosives had been carefully designed and calibrated to lift the train into the air and then, as it was starting to come apart, envelop it in gigantic balls of fire, one after another, that would rise into the sky like the mushroom clouds of an atomic explosion, while the dynamite added a ripple of concussive booms, cometizing the plushies and sending them up and outward in gorgeous fiery parabolas.

"Starting countdown," said Adair, looking at his console. "Five minutes."

Doyle looked around with a critical eye. All the camera operators were in place and ready to roll. The pyrotechnical team was poised and ready. The firefighting team was standing by in case the fire got out of control. The DP was gazing at her bank of monitors, each one showing a feed from each camera. The sun was in an ideal position in the sky, bathing the scene in a rich autumnal light tinged with gold, the shadows elongated enough to give definition and three-dimensionality. The recent snow on the mountaintops was a gift of the gods. When that dynamite went off, they were going to get fantastic, tolling echoes off those mountains, something they had tested days earlier with a noisemaker to excellent effect.

Adair continued standing at attention at the console. "Four minutes," he said.

There were twelve gas bags filled with propane, timed to go off slightly staggered, to give the impression of rolling explosions, one triggering the next. The thin, flammable skin of the bags had been dusted with various powdered chemicals to create color—copper sulfate and alum for green, strontium chloride for red, calcium chloride for orange, and iron and magnesium filings to create billions of tiny gold and silver sparks. There were specific pyrotechnical devices, similar to fireworks, also strategically positioned to enhance the display.

It was going to be the greatest explosion of his career.

"Three minutes," said Adair.

Doyle knew everyone was ready, but he questioned each person by name in turn to get their specific acknowledgment that they were ready to roll. The train gleamed in the sunlight, the foothills and mountains rising behind it, perfectly framed.

"Two minutes."

The air was fresh and bracing, the golden aspen leaves dancing in the breeze, the set quiet. Everyone had come to see it; the entire crew and cast were standing far back, behind barriers, waiting for the show to begin.

"One minute," Adair said.

"Launch drones," said Doyle.

Two drone operators had their little machines ready, and they now soared up into the sky, taking up positions at either end of the train, hovering two hundred feet off the ground.

"Quiet on set," said the assistant director, even though it was profoundly silent already.

"Roll sound."

"Speed."

"Roll camera."

"Camera speed."

"Mark."

"*Action.*"

Doyle could hear the faint sound of the drones as they began their overflight.

Three more seconds went by in silence. And then Adair touched a screen on the console, and a huge *whoosh* sound happened as the gas bags lighted, one after another in fast sequence, sending enormous roiling clouds of fire and smoke blasting upward into the blue sky. For a brief moment, the train was completely engulfed in fiery orange clouds of burning propane.

And then nothing. No booms of dynamite.

"What the fuck?" Doyle cried. He stared, unable to believe it: the dynamite hadn't gone off. There had been no concussive booms, the train hadn't lifted into the air, the flaming debris hadn't arced up and away. The propane fire dissipated rapidly, and when the flames cleared, the train was still there.

Doyle turned to Adair and saw an expression on the man's ruddy face of astonishment and consternation.

"What the *fuck*!" Doyle screamed again. "What happened to my dynamite?" He stared at the train, which should have been blown to smithereens, raining burning pieces down everywhere. But it was intact, although it had been set on fire by the gas bags. The Styrofoam was melting.

"Fire team!" Doyle screamed. "Fire team! Put out the fucking fire! My train is melting!"

The fire teams, on standby around the set, rushed in from both sides, spraying the train down with foam and water.

"What the fuck!" screamed Doyle at Adair, spittle flying.

"I can't understand it," Adair said. "I just can't—we checked it out so thoroughly last night—"

More shouting, consternation, people freaking out. Doyle wanted to see what it looked like behind the train, where the boxes of dynamite and piles of stuffed animals were. He ripped off his headset and strode around. Adair came along with him, jogging to keep up.

The animal piles, covered with netting, remained undisturbed. Not one of the dynamite charges had gone off. The train was burning, and the fire crews were well on their way to putting it out. But it was too late: his big, beautiful, life-size Western train was already half-melted. A total loss. It would have to be rebuilt from scratch.

"Don't approach!" Adair yelled as Doyle ran toward the piles of toys. "It could still go off!"

Doyle halted.

Two guys in *Hurt Locker* bomb suits, who had been standing by, now went over and began pulling apart the piles of toys to uncover the detonator boxes. They got the first one out and dragged it free, cutting through the duct tape and pulling off the lid. They stood there, staring down, speechless.

Doyle couldn't wait. He broke into a run to see what was the problem.

"Hey, are you crazy?" Adair yelled. "Get back, for chrissake!"

But Doyle was now close enough to see inside the box—and he felt his blood run cold. The detonator box was empty, with just a bunch of cut wires where the dynamite should have been.

Someone had stolen the dynamite.

51

Cash and Colcord moved slowly down the long mine tunnel, their beams playing ahead into the darkness. Once again, Cash felt her throat tightening as she contemplated the dark passageway chiseled into the mountain, braced at intervals with massive timbers, splintering and warping with dry rot.

The smell of the mine assaulted her nostrils—mold, dust, and stone, overlaid with smoke. She didn't want to think what that smoke came from.

As they turned the first bend, the light of the entrance winked out behind them. She felt a rising apprehension. It was purely psychological, she told herself—just her claustrophobia acting up.

They came to the first T, and Colcord paused at the corner and peered around. "Clear."

Cash took the opportunity to slip her Baby Glock out of the keeper and to finally rack a round into the chamber. That gave her a feeling of reassurance.

"Glad to hear you do that," said Colcord. "I always keep a round chambered. A holdover from Iraq. When shit happens, it happens fast."

"I'm not sure I like this conversation," said Romanski with a strained laugh. "You really think the killers might still be around?"

"No," said Cash, "but better safe than sorry."

They moved deliberately, pausing at every turn for Colcord to check the way ahead. They soon arrived at the first big open area with its abandoned equipment scattered about. Across the expanse, at the far side, the black timbered doorway stared at them. After pausing to scan the room, they moved quickly across and entered the low passageway. Here the air got even deader, more humid, and clammy.

Beyond, they came into the maze of passageways and dead-end tunnels marking the ore-bearing area. It struck Cash again what a perfect place this was for an ambush, with holes going off every which way, some so small it was hard to see how a human being could have squeezed through to remove ore. She felt a shudder of horror just thinking about it—what a way to die, wedged in a crawl space, unable to move. Despite their powerful flashlights, there were still plenty of dark holes from where someone could launch a spear. But as they moved along, they saw and heard nothing, no chanting or laughing

They reached the slanting tunnel, which narrowed until they had to move forward on their hands and knees, Romanski struggling with the acetylene torch, before they emerged into the larger cavity. They passed the cave-in, splashed through the stream, and came to the vertical shaft where the victim, Johnson, had been found. The evidence-gathering crews had laid aluminum gangplanks over the gap, and they quickly crossed, heading into the narrowing tunnel that caused Cash's apprehension to rise again. And then, when she almost thought they'd taken a wrong turn somewhere, their flashlight beam gleamed back at them from the steel door.

Cash held up a hand for silence, then went up to the door and pressed her ear to it and listened. Nothing. The surface was cold, and there were no sounds or vibrations coming through from the other side.

"We need to document our entry," she said, speaking in a low voice, turning to Reno. "That's gonna be your job, to take photos and video as needed of everything we do, every step we take. Think of it sort of like having a lapel camera. We're recording this is as much for our protection as for theirs—because what we do now is gonna be scrutinized."

She looked at the little group. "Once we're inside, Bart, you'll be in charge of evidence gathering. I want you to keep your eye out—and grab whatever evidence you think is relevant. For stuff that's too big to carry out now, point it out to Reno and make sure it's recorded, and then tag it for later."

"What *are* we looking for?" Romanski asked in a low voice.

"As the warrant says: evidence related to the homicide of Johnson. I know it sounds vague, and it is. Deliberately so. We wanted wording that pretty much allows us to go anywhere, see anything. I wish I could tell you what kind of evidence we're looking for—anything that looks clandestine, hidden, or weird. Use your judgment."

"Okay."

"And what's the protocol for when we encounter Erebus personnel?" Reno asked.

"It's no different from entering a house with a warrant. We can enter unannounced, but as soon as we encounter anyone, we identify ourselves and show the warrant. We'll have to state what we're looking for and where we want to go. If anyone tries to stop us, that's obstruction of a police officer, a felony. They have no right to impede us."

"Got it."

"Here's what I want you to do first," she said to Romanski. "Cut a little hole so we can see what's on the other side of this door. It might be a storeroom full of ethanol or some flammable stuff, and we don't want to set it on fire. Or there may be people on the other side and we don't want to freak them out. There's no reason to go in guns blazing. We're gonna be polite, reasonable, and calm."

"Gotcha." Romanski set down his plastic pack with the two bottles and torch and, kneeling, began adjusting them. "People, you can't look at the flame. Turn your backs."

They turned their backs, and a moment later, the cavern was brilliantly lit, with a hissing, crackling sound coming from the door.

"Okay, we're done."

Cash turned around. Romanski had cut two little holes.

"One for the light, one for your eye. Careful, the edges still might be hot."

Cash touched the surface of the steel, but it was only warm. She was surprised to see it was a good two inches thick. That was a hell of a steel door. And the holes were both dark—there was no light beyond. She put her ear to one of them. No sound.

She put the flashlight up to one hole and peered in the other.

What greeted her eye was disappointing in its ordinariness. It looked like the corridor of a school or industrial office, tiled in linoleum, with two-toned cinder block walls, darker green below, lighter above. There were light fixtures in the ceiling, but they were turned off. It went down about twenty-five feet and then made a turn, the corridor evidently still following the contour of the original mine tunnel, enlarged and squared off.

"May I?" Colcord asked.

"Of course."

He peered in. "Looks like my old high school."

Cash turned to Romanski. "Okay, Bart. Good work—now make us a door, but stop just before the final cut so I can say a few words."

They all turned their backs again and waited while the brilliant flickering light illuminated the tunnel. After about ten minutes— which seemed like an eternity to Cash—the cutting stopped.

"You can turn around."

They did. Romanski had cut a doorway, leaving just two little tabs, top and bottom. "I'll cut through those and push the door in, and then we can enter."

"Thanks," said Cash. "Before we proceed, I just want to review a couple of things. Once we're in, we communicate using hand signals only. We proceed slowly with our flashlights on low—five lumens. We want to surprise them, not give them time to stop or hide what they're doing. If we encounter any personnel, I'll announce our presence and serve the warrant." She looked around. "Any questions?"

"What if we meet resistance?" Reno asked.

"We take it slow, de-escalate, and explain."

"And if they're armed?"

"It seems unlikely they're gonna fire on us. Of course we have the right of self-defense."

Reno nodded.

"Okay, Bart, finish cutting our door."

"Look away."

They did, and after a sustained flickering of light, they heard a loud clang as the door dropped in.

Cash and the rest stooped through the opening. A cool flow of clean, fresh air greeted them, far different from the stuffy, foul air of the mine.

After a moment, Cash realized it was faintly scented with something—what was it? Flowers? Lilacs?

She held up her hand and pointed to the place where the corridor made a sharp turn. They moved down the hall in dim light, stopped at the corner, and Cash edged around it, peering, firearm at the ready.

What stretched ahead was another long, dull, institutional hallway. But then she noticed something sitting on the floor about twenty yards down. She squinted—it was hard to see in the reduced level of light. They cautiously approached.

It was an ordinary football, scuffed and worn.

52

Jack Adair stared at the empty detonation box in silent consternation. He had wired the dynamite himself—he never left a task like that to a subordinate—at eleven the previous night and then carefully covered it with the pile of prepared stuffed animals. It had been patrolled and guarded all night by Doyle's security people.

He knelt and pulled up the ending of one of the copper wires, examining it up close. The end gleamed in the light: Someone had cut it with wire cutters.

It was incredible. Someone had actually stolen the dynamite.

"This is fucked up!" he heard Doyle yell behind him. "Check the other boxes!"

Adair had worked with many movie directors. He didn't like Doyle, but the man was his best customer, and that meant putting up with a lot. But this was too much. This put at risk the reputation of his company. Something had gone wrong here, and he was pretty sure it was someone else's fault—not his.

Without saying a word, he straightened up and walked over to the next pile, gesturing for his assistants to follow, including the guys with the *Hurt Locker* suits.

"Uncover the box."

They swept away the toys and pried open the lid of the detonation box. It too was empty, showing nothing but cut, dangling wires.

"Son of a bitch!" Doyle cried. "Who the fuck messed with my movie set?"

Adair turned and, collecting his thoughts, said, "You had overnight security assigned to the set, correct?"

"Of course I did!"

"And who was in charge?"

Doyle looked around and pointed. "It was Rodney. Rodney Hammer. Hey, Hammer, get over here!"

Hammer came over. He was sweating. He was scared.

"What the hell happened? You fall asleep or something?"

"Mr. Doyle," said Hammer, "I was here all night with three people. I swear to you—*all* night. Nothing happened. Nobody entered the set—nobody."

"*Which* three? Get them over here now!"

Hammer turned. "Susan, Tom, and Sunil." The three security personnel edged out of the growing crowd of crew, gathering open-mouthed and whispering.

"Come forward!" said Doyle. "Get over here. I've got questions! And the rest of you, what the hell are you gawking at? This isn't a car accident!"

The three stepped forward. Adair stared at them. If they had been smoking pot or drinking, they didn't look it. They looked competent and alert—if nervous as hell.

"Look at this set!" Doyle yelled at them. "A million fucking dollars, and now it's ruined! How do you explain this? You!" He jabbed a finger at one of them. "What the fuck were you doing last night when you should have been guarding the set?"

"I was here all night," Sunil stammered. "Nothing happened."

Adair held up his hand. "Perhaps Mr. Hammer might care to explain the security setup last night as they were guarding the train."

"I will," said Hammer. "I placed Tom at the north end of the train; Sunil was at the south. I was on the east side and Susan on the west. We had the train in view on all sides. It was fully illuminated, with the generator and area lights on the entire night. We were in constant communication by radio. Nobody as far as I know fell asleep or was derelict in their duty."

"So it was you, Mr. Hammer, who was on the side where the dynamite was?" said Adair.

"Yes."

"You didn't see anything unusual?"

"Nothing. As I said, we had the area lights on all night, and it was brilliantly lit up. I just don't see how anyone could have gotten in there, uncovered and opened the boxes, clipped the wires, and stolen the dynamite. I can guarantee you that did not happen on my watch."

"Fuck if I believe you!" Doyle yelled.

Adair stepped forward and asked quietly, "When did your watch end?"

"At sunrise."

"And who took over then?"

"That was when the film crew arrived and started to set up."

"And then?" Adair asked.

"And so we left."

"What time was that, exactly?"

"Around six thirty."

Adair turned to Doyle. "When did you arrive with your crew?"

"I arrived around six forty-five, maybe seven. Some came earlier, others later. I don't recall."

"When you left," Adair asked Hammer, "had anybody arrived?"

"Oh yes. They were starting to come in, and as I said, they were setting up their cameras and preparing for the shoot."

Adair said, "Allow me to point out that the dynamite was hidden *behind* the train, on the far side, opposite the side where the cameras were being set up and people were arriving. So that side of the train was not visible to the arriving crew after you left—is that correct?"

After a hesitation, Hammer nodded. "I guess so."

"And so, during that moment of transition," Adair went on, "when the security team believed their watch was over and had left, and others were just arriving, the dynamite on the far side of the train was unguarded and unwatched."

Hammer stared at him, saying nothing.

Adair turned to Doyle and said, "For the record, *that's* when it happened." He was determined not to be blamed, and he intended to establish immediately that it was not the fault of him or his group but of Doyle's security people. Now he had done so.

Doyle stared at him. "So you're saying it was *my* fault?"

"I'm establishing the facts," said Adair firmly. "And the facts are these: I set up the pyrotechnics last night, ending at midnight. It was the production's responsibility to guard the set until the shoot. Now we know there was a lapse in that process—a gap—that had nothing to do with me or my team, and everything to do with your security team. That's what I'm saying."

"Don't snow me under with your bullshit!" Doyle cried. "It was your dynamite that was stolen, not mine. You're in charge of pyro. *You* got robbed, not me. Someone's gonna pay for this—it's not my problem!"

Adair gazed at him steadily. "You realize this is only the beginning of your problem, right?"

"What do you mean, only the beginning?" Doyle said.

"This has to be reported to Erebus security right away," Adair said firmly. "You've got to tell them that there are now people in this valley with a hundred pounds of live dynamite."

53

Wallace McFaul, sitting in the main room of the lodge, checked his watch. Three o'clock. The media pool had filed or broadcast their stories. The press conference had been a resounding success. It was incredible how big the story was, how widespread—at the top of every news feed he could find with his phone—*The New York Times*, the networks, CNN, Fox, Facebook, Apple News, *The Guardian*. Sitting in the lodge, McFaul had been checking and rechecking the news sites as the stories got posted. In the clips, he had spoken well and looked good, his voice calm and reassuring, his demeanor professional. (He had to get rid of that tire around his middle, though.) The lineup of law enforcement behind him looked impressive. The press had been, if not exactly grateful, at least obliged by having been let into the resort. They had rewarded him by avoiding snarky or critical coverage, at least on the major outlets. Of course, the case had better advance fast. The coverage could turn in an instant. The press were like pit bulls, tail wagging and then a sudden lunge at the jugular.

But things were going well. Absolutely. They'd cleared the mine and had the killers on the run. It was now a matter of tracking them down. Cash was temporarily out of the way, heading up to the mine with Romanski and that sheriff to collect more evidence, and he felt relieved that she was out of the loop. She was kind of a pain in the ass, not good-looking, a little heavy around the hips, and with a foul mouth—not the best look for an agent in charge. This was her first case as AIC, and she'd not done well, as far as he was concerned. He was disappointed in her. Even though she had one of the highest clearance rates in the bureau, she was lacking on the public relations side of things. A case like this, for example: the public needed to be informed and the press wanted to be fed. Or they'd turn against you. By keeping the press out for, what, almost five days? Cash had made a serious mistake and risked the press narrative going sour. By letting the press inside, he had nipped the negative stories in the bud, the press was happy, and their stories now had the right tone. The honeymoon wouldn't last—McFaul knew that: he'd better produce some results. But now that he was in charge, everything was going to be different, and he felt confident they'd wrap this up in forty-eight hours—or less.

He put away his phone and looked around. The guests had all been evacuated that morning and the press were now wandering around, starting to look hungry after having filed their stories. They'd want more. The deadline for them to leave was at four—they had one more hour. And then he'd clear them out.

He was getting ready to call Maximilian when he saw the security director striding across the big room, his face dark. McFaul didn't like that look, and he rose from his chair.

"What's the latest?" McFaul asked. "Is something wrong?"

"I just heard from Doyle. A bunch of dynamite was stolen from the film crew this morning."

McFaul felt a buzzy feeling of dread in his gut. "Dynamite? How much?"

"A hundred pounds. Apparently, they were going to use them for a movie scene with an explosion."

"Real dynamite?"

"Yes, *real*."

"You think the killers have it?" McFaul began.

"Who else? Of *course* they have it."

"What are they going to do with it?" he asked, but even before he was finished speaking, he realized how stupid the question sounded.

"What do you think?" said Maximilian, exasperated. "They're going to bloody blow something up."

McFaul felt a twist of horror in his gut. His face was now everywhere, in all the media, the man in charge. He was responsible. This would be on him. What to do? He tried to think, tried to game out how the killers might use the explosives. They'd try to blow up the lodge—that would be their first target. The lodge. But then, who else was vulnerable? For security reasons, the search crews had already been reduced, and they'd switched over to searching mostly with drones. The guests, thank God, had been evacuated. But the damn press was still there.

He realized he was starting to hyperventilate and made a massive effort to get himself under control and project composure and competence. Cash had wanted to call in the National Guard. Was it time to do that? But he'd told her that wouldn't be a good look, especially right after promising everyone the case was well under control. It would mean going through the governor, and that would take twenty-four hours. The governor had just authorized them to shut down the resort, and going back to him would be an admission of lack of progress. The press would pick up on it—you couldn't mobilize the National Guard quietly—and Jesus, that would look bad.

Maximilian was standing there, waiting for some kind of response from him.

McFaul said, "We need to make sure the lodge is protected against attack. That's the first priority. I want you to deploy Erebus security around the lodge to prevent any close approach by these crazies. We'll also redeploy half of the DPD SWAT team to the lodge."

"Agreed."

"And we need to pull all the rest of the search teams out of the backcountry, for their own safety."

Maximilian nodded. "Agreed. My men are at your disposal."

"What about the lab complex?" McFaul asked. "What kind of protection do you need up there?"

"We're good up there. I'm not worried about it. The lab complex is like Fort Knox. No dynamite's going to get through those steel doors."

"Cash and Romanski are up in the Jackman Mine," said McFaul. "With the sheriff and Reno."

At this, Maximilian looked startled. "What for? I wasn't informed."

"Routine. Collecting evidence."

"They need to get back down here ASAP."

McFaul shook his head. "Can't communicate with them while they're in the tunnels. I tried." He paused. "What about Barrow? Does he know about this?"

Maximilian nodded.

"What's his take?"

"Not happy," Maximilian said in a clipped voice.

McFaul looked around at the press bastards who were roaming about, hungry looks on their faces. "We'd better keep this from the press. And get them out of here."

"Let me remind you, Mr. McFaul, that I advised against bringing them in here at all. If there's an explosion while they're still here, with all these cameras—well, you and I, mate, are going to look bloody stupid."

McFaul felt another twinge of horror. He should have stayed back in Lakewood and left the case with Cash.

54

Colcord reached down and picked up the football, examined it, tossed it from hand to hand. It was of the best quality, a Wilson GST, well used, partly deflated. What the hell was it doing there? Maybe left by workmen, who tossed it around during their breaks? And why this long, empty hallway? He felt tense and edgy, the same feeling he'd gotten in Iraq just before things went south.

He quietly set it back down on the floor, looked at Cash, and shrugged.

She gestured for them to keep going.

As they proceeded, the corridor made a shallow turn. Colcord led the way, scouring the corridor ahead with his beam. As they went around, he saw, far ahead, that the corridor ended in a set of double doors like you might see in a hospital.

Colcord motioned for everyone to turn off their flashlights. In the ensuing darkness, a faint light could be seen seeping from the bottom crack of the door. They were approaching an area where there was light. He listened. Were those ever so faint sounds, at the edge of audibility, coming down the corridor?

He turned his beam on low and kept it angled down as they approached the set of doors. They were crash doors with no lock or handles, the kind that swing both ways, and they had stainless steel crash plates that were much dented from use. But what kind of use? They seemed strangely out of place.

He motioned for everyone to be still, and put his ear to the vertical seam where the two doors came together. He could feel, on his ear, a cool stream of fresh air flowing through the crack. Oddly, the flow seemed to carry the faint scent of vegetation, and he wondered if they were approaching an opening to the outside. He listened for a while and again heard a faint susurrus, impossible to identify—possibly the reverberations of a forced air system?

He was just about to move his ear from the crack when he thought he heard something sharper—like a distant shout. He held up his finger for more silence and listened intently. He heard it again, several emphatic voices coming from a long way off, distorted in their passage down the corridor, so faint he could only hear the high points, like cries you might hear from a distant playground. Then there ensued a silence, and he heard another raised voice, a woman's, speaking shrilly. He strained to make out the words, any words, but it was too far away and scarcely audible. But as he listened, he began to wonder—was this voice really of a woman? It was high and punctuated, rising and falling in a cadence more like a child's. But what would a child be doing deep in the Erebus labs? And then he heard a laugh, quite distinct, and a thwapping sound, like a tennis racket hitting a ball, and another high-pitched laugh.

He gestured to Cash and stepped back as she took a turn to listen. After a minute, she touched Colcord's arm and leaned toward him. She whispered, "I heard, quite distinctly, the laugh of a child."

Colcord listened again and then heard it—without doubt, the happy, high-pitched laugh of a child. There must be a day care center up ahead, perhaps for the children of the scientists and lab workers.

He tried to peer through the crack in the door but could see nothing but the continuation of the corridor to another set of double doors. With the palm of his hand, he eased open the door to get a better view. The next set of doors had windows in them, one on each side, and through them shone a bright light. He could hear the distant sounds more distinctly: faint mingled voices, shouts, cries, and laughter, like children on a playground during recess.

With a nod, he signaled they were to pass through as he held the door open. They went through at a crouch and he followed, easing it shut behind him. There was just enough light coming through the windows to allow them to turn off and stow their flashlights.

Colcord felt his uneasiness increase. He told himself it was irrational—they were approaching a day care center, for heaven's sake. But what was it doing so deep in the mines?

They walked down the corridor single file, keeping the tread of their feet as silent as possible and moving along the right-hand wall. As they approached the second set of doors, the sounds became more distinct—shouts, cries, laughing of voices raised in play, the sound of a ball being hit back and forth as if on a tennis court. No doubt now—this was some sort of playground. The light coming through the windows was cool and friendly—and it had the feeling of outdoor light, not artificial. Was this an opening to the outside? The flow of fresh air seemed to suggest so.

As they neared the set of doors, staying low to remain below the height of the windows, the sounds became more distinct. Colcord reached the doors first. He looked at Cash. This presented a problem with their plans to search the premises. Search a day care center? How silly that would be. She signaled that she was going to take a look through the window. She slowly rose, keeping her head well back in the shadows, and peered through. She looked for what felt like a long time, then she lowered herself. Colcord was surprised; the expression on her face was one of astonishment. She gestured for him to take a look.

He rose and cautiously peered out. Beyond the door was a catwalk that circled above a large interior space below. Above the catwalk was a dome, like the interior of a cathedral, painted blue with white clouds. Set into the dome were powerful lights. What lay below was extraordinary: an enormous open space with trees and grass, bisected by a stream that entered from one end of the area and flowed in a meandering course to the middle, where it had been dammed to produce a small pond with a sandy beach. The water continued flowing over the dam and ran merrily among rocks and cattails to exit on the other side. Behind the beach was a green lawn that led to a soccer field, where some children and young teenagers were kicking about a ball. On the other side of the stream were picnic tables, a playground with a jungle gym, swings, tennis and basketball courts, and some game tables.

But what floored Colcord were the children. There must have been a dozen of them, ranging from three or four all the way up to the midteens, playing soccer, making sand castles on the beach, shooting hoops. Several older kids were playing chess at the game tables.

He slowly lowered himself.

"Day care?" asked Cash.

"That place cost a fortune," said Colcord. "And it's September—most of those kids should be in school."

"Let me have a look," said Romanski.

He took a turn, peering through the window a long time. The seconds ticked on. Then he finally crouched back down. "No way is that a day care," he whispered. He took a deep, shuddering breath. "Those children aren't normal. They're . . . *strange*."

55

In the main hall of the lodge, Wallace McFaul waded into the scrum of reporters and raised his voice, trying to make himself heard over the din. It was four o'clock, the time they had all been told they would have to leave. They were supposed to be going back down to the parking garage to their damn vehicles and get out, but none of them showed any signs of leaving. This was supposed to be a press pool, which meant a select few journalists covering for the rest and sharing information and footage, but it seemed there were more than what he'd authorized. A lot more. What a clusterfuck. Cash should have been there, and that damn useless sheriff, to help manage these people. Thank God at least Maximilian and his guards were there to assist.

"Ladies and gentlemen of the press!" he called out, standing in the middle of the great hall of the lodge, raising his hands. "Can I have your attention! Please!"

Maximilian stood next to him, flanked by two security guards.

"Ladies and gentlemen!"

The press gradually fell silent, all cameras turned on him, boom mics swinging forward, cameras dollied around—a surge of interest. The vultures clearly hoped for more material for the evening's news. Well, screw them. They were just going to have to be disappointed. He'd already pushed things by letting them in over everyone's objections.

"I want to thank you all for coming out here for the press conference! We at the CBI want to make sure the public is kept informed of the latest developments in this important case, and we thank you for your role in doing that."

He paused, took a breath.

"It is now four o'clock. As we *agreed*, it is now time for the media to leave! Mr. Maximilian and his security team," he went on, nodding to Maximilian, "will now usher you to your vehicles and escort you from the resort. Thank you for your cooperation."

Nobody moved. There was a rising murmur of protest.

"Mr. McFaul—?" someone called out.

McFaul held up his hands. "I'm sorry, this is mandatory! We need to continue the investigation full speed ahead, and the extra security needs of having the press in the resort is not conducive to that. I'm sure you understand. When we organized the media pool, we made it clear this was for just the afternoon. So please pack up your equipment and depart as expeditiously as possible, so we can have the field of investigation once again to ourselves. Thank you!"

More murmurs of disappointment. The anchor of a TV crew swung out a mic. "Mr. McFaul, have there been any developments since noon?"

"Sorry, we're taking no questions."

This was met with a noisy buzz of disapproval and aggressive calling out.

"Mr. McFaul! Mr. McFaul!"

"We're making progress, excellent progress!" he said. "The case is moving toward a conclusion. We've got the killers on the run, and trust me, we are going to find them and take them into custody at any moment. I don't have anything specific that can be reported at this time."

"Mr. McFaul!" called many reporters. "Mr. McFaul!"

Christ, they were trying to turn this into another press conference. He glanced over and could see the slow burn on Maximilian's face. He held up his hands. "Thank you again. We have nothing more to comment on! Thank you! No more comments!"

"Hey!" a reporter in the back cried. "There are animals at the lake!" He pointed through the wall of glass along the side of the great hall, and there was a surge of the crowd in that direction.

"Not just mammoths," someone said loudly. The mammoths had been there all day, and the press had gotten bored with them—but now the evening parade of other megafauna had begun.

"There are more animals coming!"

The press, completely ignoring McFaul and Maximilian, moved like the tide toward the wall of glass.

"Ladies and gentlemen!"

He might as well have been yelling at a herd of cats. He could see through the glass that a giant deer with antlers had come out of the forest to drink, along with a crazy-looking armored animal the size of a car, and then—he could hardly believe his eyes—a gargantuan pigeon-toed animal with foot-long claws.

The media were now pressed against the glass, camera crews filming and jockeying with each other to get the best shots, bloggers with their iPhones out yakking away and taking selfies, a babble of excitement filling the hall.

"Ladies and gentlemen! Please!"

Maximilian came up next to him. "This is exactly what I warned you about," he said, his voice dark. "I'm going to get these bloody bastards out of here." He began waving over some guards.

McFaul was alarmed. If they gave the media the bum's rush, God knew what they'd write. "Look, Mr. Maximilian, can we just give them fifteen minutes? As soon as they've had their fill, we can move them out. You *really* don't want to force them out—they'll crucify us."

"Bloody Christ," Maximilian said, frowning. "Fifteen minutes, then."

His radio buzzed. He picked it up and stepped away, speaking into it. McFaul watched as Maximilian's face dramatically changed expression, going from annoyance to shock and then turning dark red. He spoke quietly, then hooked his radio up.

"What's going on?" asked McFaul.

Maximilian visibly struggled to maintain his composure. "Got a problem up at the labs," he said, his voice tight as a watch spring. "I've got to go. We're, ah, going to have to take some guards with us." He looked around. "You two! Help Mr. McFaul clear out the press. I'm heading to the lab."

He immediately departed, striding fast toward the elevators to the heliport on the roof.

McFaul was left with the startling memory of the expression of intense emotion on Maximilian's face of . . . what? Fear? Shock? Rage?

56

"What do you mean, strange?" Cash whispered.

"Just *look* at their faces. Look closely—there's something . . . wrong."

Cash rose and stared. They looked normal, nicely dressed, except the older children were unusually stocky, even the girls. They were very, very pale, like underground creatures. But the faces . . . She squinted. A sick feeling took hold. The faces were weird—broad and thick, with long, thin mouths, heavy brows, prominent cheekbones, and almost no chins.

Jesus Christ, what was this? What was Erebus up to? Her heart was beating like mad, with a thousand suppositions racing through her mind. Were they breeding freaks?

She crouched back down, staring at Romanski. "Who are they?"

He looked back at her.

She asked, "Are they some sort of genetic experiments?"

She could see on his face the blooming shock of understanding.

"Not exactly," he whispered.

"What? What is it?" she hissed. "You know?"

He slowly nodded.

"For God's sake, then, *what*?"

"It's another de-extinction project," he said quietly.

"What do you mean?"

He said in a quavering voice, "Neanderthals."

There was a stunned silence.

"They've de-extincted *Homo neanderthalensis*," Romanski said. "I'm pretty sure that's what we're looking at down there: Neanderthal children."

Cash was speechless. It couldn't be. Impossible.

Romanski went on, "There are a bunch of reconstructions of Neanderthal faces in museums. I've seen them. Those look like them. They're Neanderthals."

"But . . . *why?*"

Romanski returned the look with a blank one of his own. "I've no idea."

"How would they do that?" Colcord asked.

"Same way they did the woolly mammoth. They sequenced the Neanderthal genome way back in 2010—the guy who did it won a Nobel Prize."

The enormity of this began to sink into Cash's mind. Could Romanski be right? This was morally horrific, evil—but was it *illegal?*

"Look," said Colcord, "we're here to serve a warrant and gather evidence regarding a homicide. This is pretty awful, but it doesn't relate to the mission."

Cash had a sudden revelation, one that nearly floored her. "Oh, but I think this does relate to the mission," she said.

"How so?"

"I bet the killers are escaped Neanderthals."

The three returned her stare with astonished looks of their own.

"Jesus Christ," muttered Romanski. "This is some crazy shit."

"Wait a minute," said Colcord. "Aren't Neanderthals supposed to be dumb? I mean, they're inferior to humans—mentally. Those killers are way too smart to be Neanderthals."

"Let's not debate the point now," said Cash. "We've got to decide what to do." She made an effort to organize her thoughts. Should she just walk out there and announce themselves? *Not a good idea.* Should they turn around and go back? That was obviously the sensible route. None of this was going away anytime soon, and it sure as hell couldn't be covered up.

"Okay," she said. "Change of plans. We're not going to execute the warrant. We're going to get the hell out of here and come back in force. Whatever's going on here is way too big for the four of us."

Colcord said, "I couldn't agree more."

Romanski and Reno both nodded.

"But first," said Cash, "we gotta get some footage. Because otherwise, who's gonna believe us?" She took out her cell phone and rose to the window edge, peeked over. She pressed the Record button and took a slow sweep of the playground below. A minute went by, then she stopped, checked the footage, nodded, and put the phone away. "Done."

They turned around and retreated quietly down the hallway toward the back set of crash doors. Cash's mind was starting to recover its equilibrium. She began putting together how they would execute the raid, how many SWAT teams would be deployed, how they would take Maximilian and his security by surprise. The warrant was still valid all day—they wouldn't need to go back to get a new one. They could—and they should—do this as soon as possible. But what in the world would happen to all these . . . Neanderthal children? My God, what had Erebus done here?

They had reached the set of crash doors. Cash laid her hand on one and slowly opened it wide enough for the others to slip through. She went last. They paused, and Cash signaled for them to get out their flashlights and proceed under low light.

At that moment, there was a loud *chack!* and three bright lights went on in front of them, dazzling their eyes. Cash instinctively reached for her Glock, but a voice rang out.

"*We're armed and fully covering you. Don't even think about it.*"

She hesitated. It was Maximilian's voice. His figure stepped out of the blinding light, walking toward them. He was silhouetted from behind, so she couldn't see his face. He stopped.

"What in the bloody hell are you doing in here?" he asked.

Cash touched her pocket. "We're serving a warrant."

"A warrant? What kind of warrant?"

She took out the warrant and handed it to him. He snatched it, opened it, read it, and then flung it away. "My God, do you realize what you've done? You've fucked everything up. We got an intruder alarm—but had no idea it was you." His face was red. As he spoke, Cash could see that behind him, in the faintly reflected light, there was a group of armed security guards.

"Bloody fucking hell," said Maximilian. "I'm sorry—take out your weapons and place them on the floor."

"No way in hell are you disarming us."

He stared at her. "Don't you see? Look behind me!"

"We're here on a legal search, and if you stop us, you'll be committing a string of felonies."

"Oh, for fuck's sake, we're way beyond that. Why did you break in here? If only you'd continued with your normal investigation. We were well on the way to taking care of this problem ourselves. Of course we had to call in law enforcement—but I never expected this. Why? Why did you have to go get a warrant like this?"

"So you didn't expect us to find out what you're up to?"

He stopped for a moment. "And what *are* we up to, Agent Cash?"

"De-extincting Neanderthals."

He stared at her, his face growing pale. He said nothing for a moment and then shook his head. "Bloody hell, I hate to do this. Put your weapons on the floor." He turned and spoke to the soldiers behind. "Shoot anyone who disobeys."

"This is insane, Maximilian," said Colcord. "*Think* about what you're doing. People know where we are."

"I'm done talking. Look, mate, I'm sorry, but there's no other way. *Guns on the floor, now. Slow and easy.*"

They were in an impossible situation. Cash reached in and slid out her Glock, knelt, and laid it on the floor. Colcord followed suit.

"No one else?"

"We don't pack," said Romanski.

"Turn around and place your hands on the back of your heads."

They did so.

"Now walk back to the doors."

Cash put her hands on her head, and they walked back to the set of doors with the windows.

"Stop there. Wait."

Behind them, two men with assault rifles came forward. They were searched and their radios and cell phones removed. The soldiers then held open the doors for them.

"Go through," said Maximilian.

They went through and came out on the catwalk above the playground. At that moment, a bell went off, an ordinary school bell. Cash could see below as the children gathered in several lines and began filing out various doorways, adults escorting. With a start, she saw that some of the adults also looked strange.

"Turn around."

Cash and the rest turned around. Now, in the light, they could see. Maximilian stood in front, along with Karla Raimundo, the Erebus CEO they had interviewed earlier. Behind stood Barrow, sweating and pale, with a line of security officers armed with AR-15 rifles and sidearms.

"Looks like the whole gang is here," said Colcord.

Cash said, "You're making the mistake of your life."

"You brought this on yourselves," said Maximilian. "Curiosity killed the bloody cat."

57

Slavomir Doyle was hoarse from yelling all afternoon at the crew breaking down the set and storing everything in the prop trailers. The crew had finally finished up around four thirty and gone back to the lodge to pack up and leave. Doyle had stayed behind to do a final check and make sure everything was buttoned up tight. He strode about, furious, thinking of the hole this was going to blow in his budget. Millions of dollars thrown away and now a gang of killers roaming around with their dynamite. What a fuckup. After the confrontation, Adair had disassembled his gear and equipment, packed up, and left with his crew. Ballou had retreated to his trailer and locked himself in—saying he had to talk to his agent. Doyle had no doubt why: they were figuring out ways to chisel more money out of the production by invoking the schedule-delay penalty clause in the contract. The greedy bugger had been in there for hours.

The supposed drop-dead deadline for them to be out of the valley was five p.m. But he didn't give a flying fuck about the deadline. He'd already paid Erebus over three million dollars, and as far as he was concerned, that entitled him to take all the time he needed. Still, he wanted to get this shit show wrapped up as soon as possible because he was just bleeding money, racking up meal penalties and overtime.

His eye fell once again on his big beautiful train, now a Styrofoam slag heap. A new one would have to be rebuilt from scratch off-site and brought in to be assembled. But when would that be? And how long would it take? No one could tell him when they might be able to return—it could be a day or two, a week, a month. Meanwhile, if he wanted to retain his crew, he'd have to keep paying them—otherwise half of them would go off and take other jobs, and he'd have to round up another crew at even more expense and time.

He looked at his watch. Almost five o'clock. In the distance, in base camp, he saw the door to Ballou's trailer finally open, and out came the actor, still dressed in that ridiculous Gene Autry getup, a sycophantic assistant dancing behind him with a clipboard.

He came striding over, looking as cool as ever. "How's it going, Slavomir?" he asked.

"It's fucked. Very, very fucked."

He nodded politely. "Any word on when we can resume?"

"They say in a few days," Doyle said, lying.

"I see." Ballou took out a silver cigarette case, opened it, removed a cigarette, tapped it on the case, placed it in his mouth. Then he extracted a lighter and lit it, exhaling a long stream of smoke. "You can imagine, Slavomir, how much this has disrupted my schedule."

Doyle made a huge effort to cover up his irritation and let Ballou get on with his small talk before dropping the bad news. Getting mad at Ballou would be colossally counterproductive. The man was as sensitive as a blubbering baby. "I'm so sorry, Brock. I'm sure you understand that all this is out of my control."

Ballou nodded, taking another drag and looking out over the set. "Really too bad about the train. It's a shame the scene didn't go as planned."

"You can say that again."

"Any idea who stole the dynamite?"

Doyle shook his head. "I think it was some rogue Erebus employee. This whole place is a disaster."

Another thoughtful nod. "I was just talking to Billy."

Billy was Ballou's agent, a hair-plugged, braying jackass. Doyle despised him.

"I hate to say this," Ballou went on, "but Billy's insisting that we invoke a scheduling penalty, depending on how long this delay goes on. I tried to talk him out of it, but you know agents . . ." His voice trailed off, and he sucked in more smoke.

Tried to talk him out of it. What bullshit. Tried to talk him *into* it, more likely. The two bastards were slavering at the mouth, thinking about the juicy addition to Ballou's already bloated compensation.

The leading man went on, "I just wanted to give you a heads-up so there're no hard feelings. Billy's people will be in touch with your people, but I wanted to let you know personally—because of our good relationship."

"Thank you, Brock, that's much appreciated." *Fuck you too.* How does a guy like that smoke and keep such clear skin? Nobody in Hollywood smoked anymore except him. Doyle hoped he'd get cancer—but not until shooting was over.

Doyle saw one of Erebus's jeeps draw up and park next to the gate. A man in a uniform got out. It was the assistant director of security, no doubt coming to hassle them again about being out by five.

"Well," said Ballou, "I'm going to head back to my trailer and start packing up. Thanks for your understanding."

"Of course," said Doyle, mustering a pleasant expression.

Ballou moved off, nodding a perfunctory greeting to the security person, who was striding over, looking angry.

The man came up to Doyle. "Can't this go any faster? You're supposed to be out of here by now."

Doyle looked him up and down. He wasn't about to be pushed around by some door-shaker.

"To paraphrase Yogi Berra," Doyle said, "we ain't gone till we're gone."

58

Cash stared at Barrow. The man was pale and sweating. "We came in here with a search warrant," she said. "We're law enforcement. Our purpose here is to search the premises for evidence related to the homicide of Officer Lane Johnson. The warrant's a matter of record—they know we're here."

Barrow looked flummoxed, speechless.

"They know what we're doing," said Maximilian. "They saw the playground and—"

"I'll take care of this," said Raimundo, cutting him off. She turned to Cash. "You've got more balls than common sense, Agent Cash."

Cash looked at her and then back at Barrow. He looked like he was cracking. She might be able to work on him. "The felonies you and your men are in the process of committing are, so far: assault, kidnapping, conspiracy, impeding law enforcement officers serving in their official capacity—"

"Shut up. Just *shut the fuck up*!" Barrow screamed. "Or we'll gag you. Understand?" He grasped his head in both hands. "Oh my God, what are we going to do with these people?" He looked up. "Why did you break in here? This ruins everything." The billionaire was unhinged, his face flaming, sweat streaming down.

But Raimundo remained cool and collected. She said quietly, "Nothing has been ruined, Mr. Barrow. We've got the situation under complete control."

"How?" he cried. "This was so"—he almost spluttered with rage—

"*unexpected*. What have you done? Cutting through that door! My God, what a mess you've created coming in here!"

"I will handle this," said Raimundo crisply. She turned to them. "I spoke to McFaul just now; he thinks you went into the mine to collect evidence from the crime scene. You didn't tell him that you were going to cut through the steel plate and see what was behind it, did you? You didn't tell him you had a search warrant. He's not concerned about you, and neither he nor anyone else has any idea where you went in the mine or what your real purpose was here. Inside the mine, you haven't been able to contact anyone. The search warrant no doubt is vague about where you'll be searching. So nobody knows you came through that door or what you've seen—and nobody *will* know. Within the hour, we're going to seal that steel door back up and polish it in such a way that there will be no evidence you even went through it."

At this, Cash felt a creeping chill. "So, you're going to kill us?"

"Wait. We can't do that," said Barrow loudly. "If we kill cops, the investigation will land on us like a ton of bricks!"

Raimundo turned to Barrow. "The investigation will merely show that mines are dangerous and the air is often contaminated with carbon monoxide and other deadly gases."

Barrow was breathing hard, his face twisted in indecision and agony.

Raimundo added, "Do you understand what I'm saying, sir?"

Barrow shook his head and kept shaking.

"Enough talk," she said. "Let's just get this over with. Mr. Barrow, pull yourself together."

"I don't like this solution," Barrow said. He was sweating like a stuck pig.

She said calmly, "Once you've had a chance to consider it, you'll see there's no choice, sir. You won't be a party to it, and you'll never hear of it again."

Cash glanced at Colcord, whose face was white.

"I don't know . . . ," Barrow moaned.

"Are you going to let me and Mr. Maximilian take care of this little problem, Mr. Barrow? *Think* what's at stake. You know I always have your best interests at heart. We've come a long way."

After a moment, he nodded dumbly.

"Good." She turned to Maximilian. "Take Mr. Barrow back to his quarters. Assign a guard to make sure he remains there for the next hour—and makes no calls."

"Yes, ma'am." Maximilian took Barrow's arm. "Sir? This way."

The billionaire was led off, passive and unprotesting, his shoulders drooping. Cash watched him shuffle off like a browbeaten child. She was incredulous—what a change from the blustery, assertive business-man. It was clear where the real power lay.

Raimundo turned back to the soldiers. "Take them to the CO."

Cash wondered who the CO was—commanding officer?

"Should we restrain them?" the head soldier asked.

"No restraints. The marks might be noted later. If anyone resists or tries to escape, shoot them."

"Raimundo," said Romanski loudly, "why are you breeding Nean-derthals up here?"

Raimundo looked at him sharply. "I see you've made a clever deduc-tion. Congratulations." She turned to the guards. "Take them away."

59

In his personal quarters deep in the Fryingpan Mine complex, Karman finished playing the second violin part of Pachelbel's Canon in D. He lowered his violin and looked at his pupil, who was lowering her violin as well, looking up at him hopefully, waiting for praise or a kind word.

"That was an improvement," he said with an encouraging smile. "How did the music make you feel?"

"Good," she said.

"Did it bring up any particular thoughts or feelings?"

"I felt like I was walking in the mountains."

"Oh, that's beautiful. That's perfect." Karman felt an enormous swelling of pride as he looked into her funny little twelve-year-old face—she had played acceptably, but more importantly, with phrasing and sensitivity to the music. And she managed to stay in tune some of the time. *Like walking in the mountains.* That was poetry. Neanders understood and loved music as much as Sapiens. And it was amazing how well they responded to the Suzuki method. The fact that they could play a violin at all was quite remarkable, but it was just one more surprise in what had been two decades of surprises, which had shattered every preconception of what Neanders were like or what they could do. Karman had come to prefer their company to Sapiens—Neanders were direct, frank, and ingenuous. They were much less manipulative than humans and were not at all good at lying and cheating. Humans had partly mitigated their violence problem through lying, manipulating, and deceiving their way out of potentially violent situations.

He looked down at her shining, eager face, her straw hair and green eyes, wide mouth and puggy nose. A Sapiens would find her looks off-putting, strange, even ugly, but he didn't. She was beautiful in her own childlike way. As were they all.

"Shall we try to sight-read a little Vivaldi?" he asked, raising his bow questioningly.

"Yes, Professor."

"Good. Let's play the A-minor Concerto, second movement." He took out the music and set it on the stand, opening it to the page. "Vivaldi wrote this music in a place called Mantua, in Italy, three hundred years ago. It's a beautiful piece. You'll love it."

She nodded, her short bob swaying.

"Now before we begin, let's look over the music. First, what key is it in?"

She stared at the music notation and touched the key signature with a stubby finger. "One flat."

"That's right."

"F major?"

"Are you sure? Look at the first note."

"D minor."

"Excellent! And the tempo marking?"

"Largo."

"Meaning?"

"Slow."

"And now, can you read to me the description below the stave?"

"*Cantabile e molto sentito.*"

Her Italian accent was atrocious, and she stumbled over the words—Neanders were certainly not linguists—but Karman didn't bother correcting her. That wasn't the important thing. "What does it mean?" he asked.

A long silence. She scrunched up her face, her nose wrinkling. "I don't know."

"Do you know what language it is?"

"Italian."

"Good! Italian is the language of music. It means 'singing and with great feeling.' It was Vivaldi's way of telling the violinist *how* to play it.

He wants you to think of the violin as an extension of your own body, so that through it, you are singing as if with your own voice and pouring into the violin your own feelings."

"Yes, Professor."

"So what we have here is a piece of music that is slow and singing and a little dark and mysterious."

"Sad?"

"Not sad—no. Not happy either. Something that gives you . . . a shiver."

At this, the girl smiled. "A shiver," she repeated. "I like shivers."

"Exactly. Now—shall we begin?"

She raised the three-quarter-size violin and tucked it under her chin, poising the bow, her eyes on Karman, waiting for the signal.

Karman nodded and made an exaggerated downward bowing motion, and they began, playing together.

He closed his eyes as they played, his ears listening lovingly to her squeaky, scratchy notes and awkward corrections as the girl struggled with the music, trying to stay in tune—but all the same, it was a remarkable thing, a truly remarkable thing.

A loud knock came at the door.

60

"You're playing God," said Colcord, "and you're going to go down in flames."

"We aren't interested in your petty judgments," said Raimundo. "We're done with talk." She turned to the head guard. "The next time a prisoner speaks, shoot him."

"Yes, ma'am."

"Take them to the CO and be done with it. Now."

The guards prodded Cash and the others with their rifle tips. "Get going."

As they were escorted down yet more long hallways—the place seemed endless—Cash tried to assess their chances in a fight. It would clearly be hopeless. There were eight guards, armed to the teeth, versus the four of them, unarmed, and they were deep in the enemy's terrain. Once again, Cash wondered, who exactly was the CO and what was his role? Was this some kind of military or government operation? They could have turned Barrow, but this Raimundo was as cold as ice. Maybe the CO would be more amenable.

She glanced at Colcord and got an answering look in return.

The guard contingent, led by Raimundo, escorted them down a series of hallways and corridors. At one point, Cash heard the faint sounds of a violin, but that faded away. Through a locked door, they entered an attractive, hotel-like corridor with carpeting, pleasing wallpaper, and light fixtures. Doors lined either side: thick glass doors. As they walked through, Neanderthals came to the glass to watch them go past—all were adults, dressed in the same preppy L.L.Bean clothing. They pressed their faces and hands against the glass, and some of them looked misshapen and freakish, with distorted features and twisted bodies. Those with their faces against the glass started making sounds with their lips—buzzing, razzing sounds, ugly sounds, or they licked the glass with grotesque tongues. Others drummed softly on the glass, staring with bug eyes, their mouths twisted, like inmates in an asylum. It was like an asylum, except that through the glass, Cash could see clean, hotel-like living quarters. It didn't look like quarters designed to house prisoners, but these Neanderthals were clearly locked in. The experience was unnerving and disturbing—who were these people? Some of them were not normal even by Neanderthal standards. They were freakish, abnormal in body and mind.

At the end of the "hotel" hall, they came to another locked door. The lead guard punched a code into a keypad and opened it. They were prodded at gunpoint into another dingy corridor, concrete and cinder block, which made a turn and dead-ended in a steel door with a glass porthole. That door was opened with another keypad.

"Inside," the lead guard said.

They were herded into the room. It was small and empty, with a drain in the middle and a light set into the ceiling.

"What *is* this?" said Colcord. "Where's the CO?"

"Get them in the back of the room," Raimundo said to the guards. "Push them back and get out."

The guards jabbed at them with their rifles. "Get back. *Back.*"

Cash shoved a rifle to one side. "What's this bullshit? You said we were going to the CO."

Raimundo issued a harsh laugh.

Romanski said, pointing to a nozzle in the wall: "CO. *CO.* Carbon monoxide. That's what this is. A fucking gas chamber. They're gonna make it look like we died of gas poisoning in the mines."

Cash took this in with an electric shock. She exchanged a glance with Colcord and saw the same idea in his eyes: it was now or never. She charged Raimundo, slamming into her and taking her down hard. Colcord simultaneously took a swing at the lead guard and grappled with him. Cash landed on top of Raimundo and wrapped her hands around her throat, seeing the look of terror in the woman's eyes. But someone smashed Cash across the back of the head, and she saw a burst of stars and everything went far away. She felt herself being dragged, heard distant voices and a loud clang, and then swam back into consciousness. Colcord was lying beside her, his face bloody, nose crooked, blood pouring out—broken. Romanski and Reno were also on the floor, beaten but alive. It was over almost as soon as it had begun.

Cash struggled to get up. The steel door with the porthole was shut. She staggered to her feet, fighting a wave of dizziness, and dragged herself over to it, turning the handle, but it was locked. She looked through the porthole. The hallway was empty. Everyone had gone.

She pounded on the door and yelled, the solid steel muffling her blows. She threw herself against the door, but it yielded not at all. Her head pounded and swam from the sudden effort, and she had to steady herself by leaning against the wall. She looked around the room, but it was bare and the walls and floor were made from smooth, welded stainless steel plates, with just the one light inset into the ceiling, a drain in the floor, and the nozzle in the far wall, up high.

They were going to be gassed in there. Gassed with carbon monoxide.

And even as she realized that, she heard a hiss from the nozzle and felt a stream of air issue from it—cool, colorless, and strangely fresh-smelling.

61

Wallace McFaul watched the press gathered at the glass wall, wondering where Maximilian and most of his guards had suddenly rushed off to—leaving him shorthanded to deal with this shit. And where was Cash and that sheriff when he needed them most? He had been calling her regularly on the radio and cell phone, but she must still be up in the mine, gathering evidence with Romanski. She'd been up there for hours. What was so important that she had to leave the main investigation on such a minor errand? Had something happened to her? If he didn't hear from her in two more hours—by six p.m.—he'd send some people up there to investigate.

The eager throng of reporters crowded at the glass wall. The video media was particularly excited—this was hot footage. Erebus had always been restrictive with footage of their creatures, building up a sense of mystique.

He stared out at the huge animals gathering at the lake with a sour, aggrieved feeling. The woolly mammoths were gigantic, but they weren't even the most spectacular of the animals on display down there. There was one animal waddling along with huge claws, which he thought must be a giant ground sloth. And then out came a rhinoceros that was staggeringly huge, twenty feet tall, looming above the tops of trees it just walked over, flattening them as if they were sticks, the ground trembling with every step it took. The sun had just set, leaving the surrounding peaks painted in red, filling the valley with a soft warm light. Hard to believe such a place could be the scene of murder and cannibalism. But this had to stop. They had to leave. They'd *promised*.

"Ladies and gentlemen of the media!" he yelled, wading in among them. "May I have your attention, please!"

Now that they knew he had nothing new to report, they ignored him completely.

"Ladies and gentlemen!"

It was hopeless. Should he start issuing citations? That would backfire, negate all his efforts at cultivation. It was enraging. He pulled out his radio and called for Graves, the leader of the SWAT team. She came on immediately.

"Graves here."

"Lieutenant, I need some muscle up here in the lodge, main hall. The media were supposed to leave at four, but they won't go."

"Copy that. But we've only got six guys patrolling the lodge perimeter. Okay to reduce that to four, send you two?"

"Send me three."

"Copy that. Sending up three guys."

He hung up. The DPD guys would show he meant business, get those press bastards out.

He heard a deep voice behind him. "You in charge here?"

He spun around. A man in a blue suit, with a white beard and red face, came up behind him, breathing hard and swaying on his feet. He looked vaguely familiar.

"Who are you?"

"Gunnerson," the man said. "Father of the victim. Those bastards guarding my room seem to have vanished."

The billionaire. "Yes, Mr. Gunnerson, I'm so sorry for your loss—"

"Cut the crap and tell me what's going on."

And he was drunk, McFaul realized as a wave of whiskey-laden breath washed over him. "Mr. Gunnerson, we're making excellent, *excellent* progress on the case—"

"I already heard your bullshit on TV," he said. "You got any of those murdering sons of bitches yet?"

"We're on their trail, got them on the run." He didn't say anything about pulling the search teams out of the valley or the stolen dynamite. "I expect to wrap up in twenty-four hours."

The man staggered closer and pressed a finger to McFaul's chest. "Lemme tell you—"

McFaul brushed the hand away; he wasn't going to put up with being touched, even by this man. "Sir, stand back, please."

"Stand back?" he said loudly. And now, McFaul saw some media people nearby were turning, their attention attracted by Gunnerson's loud voice.

"It's Gunnerson!" one of them suddenly exclaimed, hustling over with a microphone. "Mr. Gunnerson, I'm from KBUT in Laramie—"

"Get that fucking thing out of my face!"

"I'm so sorry for your loss. Could we ask a few questions?"

Now everyone was converging on them. "Mr. Gunnerson—so sorry—I'd like to ask you—"

They were surrounded by an excited mob, mics thrust in their direction.

"Hey, hey, give the man some space!" McFaul cried as Gunnerson shoved a cameraperson who had stepped too close.

"Mr. Gunnerson! Mr. Gunnerson!"

There was a sudden flash of light beyond the windows, almost immediately followed by a terrific boom. The entire wall of glass shattered and dropped like a curtain, and the building rocked violently on its foundations. McFaul was thrown off-balance by the shock wave, and Gunnerson went down like a sack of cement, amid gasps and cries from the crowd.

A moment later, the lights flickered and went out, leaving the great hall in a twilight gloom, except for the lights of the cameras on battery power, which danced and staggered around as their operators recovered from the explosion.

McFaul was frozen on the spot with horror. The killers, the crazies, had blown something up—sounded like it came from down the valley, near the Mammoth Gates.

Gunnerson clawed himself up from the floor with an incoherent roar, and the media crowded around both him and Gunnerson, cameras running, yelling out questions, already recovered and thrilled to be on the spot of the disaster.

McFaul pulled out his radio, calling Maximilian. He could hear Gunnerson yelling. The press were jostling and bombarding him with questions.

"What happened?"

"Was that an explosion?"

"What blew up?"

"Who did it?"

The emergency channel was overloaded with chatter. He tried Graves; that channel too was jammed. Where the hell were his three guys?

"What's your comment?" they were shouting and crowding into him. "What's happened?" The shouting went on and on, question after question. The press were in a frenzy, going to milk the disaster for all it was worth.

"I don't know what happened!" McFaul cried, switching through the emergency channels. "We're on it. We're *addressing* it!"

"How? *What* are you doing? *What* blew up?"

He backed away from them, calling Cash on the emergency channels, and then he tried Maximilian and Graves again, but all the channels were either jammed with traffic or were down, just static. Where was everybody? Where had Maximilian taken the guards? Where were his three SWAT guys? He could hear Gunnerson cursing and hollering at the media—and of course they were getting it all on tape, loving every minute, surrounding and tormenting him as if he were a circus bear.

McFaul felt overwhelmed, gripped by a rising panic. Where was the security that was supposedly protecting the lodge?

He saw, as if in answer to his wishes, four security guards running across the room, carrying their radios. He shouted at them, "You, hey! Stop!"

But they ignored him, racing past and into the staff area. McFaul shoved a reporter out of the way and followed at a jog. He would go down to the security area and rouse those people and find out what happened and get some coordination going.

He held the key card he'd been given to the security door entrance, but nothing happened. Of course—there was no power. He pushed open the door—it had unlocked—turned and shut it in the face of the surging press. He tried to hold it shut, but the damn reporters pushed it open anyway.

"This is a restricted area!" he shouted and was ignored as they streamed in.

Fuck it. He turned and headed down the hall, down the emergency stairs, and entered the security area. He was astonished: it was almost empty. Where had everyone gone?

"You!" He seized a young man sitting at a video screen. "What's going on? Where is everybody?"

The poor man was in shock. "There's some kind of emergency up at the labs. Everyone was called up there."

"What kind of emergency?"

"I don't know. All these video feeds went dead—no power."

"Don't you have emergency generators?" McFaul cried.

"Yes—but they're not kicking in."

"Why? What's going on?"

Now the press were streaming in. It was enough to drive you mad.

"I don't know."

Jesus, this was going nowhere. He felt gripped with panic. They should have called in the National Guard—in fact, that's what they needed to do right now. He whipped out his cell phone—no bars. He got back on the radio—how to connect with the governor's office? The emergency channels were hopeless.

He had to get back upstairs; maybe he could pick up cell reception higher up. He ran out of the room, pushing past the scrum of press, and headed back up to the great hall.

He found it a complete scene of chaos.

Still no bars. With the loss of power, there must have been a loss of cell coverage too.

What to do now? The emergency channels on his radio were still overloaded. He went to 154.905 gigahertz, Colorado State Patrol, and found it was quiet, broadcast an emergency call, waited for a response, broadcast again, tried several other state and county law enforcement frequencies, but could get no response. The problem was, most of the frequencies weren't monitored, and the working ones were either jammed or down.

And then he paused. Was that smoke he smelled? He looked around wildly. That *was* smoke. Where was it coming from? He scanned the room, and what he saw chilled him: smoke was issuing from the seams of the main elevator doors, getting thicker even as he stared. There was a fire below, and smoke was coming up the elevator shafts. He spun around and looked toward the shattered windows, and he could see more clouds of smoke billowing up from the outside.

Son of a bitch, the building—the huge wooden lodge—was on fire.

62

Cash stared at the nozzle in horror and tried to cover it with her hands to block the flow of gas, but it was under pressure and would not be stopped. She backed away to avoid breathing it in.

Colcord sat up. "Oh my God," he said, holding his head. Reno and Romanski were also stirring. They had all been beaten.

Cash took another step back from the nozzle. She recalled from somewhere that carbon monoxide was a heavy gas. It would settle at floor level and fill up the room from there.

"Hey!" she said. "Everyone—stand up. Off the floor, get up on your feet!"

They did so, groaning and stumbling. She then thought, *What's the use?* They were dead regardless. There was no way out of this metal box. It was monstrous—their bodies would be arranged in some mine tunnel, and everyone would assume death by carbon monoxide poisoning—a common fatality in mines.

She realized she was hyperventilating. How stupid was that? Were they going to die? Of course they were.

Colcord came over and put his arm around her. "Agent Cash, there's something I've been wanting to tell you—"

"Don't say anything," Cash interrupted. "Not now."

He shook his head. "Okay."

"I can't believe this shit," said Romanski. "These people—this is what the fucking Nazis did. Eugenics meets the twenty-first century. I'm not ready to die like this."

Cash swallowed. Neither was she. But only a miracle would save them now.

The light in the ceiling flickered, and a vibration passed through the floor, followed a few seconds later by a rumble, a deep and distant thunder.

And then the light blinked out entirely, plunging the room into absolute blackness.

For a moment, Cash was stunned. The blackness was so absolute it was disorienting. But then she realized the hissing had stopped. A power failure. She took a step forward, and another, and found the steel wall with her outstretched arms. The door to the room would be to her right. She fumbled along the wall until she found the door and then groped down to its handle—and turned it.

The door opened.

"Hey," she said. "*Hey!* The door's unlocked." Hardly believing it, she pulled the door all the way open—a miracle. An insane miracle. The hallway beyond was also as black as night. She lowered her voice. "Everyone get over here. *Quietly.*"

A light came on; Romanski's face appeared in the dimness. She realized: of course, they still had their flashlights.

They gathered around him in a tight group.

Cash whispered, "Emergency power might be coming on any moment. We've got to get out of here, move fast and silently, and use only the one five-lumen light. Is everyone okay to move?"

Everyone nodded.

"Sheriff, can you retrace our steps out of here?"

"I'm not sure."

"Let's all try to remember." She kicked herself for not paying more attention as they were being led through the maze of hallways; she'd been too traumatized.

She paused. There were sounds coming down the hall, a hubbub of excited voices. She had a sudden fear that it was the guards coming back to check on them, but as the sounds got louder and closer, she realized these were no guards; it was a mingling of yells, clapping, laughter, and whistles. It sounded like a mob.

The power failure that had unlocked their door had, perhaps, released the locks everywhere—including in that hotel-like hallway, freeing all the inmates or whoever they were.

"What's this?" said Romanski. "What's going on?"

"The Neanderthals are out of their quarters," said Cash.

Now they could see the glow of faint, indirect light coming from around the corner as the hubbub of voices came closer—yells, expostulations, whistles—the sounds of a mob growing excited. They were coming their way.

Cash said, "We'd better hide in here until they go past. Understood?"

A murmur of agreement. As the sounds got louder in the hallway, Cash eased the door almost shut. But not all the way. She realized that if emergency power came on, they might get locked in again, the gas resuming—so she propped open the door slightly with her foot, hoping that it wouldn't be seen.

The rowdy noises came closer, and a reddish light shone through the porthole window. The silhouette of a man—a Neanderthal, with that big, long mouth and no chin—passed by, carrying a burning torch. And then there were others, streaming past, not just men but also women, some with torches, others with flashlights. A few of the women were carrying children and babies. All came streaming past in a hurry, their pale faces grimly set as if with a singular purpose.

63

Marius Karman left his quarters and was on his way to the entrance of the mine when the rumble passed through and the lights flickered and went out. He froze in the darkness, waiting for the backup power to kick in. When nothing happened, he realized this must have been a deliberate act and not just a standard power failure. He also knew that the default position of the locks throughout the complex was set to be unlocked—a precaution to make sure no one would be trapped in case of a fire, cave-in, or other emergency. Which meant, with the failure of backup power, the Neanders would get out and could go anywhere. Especially the defective adults.

That was bad news. The Neanders, who had stolen the explosives—he had recently heard about that—had dynamited the valley's power grid. Which meant they had a plan. He wasn't completely sure what that plan was, but he had a pretty good idea. And they also had a leader, equally disturbing, since previously the Neanders had been disorganized and unsystematic. Now they were organized.

It was pitch-black in the hallway, and he had no light. He was alone. He felt in his pockets but of course he had no matches or lighter. But he did have his cell phone. Pulling it out, he checked the battery life—half—and turned on the flashlight.

He stood in the dim corridor, the light barely illuminating ten feet in front, his mind churning through all the possibilities, the likelihoods, exploring the outcomes. Part of him was frightened, part of him was full of sorrow. But another part of him was . . . gratified. The others had been underestimating the Neanders for so long, denigrating them, dismissing them, treating them like children—it had almost driven him mad. Now they had better take them seriously.

Of course, it was way too late for that to make a difference. What was going to happen now, Karman had no idea. But it was going to be big.

It was quiet in the passageway, off the beaten path between the front labs and the back living quarters. He had some time before the Neanders came this way. They would be roaming. They would be hunting. And they would be killing.

It was clear he needed to get out of the mountain as soon as possible, because the place was now a death trap for Sapiens. The shortest route would be to continue toward the front portal of the Fryingpan Mine, but that's where he'd be most likely to run into Neanders. Better to go out some back way. In fact, the best way—the way least likely to run into anyone—would be through the Jackman Mine, where—he had just heard from Maximilian—Cash and her team had cut through the steel door blocking the adit that connected Jackman to Fryingpan.

He placed a hand against the cool wall of the tunnel and visualized in his mind the layout of where he was and where he wanted to go. He could find his way if he kept in his head a strict dead reckoning of every step he took.

And so Karman began . . . straight ahead, seventy-five feet—thirty steps at two-point-two-feet per stride—and then turn right and go another one hundred feet . . .

64

As the distant rumble and vibration died away, Karla Raimundo froze in the sudden blackness. A moment later, Maximilian's flashlight turned on, and she reached down and pulled hers from her utility belt and turned it on as well.

"The emergency power will kick in any moment," said Maximilian, who had rejoined her after taking Barrow to his quarters.

They waited.

"The transition to backup should have been seamless," said Raimundo. "It should have happened instantly."

"What are you saying?" Maximilian asked.

"This is no accident," said Raimundo.

"You think the Neanders cut the power?"

Raimundo looked at him. Could he really be that thick? Now she could hear sounds, faint noise, echoing down from afar in the hallways. The locks were electronic; with the power failure, they had all unlocked. This was never supposed to happen.

"We've got to get ourselves to a secure location," she said to Maximilian.

"Are they out? The bloody Neanders are out?"

"Obviously."

"What happened to the two independent layers of backup power? It's supposed to be redundant!"

She didn't bother answering. Her mind was preoccupied with their present situation. The living quarters where Barrow was holed up—that was the securest place within reach. That's where they had to go. Not only that, but there were two guards with Barrow, armed with AR-15s. She bitterly regretted deploying the rest of the guards up to the front of the mine or guarding the sequencing labs. She instinctively reached for her comms, but then realized that, without power, the underground comm system with its network of repeaters wouldn't work.

"We need to get to Barrow's quarters," she said, moving into a swift walk. "We'll be safe there."

She could hear the growing commotion of the Neanders echoing through the corridors. They were bent on bloody work, no doubt. These were the worst, the error-ridden early failures of the de-extinction process. She had told Karman time and time again to put them into the CO room, which had been built especially for the purpose of putting the misbegotten to sleep. But Karman was sentimental and Barrow was weak, and she had been overruled. She had been dealing with this for ten years. Almost all of Erebus's problems had been caused by Barrow's indecision and Karman's unaccountable affection for the brutes. And this was the result. Worst of all—absolutely the most disastrous decision Karman and Barrow had made—was to educate the Neanders. They were bred for only one purpose: their genes. But no, Karman had insisted on raising them like human children, putting them in classrooms, showing them movies, teaching them how to read and play music and do math and paint and sing and play games—and *especially* giving them access to computers and technology. None of this would have happened if the Neanders had been kept in happy ignorance and illiteracy. She had argued time and again that Neanders with knowledge would be dangerous, that they'd figure things out and rebel. She'd been overruled every time. And this was the result.

Reaching the elevator, she realized that, of course, it wouldn't work without power, and so she diverted to the nearby stairwell, heading down to the living quarters. The high-security locked doors of the stairwell were also unlocked—everything was unlocked.

Maximilian followed in silence. The growing commotion of the Neanders now seemed to be spreading. The sounds were coming from everywhere and nowhere at once as the brutes, elated no doubt with their freedom, fanned out. What were they doing? She didn't need to guess: they were looking for humans.

The stairwell came out to the lower level where the high-security door protecting this level was also unlocked. The weakness of the system, so dependent on power for security, surprised and enraged her. She had no idea that such a thing could happen, that a mere power failure disabled all the locks. More incompetence from some low-level engineer.

This lower level was off-limits to the Neanders, and indeed, it had been kept secret from them. It was the Sapiens level, the executive offices and living quarters, gym, and dining room. The elegance of the hallways on the Sapiens level—the beautiful wallpaper, the antique sconces, and hall tables with fresh flowers, all of which Barrow insisted upon—did not reassure her in the slightest. On the contrary, when the Neanders discovered this, it would not only confirm that this was where the Sapiens were, but it would also enrage them. This would be the level they would search first, and thoroughly.

She wondered briefly how in the world the Neanders knew to disable the backup generators. How did they even know where they were? They were clever, those brutes.

A final turn brought them to the steel door to Barrow's quarters. It was closed. Raimundo knocked and called out—she didn't want to be shot full of holes by some trigger-happy guard. "Mr. Barrow? It's Karla Raimundo. Open up."

She heard the rattle of something, and the door was opened by one of the guards. They came in, and the guard shut the door and replaced a jerry-rigged bar across it.

"Where's Mr. Barrow?" she asked the guard.

"He's in the back library, ma'am," he said.

She and Maximilian hustled back through the darkened residence. It was a masterpiece of sleek minimalism, titanium and polished wood surfaces everywhere, almost no furniture, gleaming stone floors. They passed through a foyer, a hall, and through a titanium archway into the library. Barrow, sitting by a gas fire burning through spheres of glass, jumped up and came over. The other guard was there, standing at attention.

"Thank God you've come," he said. "The Neanders blew up—"

"We know," said Raimundo. "The Neanders are out; the cell doors are open. They're overrunning the place."

"What do we *do*?" Barrow shrilled.

"We stay here," she said calmly. "Leaving is not an option. The Neanders are spreading out, and we don't know where they are."

"Will we be safe?"

Raimundo felt as if she were reassuring a child. "There's only one door, it's steel, and it's barricaded. We've got two armed men. The Neanders have got nothing but torches, knives, and spears. So yes, I think we'll be safe."

"Maximilian?" Barrow asked, turning to the security director. "Is this what you think? That we should stay here?"

"I agree with Karla. We need to hunker down. I don't see another option."

"What's happening outside? At the lodge?"

Maximilian shook his head. "I don't know. All comms are down. When I left, the press was still there, and McFaul was trying to get them out."

"The goddamned idiot," said Barrow, "inviting the press in like that." He passed a trembling hand over his head of white hair. "What do you think the Neanders are going to do?"

Raimundo said, "Let's just focus on what *we* need to do. We need to reinforce that door." She didn't add her next thought: that the Neanders would certainly be looking for them. They would be a target, if not the prime target.

"Very good, then," said Barrow. "Go reinforce that door. Maximilian, you go with her, make sure it's rock solid."

Raimundo turned and left, with Maximilian following. She went back through the residence to the entry door, which she carefully examined with her flashlight. The door was steel, and it opened inward. The door was set into a steel doorframe. While it was unlocked, the guards had barred it with a piece of angle-iron wedged into both sides of the doorframe.

"This isn't strong enough," she said. "We need a second bar across this, one that's more solid."

She examined the doorframe more closely. They would need to cut slots or holes in it to add another bar. "Are there tools or a workshop in the residence?" she asked the guard.

"Yes, ma'am, there's a workshop."

"There wouldn't be an acetylene torch, by any chance?"

"No. There's an arc welder."

That would be useless without power. "How about a power drill that runs off a battery?"

"I believe there's one there, ma'am."

"Bring it up with some metal drill bits. And get me a stronger bar to put across here—like a metal pipe or something."

"Yes, ma'am."

The guard disappeared. Raimundo pressed her ear to the door. Were the Neanders in the lower level yet? All was silent. Maybe they wouldn't find it. But no, she told herself, that was wishful thinking. They would explore every nook and cranny of the tunnels, they would find the staircase to the lower level, and they would search it. And then they would find their way out of the mines as the previous escapees had. They would get out into the world—and God knew what havoc they'd wreak.

What a catastrophe.

A few minutes later, the guard returned with a toolbox, chisels, a drill, and a stout section of pipe.

Raimundo inspected it. It was a good thick galvanized steel pipe, right for her purposes. She measured it out and drew two holes on the frame into which the pipe could be inserted. The pipe would have to be cut down to size, but there was a metal saw in the toolbox.

"Cut the end off this pipe, here," she said to Maximilian, indicating where it needed to be cut.

She took up a power drill, pressed the trigger, and heard a most satisfying whine. Thank God the battery was charged up—at least somebody had been competent. She released the trigger, inserted a metal drill bit, and began drilling into the steel frame, one hole after another, connecting them, until she'd drilled out a round opening to insert the pipe. Meanwhile, Maximilian sawed off the end of the pipe.

When the whine of the drill stopped, she heard muffled noise beyond the door—yelps and cries, whistles and yodeling.

"Listen to those buggers," said Maximilian, sweating. "Looks like they found the lower level."

"Of course they did." She began drilling a hole on the other side of the frame. They were making a lot of noise that was sure to attract attention. They'd better finish up fast. She heard loud voices in the hall outside the door.

Thump! Someone pounded on the door. *Thump! Thump!*

"*There's someone in there!*" she heard yelled in that breathy Neander voice she hated so much. "*I heard them. They're in there!*"

Fists began to pummel the door, and the handle turned frantically. The door moved, but the original bar held.

More pummeling and yelling.

"*We're gonna kill you!*"

"Done," she said, pulling the drill out. "Shove that pipe in there."

Maximilian, holding the steel pipe, jammed it in one hole, slid it in, then went to insert it in the other end. It didn't go—there was still a small corner of steel blocking it.

"Take it out!" Raimundo said. "I'll drill that burr off."

A coordinated push on the door caused it to rattle in its frame.

She smoothed off the last corner of steel with the drill, and Maximilian rammed the pipe in. Now it fit snugly. The other end went into the opposite hole.

She stepped back and shined a light over it. Solid. The other bar was not as sturdy, but the two of them together would hold. For sure they'd hold.

Now she could hear another muffled *whump!* on the door, as the Neanders beyond evidently had gotten together and were using their combined shoulder power to try to force it open. She was satisfied to see the newly reinforced door hardly move. It would take a tank to break it down.

The handle turned again, rattled, and another coordinated *whump!* took place. The commotion on the other side increased, whoops and yells and excited chatter as the crowd seemed to grow amid much loud discussion.

"*They're in there. They must be. Hey, you! We're coming to get you!*"

More thumps as they tried to shoulder themselves in. The pipe rattled but held firm.

"*The door's blocked!*"

"*Hit it! Hit it!*"

Bang! The door was struck with something heavy, and the bar jumped in its seating.

Bang! Bang!

Muffled conversation was followed by a period of quiet.

Maybe they'd given up. But no, that was not like them at all.

BOOM! sounded from the door, both bars jumping now. *BOOM!*

What the hell were they hitting it with?

BOOM!

It was something big and heavy, and she could see the steel door was slightly deformed in the middle by the blow. Cracks were forming around where the doorframe was cemented into the wall.

BOOM!

They were using some kind of battering ram, something heavy from the playground, maybe. The pipe bar bent slightly from the blow. Raimundo felt her blood run cold.

"*You're gonna die!*" came an enraged, breathy voice. "*Die! Die!*"

BOOM!

It was just so crazy. It was like a horror film. For the first time, she felt afraid for her life.

"I'm getting the other guard," Maximilian said.

BOOM! The entire door shook as if hit by a car. It deformed again, the plaster on the walls surrounding the doorframe cracking and splitting and dropping in pieces.

Maximilian returned with the other guard. She could hear Barrow's voice from the back of the residence, raised in fear and complaint. Barrow, weak, mewling Barrow. It was his fault, his and Karman's. Too late to dwell on that now.

"Position yourselves on either side, left and right," Maximilian said. "Ninety-degree angle of intersecting fire, weapons free."

"Yes, sir."

BOOM! A crease appeared in the steel, and more plaster fell. The whole residence shook from the blow.

BOOM! The crease deepened, and a small seam opened in the steel as plaster flew off the sides, the doorframe itself moving.

BOOM! The seam grew larger, and the frame buckled inward, plaster showering to the ground.

At that point, Raimundo realized the door was not going to hold.

65

When the group of Neanderthals had passed, Cash eased open the door and listened. She heard the receding sounds of chaos echoing down the hallways.

"Okay," she said. "Coast clear."

They passed through the doorway into the corridor, moving cautiously, flashlights dimmed. From there, they entered the living quarters. All the glass doors were open, the occupants gone. Beyond, the hallway branched, and Cash tried to remember which way to go from there. They had a quick discussion and decided to go left. But after half a dozen more turns, Cash realized they had gone wrong somewhere and were lost in a warren of tunnels that seemed to go every which way and nowhere at the same time. But wherever they were, they couldn't seem to escape the distant sounds of the marauding Neanderthals. It was hard to tell from which direction the sounds were coming, due to distortion through the maze of tunnels. She called a halt.

"We're lost."

Nobody disagreed.

"We need to figure out a system for finding our way out of here," she said, "or we're gonna go around in circles until we run into those crazies and get torn apart."

As they discussed their predicament, the staccato sound of automatic weapons fire reverberated down the corridors, a furious explosion in some distant part of the complex.

"What the hell?" breathed Romanski as they all froze, listening.

It went on, stopped, started again for a moment, and then silence fell again, broken by just a few isolated shots. As they waited, straining to listen, an attenuated and desperate scream came echoing down, going on for longer than seemed possible before dying away.

Cash could feel a cold trickle of sweat creeping down her neck. If they could find their way back to the giant playground, from there they could retrace their steps to the steel door and escape the mine.

Now the cries and whoops of the Neanderthals began again, filling the silence left by the firefight. There was another brief sporadic burst of gunfire.

"We can use airflow as a guide," said Romanski.

"How so?" Cash asked.

Romanski licked his finger and held it up. "Air is flowing that way."

"Yeah," said Cash, "but do we go toward it or against?"

"We go against," Romanski said. "Cool air was flowing away from that playground space as we approached it. So air is being drawn into the large space and then pushed out through the tunnels. QED, if we go against the airflow, we will arrive back at the large space."

"But there's no power," said Cash. "No more airflow."

"Doesn't matter. We're talking natural airflow. These mines were ventilated back in the old days not with HVAC but with shafts."

"Okay," said Cash. "Let's try it."

Romanski pointed in the direction they should go, and they continued on. At each turn, Romanski tested the air and directed them. Cash was surprised at how large the complex was and how much room Erebus seemed to have created for expansion.

As they moved in silence, Cash tried to wrap her head around the idea of bringing Neanderthals back to life. How could they possibly have justified it? These Neanderthals were clearly human. They had speech, they could reason, they were *people*, not animals—and yet here they were being treated like chimpanzees in a medical lab, or like the guy in *The Truman Show*, kept ignorant prisoners—to what end? The whole grotesque project was rife with profound moral repugnance. No wonder the Neanderthals were enraged and full of hatred. But to take it to the extreme of beheading innocents, cooking and eating them . . . ? A moral horror show on both sides.

As they moved down the empty hallways in silence, always into the flow of air, Cash realized, from the voices and cries, that they were also getting closer to the Neanderthals. They were walking straight into the hornets' nest.

They proceeded cautiously, staying close to the walls, pausing at each turn to check ahead and make sure the way was clear. After what felt like an interminable set of empty hallways, a set of double doors appeared like the ones that led into the playground catwalk, with two small windows. Cash gestured for everyone to turn off their flashlights. In the darkness, she could see light coming through those two windows. The smell of acrid smoke drifted down the hallway.

They crept up to the door, and Cash rose and peered through. They had reached the playground. Beyond the catwalk, in the open area below, Neanderthals were gathering—men, women, and children. Some were carrying burning torches, others flashlights and spears. One, she saw with a chill, had an AR-15 rifle slung over his shoulder—and with a start, she recognized him as the tall pseudo-priest in the video with a massive, braided mane of blond hair. He was clearly their leader, directing the show. A big bonfire had just been lit, and people were cutting down trees and throwing limbs into it, plastic toys from the playground, benches, tables—anything that would burn. The smoke rose and was drawn into a ventilation opening in the domed roof.

Near the fire, group members were carrying large jugs of clear liquid from an adjacent corridor and stacking them on their sides, openings pointed toward the fire. What did they contain? Water, in case the fire got out of control? No . . . it must be ethanol. It seemed they were getting ready to blow up the place.

She lowered herself and turned to the others. "We're there," she whispered, "but on the wrong end of the catwalk. We're going to have to circle around to reach the tunnel we came in on." She looked around in the dim light at their faces. "We stay low, moving on hands and knees and keeping to the inside wall. When we open the door, anyone looking up might see us. So we ease it open as slowly as possible and crawl out one at a time. I'll hold it open and go last. Ready?"

Everyone nodded.

"Let's go."

Still crouching, she eased open one side of the door with her right arm. When it was open enough to admit a person, she tapped Reno, and he crawled out. Colcord followed, then Romanski. She went last. Once out on the catwalk, she eased it shut.

No one below had seen.

They began crawling on hands and knees along the wall, keeping away from the railing. Below, Cash could hear the murmuring and chatter quiet down, and then a sound rose like a hum that quickly evolved into a sort of chant, high-pitched and menacing. The gathering had the feeling of organization—of a plan. Maybe even the beginnings of some sort of ceremony.

She thought that the events of the past six days weren't as random and crazy as they seemed. The kidnapping and killing of the two hikers, the killing of the baby mammoth, mocking them with the drone video transmission, luring them up to the cannibal site and the murder of Johnson, the carefully calibrated explosions that took down the power and backup, and now what seemed like setting up a gigantic fire or explosion—this was a coordinated plan. What had happened to the nine armed guards who had escorted them to the CO room? Was that shooting some sort of firefight? What had happened to Barrow, Maximilian, and Raimundo? Had they escaped?

The chanting increased from below, and a flickering light rose up, painting the fake sky ceiling above them with yellow light as a huge column of oily smoke intensified. The bonfire was growing larger. The chanting grew louder. Something was happening. What were they doing?

Cash felt it was important to know.

She touched Colcord and, with a hand signal, indicated she was going to creep over to the edge of the catwalk and look down. He shook his head vigorously, but she didn't agree. She felt she would not be seen; the Neanderthals were too absorbed in what they were doing, and the fire filled the space with a chaotic pattern of light and shadow, providing cover.

While the others waited, she crawled over to the edge and, with infinite care, peered over.

The bonfire was leaping up, and more jugs had been stacked—hundreds of gallons of clear liquid. An enormous pile was turning into a massive bonfire, sending up a plume of acrid smoke. The man with the braid stood at a makeshift altar, two poles on either side, each with something mounted on top.

Some of the Neanderthals were standing in a choir-like formation, swaying and chanting, their hands reaching upward, not unlike what they had done on the drone video. Others watched—mostly women carrying babies, toddlers, and children.

She peered down, squinting. What were on those poles? The horror of it dawned on her—they were human heads. In the flickering fire-light, she saw that they were the heads of Maximilian and Raimundo.

She heard a cry of despair and saw a man being led by two Neanderthals into the circle of chanters. It was Barrow. He was trussed with his arms tied behind—and his face in the firelight was a mask of terror. He was not gagged, and she could hear his thin wail of fear, rising and falling with the chanting as they marched him toward the bonfire. Meanwhile, the pseudo-priest led the congregation in a loud, humming sort of chant while everyone waggled their hands over their heads.

What a scene of horror.

She crept back from the edge and rejoined the group.

"What did you see?" Colcord whispered.

"Heads on pikes, Barrow tied up. And there's a guy with an automatic weapon. They're . . . getting ready to blow the place." She gestured. "We'd better get the hell out of here."

They crept around the perimeter to the double doors leading off the catwalk. Now they faced a second moment of peril—opening a door and crawling through, where, again, the door's movement might be seen from below.

Staying low, Cash grasped the bottom edge of the door and eased it open, ever so slowly. Romanski and Reno quickly crawled through, followed by Colcord. Then she went through herself and began easing the door shut from the other side.

She heard a sudden shout from below—and then a chorus of cries in those weird, breathy, high voices. *"Hey! Someone's up there!"*

66

Doyle stared over the movie town, plunged into sudden darkness by the explosion. The set had mostly been put to bed, everything battened down and locked up, and the crew gone back to the lodge. There wasn't much more to do.

It made him angry and anxious to think that the explosions he had just heard, which evidently killed the power, would be blamed on him. He hoped to hell no one had been killed. But regardless, it was not his fault. Adair was in charge—they were his explosives. Adair let those crazy motherfuckers steal his dynamite. But after their confrontation, Adair had quit and left, driving straight out of the valley with his team. Well, good riddance. It made his head spin just to think of the lawsuits that were going to come out of this. The lawyers would be feeding at the trough for years. His film might never get made.

He looked over at Ballou's trailer. The actor had been holed up in there with his PA at the time of the blackout, doing God knows what. He was one of those stars who lived in his trailer—a super-expensive honey wagon—rarely leaving it or mingling with the crew. But now that the power had failed and it was suddenly dark, it flushed Ballou out. Doyle saw the movie star exit and come striding over, a displeased look on his face, his PA following him carrying a cell phone and clipboard.

Ballou was still dressed in cowboy chic: embroidered cowboy shirt, leather vest, bolo tie with a chunk of turquoise, snakeskin boots, skin-tight black leather pants, engraved silver buckle almost the size of a dinner plate, and a 100X cowboy hat with a rattlesnake hatband. He looked ridiculous, like Gene Autry, except he couldn't sing worth shit. That's what he must have been doing all that time in his trailer, dressing and preening. He wished he could have seen Ballou's annoyance when the lights in front of his giant mirror went out.

"How in the heck am I supposed to do anything in the dark?" Ballou said as he planted himself in front of Doyle, his deep voice edging into a whiny tone. "I'm not finished packing my things. The phones aren't working, and the internet's down!"

Doyle put back on the pleasantest expression he could muster. "Brock, I'm sorry. I don't know what to say, except we're doing the best we can. I'm about to leave myself—we can't do anything without power."

"How much have we paid these people already? This is bullshit!"

"I couldn't agree more." And he did agree. Three million dollars thrown away. "Let's get down to the lodge. I'm sure they've got power there—backup power at least." He glanced in the direction of the lodge, a few miles down the valley, the view obscured by a ridge covered with fir trees.

"Mr. Ballou," said the assistant, carrying his cell phone, "I still can't get through. There are no bars."

Ballou waved a hand. "Screw it. Lock up the trailer, bring the car around, and let's go back to the lodge. We'll leave that stuff behind."

"Yes, Mr. Ballou."

Doyle's eyes strayed back to the wall of fir trees below the movie set. There was something funny down there. A low cloud was rising above the trees, a dark pall looming against the twilight sky.

"Hey, Brock. Take a look down the valley."

Brock turned and looked, squinting. "Is that smoke?"

"I think so."

Even as he stared, a black cloud billowed up above the trees. And now he could see a faint ruddy glow reflecting off the bottom of the clouds.

"Is the lodge on *fire?*" cried Ballou.

There was a muffled rumble, and a second dark cloud roiled up, followed by licks of orange. Something had exploded down there, and the fire was mounting fast.

"Oh my God," said Doyle, staring, horrified. The motherfuckers had set the lodge on fire. "Brock, go get your car. We're getting out of here. Now."

The movie star whirled around to his PA. "You heard him! Bring the car around!"

Doyle had driven up in one of the vans, of which there were several still sitting in the parking lot. The keys were hanging in the set production trailer. As the PA went jogging off to get Ballou's car, Doyle strode down to the production trailer. He went inside, grabbed the set of van keys, and exited, locking the trailer door behind him. As he did so, he heard a short scream.

He spun around. In the dimming light, he saw the PA sprinting away from Ballou's honey wagon. What the hell was going on? Then he saw the man was being chased by two figures wearing masks, dressed in camouflage.

The PA screamed again as the figures ran him down, caught him, and—oh, Jesus—twisted his head around like a chicken's, cutting—

In a surge of terror, Doyle sprinted for the parking lot, clutching the keys in his hand. And there was Ballou, also sprinting toward the lot, his hat tumbling off. They arrived at the van at the same time; Doyle dove into the driver's seat and thrust the key into the starter as Ballou scrambled into the passenger seat. The van roared to life, and Doyle stomped on the accelerator even before Ballou had gotten the door closed.

"Did you see that? *Did you*—?" Ballou screamed.

"Shut up. I got to concentrate," Doyle said as the van spun its tires in the dirt and fishtailed out of the parking area. He saw, out of the side window, those same two figures running toward the road ahead of them—to cut them off.

Doyle accelerated, the van churning up a stream of gravel. They roared down the road, just passing the two figures as they converged. He saw them in the rearview mirror, now running down the road after them, the crazy motherfuckers dressed in weird camouflage. Good luck. They'd never catch up.

Ballou was in his seat, hyperventilating. He'd lost his hat, and his formerly slicked back hair was all askew, filling the car interior with the smell of Clubman hair tonic.

Doyle kept his eyes dead on the road. What happened to the PA was the most horrible thing he'd ever seen, and he had no intention of remaining in this valley one more second. He focused all his attention on staying on the dirt road, which wound down through the forest in gentle curves. But he knew up ahead it would drop into a series of hairpin turns and then loop around the lodge on its way to the Mammoth Gates.

Ahead, over the treetops, he could now see flames leaping up into great billowing clouds of smoke. Ballou, in the passenger seat, was hunched over, gasping, weeping, hyperventilating, a complete wreck.

The road emerged from the forest and came to the hairpin descent. Now, free from the trees, he had a clear view of the lodge, about a mile away. The huge wooden structure was completely consumed in fire, burning like a son of a bitch, the flames leaping hundreds of feet into the air, with small explosions inside the inferno sending up extra gouts of fire and smoke. The forest had caught fire on the other side of the lodge and was spreading.

He slowed the van to take the first hairpin curve and slowed it even more to take the next. There were guardrails, but it was damn steep, and if he went off the side, that would be the end for sure. A third turn, and then the lower, more level part of the road suddenly came into view. He jammed on the brakes, the van screeching and slewing to a stop just before a big fir tree lying across the road, blocking it. He stared in horror: the tree had been freshly cut, and there was no way around it because of the guardrails on either side.

"God help us!" Ballou cried. "What now?"

Doyle jammed the van into reverse, laying rubber as he backed up, and swung the wheel to execute a three-point turn. He backed into the roadcut with a crunch, floored it, and lurched forward, expecting an ambush at any moment. It was going to be a five-pointer, no way to avoid it—the van was big. Another screeching lurch back and forward, and he gunned the engine, heading back up the hill.

"What are you doing?" shrieked Ballou. "You're not going *back*?"

"Did you see the fucking tree?"

"Those . . . *monsters* are back up there. My God!" Ballou's voice fell into a wail and he bent over, blubbering all over his leather cowboy vest.

Doyle tried to get a handle on what was happening. The crazies had blocked the road—the only way out of the valley. They had to get away from them . . . but where? How high up did the road go? He hadn't ever driven past the movie town, and he had no idea how much farther the road went. But it must dead end somewhere.

As long as they were in the van, moving fast, they couldn't be waylaid, but when they reached the end of the road, what would they do? Get out, climb into the mountains, try to hide? But that might be up high, even above the snow line, and they had no decent clothing. Should they ditch the van lower down, get out, and try to hide in the forest? Or hide the van somewhere and stay in it all night?

He tried to control his own breathing and pounding heart. The van was now approaching the old movie town. The road circled past it, taking a big curve around the town through a forest, and then—where did it go? They needed a map. And a strategy.

"Brock!"

Brock was moaning. What a helpless baby.

"Brock! Wake the fuck up and look in the glove compartment and see if there's a map!"

Brock's head came out of his hands, and he fumbled with the glove compartment, opening it and shuffling through the papers. No map.

"Keep looking!"

While Brock rummaged through the side compartments and center console, the van emerged from the forest, and the movie town now came back into view. He was shocked all over again—the motherfuckers had set the town on fire. Flames were leaping from the old wooden church at the north end, and more fire billowed from the windows of the livery barn in the middle. It was going up fast.

"No map!" said Ballou. "I can't find any maps!" He looked up and cried out at seeing the burning town. "They're there! Don't stop!"

Doyle didn't even bother to reply. The tires screeched as he took the curve that looped around the town. The road now climbed up over a low rise and plunged back into a dark forest, the trees whipping by, the headlights illuminating the trunks as they flashed past like endless rows of columns. The engine screamed.

The road now curved again, looping through a particularly dense part of the forest. Around the curve, he jammed on the brakes as his headlights illuminated another massive tree across the road. And he saw movement—the same two figures who had attacked the PA in the town raced out of the darkness into the headlights, crazy fucking maniacs with masks, their bodies covered with leaves and bark and grass.

"Help!" screamed Ballou.

Doyle threw the van into reverse and stomped on the accelerator. With a scream of rubber, the van accelerated backward, leaving a cloud of smoke as the figures chased them. He continued backing up, not daring to take the time to turn around, driving as fast as he dared. But those crazies were running down the road like bats out of hell, grotesquely illuminated by his headlights. He must be driving backward at close to twenty miles per hour, and yet they were keeping up—how was it possible? He gave it more gas, trying desperately to stay on the road, driving using the rearview mirrors. But the backing lights were weak and the forest was dark, and he could only go so fast. If he went off the road, crashed—he couldn't think about that.

"They're getting closer!" screamed Ballou.

There was another thing he could do. He jammed on the brakes, came to a screeching halt, threw the shift lever into drive, released the brake, and instantaneously stomped on the accelerator. The van leapt forward, and he steered straight for the two motherfuckers.

67

McFaul stumbled onto the lawn along with a mass of panicked media people, everyone scrambling madly to get away from the inferno. The huge wooden structure had gone up like a tinderbox, engulfed in flames so fast it almost felt like a bomb had gone off. There had been no sprinkler system going on, no firefighting effort, nothing. It had been crazy how fast the flames burst out of the elevator shafts, punching down the doors. It had been everyone for themselves, crews dropping their cameras and mics and whatever and running for the exits, the terrible screams as the flames boiled across the room, engulfing people.

He crossed the lawn, half running, half stumbling, feeling the heat of the conflagration on his back. He had to get far enough away from the fire to be safe. The lawn ended at a low stone wall, beyond which ran a lush meadow that sloped down toward the lake, framed on either side by groves of aspen trees. McFaul staggered to the wall and rested on it for a moment, coughing and spitting. He stank, and his lungs felt raw from breathing in the searing smoke. A few other media people had collapsed on the wall. And here came a stocky figure in a suit, lumbering and swaying. He recognized the white beard, the red face. Gunnerson.

The man sat heavily on the wall and put his face into his hands.

McFaul looked back at the lodge. It had become an inferno, a column of fire boiling a thousand feet into the evening sky. He could feel the heat on his face, and he was racked with another cough. The heat was intense—he had to move farther away. Others around him were doing the same. He rose unsteadily to his feet and climbed over the wall and walked through the long meadow grass toward a stand of aspen trees. Past it, he could see the lake, now vacant. The animals had all fled.

"Hey, McFaul! Hey!"

It was the billionaire, Gunnerson.

McFaul tried to quicken his stumbling walk, but Gunnerson fell in beside him.

"What the fuck happened?"

McFaul didn't answer.

"Hey, you know who I am? Talk to me," the man bellowed.

"The crazies got their hands on dynamite," said McFaul, still walking. "Stole it from the movie set."

"That was the explosion?"

McFaul nodded.

"And the fire? Did the crazies start the fire too?"

He shook his head. "I don't know. Erebus security was supposed to be guarding the lodge. That wasn't our responsibility. The security just . . . disappeared."

Gunnerson shook his shaggy head. "Fucking incompetents. They killed my son."

McFaul coughed again. He just wanted to get away, lie down, and curl up. They were almost in the grove of aspens. The rest of the media corps had dispersed over the meadow, away from the fire, shell-shocked, some sitting or lying down, waiting to be rescued.

"Where's the cavalry?" Gunnerson asked. "I mean, when are we gonna get some help here?"

"All the comms went down with the explosion," said McFaul. "I can't get in touch with anyone. But I'm sure they're scrambling a response. I'm sure we're going to see some action soon."

They reached the grove. McFaul walked into it, intent on getting somewhere in the middle, somewhere dark and anonymous, far away from everything. Gunnerson followed, much to his dismay. McFaul found a spot and eased himself down on a fallen tree trunk and put his head in his hands. His mind seemed to have stopped working.

"What about the CBI?" asked Gunnerson. "What about Cash? What are you fuckers *doing*?"

"I don't know," McFaul said, speaking through his fingers. He thought of Cash and Romanski up at the mine. God knows what was going on up there. He lifted his head. Through the trees, he could see the fire still raging, bathing the surrounding area in a malevolent glow and casting bloody reflections over the water of the lake. As he stared, he saw something moving cautiously along the far shore of the lake— two small figures.

"You see the people down there?" Gunnerson asked.

McFaul shook his head and didn't answer. He really didn't give a damn now. He felt numb.

"Where'd they come from?"

"We had a report," said McFaul wearily, "of some media people sneaking out of the lodge to film the animals." He glanced up at the sky. The stars, just starting to come out, were almost washed out by the orange glow of the fire. There was a muffled sound then a sudden roar; he watched with incredulity as the roof of the lodge buckled and collapsed inward with an enormous rumble, sending up a trillion sparks that danced and whirled upward as if to replace the stars themselves.

Through the slender trees, he could see the two people down by the lake coming around the shore and heading up toward the meadow where most of the refugees from the lodge were waiting. There was something odd about those figures; they were moving cautiously and, it seemed, almost furtively. As the two figures got closer, they became more visible in the glow of the fire, and McFaul could now see they were wearing masks and what looked like bodysuits.

"Jesus, they're two crazies!" Gunnerson said loudly. "They're two—"

"*Quiet*," McFaul said, crouching. He watched as the figures moved swiftly across the field toward several refugees from the fire, who were huddled together in the meadow about two hundred yards away, waiting to be rescued.

"You have a sidearm, right?" whispered Gunnerson.

McFaul ignored the question.

"Give me your gun," Gunnerson said.

McFaul shook his head. He didn't have the energy to engage further with this son of a bitch.

"Hey, you listening?"

"No." McFaul shook his head. "No."

McFaul's eyes remained fixed on the two figures, now approaching a seated group of people. The people, unaware of the approach until the last moment, sprang up and backed away, but the two figures rushed them. There was a brief struggle and several piercing screams, abruptly cut off into silence. Others waiting in the field saw what had happened and broke into a panicked flight, running every which way, while the figures, silhouetted against the fire, hunched over their struggling victims, and then one of the figures abruptly stood up, holding aloft a round, dripping object by its hair, and letting loose a cry of triumph.

"*Get down*," whispered McFaul. "*Lie flat. Hide.*"

He quickly lay flat on the leaf-strewn forest floor, face up. In a flash, Gunnerson was down beside him, his breathing heavy, breath laden with whiskey. Slowly, McFaul eased his sidearm from its holster and placed it on the ground next to him. He could hear, in the meadow beyond, more commotion and screaming and the thudding sound of feet. *Don't come in here*, he prayed. *Please, God, don't let them come in here.*

"Cover yourself," he whispered to Gunnerson. And slowly, trying not to make any noise, he began raking leaves up and around him with his hands, covering his body. He heard the billionaire next to him doing the same. After a minute, he was sufficiently covered, and he rested his hand once again on the cold, reassuring steel of the 9 mm at his side. Staring straight up into the dim crowns of the trees above him, licked in red from the fire, he told himself they were well hidden in the shadowy grove, lying among fallen trees where they'd be almost impossible to spot. Surely they would not be found.

"*I want your gun*," whispered the hoarse voice of Gunnerson in McFaul's ear.

68

Cash and the others sprinted through the tunnels, the sounds of the pursuing mob echoing behind them. The mob was making an unholy din, screeching, whistling, and ululating. It was hard to tell, from the echoes and distortions, how far back or how many there were, but the clamor seemed to be getting closer.

The corridor made a gradual turn, and there, up ahead, their flashlights illuminated the steel door, still with a hole cut in it. They leapt through the gap and continued, Colcord taking the lead. They took each turn running as fast as they could, the clamor of their pursuers ever closer. Cash's lungs felt like they were on fire.

They came out into the large open area and sprinted across it, but even before they'd reached the other side, the pursuers burst out of the tunnel they had just exited, with torches and flashlights, the big chamber magnifying their shrieks and yells.

"There they are!" one of them screamed.

The mob was only fifty yards behind. A spear came flying past them, going wide. Cash glanced back and was shocked to glimpse, among the mob, women and teenagers. They were dressed in regular clothing, no weird camouflage outfits, and they looked normal, except for their peculiar faces and the way they ran. Another spear came soaring past.

Colcord was slowing, gasping for air in the high altitude, and Cash felt she too was nearing collapse, the only thing driving her on was pure adrenaline. One turn, another, and another, and then—thank God—

the bars of the entrance gate came in view. She was shocked to see a person was there, trapped in the mine, banging on the bars and shouting into the night.

It was the scientist—Karman. He spun around. "The gate's padlocked!"

"Get out of the way!" Cash yelled, fumbling into her breast pocket and removing the key. The guards who had been outside were nowhere to be seen. She fell to her knees and reached through the bars. She grasped the padlock in one hand and slid the key into the hole with the other, giving it a twist. She struggled with the lock, thinking of the man she'd seen with the AR-15. He'd be in that mob somewhere, she felt sure.

The lock sprang open. She slipped it off the hasp and yanked open the door.

"Out!"

Karman crowded out the door first, with Romanski and Reno following.

The mob was practically on top of them, in a chorus of crazy yelps and whistles. Cash exited and held the door open for Colcord, then followed. She slammed the door, seized the padlock, and slipped it through the hasp, snapping it shut as the surging mob hit the bars. A moment later a spear came flashing out, just missing her neck, while arms and hands reached wildly through the bars, slashing at her with knives as she skipped back out of reach. She pivoted and ran as more spears came flying out.

"Go, go, go!" she cried to the others ahead of her, and they went scrambling down the scree slope below the mine entrance, loose rocks sliding and tumbling in the dark. Behind, she could hear their pursuers, now bottled up behind the locked door, yelling and banging.

"*You can run,*" a voice whistled out, "*but you can't hide!*"

"*We'll hunt you down like dogs!*"

The voices and noise became fainter as the group descended. They finally reached the meadow that also doubled as a landing zone. But now their flashlights illuminated a grim sight: the burnt hulk of the CBI's A-Star helicopter, lying on its side, flames and smoke still licking up from it. And lying around it, half-hidden in the long grass, lay the dead bodies of three people. She recognized the two guards, Hadid and Watkins, the other body evidently being the pilot.

"Look down the valley," said Colcord, pointing.

Cash lifted her eyes from the bloody scene. Way down in the valley, she could see the bright glow of a fire—actually two fires. Huge fires. The lodge and the movie town.

"They're burning the place down," Colcord said.

"Yeah," Cash said. The sight had really taken away her breath. They had no radios, cell phones, or weapons—they were in trouble. "We'd better keep going. Those bars aren't going to hold them forever. I saw one guy back in there with a rifle."

Colcord jerked his chin toward Karman, the scientist, who was standing to one side, bent over, his white hair dangling, gasping for breath. "What're we going to do with him?"

She said, "He might . . . be helpful."

"So what now?" Reno asked. "We can't go down. I'm sure they blew the Mammoth Gates along with everything else. We're trapped like rats."

There was a silence.

"Up," said Cash. "We go up and over the pass."

69

The van careened toward the sprinting figures, Doyle fanatically gripping the steering wheel, determined to run down at least one of the bastards. He expected them to split and dive off to either side—in which
case he was ready to swerve and hit one at least—but they didn't: they
came straight on.

"Die, motherfuckers!" he screamed as the van closed in, the two
men running side by side at him down the center of the road. He
braced himself for the impact—and then nothing. He was past them.
No blow or crash—they seemed to have dodged away at the last minute. But where?

He looked in the rearview mirror and was horrified to see one of
the masks leering back at him from only a few feet away—the brute
was clinging to the side of the van. And from the opposite mirror he
could see the other bastard. They'd somehow clutched onto the van as
it passed. How had they done it? It was the kind of thing only a highly
trained stuntperson could do.

"They're on the van!" Ballou screamed. "Do something!"

Doyle swerved the van, weaved it back and forth, trying to shake
them off, but the two figures clung like limpets. The van had a railing
on top for property stowage, and they were holding onto that while
making their way along the running boards, hand over hand toward
the front. The one on his side reached down and grabbed the door
handle—locked. He turned and with his arm cocked slammed his

forearm into the driver's-side window, the muffled thump turning it into a spiderweb of cracks.

Doyle would scrape them off. His headlights illuminated the road ahead, lined with bushes and little trees. He swerved to the left side of the road and ran into the vegetation, the shrubbery slapping and scraping the sides as he floored the accelerator, the wheels spinning and the van lurching and fishtailing. Then he jerked the wheel to the right and brought the van back to the road.

The son of a bitch was still there. The brush had ripped off his mask and some of his camouflage covering, and what Doyle saw frightened him more than anything—a pale, bloody face of freakish ugliness, with massive brow ridges and a giant grimacing mouth full of huge flat teeth, the man's long, blond hair in braids whipping about in the wind like some crazy Viking's.

"What the fuck?" he screamed as the figure slammed his forearm again into the window, knocking it partway in, the glass held together only by the layer of sealant. Then the crazy pulled and scratched away the gummy glass fragments and reached in and down to unlock the door.

"Fucker!" Doyle, keeping his right hand on the steering wheel, grabbed the door handle with his left and jerked the door open, slamming it into the man and partly knocking him off, the son of a bitch hanging onto the railing at the top of the van with his legs swinging free.

He shut and opened the door, again and again, battering the man's body as he clung to the roof, but he just wouldn't let go.

"No! No!" Ballou screamed on the other side, where something was happening, but Doyle was too busy trying to knock the man off on his side and pay attention to the road to see. The van swerved and fishtailed, almost going off the road as Doyle jerked the wheel back and forth.

"Fucker!" Doyle screamed again, shutting the door and pounding down the lock. He would do another off-road detour, scrape the man off. But now the bastard, still gripping the railing, reached inside again and managed to grasp the door handle, and yanked the door open, trying to climb in.

One hand still gripping the wheel, Doyle tried to grapple with the man, swatting at him several times and trying to shove him back out with his shoulder, the van careening along, but he was like a damn octopus, his hands everywhere grasping and pulling himself in, and Doyle couldn't reach the handle of the open door to shut it.

While he was struggling, he heard a scream come from Ballou and felt a spray of hot blood on the side of his face. Ballou's scream abruptly cut off.

He swerved again and stomped on the accelerator, driving off the road and straight into a brush thicket. The van plowed into the vegetation, crashing and bucking through it before striking a tree stout enough that it threw the van sideways, and it rolled up and over. Simultaneously, there was an explosion, and Doyle felt himself punched back, momentarily stunned as the van came to a rest. For a moment, he was in a panic, clawing at the thing in his face, when he realized it was the airbag having gone off. He gasped for breath, trying to recover his sanity. Everything hurt, but as he moved, nothing felt like it was broken—and the airbag had finally knocked off the bastard who had been trying to climb into his side of the vehicle. He felt something dripping on him and looked up, and nestled amid a deflated airbag in the passenger seat now above him—the vehicle lying on its side—he saw a horrible sight: Ballou, his throat cut. Behind, he could hear scrabbling in the brush and a grunting sound.

Get up and out and run.

He reached up and, grasping first the seat rest, the deflated airbag, and then the door handle, he managed to climb up past Ballou's body and crawl out the broken passenger-side window, hoisting himself up onto the side of the overturned van. Kneeling, he saw that one of the brutes was twenty feet behind the van, impaled on a broken tree trunk. The other—where was the other? Doyle looked around wildly. Was he gone? Was he the one grunting earlier? The forest was quiet.

Just get the hell out.

He jumped down from the side of the van and thrashed his way through the vegetation, heading away from the road and into the densest part of the forest. It was dark, he couldn't see, he had no idea where he was going, everything hurt like hell, and he was being scratched to pieces—but he was so focused, so pumped up with adrenaline, that he felt nothing, only the drive to run, to escape, to get away from those murdering freaks.

70

McFaul hid in the grove of aspen trees, his heart pounding so hard he felt sure they could hear it. After Gunnerson's threatening demand for the gun, he tightened his fist around the handle and moved it away from Gunnerson's reach. "Stay away from me."

He wanted to get away from this man, but he didn't dare move or make a sound. His hand gripping the weapon, McFaul looked up into the crowns of the trees, painted in orange and red light from the burning lodge. The smell of earth and leaves was stifling, and every time a breeze sifted through the treetops, more leaves came fluttering down, settling around him with little rustling sounds. He could hear Gunnerson breathing heavily near him.

The man did not renew his absurd request. Maybe he'd given up on the idea.

McFaul tried to slow his pounding heart. He thought of his office back at the CBI, and he thought of his home in Lakeview, where the lawn needed cutting and the hedge trimming. He thought of his wife and children back there. What were they thinking? Did they know about what was going on up at Erebus? They must have heard something; the news would be all over. It would be huge, especially since the national press was already in here and broadcasting at the time of the explosion. They had satellite uplinks despite the power failure—they often carried their own generators with them.

Oh yes, the world certainly knew what was happening. So where were the rescuers? Where were the SWAT teams, the National Guard rapid response teams, the helicopters flying in with soldiers? Why hadn't they come yet? It had been at least twenty minutes since the explosion—but it seemed like an eternity. But McFaul knew why they weren't here; he knew, from his many years in law enforcement, that the bigger the crisis, the longer it took to mobilize. Certainly, the crazies had blown up or blocked the Mammoth Gates, so the only way in would be by chopper. Right now, there would be SWAT teams gearing up, National Guard troops being called up and assembling, helicopters warming up, and a lot more happening besides. Something this big required a massive response, and a massive response always meant more coordination among branches of law enforcement and a longer prep time. Which meant it could be ten, twenty, or thirty more minutes before the helicopters arrived.

A lot could happen in that time.

Please, God, don't let them come in here.

From his position lying on the ground, he couldn't see what was going on in the field—the killing field—except what he could glean from the commotion coming from that direction—screams, desperate pleading, horrible sounds. The killers were at work, hunting people down. They were methodical. And no one seemed to be around to fight back. Where were the Erebus security guards? They had been there before, but then they suddenly seemed to vanish. Had they run? What about Cash and Romanski?

His mind was churning like a whirlpool. He had to stop thinking and calm himself down. The blood was pounding in his ears. Was he having a stroke? McFaul felt the steel of his 9 mm under his sweating hand. He would take one or more of the bastards with him if they came in there. But this thought scared him. He didn't want them to come in there. He didn't want to die a hero with a memorial wall of blue and a band and a flag-draped coffin. He just wanted to live to see his wife and kids. Tomorrow. That's all.

Please, God, keep them out of here.

He heard more horrible sounds from the killing field and wished he could stopper his ears, but he didn't dare move even to do that. So far, the killers hadn't entered the grove, at least from what he could hear. There had been a lot of people in the field—that's where most of those fleeing the fire had gone, collapsing on the grass, waiting to be rescued. No one had come into the grove, as far as he was aware, except Gunnerson. They were the only two.

All he had to do was survive the next ten, twenty minutes, and then the helicopters would arrive. They'd come down in that very field. That was the obvious landing zone.

Please, God, don't let them come.

He heard Gunnerson's gravelly breathing next to him. *What a coward*, McFaul thought, trying to get this gun. The rich bastard thought whatever he wanted should just be his. Staring upward, beyond the painted treetops, the sky glowed a dirty red against the huge column of fire and smoke—but beyond that, he could see a single star. He prayed to the star, he talked to the star in his mind, he beseeched the star: *Please don't let them come in here.* They wouldn't come into the grove. There was no reason to think anyone was in here. It was crisscrossed with fallen timber. Nobody else had taken refuge. The killers would stay in the field. They wouldn't search the surrounding woods and trees.

He heard a sudden grunt next to him, and all of a sudden, Gunnerson was on top of him, wheezing. Before McFaul could react, the man had seized the arm that held the weapon and was trying to wrench the gun away. The two struggled for it, thrashing around in the leaves. McFaul tried to heave the man off him, who was as heavy as a boulder. The man shook his arm, grunting like a pig, trying to pry the gun loose, making a lot of noise. He twisted hard back and forth and, with a great heave, managed to throw Gunnerson partly off. With his other arm, suddenly freed, he punched the man in the side of the head and punched again, hard, and finally got Gunnerson fully off him; McFaul yanked his gun arm free and rammed the muzzle into the man's gut and pulled the trigger.

A loud explosion took place, spraying his face with blood, blinding him. Gunnerson grunted once and lay still as McFaul frantically wiped the blood out of his eyes. Crouching, trying to control his breathing sounds, he waited and watched, trying to locate the two figures out in the meadow. There they were, on the far side—maybe they hadn't heard the gunshot. But no, now they were turning and coming toward the aspen grove, cautiously, one careful step at a time, walking as softly and deliberately as cats.

71

Standing in the meadow, Cash looked up at the thirteen-thousand-foot ridgeline.

"There's a way up," said Colcord. "Diagonally, through the second scree slope and between those outcrops. If we can get to the ridgeline, we can follow it northward to Espada Pass—and then over into the Flat Tops Wilderness."

In the dim moonlight, Cash could make out the line. It was steep but not technical. "I see it. Let's go. You lead."

They started up the slope, moving fast and silently, flashlights off. In twenty minutes, they had cleared the last patch of stunted trees and come out above the tree line. Above them rose barren scree slopes and couloirs to the ridge, the last part in snow. That would be a bitch to climb, Cash thought, but the snow probably wouldn't be very deep, being the first of the season. It would be cold—it was already cold—and they'd have to keep moving. Thankfully, they had all worn good hiking boots into the mine—all except Karman, and she didn't really give a damn about him. Once they were on the ridge, they would need to get over and down into the Flat Tops as quickly as possible. From there, Colcord said—who had backpacked in the Flat Tops in his younger days—it would be a long hike out to the nearest road—twenty miles.

She glanced down to see if they were being followed, but there was no sign of it.

The slope they were ascending consisted mostly of rocks and

gravel—nothing lived up there, not even plants. She could feel the altitude acutely, breathing hard in the thin air, her breath condensing with every exhale. The air was cold and getting colder. As they climbed, Cash could see, far down the valley, the orange glow of the fires. Unbelievable. It was like a war. It *was* a war.

Cash turned to Karman. "Why bring back Neanderthals? What was the reason?"

Karman, breathing hard as they climbed, did not respond, his long shock of gray hair hanging down over a smooth forehead. He was wearing an elegant Italian suit, silk tie pulled down, collar unbuttoned, a jacket zipped tightly over that. He was going to be cold.

"Maybe we should have left you behind," said Colcord, "to be torn apart by those monsters you created."

"They're not monsters," said Karman.

"Oh yeah?" said Romanski. "They *are* monsters, and you're their Frankenstein."

Karman said, "You are an ignorant fool." His blue eyes glittered like sapphires in the moonlight.

"But . . . *why*?" Cash asked again.

"We're transforming the human race. No longer does chance control our evolution; *we* control it."

"But how," asked Cash, "is de-extincting Neanderthals going to do that?"

Silence from Karman.

"You piece of shit," said Romanski. "We saved your life. Answer her question."

Cash gave a sign to Romanski to cool it and looked back at Karman, toiling up the slope. This man was remarkably fit for his age, having little trouble hiking up a steep ridge at eleven thousand feet. He knew what they were up against far better than they did, and she needed him to provide that knowledge to them. She needed to get him talking.

"I was taught Neanderthals were dumb, ugly brutes," said Cash.

"They are *not*," Karman said. "Neanderthals are grossly misunderstood. They were not the primitive hominin of popular culture, communicating by grunts and living in caves."

"Those first killings—they were escaped Neanderthals, weren't they? They're murderous goons, it seems to me."

"They are . . ." He hesitated. "Confused. Some are early mistakes, aberrations. They fell under the sway of a charismatic leader."

"I don't get it," Colcord said. "What does resurrecting Neanderthals have to do with improving the human race?"

"Neanders are stronger, faster, and more robust than *Homo sapiens*," said Karman, his voice rising. "They have human vocal cords—they had the gift of speech. Just like Sapiens, they had language, religion, art, and music. What's more, their brains were bigger than ours. This has been known for over a hundred years—the average cranial capacity of a Neander is seventy cubic centimeters *larger* than Sapiens'."

"So you're saying they're smarter?" Colcord asked.

"Not in logic and analysis. But in shrewdness and tactics, yes. And they're superior in other ways too."

"So why'd they go extinct, if they were so much better than we are?" asked Colcord.

"Because humans have one key quality they don't: *empathy*. That is something we discovered when we began to raise them as children."

"Empathy? How would that make a difference?"

"It makes all the difference in the world. Out of empathy springs cooperation, compassion, and altruism. We had each other's backs. We could organize ourselves into much larger and more cohesive social groups—which meant bigger war parties. But empathy also allows us to lie and deceive and manipulate—because empathy helps us to see into another person's mind. With empathy, you can anticipate what others are thinking and feeling. That's a huge advantage in warfare and conflict. Empathy is what gave us the decisive edge in the war with the Neanderthals."

"Humans had a war with the Neanderthals?" Colcord asked.

"Not in the modern sense. A nine-thousand-year war. When our ancestors arrived in Europe around forty-five thousand years ago, they found a rich continent that had only one problem: it was fully occupied. A brutal struggle for resources began. Paleo sites all over Europe show this struggle was violent. There was widespread cannibalism—on both sides. The conflict lasted five thousand years, but eventually, we drove *Homo neanderthalensis* to extinction. It was a terrible thing we did."

"Why do they look so Nordic?" Colcord asked.

"They *are* Nordic. The Neanders we resurrected came from DNA recovered from sites in Western Europe. These Neanders evolved in a high-latitude environment with little sun and extreme cold—back then, it was much colder than today. Pale skin, of course, is necessary for vitamin D production in regions with little sunlight."

"As far as empathy goes," said Colcord, "there are still a lot of humans who lack it."

"Indeed," said Karman. "As with any recently evolved characteristic, there are some born without it. We call them *sociopaths*. But you have to understand, absence of empathy is almost universal in the animal kingdom. Evolution does not normally produce it. *Homo sapiens* is an exception."

"*You're* a sociopath," said Romanski. "A worthless sack of shit."

"I will not respond to your provocations," said Karman.

"But you still haven't answered the question," said Cash. "How is resurrecting Neanderthals going to improve the human species?"

"We needed to de-extinct them to identify and isolate the Neander genes for the physical skills we desired—strength, coordination, speed, endurance. You have to see how these genes are expressed in vivo—it's not something you can do in a test tube."

"And then what?" asked Colcord. "What are you doing with those genes? Who's getting them?"

Cash had a sudden revelation: she knew the answer. "Erebus bills itself as a honeymoon destination," she said.

A sudden silence.

"Oh my God," said Romanski, "you're making *designer babies!*"

"Exactly," said Cash. "For superrich people like Olivia and Mark Gunnerson. She was pregnant—remember? That's what's going on here—they're sticking Neanderthal genes into human babies."

"They are *not* 'designer babies,'" Karman erupted angrily. "We're guiding our species to a brilliant new future. No more sickness, genetic disease, obesity, addiction, or cancer. No more ugly, weak, or stupid people. No more depression or mental illness. These brave young couples are phase one in the plan, and their fees are financing our vital work!"

"Do they know you're putting Neanderthal genes into their babies?" Romanski asked.

"Of course not. They think they're getting gene editing to make their children stronger and faster. And they are!"

"This is grotesque," said Colcord. "Unspeakable."

"Come now! Humans crossbred with Neanderthals already. We're two to three percent Neanderthal—much to our benefit!" Karman was practically shouting. "All we've done is extend that natural process!"

"So—why are they hunting and killing us?" Cash asked. "Why this hatred?"

Karman's voice suddenly dropped in tone. "Revenge."

"You mean revenge on Erebus?"

"No. Revenge on all of us . . . for what we did."

"What did we do?"

"Just what I said: we drove them to extinction. They figured that out on their own with their access to technology, and now they want to extinct us."

72

McFaul braced himself, kneeling, the 9 mm Colt in both hands, taking aim at the two approaching figures. He lightly rested his forearms on a fallen tree. He was going to smoke these bastards as soon as they came into range.

And then he heard the rescue choppers. He felt relief course through his entire body; never had a sound been so welcome. He looked up and through the treetops saw the first aircraft pass by, its running lights blinking. A moment later, a second one arrived. They both slowed and began to circle, two big Black Hawks with Air National Guard markings, no doubt full of troops armed to the teeth. Just as he hoped, it looked like at least one was going to use the field as a landing zone. He turned his head and saw, farther away, the lights of a third and fourth helicopter going up the valley. What a beautiful sight. The nightmare was over.

He turned his attention back to where the two figures had been. They had vanished. Run away? With the arrival of the choppers, the killers would be scattering in fear back into the forest. They weren't going to stick around and fight the Air National Guard with spears and sticks. And now, those bastards would be hunted down. This shitstorm could still be fixed.

One chopper was slowing and turning to land. As soon as it touched down, he'd rush across the field and get the hell out of there. They'd take him far away from these crazy bastards. But as these thoughts passed through his mind, he knew it couldn't be; he was supposedly the incident commander on-site. That's how he'd presented himself at the press conference. And here he was, hiding in the trees, covered with leaves. But what else could he have done? He had no options. His gaze fell on the dark bulk of Gunnerson. The man, drunk, had attacked him and tried to take his weapon. His actions had been justified and by the book—protocol in dealing with a perp trying to take the weapon of a law enforcement officer.

He thought fast; they'd be debriefing him almost immediately. He had to organize his thoughts, lay out his story. The key point was that the attack was coordinated and had taken everyone by surprise. The crazies had dynamited the power station and set the building on fire. Much of the failure could be laid at the feet of Erebus; the two dozen vaunted security personnel that Maximilian had promised would guard the lodge had melted away at the crucial moment. And the SWAT team—where the hell had they gone? They'd run too, it seems, or something had happened to them. He was on record trying to persuade Maximilian and Barrow to call the governor to get the National Guard in there. They nixed it. As director of the CBI, he had no authority to command troops or call in the National Guard; the CBI was an investigative agency, not an agency with ranks of military personnel or large law enforcement dispositions.

The other thing to be emphasized was this: he was not the agent in charge, Cash was. She had made an ill-timed and marginal evidence-gathering trip, at the most unpropitious moment, taking that useless sheriff with her. Who the hell knew where she was, even now? Cash was *still in charge*—he'd been careful not to make the change of command official. He'd gone up there to direct the presser, to interface with the public, not to run the investigation. When you got down to it—when you really examined how the investigation went off the rails—it was her fault. She was out of her depth. She was nowhere to be found at the crucial moment. She and that good-old-boy sheriff. Not only that, she was supposed to evacuate the civilians from the valley, and yet the film crew had not left. That was where the crazies had gotten the dynamite. No way was he going to take the fall for her failures. He would make that crystal clear at the debriefing.

His thoughts were brought back to the present by the thud of the rotors as a Black Hawk chopper, lights playing on the ground beneath, descended, while the other circled farther above.

Thank God. McFaul eased himself up to see better. Yes, one was definitely coming in for a landing. Christ, they were taking their time. But they'd at least chased away those two crazies, who must've run away like gazelles when the lion shows up. Nobody would pick a fight with the Air National Guard, especially spear-toting nutjobs covered in leaves and grass.

Hurry up. Hurry up and land.

He watched through the tree trunks as the Black Hawk settled down, lights brilliantly illuminating the LZ. In the glare of the landing lights, he could see several dark shapes—bodies lying in the grass. Victims of the crazies. His eye strayed to Gunnerson, a dark shape lying next to him in the leaves.

A loud rattle of gunfire startled him, and he snapped his attention back to the helicopter. There was a sudden roar of engine power from the chopper and, just ten feet from the ground, it started to rise abruptly.

What the hell?

Another three-round burst sounded off to the side, and the chopper, twenty feet from the ground, suddenly tilted crazily, its rotors tipping over and its tail swinging around. There was another torrent of gunfire, and he could see the rounds flashing off the Black Hawk's armored sides. The aircraft struggled to right itself, but one of the rotors was hit in a shower of sparks, and pieces of it flew off with a singing sound, the engine roaring even louder with the sudden application of power from the pilot attempting to bring it back under control.

Who was shooting? Did those bastards have guns?

The other chopper circling above responded, swinging around and swooping down, doors open, and he saw muzzle flashes in the doorway as they returned gunfire, opening up with a deafening .50-caliber machine gun, the tracers showing they were firing at a group of trees at the far end of the meadow, and now he could see return gunfire from those trees. The .50 caliber literally tore the trees to pieces, chopping through and sending the branches and trunks falling every which way, like a giant wood chipper.

This was unbelievable: the crazies had weapons. And how many of them were there? They were insane. It was suicide, firing at Black Hawks like this. And they had waited until the last minute, when the National Guard hadn't expected to take fire.

Meanwhile, the Black Hawk's engine roared as it struggled to right itself, to rise, but it was too late—the aircraft was close to the ground and unable to recover from the rotor damage, and it came down sideways and hit hard, the rotors flying off, the tail slamming into the ground, troops spilling out of the open doors and running—followed by a huge explosion and a ball of fire. He felt the sudden heat of it on his face, the brightness flooding the trees. In the glow, he saw something that practically stopped his heart: one of the crazy killers was crouching in the woods not fifty feet from him. In the sudden bath of light, the brute's head snapped around, and in an instant, the figure rushed at him, leaping like a deer over the fallen trees and brush, carrying a short spear.

McFaul raised his weapon in a spasm of fear, and he pressed off one, two, three shots—but in his panic, he wasn't taking the time to aim properly, and his shots missed. The crazy launched his spear, and McFaul felt a terrific blow to his chest that knocked him to the ground. He looked down in astonishment to see the shaft of the spear sticking out of his chest, right above where his heart was—and then darkness shut him down.

73

Doyle finally couldn't go any farther, and he collapsed to the soft forest floor. He lay on his back, arms thrown out, gasping for breath, wheezing and coughing, suppressing the urge to vomit. He had run like a madman for God knows how far, tripping, falling, getting up again, thrashing through brush, and stumbling across streams. He was torn to pieces, cut and bleeding, his clothing in tatters. But he was alive.

As he lay there, he realized he'd escaped the crazies. Maybe he hadn't even been chased. One of the motherfuckers was dead for sure, but the other? Maybe he too was dead—or at least too injured to give chase. Whatever it was, he'd beaten those mofos, he'd escaped—he'd survived.

The thought calmed him down as he began to recover his breath. He tried to slow his gasping enough to listen. He could hear nothing but the sighing of the wind. Looking upward, he saw the dark forms of the trees against the night sky and, beyond them, a smattering of stars. There were little patches of moonlight here and there speckling the forest floor and tree trunks, and everything smelled of pine needles.

His breathing gradually slowed. He felt the cold mountain air flowing over him, turning the sweat on his face icy.

He took a deep breath and then, wincing and trying to stay quiet, he raised himself up on an elbow. He was near the base of some kind of gigantic pine tree, or fir, or whatever—with a bunch of gnarly roots. He scooted over and propped his back against one of the roots. Now which way had he come? He looked around and realized he had no idea. With all the tall trees around, he couldn't see any mountains or landmarks, and the dark forest floor showed no tracks.

How far had he run? A long fucking way. He'd crashed through dense vegetation, crossed open areas, run like hell through big deep forests of tall trees, climbed over rocks, fallen in a stream, traversed wilderness. He must've gone miles and miles. Mostly, it had been downhill, but there were uphill portions, ravines, scrambles. He was as lost as a person could get.

The important thing was, he'd escaped those motherfuckers. Jesus, the image of Ballou above him, tangled in the airbag with his throat cut, blood still draining—that horror would live with him for the rest of his life. It was insane what had happened . . . And it would make a hell of a documentary. He was there. He was attacked. He escaped. He was the guy who survived.

What now? It was going to get cold—very cold. The temperature was already dropping fast. Might even go below freezing. At least he had put on a light jacket to ward off the evening chill of the mountains. But it would get colder, and the jacket would not protect him against below-freezing weather. On the other hand, no way was he going anywhere. He was going to spend the night right here, in this deep forest, where he'd be safe, far away from what was happening down there around the lodge and the movie town. No way was he heading back to the road or anywhere near those fuckers. He would wait for a rescue, which he knew would be coming soon. He would spend the night here and wait until it was safe, and only then would he come out. A body could survive weeks without food, that he knew. And there was no shortage of water. As long as he didn't freeze to death, he would survive.

He sat up a little more, adjusting his back against the massive root. This was not a bad place to spend a night. He thought once again, this time with a glow of pride, that he had escaped the mofos. He was a survivor, always had been since his hardscrabble childhood in the Burren in County Clare. He had spent the night out before, many times, when he got in trouble and was kicked out by his da, or with his friends getting drunk and smoking cigarettes.

He breathed in the night air, filled with the scent of pine. He could already see the documentary. He began writing the voice-over in his head.

And then he froze: there was a distant noise. Suddenly alert, his heart pounding, he listened. And he heard it again: a footfall in the forest, the crackling sound of twigs and needles being trod on. And another. And another. Slow and stealthy—and getting closer.

In a sudden panic, he crouched, trying to hide himself among the roots, hardly daring to breathe. They were coming. They were moving around in the dark, no doubt looking for him. He thought of running, but they were already too close, and they'd hear him and catch him.

Doyle stared in the direction of the sounds, straining to see, but there were no lights. He huddled in the darkness at the base of the giant fir tree, among the roots. They were moving at such a slow pace that he figured they hadn't seen him yet. He couldn't outrun them, especially in his condition. He prayed they would pass on by without seeing him. It was dark and he huddled, trying to cram himself in among the roots, become as invisible as possible.

The sounds got closer. They were heavy, like they were marching in unison, brush and branches cracking and falling. It was noisy—there must be a lot of them. Closer now . . . closer . . . He strained to see through the gloom. A huge shape loomed out of the dark—a gigantic lumbering monster that blotted out the night sky.

What was this? He felt such relief he almost laughed. It wasn't the mofos; it was an animal. A gigantic, stupendous creature. Not a mammoth—Jesus, Mary, and Joseph, it was twice as big as a mammoth, the biggest animal he'd ever seen, a giant shaggy rhinoceros, moving in slow motion, a living mountain in the night. In awe, he watched it pass by, each footfall shaking the earth, its breathing deep and ponderous, forming swirling clouds of condensation behind it.

After a few minutes, it had passed, and he could hear its bulk moving down through the forest, the sounds of its passage gradually fading away into silence.

Doyle was spellbound. He felt like he had just had a religious experience. He had escaped death, and now he had witnessed this gigantic extinct animal going he knew not where, thinking its lonely, ancient thoughts, resurrected and given a second chance to live its prehistoric existence.

He leaned back against the tree and shivered. It was going to be one cold mother of a night. The forest floor was covered with dry, soft needles, and he began scooping them up and stuffing them into his jacket, packing them all around for warmth and then zipping it up tight. It didn't take him long to realize that, even though the stuffing was a bit prickly, it was going to work well. He felt himself warming up already. He might be lost in buttfuck nowhere, but he was safe. He was warm. He had escaped death. He was a survivor.

Even though Doyle had rejected Catholicism a long time ago, he thanked God most fervently for having been delivered.

74

The word *extinction* hung in the air. Cash was stunned by the scientist's revelations. Everything finally made sense—the craziness of the killers, their hatred and brutality, the rituals, the taunting. And it even explained Gunnerson's mysterious comment about asking Barrow what he thought he was doing up there. Along with his refusal to explain the same question—because it would have exposed his son and daughter-in-law as having come to Erebus to get themselves a designer baby.

The thought of babies gave her an idea. "You told us earlier that your resurrected animals couldn't reproduce. But . . . can the Neanders reproduce?"

At this, Karman's eyes seemed to glitter. "Yes. We thought not and tried to stop any liaisons of that kind. But you know how it is: the Neanders themselves showed us they could. And the babies they had were perfect—fully Neanderthal, of course."

Cash tried to wrap her mind around this idea—that they could reproduce. "Can they . . . interbreed with humans?" she asked.

"They did before," said Karman. "There's no reason why they couldn't do so now."

A brief silence fell on the group while they contemplated this.

Colcord asked, "How did word get around that people could get a souped-up baby at Erebus?"

"A genetically enhanced baby."

"Whatever. How did people learn this service existed?"

"Through Barrow. He lives in an exclusive world of billionaires. They move in cloistered circles in places like Davos and Bohemian Grove. Very quietly, he spread the knowledge of our gene-editing platform for couples wishing to conceive. Barrow recruited the rich families—that was his role. He was the salesman. And of course, the customers had every incentive to keep the secret."

"And how much does this . . . baby enhancement cost?"

"Twelve million."

"Twelve million dollars for each baby?"

"The megarich will pay anything to have perfect children."

"The parents had no idea Neanderthal genes were being stuffed into their precious little embryos?"

"They wouldn't have understood. But let me be clear: resurrecting the Neanders wasn't just to exploit their genetic heritage."

"What else?" Colcord asked.

"To right the great wrong we did to them. They're humans too, of course. Now that we have the technology to do it, I believe it is a moral imperative to bring them back. This was the reason I became involved."

"They don't seem grateful for being de-extincted," said Romanski.

"Of course they are! It's just that a poisonous ideology took hold. We gave them wonderful lives. You saw the playground. That was just one of several, and they had excellent teachers and classrooms, books and movies, world-class sporting programs, nice clothes, and good food. They put on Shakespeare plays, they had a chess club, some of them played music and had a rock band—we gave them the best of everything. Of course, we had to be careful what knowledge they had access to. It was decided—against my wishes—that they shouldn't know who they were or where they came from. They would live their lives in a walled garden, content with the carefully curated information we gave them."

"How did it go wrong?"

"We consistently underestimated their cleverness. They learned enough—little clues here and there—to fill in the gaps, piece things together. They realized they were experimental subjects. They figured out they were Neanderthals, that they were being held prisoner, and that they were being used by us Sapiens for some purpose. It was quite astonishing how clever they were. Perhaps . . ." He hesitated. "Perhaps

I was partly responsible. I encouraged iconoclastic thinking in some of the brighter ones. I see now it was a mistake to teach them so much about science and technology and give them computers. I truly regret that—I thought I was doing good. But they figured out so much more than we expected and turned it all against us. Making it worse, Neanders are susceptible to conspiracy theories and magical thinking. They turn too quickly to violence as a way of solving problems. This cannibalism thing is horrific—I had no idea they were capable of that."

"So it was a little like *The Truman Show*," said Colcord. "Until they found out what was really going on."

"You might say that."

"I can't believe you would think resurrecting Neanderthals would be a good idea," said Colcord.

"I *raised* these Neanders—some of them are like my own children. They're not evil or murderous. We had no idea they would create a religion out of taking back the earth from Sapiens. And in the early days, genetic errors led to some mental issues. I refused to let those unfortunates be put down. But because they were dangerous and unpredictable, we had to keep them in secure conditions, humane conditions. Some of those were among the ones who initially escaped—and poisoned the minds of others."

"Hey," said Reno, who was taking up the rear. "Down there— lights."

They stopped and looked back down the slope. Cash could see a patch of distant, flickering lights from where they had come, maybe half a mile away.

"Son of a bitch," said Romanski. "Your dear misunderstood friends are chasing us."

"You know these Neanderthals," said Cash. "You got any ideas on how we might deal with them?"

Karman looked pale in the moonlight. "We can't outrun them. We can't lose them—they're expert trackers. They have a keen sense of smell, so it won't do any good to try to hide. They're far more adapted to the cold than we are."

"Nice," said Romanski. "So let's just give ourselves up to be cooked and eaten. With fava beans, of course."

"So what *can* we do?" asked Cash.

"I can talk to them," Karman said.

Romanski laughed bitterly. "And earn your own personal decollation."

Karman didn't answer.

"We'd better just keep going," said Colcord. "Standing around jawing is not an option."

Karman said nothing and turned away. They continued up the slope, struggling to move as fast as possible. Cash found herself gasping for breath in the thin air, and Colcord wasn't doing any better. The lights were coming up the ridgeline fast. There were a lot of them—it was a mob.

"What are their weaknesses?" Cash asked Karman. "Aside from a lack of empathy."

"Weaknesses?"

"What I'm getting at is: How can we use those differences between us to our advantage? We were able to defeat them once—can't we do it again?"

Karman shook his head. "No. We can't. They're really fixated on wiping out the Sapiens—that's given them a purpose. They might end up squabbling and killing each other later, when they're sitting around a campfire, but right now—forget it."

"So you're saying there's nothing we can do," Cash said.

"Except he's going to *talk* to them," said Romanski.

"They know me. I understand them."

Cash looked down the slope. It was frightening how fast those lights were coming up—and how many there were. It was almost as if they were running uphill—in fact, they probably were.

"Listen," Cash said to the group. "We don't have a lot of time until they're on top of us. We'd better find a defensive location and get ready to fight."

"Fight? With what?" Romanski cried.

"Rocks," said Cash.

"Rocks? Is that a joke? We're gonna throw rocks at them?"

"I'm going down fighting."

The lights below them were now spreading out in a line. They were no more than a quarter mile below. It looked like the whole mob—everyone.

And then came a muffled rumble from deep within the mountain. It grew rapidly in intensity, and then a blast of fire shot from the mine entrance far below with a roar, and elsewhere among the nearby mountains fire and smoke jetted out like great cannons blasting into the night, the thunderous echoes bouncing off the peaks. The entire side of the mountain to their right cracked and began to slide, collapsing into a giant, fiery avalanche.

The laboratory complex had been blown up.

75

The earth shook so violently that Cash and the others had to brace themselves against rocks and each other to avoid being thrown to the ground. She heard, in the background, cheering and whistling from the pursuing mob. After a long moment, the earthquake subsided enough for them to move again, and she looked around for a defensive position. Not far above them was an outcrop and a cluster of fallen boulders that they could take cover behind. It wasn't great, but it was the best they were going to get.

"Up there. That outcrop."

They turned and angled toward it, running and gasping for breath. Cash stumbled. Her strength was ebbing fast, and she struggled to suck in enough oxygen to keep going. Below, the lights were spreading out in the mob's apparent flanking maneuver to trap them.

Romanski reached the outcrop first. Cash heard a burst of gunfire from below, and rounds snicked up around her as she threw herself behind the protection of the rocks. A moment later, Karman came sprawling in with Colcord and Reno. They huddled behind the boulders. As a defensive redoubt, it was not what she had hoped, but they were out of time, and it would have to do.

"Collect stones," she whispered.

They began scouring the area, grabbing and piling up rocks. It was pathetic, but it was all they had. They were totally screwed.

Through a narrow gap in the boulders, Cash could see the Neanderthals spreading out on the slopes below the outcrop. Most of them were dressed in preppy outdoor clothing, with Nike athletic shoes, some carrying burning torches, others with flashlights. Many had spears, and one, the leader with the braid, toted an assault rifle.

The leader came to a halt at the bottom of the outcrop below them, an enigmatic smile spreading across his odd-looking face, no longer covered by a mask. Instead of the homemade camo outfit, he was wearing a button-down shirt, a down Patagonia jacket, and cargo pants. His face was so pale it almost glowed in the moonlight, his white-blond braid descending to his waist. There was nothing "primitive" about him, not in the alertness in the eyes, in his charisma, or in the smile playing about his lips. He was all too human.

The others were dressed in similarly neat clothes, some with long hair, braided or loose, others with shorter cuts. It appeared this was the same group she had seen around the bonfire in the mine—around twenty men, women, and children.

The leader raised the assault rifle and pointed it at them, casually spraying fire, the rounds smacking and zinging off the boulder they were huddled behind, showering them with chips.

The firing stopped, and the man said, "Greetings, Sapiens!" his strange whistling voice cutting through the thin air.

The other Neanderthals had moved up the slope on either side of the outcrop, and now Cash and her group were essentially surrounded.

"Come out, come out, wherever you are," the leader sang, imitating the warbling voice of Glinda, the good witch from *The Wizard of Oz*.

"We're not gonna stand up to be mowed down," Cash called out. She tried to think of how to engage him. "Can we talk? We mean you no harm."

The leader's head tilted back, and he let out a thin, whistling laugh. "You mean us no harm! Now that's a really funny joke!"

Cash glanced over at Karman. His face was covered with sweat, his eyes glittering strangely.

The leader went on, "I see you've been gathering rocks to throw at us. Really? Rocks? What are you, a bunch of dumb Neanders?"

He and the Neanders all laughed uproariously. He was clearly enjoying himself.

"Dr. Karman! You remember me?"

"Of course I do," said Karman weakly. "How are you, Joey?"

"You read me pirate stories. Walking the plank, keelhauling, all that good stuff. And then later you taught me Shakespeare, remember? *And yet to me, what is this quintessence of dust? Man delights not me; no.* I have not seen you in a long time, Dr. Karman. Come out. I want to have a look. For old times."

Karman didn't move.

"Afraid?"

"Yes, to be frank."

"I won't shoot you. Promise."

Karman was shaking.

Suddenly, Joey fired his weapon again, three rapid shots, the bullets smacking the rock, whining off into the dark. "Stand up. Now."

Cash looked at Karman and shook her head. He was going to be shot.

Karman started to rise.

"*Don't,*" Cash said.

"I have to."

He stood up, his legs shaking.

"The good doctor!"

Karman said nothing. At any moment, Cash expected a burst of gunfire to cut him down. But it didn't come.

The leader turned to the group. "Who's your daddy? Karman is your daddy!"

This was going from bad to worse. None of them were going to get out of there alive. She tried to drive out of her mind not only the thought of dying but what they might do to her body afterward.

Karman spoke. "All right, Joey. Easy now."

"Sure, it's all right," said Joey sarcastically.

"I want you to think about something."

"Of course! Here comes the lecture!"

Karman stepped around the boulder and began walking slowly around the outcrop and down toward the man. "Not a lecture but a thought."

"What thought?"

"We kept many secrets from you."

This caused a brief silence. Joey frowned.

Karman quickly went on, "They were very careful with how you were raised—with what knowledge you were allowed to have. They allowed you to learn *only so much*—and no more. They were afraid of what you might become when you grew up. They shut off your education just before critical mass. But you! You all were too clever for them—especially you, Joey. You filled in some of the gaps and figured out things that made you angry. And rightly so. I was not part of throttling down your education. I argued that you should be taught your heritage and learn to be proud of it. I was on your side. Always."

"All lies. You're just another Sapiens."

"No, I'm not. I'm your friend, and I think most of you know that. There is still much I can teach you." He took a deep breath. "Do you remember the story of Adam and Eve and the tree of the knowledge of good and evil?"

Joey stared.

"God created Adam and Eve and put them in the Garden of Eden. They were told they were free to do whatever they wished, except to eat the apple of the tree of the knowledge of good and evil. But . . . they picked and ate it. They couldn't help themselves. They ate the apple."

A silence had fallen over the group.

"That choice has now come to you. I am offering you the apple from that tree. Will you take it?" Karman took a step toward Joey, his hand outstretched.

At this, Joey laughed—but it had a note of uncertainty in it. He raised his rifle and pointed it at Karman. "Keep your apple."

Here it comes, thought Cash.

Karman said, "Take the apple and eat of it. Ye shall be as gods, remember? Learn the secrets of being human."

Joey's sarcastic laugh cut through the night air. "You've got it all wrong. You actually think we *want* to be like you? You Sapiens, with your bleak and apocalyptic history? What a grim and self-loathing species you are! Look at what you worship as progress. The agricultural revolution turned you from free wanderers into slaves to the land. The Industrial Revolution robbed you of your souls and made you cruel.

And the IT revolution gave you loneliness, hatred, and misery. What's next for Sapiens in the glorious march of progress?"

A murmur of approval rose among the Neanders, like a congregation responding to a preacher.

"You're the species of the apocalypse. You exterminated us, and you're doing the same to thousands of other species. You've mortally wounded the earth. You didn't just eat the apple; you destroyed the garden. And yet you go on and on, consumed with greed, addicted to comfort, soft and degenerate as grubs. You think we want to be like you?"

His whispery voice had taken on the cadence of a preacher, generating sharp murmurs and expostulations of approval from the crowd. Some began to raise their hands in a fluttering motion to the sky.

"You speak of eating the apple? No! We're starting over with God. We're going back to His garden. We're returning to His wilderness. We're rewilding ourselves, and we're going to start anew, in harmony with His creation."

Harmony, murmured the crowd, swaying. *Harmony*.

Karman didn't respond at once. He stood a little unsteadily on the slope as Joey raised the weapon and aimed it at him. "We have our God, Doctor. Time to pray to yours."

"No," said Karman. "No. Please don't."

Joey aimed slowly, his eye on the scope.

"Joey," said Karman, shifting his tone into something soft and cajoling. "Wait. I can tell you where we found the DNA that made you."

At this, Joey became still.

"You want to learn it? If you kill me, you'll never know."

A long silence. Joey continued aiming the weapon but did not fire. The others fell silent.

"Your DNA came from a burial found in a cave in France—a cave with beautiful paintings in it. Those bones were the remains of a Neanderthal man, one of the last of his kind. We used to think those paintings were done by Sapiens. No longer. Now we know Neanderthals created the oldest of those paintings and the bones in the cave belonged to one of those artists. We extracted DNA from the skull—drilling out bone powder from the cochlea, to be exact—and with that DNA *we made you.* That person buried in the cave, that artist, is *you.*"

The weapon faltered. Joey wobbled on his feet. He seemed completely unnerved by this.

"Do you remember the pictures you drew as a child, which I framed? They were remarkable." Karman looked around at the others. "And all of you? I have your stories too. I can teach you what was withheld for so long—your patrimony. Your origins. Who you are. Each one of you."

Nobody moved.

"You mentioned those pirate stories I used to read to you," said Karman. "Remember what they did when they captured a ship? They invited the sailors to join them. If they did, they had to sign the articles and swear to become a pirate. If they didn't, they had to walk the plank and die. I'll sign the articles."

More silence.

"What I'm saying is, I'll join you. I understand you. I believe in you. I was the one who always protected you against the Sapiens." He took a deep breath. "I *created* you, each one of you, from dust. Literally. Each one of you came from dust drilled from secret pockets of DNA trapped in ancient bones."

There was a confused murmuring from the group. They had dropped their hands. They were uncertain, nervous.

"The Sapiens are coming to get you. It will be awful what they'll do to you. Very soon now, their helicopters will be arriving in the valley, and heavily armed men will be coming up here in force to capture you and return you to bondage. You need to escape."

Joey's face twisted with emotion.

"Above us," said Karman, raising his voice and pointing, "among those mountain peaks is a hidden pass out of this valley. It goes into a vast, uninhabited wilderness. Beyond that pass, there lies your promised land. No Sapiens live there—it's all for you. I know the way. I will lead you. But we've got to hurry, because they're coming. I will lead you to the promised land. I will share your destiny—if you'll accept me. The decision is yours to make—now."

Joey stared at him and finally, after a long moment, nodded sharply. "Yes," he said. "We accept."

A murmuring of approval came from the congregation. *Accept. We accept.*

"I must ask for something in return," said Karman. "You will let these people go."

"No," Joey said.

"Joey? *Let these people go.* Empathy, remember? You need to practice it. You all do."

"No."

"It's the price of my cooperation."

Joey said nothing. The others looked uncertain, agitated, looking to Karman and then to Joey.

"Empathy," Karman said. "Compassion. Practice it. Let them walk away. They had nothing to do with how you were abused and misled."

Joey paused and then brusquely turned to Cash and the group. He waved his rifle. "Go!"

Nobody moved.

"You're going to have to lay down the rifle before they'll come out," Karman said.

Joey laid the rifle on the ground.

Cash was the first to stand up, then the others.

"Go," said Joey. "Get out!"

Cash began to edge out of the rocky outcrop, the others following. They walked around the outcrop and downhill, toward the line of Neanders. The line opened up to let them pass through, the Neanders glaring at them with fierce expressions as they passed by.

They continued past them, walking fast down the steep slope, trying to keep from stumbling. Nobody said a word—they just kept moving, not daring to look back, leaving the Neanders behind. Cash picked up the pace, angling away from the Jackman Mine entrance, from which smoke and fire were still pouring. She felt numb. Far down the valley, she could see the lodge continuing to burn, along with the movie town. And then, she heard the distant throb of helicopters and could see their blinking lights coming up the valley.

The rescue had finally begun.

Half an hour later, when they reached the tree line, Cash stopped, and they regrouped, recovering their breaths. She finally turned and looked up at the mountainsides. Far above, along a snowy ridgeline, framed against the stars, she could see a wavering band of lights moving northward toward the pass—and into the great wilderness beyond.

76

The conference room at CBI headquarters in Lakewood was already packed for the debriefing when Cash entered and took a seat at the front next to Romanski, Reno, Colcord, and others involved in the Erebus investigation. The CBI's new director, Blaisdell Holmes, stood at the podium, waiting for the hubbub to quiet down and the debriefing to begin. Holmes had been deputy director of the CBI, and her elevation to the top spot after the demise of McFaul was expected and uncontroversial.

Over the past month, the media had dragged the CBI through hell, but Holmes had handled it well, admitting fault where blame was due, quietly resisting the many unfair and inaccurate accusations, and calmly refuting the mind-boggling proliferation of conspiracy theories that arose, each one more outlandish than the last—as if the incident hadn't been crazy enough to begin with.

When the digital clock behind the podium registered three p.m., Holmes stepped forward to the podium, tapped on the mic, and said, "I extend a warm welcome to the CBI and the Eagle County Sheriff's Office."

The purpose of the debriefing was to update CBI on the progress of the investigation. The crisis at Erebus was over—but the investigation itself continued.

Holmes reminded everyone that the details that would be discussed at the debriefing were confidential, restricted to law enforcement only, and that no recording was allowed. Then she placed a portfolio on the podium to refer to, opened it, and looked around the room.

"We have what we believe is a final tally on the dead and missing," she said. "Nine of the experimental subjects are deceased. None were able to be taken alive. They were killed fighting with the Air National Guard units sent into the valley. An unknown number of experimental subjects, perhaps as many as two dozen, escaped over the mountains and are still at large in the Flat Tops Wilderness Area."

Experimental subjects was the phrase officially adopted to refer to the Neanders. It somehow seemed less threatening. The idea that they were resurrected Neanderthals had only been accepted with the greatest reluctance and only after incontrovertible DNA sequencing had been completed. Most of the rest of the de-extinction evidence had been wiped out in the destruction of the labs. The federal government had stepped in and dropped a classification order on most of the information being recovered.

"The numbers of casualties and missing are significant," Holmes went on. "They include Maitland Barrow, CEO of RxB, the holding company of Erebus, presumed dead; Erebus CEO, Karla Raimundo, presumed dead; security director, Andrew Maximilian, presumed dead. Missing are sixteen Erebus security personnel and fourteen other employees, presumed deceased from the explosion and collapse of the laboratory and mine complex. The chief scientist of Erebus, Marius Karman, is believed to be alive, having joined with the experimental subjects in the Flat Tops Wilderness Area. The deceased include the actor Brock Ballou; four other employees of the film company; and twelve members of the media. Five Air National Guard members died in the assault on the valley, along with six members of the Denver PD SWAT team. My predecessor, Wallace McFaul, lost his life in the incident, as did businessman Rolf Gunnerson, and of course his son, Mark, and daughter-in-law, Olivia, whose deaths initiated this investigation."

She paused and swept the room with a grave expression. "In short, there was a shocking loss of life, not to mention the many others who were injured and traumatized. I'd like to call for a moment of silence for those victims."

A hush fell.

Then she resumed. "I would like to acknowledge the important roles in the case played by Agent in Charge Frances Cash, Sheriff James Colcord, Forensic Services detective Bart Romanski, and forensic technician Michael Reno."

Cash heard this and colored. She wasn't fooled. She was in the doghouse internally, but what was worse, she blamed herself. She'd retained her job only because the CBI needed something positive to point to after the McFaul disaster, and she was that thing. Colcord hadn't fared as well; he'd been slammed in the press, and it seemed likely he'd lose the upcoming election in November. The media, having lost so many of their own, had been hammering everyone pretty good. And then there was that filmmaker Doyle, who'd witnessed Brock Ballou's killing but managed to escape the crazies. He was now making hay on every talk show in America. The governor had taken a big hit when it became known he'd been reluctant to close the resort and had delayed calling in the National Guard. There were no actual heroes in Cash's mind except for the National Guard and the Denver PD.

Holmes went on, "As we know, Erebus was engaged in the so-called de-extincting of Pleistocene megafauna. They were also engaged in a secret project to manipulate the human genome as part of a commercial program offering prospective parents the ability to create designer babies with enhanced physical characteristics. They did this, apparently, through resurrecting *Homo neanderthalensis*, an extinct hominin species that occupied Eurasia hundreds of thousands of years ago. Erebus harvested some of their genes to insert into human embryos. The families who opted for this genetic enhancement paid many millions of dollars to receive it—without knowing their babies were getting Neanderthal genes." She paused. "We are in the process of identifying those families and notifying them of that fact. You can imagine the news is an unwelcome surprise. The children who were born with these genetic enhancements, some of whom are as old as nine years, are being evaluated by medical professionals for any side effects or unexpected presentation of disease or infirmity. It appears there may in fact be issues with regard to a propensity toward violence—but that is beyond our purview. Unfortunately, the identities of many of these families have leaked to the media."

She shifted another piece of paper.

"The laboratory where this work occurred was completely destroyed in an explosion and landslide. The area is still closed off and under investigation, and it will be for some time. The resort lodge burned to the ground, as did the historic mining town of Erebus, which had been converted into a movie set. The entire valley is closed as a crime scene and is being examined for evidence."

She paused and took a deep breath.

"With regard to my predecessor—all of you have seen the media reports. It appears he shot and killed Rolf Gunnerson. That is still under investigation. His conduct has cast a shadow over the CBI, and we will need to work hard to regain the trust of the public and media. I call on all of you to undertake this task.

"The investigation is ongoing, and there is still much more to be done. The Flat Tops are being searched. So far, the experimental subjects, led by Karman, have evaded our searches. The area, although large, is finite. We do expect to eventually track them down, especially as winter closes in and they become easier to track."

She closed her papers and said, "That is all I have to say for now. We will take your questions. I will ask those in the front row, who participated in the case, to come to the stage to be available for any questions that might arise."

Cash, Colcord, and the rest stood up and filed onstage. Cash looked over the sea of law enforcement and Forensic Services people looking back at her. It was painful for her to think about what might be going through their minds about her role in the debacle.

But the questions were not too challenging, and if people were thinking bad thoughts, they kept them to themselves. An hour later, the room had finally run out of questions, and the meeting was adjourned.

As they filed out, Colcord fell into step beside her, and they walked out together into the parking lot.

"Well, partner," said Colcord, "that wasn't as bad as it could have been."

She shook her head. "Yeah." And then she hesitated. "There's something I've been wondering about."

He raised his eyebrows. "Yes?"

"Back there, when we were locked in that chamber and thought we were going to die, you wanted to say something to me—some last words. Remember that?"

He nodded. "Sure do."

"What was it?"

He gave her a slow smile. "Ah! *Now* you'd like to know?"

She looked at him. "I would."

"I'll tell you what. Why don't you come by my coffee shop in Eagle one of these fine days, and we'll have a cup of joe and talk about it?"

She took in his friendly face, crinkled blue eyes, and cowboy hat. "Deal."

77

Frankie Cash stamped the snow off her boots and pushed open the door of the cafe, the scent of brewing coffee and freshly baked pastries enveloping her along with the welcome heat from a woodstove. She unwound the scarf from around her neck, hung up her coat on the rack by the door, and looked around. It was more like a comfortable living room than a coffeehouse, with old leather sofas and chairs, wooden tables, a counter along one side, and an antique woodstove with silver trim in the center.

Sheriff Colcord rose from a grouping of chairs near the stove and strode over to her, no longer in his uniform but wearing jeans, a checked shirt—and the cowboy hat.

"Hello, Agent Cash," he said, extending his hand. "Welcome to the Ore House."

She took the hand. "How about dropping the *sheriff* this and *agent* that? Call me Frankie."

"And I'm Jim. Let's get you something."

He led her over to the counter. She ordered a triple espresso—and declined the pecan sticky bun he was having, although it looked fabulous. They took their beverages to a pair of beaten-up leather chairs near the stove, walking across the creaky wooden floor.

Cash settled into the chair, absorbing the warmth. It had snowed overnight, and the temperature outside had barely crept above five degrees. The plate glass windows, decorated with Christmas boughs and ribbons, were all frosted up, the cool light of winter filtering through. She could hear a snowplow scraping past on Eagle's main street, which contributed to the cozy feeling inside.

She sipped the coffee.

"You like?" asked Colcord.

"Perfect," she said. "And this place—I love it. It's just like what you described."

"Thanks." He tucked into his own coffee and then took a bite of the sticky bun. "I dreamed up this place on my last tour in Iraq. Over that year, I built it in my mind, bit by bit, piece by piece, as a way to keep my thoughts from . . . all the other things going on."

She nodded. "I guess congratulations are in order—I mean, getting reelected."

Colcord nodded. "It was a close call. The Erebus disaster took its toll, but my opponent was . . ." He chuckled and circled his finger around his temple. "I was lucky."

"Lots of idiots running for office these days." After a moment, she said, "So . . . I'm still curious. What was it you wanted to say to me?"

He gazed at her, smiling. "I wanted to tell you that I had a deep respect for you and that I was sorry I wouldn't get the chance to know you better."

"That's it?" She felt vaguely disappointed.

"What did you expect, a confession of love?"

She flushed. "No, no," she stammered, "but thank you. I feel the same about you."

"How do you feel about the get-to-know-you-better part?"

"I . . . don't have an objection to that."

He looked at her intently. "Okay. Good to know."

She covered up her embarrassment by tossing down the last of her coffee.

"So how about you?" he asked. "Any fallout?"

"I guess I was lucky too. McFaul made a huge deal of taking over just before the shit hit the fan—with the media right there, recording it all. Those reporters who survived just crucified him. It diverted the unfriendly fire away from me, so to speak. And the CBI needed a couple of heroes after McFaul's disgrace to parade around, so they chose Romanski and me. It was pretty mortifying and totally undeserved, and everybody at the CBI knows it."

"You're being too hard on yourself."

Cash shook her head. "I could've—*should've*—done better. I should have insisted on getting the SWAT teams and National Guard in there earlier. I should have insisted on shutting down the resort earlier. If it weren't for you finding out about the Jackman Mine and getting those maps, I don't know where we'd be."

Colcord shook his head. "You're the one who got that warrant that blew the case wide open."

"Yeah, but it was too late," she said. "It didn't stop the uprising or whatever you want to call it. I can't believe Erebus knew all along what was going on and who the killers were. Unbelievable. How did they think they'd get away with it?"

"They were arrogant. They believed their own security would find them and take care of it themselves." He sipped his coffee. "But what I find puzzling is why McFaul killed Gunnerson. Does CBI have any idea what that was about?"

"Hard to know what happened between those two, but I bet Gunnerson was the instigator."

"De-extincting Neanderthals—what a batshit crazy thing to do," said Colcord.

"That's the problem with science," said Cash. "If something *can* be done, it *will* be done—no matter how dangerous. I have no doubt that in China or Russia or even somewhere else in America, Neanderthals are being resurrected. There may be a lot more of them out there. They sequenced the Neanderthal genome in 2010—it was only a matter of time before someone started cloning them."

"It's the Tower of Babel all over again," said Colcord. "It's what happens when you play God."

"Exactly right. And it's pretty astonishing they can't find them in that wilderness—especially now that it's winter. I know they're tough, but there must be five feet of snow out there, twenty below zero at night, blizzards. How the heck are they surviving?"

"They're committed," said Colcord. "And consider how big the area is. If you add up the Flat Tops, plus the surrounding National Forest and BLM land, that's over a million acres in the heart of the Rockies. And the Rockies stretch from New Mexico to Canada—so if they're traveling, they could be anywhere." He paused. "They don't look so different from humans that they might be able to pass for us. Sure, they're weird-looking and talk funny, but a lot of people are weird-looking and talk funny. There's no deficit with their intelligence."

Colcord took another bite of his pecan bun. It was driving Cash crazy, watching him eat it, smelling the sweet, buttery, nutty aroma.

"You want half?" he asked, aware of her look.

"Oh, hell, why not?"

He cut half the bun and passed it to her. She sank her teeth into it. "Wow," she said. "Who makes these?"

"We do—in-house. It's a family recipe from my mom."

She savored the flavor. It shot her diet to hell, but she'd make it up by skipping dinner. This was just too good to pass up.

"What do you think they're planning out there in the wilderness?" he asked.

"You heard it. Extinction."

"Good luck. There are eight billion of us—and twenty of them."

Cash leaned back in the sofa chair. "All I know is—this ain't over."

AFTERWORD

WELCOME TO THE ISLAND OF DR. MOREAU

When the first Neanderthal bones were discovered in a cave in the Neander Valley of Germany in 1859, some scientists claimed they must be
the bones of a lost Cossack who had bow legs from spending too much
time on horseback. But it was soon understood that these were fossils
from a species that was almost—but not quite—human. It was named
Homo neanderthalensis.

Similar discoveries of Neanderthal fossils were soon made in other
parts of Europe. The bones were thicker and heavier than those of
Homo sapiens, and the skulls had heavy brow ridges and sloping fore-
heads. Scientists soon painted a picture of "Neanderthal man" as a
brutish, beetle-browed, knuckle-dragging primitive with a brain that
could function only at a "purely vegetative or bestial" level, as one early
paleoanthropologist wrote. They lived in caves, were covered with hair,
and did not have language beyond grunting and bellowing. They were
opportunistic scavengers rather than noble hunters.

One curious fact, however, made it difficult to completely relegate
Neanderthals to the level of beasts: they appeared to have a larger cranial capacity than *Homo sapiens*—their brains were bigger than ours.

This disparaging view of Neanderthals dominated scientific and
popular imagination until the 1950s, when a string of discoveries in
Eurasia and new, careful examinations of Neanderthal bones and arti-
facts led to the emergence of a more complex view of the species. The
knuckle-dragging idea, for example, was shown to have come from
a Neanderthal who was stooped because he suffered from crippling
arthritis; Neanderthals actually walked as fully upright as we do. They
were probably not covered with hair, as evidence emerged that they
scraped hides and made leather pliant by chewing on skins, which

meant they wore clothing—a necessity in the bitterly cold Europe of the distant past.

Studies of Neanderthal anatomy and genetics reveal that they had language ability. Not only did Neanderthals have the hyoid bone of the neck in the right position for speech, but they also carried the *FOXP2* gene, which in humans is linked to speech. What's more, they possessed an expanded Broca's area in the brain, the region governing complex speech, the formulation of sentences, and the vocal and breath control necessary to speak words.

And their brains were indeed bigger. One of the largest hominid crania ever measured, in fact, belonged not to a modern human but to a Neanderthal who lived 55,000 years ago in what is today Israel. Neanderthal brains, however, had a smaller cerebellum and parietal lobes, which suggests that they were less capable than we are in terms of tool use, creativity, higher-order conceptualization, and social abilities. Their occipital and temporal lobes and olfactory bulbs, however, were bigger, implying they were superior to humans in smell, eyesight, and hearing. They were especially adapted to seeing in low light, and they may have been more crepuscular than diurnal—in other words, they were most active at dawn and dusk.

Far from being scavengers, Neanderthals were apex predators. They lived mostly on meat, and they hunted the most dangerous game on the planet, including mammoths, woolly rhinoceroses, aurochs, and boars, as well as wolves, cave lions, and cave bears. They had fire, with which they roasted, boiled, and smoked their food. They made houses out of mammoth bones. They flaked stone tools, although over the course of 150,000 years, their tools stayed the same, showing almost no innovation or evolution. They buried their dead. They took care of the crippled and infirm. They probably had religious beliefs and some concept of an afterlife, because they placed offerings in graves—especially those of children—and in one case, they appear to have scattered medicinal plants and flowers in an adult's grave, which some think might mean the individual was a healer or shaman. They probably adorned themselves with shells, claws, bones, and feathers and painted their bodies. They created abstract images on cave walls, including hand stencils, dots, and lines. They collected fossils, quartz crystals, geodes, and other pretty rocks for no apparent reason except to admire their aesthetics. They had music. Fragments of bone flutes have been found at some Neanderthal sites, and the placement of the holes indicates Neanderthals may have used a pentatonic (five-note) scale. They knew how to make boats; Neanderthal tools found on Greek islands prove that they could sail short distances—but they never made the insanely dicey over-the-horizon voyages that modern humans did, such as the aborigines who used boats to reach Australia 45,000 years ago. Neanderthals were so close to us that many paleoanthropologists today think they may not have been a separate species but a subspecies.

In Europe, living in regions with a deficit of sunlight, Neanderthals probably had lighter skin color to make sufficient vitamin D. We know that at least one Neanderthal woman had red hair, and it has been theorized that the rare red-hair gene entered the modern human population through interbreeding with red-haired Neanderthals.

The gradual evolution in our understanding of Neanderthals took a revolutionary turn when it was discovered in 2010 that most of us *are* part Neanderthal. In that year, Svante Pääbo, an evolutionary geneticist at the Max Planck Institute for Evolutionary Anthropology in Germany, sequenced the Neanderthal genome. He and another geneticist, David Reich at Harvard, showed that Neanderthals interbred with humans. As a result, most humans carry a small percentage of Neanderthal genes, especially people from Europe and Asia. (Pääbo won the Nobel Prize in 2022 for this work.) It appears that around twenty percent of the Neanderthal genome survives in modern humans in bits and pieces, with each non-African human carrying two to four percent of Neanderthal genes.

Neanderthals were different from modern humans in important ways. One dramatic difference was in strength: Neanderthals were immensely stronger than modern humans, with much heavier bones and bigger muscles. Elizabeth Kolbert noted in "Sleeping with the Enemy," a remarkable essay about Neanderthals in *The New Yorker*, that in any sort of physical contest, Neanderthals were "probably capable of beating humans to a pulp." They had a higher metabolism and matured more quickly than modern humans. We know from assemblages of bones found in caves and group trackways that they probably lived in smaller groups than we did in our hunter-gatherer days. In 2022, the remains of a family of Neanderthals—a father, daughter, and some cousins—were found in a cave in Siberia, where they had probably starved to death during a harsh winter.

Our social interactions are without doubt one of the most complex mental activities that modern humans engage in. Even in our days as hunter-gatherers, we lived in groups large enough to require a great deal of astuteness and intelligence in navigating social relations. This may not seem obvious at first, but when you consider how difficult it is for human beings to interact effectively, get along, be productive, resolve conflicts, maintain a good reputation among peers, engage in remunerative work, navigate marriage and child-rearing, and avoid transgressing social norms, you'll begin to see just how mentally challenging it is to be a successful human being. We devote most of our day not to solving math equations, driving cars, or writing books but to curating our interactions with others. Much of our brainpower, scientists believe, evolved to deal effectively with social interactions, which allowed us to live successfully in ever-larger groups. Chimpanzees have enormous social problems living in even small, simple troops; they are horribly prone to violence and have poor conflict resolution skills, constantly jockeying for dominance, squabbling, and beating each other up. They cooperate only with great difficulty. There is some genetic evidence that autism may be linked to atavistic Neanderthal gene variants cropping up in modern humans. One of the symptoms of autism is having difficulties in social interactions, suggesting that Neanderthals might have been similarly disadvantaged. This is one reason, perhaps, why they lived in smaller social units than modern humans—and why they could not compete when we arrived with our bigger and more cooperative groups.

What about some of the more controversial depictions in my novel, starting with cannibalism? This is also based on fact; cannibalism among Neanderthals was widespread, judging by the sheer number of sites found across Europe and Asia of cannibalized Neanderthal remains. In the French cave of *Grotte de* Moula-Guercy, for example, the bones of five cannibalized Neanderthals were found, in which the arms had been chopped off and disarticulated, legs stripped of flesh, and the chest cavity scooped clean of organs. In another French cave with Neanderthal remains, some thirty-five percent of the bones showed stone tool marks that indicated they had been butchered.

The practice was not limited to Neanderthals; many sites of *Homo sapiens* also show clear signs of cannibalism. There was, for example, widespread cannibalism in the prehistoric American Southwest, which I wrote about in an article for *The New Yorker*. Much of this was not starvation cannibalism—it was cannibalism employed as a tool of terror and control, a way to frighten and cow your enemies. The discovery of a peculiar gene in the human genome hints that cannibalism might have been widespread among our ancestors. Most modern humans carry variant 129 of the *PRNP* gene. (This is a gene that controls the manufacture of certain proteins.) Variant 129 makes humans immune to prion diseases. Prion diseases, also known as *transmissible spongiform encephalopathies*, are transmitted by the cannibalistic eating of human brains. The mere existence of such a gene indicates that cannibalism among our forebears might have been widespread enough to trigger pandemics of prion disease, which would cause the spread through the human population of the protective variant 129. A British investigator, Simon Underwood, noted that Neanderthals lacked variant 129. He concluded that Neanderthals, in killing and eating modern humans, might have contributed to their own extinction by being infected with human prion diseases to which they had no natural defense.

Did we drive Neanderthals to extinction? While there is no proof, the answer is almost certainly yes. When modern humans arrived in Europe is debatable, but the earliest modern human bones—found in Bulgaria, Italy, and Britain—date to around 45,000 years ago.* Following that time, modern humans began pouring into Europe and reproducing at an ever-increasing rate. Neanderthals, who had successfully lived in Europe for over 300,000 years, went extinct 39,000 years ago—that is, around six thousand years later. The timing of our arrival and their extinction is just too close to be coincidence. How would

---

* This picture is complicated by the fact that we know that *Homo sapiens* and Neanderthals were in contact with each other much earlier than that, since humans and Neanderthals interbred at least 100,000 years ago, according to genetic evidence. In my novel, I use the time period of *Homo sapiens*'s probable arrival in Europe, not in Asia or the Levant.

Neanderthals have reacted to this new, ugly, and physically weaker species arriving in their lands, hunting their animals, living in their caves, fishing in their rivers, and collecting their edible and medicinal plants? And how would a migrating band of Sapiens have reacted to finding a rich valley filled with useful animals and plants, and a fine cave for living, which just happened to be occupied by some trouble-some Neanderthals?

There would be violence.

The paleoanthropological world seems curiously reticent about stating outright that humans drove Neanderthals to extinction. Some researchers assert that the mass migration of modern humans from Africa simply interbred Neanderthals out of existence and assimilated them. Others point to rapid climate change as the cause of Neander-thal extinction, although Neanderthals had lived through ice ages and abrupt climate changes many times before. Some speculate that diseases brought by modern humans from Africa might have swept through Neanderthal populations, much the way European diseases decimated Indigenous populations in the New World. Some say that Neanderthal populations were so low that they were weakened from inbreeding. All these might have been contributing factors. In my view, absolutely everything we know of human history and behav-ior points to a violent struggle between Neanderthals and modern humans for land and resources. This has been the way of the genus *Homo* forever. The bottom line is that archeological digs across Eu-rope show that when modern humans arrived in a particular region, Neanderthals soon disappeared.

As for interbreeding between Neanderthals and Sapiens, I doubt most of the Neanderthal DNA in our genome came from consensual liaisons between loving partners. Mass rape has been a tool of conflict throughout history. Violence between bands of humans of the same species is common; think how much more likely it would be between bands of different species. Human beings may have been weaker than Neanderthals, but they compensated with cleverness, cooperation, and advanced technology—and among their advantages might have been a greater sense of empathy, which is the ability to know what another person is thinking and feeling. Empathy also gives us insight into our own selves and inner motivations. As Sun Tzu wrote in *The Art of War*: "Know your enemy and know yourself; in a hundred battles, you will never be defeated."

The genomes of both Sapiens and Neanderthals record a severe genetic chokepoint some time prior to sixty thousand years ago. Both species were almost wiped out, but managed to squeak by with mere thousands or hundreds of individuals. The Sapiens population seems to have crashed to less than ten thousand "breeding pairs," and one study estimated that the human species survived for several centuries with only around forty females at any given time of reproductive age. We don't know where these modern humans eked out their precarious existence or whether it was one small band or a few scattered ones.

This near extinction of our species was likely caused by a single dramatic event: the Toba eruption. On the island of Sumatra, the Toba volcano exploded around 74,000 years ago in one of the largest eruptions known to have occurred on the planet. It blasted billions of tons of ash and soot into the atmosphere, which spread over the earth in a dark cloud that took perhaps six years to settle out. The dust triggered a brutal volcanic winter, freezing the earth for months, causing huge snowfalls where snow had never been, vastly increasing sea ice, killing almost all the tropical forests and many of the temperate ones, and chilling the earth for years afterward. The volcanic winter caused population crashes in other mammal species, including chimpanzees, and it appears to have triggered the extinction of some half dozen hominin species living on the earth at the time.

In the end, the Toba disaster was a gift to our species. The population crash of Sapiens was soon followed by rapid population growth, a flowering of technological innovation, and a flood of humans out of Africa and across Europe and Asia. The Toba eruption contributed to who we are, along the lines of the old adage that what doesn't kill us makes us stronger. In clearing the earth of other hominin species, the

Toba eruption left the world open to two hominin species alone, who would soon face off.* It set the stage for the final conflict to come.

Why should we care about Neanderthals and their annihilation? Kolbert, in her Pulitzer Prize–winning book, *The Sixth Extinction*, lays out a convincing argument that our species is responsible for an ongoing destruction of animals and plants that is reaching the staggering levels of the earth's previous Big Five mass extinctions. With our marvelously clever yet weirdly oblivious brains, we have managed to become an agent of mass extinction as powerful as the asteroid that wiped out the dinosaurs. It is both fascinating and troubling that the first major extinction we caused was that of our own cousins, the Neanderthals. It was the prototype of so many conflicts to come. We've seen across history that when two cultures meet, the stronger culture usually destroys the weaker. This is a fundamental characteristic of our species. So many of our contemporary conflicts, our tribal divisions, our clannishness, our willingness to dehumanize our opponents, our fear and hatred of the "other" are clearly rooted in our evolution. These qualities that so bedevil us today found an early and vivid expression in the deadly conflict between Sapiens and Neanderthals. If we want to know ourselves, our place on the planet, and how we must change if we wish to survive—we must also understand our Neanderthal cousins and the ancient conflict that led to their demise. And we must know Neanderthals because we *are* part Neanderthal. In this sense, Neanderthals did not go completely extinct but live on in our own bodies and minds.

Will scientists bring Neanderthals back to life someday? Geneticists are already on the cusp of resurrecting several extinct creatures. The woolly mammoth and the thylacine, also known as the Tasmanian tiger, will be the first to be revivified, probably by a company called Colossal, founded by George Church, a brilliant geneticist at Harvard Medical School. The Colossal website declares: "Colossal, a bioscience and

---

* With the exception of some isolated populations of hominins on islands that would go extinct later.

genetics company co-founded by world-renowned geneticist George Church, Ph.D., and technology entrepreneur Ben Lamm, is focused on rapidly advancing the field of species de-extinction. Using CRISPR and other genome editing technologies Colossal will pioneer a practical, working model of de-extinction to apply to the Woolly Mammoth and other species."

In his book, *Regenesis,* George Church describes in detail how he would go about resurrecting Neanderthals, possibly using the services of "an extremely adventurous female human." To accomplish this, he writes,

> You'd start with a stem cell genome from a human adult and gradually reverse-engineer it into the Neanderthal genome or a reasonably close equivalent. These stem cells can produce tissues and organs. If society becomes comfortable with cloning and sees value in true human diversity, then the whole Neanderthal creature itself could be cloned by a surrogate mother chimp—or by an extremely adventurous female human.
>
> Any technology that can accomplish such feats—taking us back into a primeval era when mammoths and Neanderthals roamed the earth—is one of unprecedented power. Genomic technologies will permit us to replay scenes from our evolutionary past and take evolution to places where it has never gone, and where it would probably never go if left to its own devices.

What a vision of the future of the human species, indeed. Church later gave an interview to *Der Spiegel* magazine, in which he elaborated on his views.

> *Der Spiegel:* How do we have to imagine this: You raise Neanderthals in a lab, ask them to solve problems and thereby study how they think?
> Church: No, you would certainly have to create a cohort, so they would have some sense of identity. They could maybe even create a new neo-Neanderthal culture and become a political force.

Among the seed investors in Colossal are the Bitcoin billionaire twins Cameron and Tyler Winklevoss and other celebrities.

In 2022, Colossal offered a wider financing opportunity, which was swamped with money from eager investors, who oversubscribed to the offering by millions of dollars. Colossal's efforts to de-extinct the woolly mammoth will almost certainly succeed, possibly in less than five years, and more resurrections will follow. I believe this will be a brilliant and wonderful achievement—but every extraordinary advance in technology offers a dark side. It is this dark side my novel explores.

As Church notes in his book, the same CRISPR technology being employed at Colossal to resurrect mammoths could be used to de-extinct *Homo neanderthalensis*. Elizabeth Kolbert, in her *New Yorker* article, wrote that it would be easy to put Neanderthal genes into a human embryo and see what happens—which is, of course, what I depict in my novel. She wrote: "From an experimental viewpoint, the best way to test whether any particular change is significant would be to produce a human with the Neanderthal version of the sequence. This would involve manipulating a human stem cell, implanting the genetically modified embryo into a surrogate mother, and then watching the resulting child grow up. For obvious reasons, such *Island of Dr. Moreau*–like research on humans is not permitted . . . But it is allowed on mice. Dozens of strains of mice have been altered to carry humanized DNA sequences, and new ones are being created all the time, more or less to order." You heard that right: we're putting human DNA into mice to see what happens. Might someone, somewhere be asking: Let's put Neanderthal DNA into humans to see what happens?

As Frankie Cash says at the end of my novel, "If something *can* be done, it *will* be done—no matter how dangerous. I have no doubt that in China or Russia or even somewhere else in America, Neanderthals are being resurrected."

While *Extinction* is fiction, the science in it is real. It is here, and it is now. If Neanderthals haven't already been de-extincted somewhere on earth, they will be soon. *Extinction* is a way for me to say to readers: welcome to the Island of Dr. Moreau.